TWINNED : BOOK 1

COMMIT TO THE KICK

TRIS LAWRENCE

DUCK
PRINTS
PRESS

Schenectady, New York

COMMIT TO THE KICK
Copyright © 2023 Tris Lawrence

ISBN 978-1-946472-88-5 (trade paperback)
ISBN 978-1-946472-90-8 (ePub)
ISBN 978-1-946472-89-2 (PDF)

Cover art © 2021, 2023 Jade Hallett
Edited by Ruth Hadad and Nina Waters
Paperback layout by Hermit Prints
E-Book layout by Claire Houck

Published by Duck Prints Press, LLC. Schenectady, New York. Find our other publications and learn more about us at https://duckprintspress.com.

Tags
Genre: Modern with Magic
Rating: General Audiences
Trigger Warnings: alcohol use, death of a sibling (off-screen), harm to children (mentions of), major character injury, minor character death, micro-aggressions (racist), speciesism
Relationships: f/f (background), family, found family, friends with benefits, friends to lovers, m/m, parenthood (single parenting) (background), siblings, twins
Character Features: anger management issues, asexual, bipoc, bisexual, child (background), creature transformation (animal), creature transformation (bird), creature transformation, creature transformation (dog), demiromantic, gay, ghost, memory loss, magic use, masochist, musician, neurodivergent (background), oblivious, pansexual, polyamory (background), precognition
Other Tags: angst, bed sharing (platonic), break-up, college, emotional hurt/comfort, fraternity, fraught family dynamics, funeral, grieving, hurt/comfort, new york, politics, present tense, sexual content (non-graphic descriptions), sports (football), sports (martial arts), third person limited

ORIENTATION

1

THE THING ABOUT email is that it doesn't really tell you about a person. Oh, it tells you everything they want you to know, but there are no tells, no scents, no skipping heartbeats and little bits of body language to give hints for the things they hide inside their mind. Alaric knows this better than anyone; he knows the things he left out when he emailed with his roommate over the summer. He made sure they got the important topics on the table: that they're both Talented, who's bringing the TV and who's bringing the fridge, whether they have early morning classes (they both do) and like to stay up late (his roommate does, and Alaric can sleep through anything anyway).

Other than that, Alaric doesn't know much more about Harrison Everett other than that he prefers to be called Rory, and he's apparently a guitarist in some band which is why he hasn't had time to email much.

Alaric can't get upset about Rory hiding things. It's not like Rory knows much more about Alaric.

But it's the not knowing that makes Alaric's skin itch. He can feel his power rippling under his skin, hear the baying in his mind that means the shift is coming whether he wants it to or not. Fur covers the backs of his fingers; his nails elongate into claws as he flexes his hands and growls softly.

He has to push it back.

He reminds himself that he's just waiting for his roommate. He's just waiting to meet the person he will share living space with for their freshman year here at PHU. It's nothing. *Nothing.*

There's a quick rap on the door and a creak as it slides open. Alaric jumps off his bed, able to shake off the shift as he catches the familiar scent coming through. He catches his twin in a hug as soon as Drea opens her arms, pulling her in close and pressing his cheek to hers. She lifts her hand to his head, threads her fingers in his hair, and rubs her cheek along his. "We got to campus about an hour ago, Ric," she says, and Alaric looks beyond her as if his parents might walk in at any moment. "And they already left," she continues with a rueful smile. "They helped me get everything moved into Davison, but Dad knew you wouldn't—"

"He's right." Alaric pulls out the chair from his desk, gestures to it for Drea, but she ignores him and hitches herself up onto his bed instead, her feet dangling. It settles the beast under his skin to have her here—not to mention knowing that his parents have been and gone without him having to play polite games. He came to school two weeks early to start training with the team, and it's been a welcome respite from dealing with the pressure of home life.

He's got his hands on the bed, about to push himself up to sit beside her, when the door crashes open behind him. His lip curls, a fresh growl starting. Claws tip his fingers as he turns on light feet, the change trying to rush through him.

"Whoa, hey, um, down boy?"

Alaric can barely see the guy standing there. He sees a bright shock of red hair, almost hidden by the stack of boxes he's carrying. The boxes drop, and the guy is stocky, freckles spattered across his face and his hair a bushy mess around his face. Definitely not Rory; they did at least manage to exchange pictures. The redhead grins easily, obviously not afraid as he steps around the boxes, one hand held out.

"Rory said you were Clan. Cool. I'm Thorne, Rory's brother. We're getting him moved in before we go get my apartment set up. Dad offered to take me over to mine"—he gestures with his right hand—"but I wanted to make sure Rory's settled first. Besides, I know Dad"—he gestures with his left hand—"would rather we do this as a family."

Alaric takes that to mean that Rory and his parents can't be too far behind Thorne's arrival in the room. He cocks his head, listening for voices approaching, but he can't separate anything out from the general hubbub in the hallway.

He'd liked this place until today. It was quiet. Peaceful. Now it reeks of anxiety and exhaustion, and he can't make anything make sense.

Drea's hand falls on his shoulder, and he realizes that he hasn't taken Thorne's offered hand yet. Alaric inhales, manages to convince the claws to become short, blunt nails as he wraps his hand around Thorne's. He squeezes once, notes the callouses on Thorne's fingers and palms and the warmth of Thorne's hand as he squeezes back.

Suddenly uncomfortable, Alaric pulls his hand free and steps back, stopping short with the bed in his way behind his shoulders. There's a rush of amusement in the air, and he swats at Drea's hand in answer.

"213. This is it." The voice is cheerful, female, and Alaric has just enough time to brace himself before the small dorm room is suddenly full of too many people. "Hi there. I'm Lucy Wilson." Lucy has an easy smile as she sets down the suitcase she's carrying. "You must be Alaric."

Alaric can't find his voice. He blinks, because there's Rory—he recognizes him from the pictures, tall and whipcord thin, his dark hair long and falling slightly in his face—but there's Lucy, and two other men, one who looks like Thorne and one who looks like Rory. And it's too many and too much all at once.

"I think we're overwhelming him," the taller man says softly, and Alaric glares at him. It's true, but he doesn't need it pointed out.

"Mom, Dad, Dad," Thorne says, pointing quickly at Lucy and the two other men.

Rory pushes past them, sets the guitar case he's carrying on the remaining bed. "Lucy, Daniel, Rowan." He points to the same three, offering names. "Why don't you guys go get the rest of my instruments and I'll start unpacking." Rory stands with his shoulders lightly hunched, body curled in on itself, and Drea makes a soft noise. Alaric can smell the discomfort as much as Drea can read it in his body language. He doesn't quite smell like prey, but he's not strong right now, either.

He's not what Alaric expected.

Rory sinks down on the bed, closes his eyes, and exhales as soon as the others leave. "We are overwhelming. I'm sorry," he says, and Alaric snorts softly.

"Mages," he says. "Mages and Clan haven't ever really gotten along."

Rory licks his lips, shrugs one shoulder before he looks at Alaric. "I told you what we were over the summer," he says.

"And I said it wasn't a problem," Alaric counters. "Is it going to be a problem for you?"

Rory shakes his head. "And you can see how fascinated my brother is," he adds dryly. "He's more likely to be a problem for you than I'll be. He gets excited about things sometimes, and he doesn't always have a great sense of personal boundaries. But if you say no, he'll listen. He's good about that."

Alaric nods. He's supposed to say something else, he figures, but he's never been good at small talk or extending conversations. Instead he looks back at Drea, and she lifts one hand, shrugging. "You need help bringing things in?" he finally asks, glancing at the door. He knows the rest of them will be back soon, and a part of him is braced for the impact of their arrival.

"Let's focus on getting our room set up so we're not tripping over each other. My family can do the carrying." Rory comes to stand in front of Alaric's bed, looks at the way he has it lifted, with his bureau underneath. "I need a place for my instruments, but I need to make sure I don't bang my head every time I get into bed."

Alaric rarely feels short, but Rory's a solid three inches taller than him, at least, and he's so thin that he looks even taller. "Fine Arts," he says, because it's one more fact that Rory had offered over email.

"With a side of Magical Studies, yeah." Rory moves his guitar case to the side, motions for Alaric to help him with the bed. "And you?"

"Undecided." Alaric's tone is flat, because that's really the best way to describe a lot of things in his life right now. "I've got time to figure it out. Right now, it's all just about the football."

It gives him something to focus on, a reason to keep going forward for the moment. He'll figure out the rest when he has to, and not a moment before.

2

THE DORM ROOM feels crowded once everything's in its place. Alaric helps Rory turn his bed into a loft and stow his bureau and the fridge under it. They share space on the shelves Alaric placed under his own bed and do their best to reconfigure the rest of the room into something that will fit all of Rory's instruments along with study space and room to walk.

"I think we should get rid of one of the desks." Rory turns slowly, surveying the room. "It's the one thing that doesn't fit, and I'll either do my homework on my bed, or I'll be sitting on the bed or floor while I work on music. I don't like desks unless I'm really deep in working on a ritual."

Alaric makes a noise of agreement. He's not sure he'll use a desk, either. "I don't like studying in my room," he grumbles, which is only half a truth. He doesn't like studying in general, but it's a necessary evil if he's going to play football. Or go home again. Clan doesn't like deadbeats, even if Alaric thinks he can come up with other ways of serving their community.

"I'll ask the RA," Alaric says. He pulls open the door, starts to step out, and pulls back when he realizes someone is standing there, hand raised to knock.

"Floor meeting in fifteen," the guy says. He's got a charming smile. It's the only word Alaric can come up with for it, that kind of smile where Alaric feels like he should smile back; he's half looking for the lens flare reflecting off the guy's teeth. At least it smells genuine.

"I've ordered pizza, and if you want to bring any snacks with you, go ahead," the guy says. "We'll be introducing ourselves, going over the ground rules, getting to know each other. Don't be late."

"Dining halls open tomorrow," Rory comments. It's a good point. Pizza will be welcome, and Alaric hopes that the RA took Clan appetite into account when he was ordering for the floor.

Alaric stands in the doorway, watching as the stranger moves on to the next room. The guy has a nice—Alaric almost stops himself, but no, he can think anything he wants in the privacy of his own mind. The guy has a nice ass. And he moves in such a fluid way. Liquid. More like dancing than with a predator's easy grace. It's the kind of movement that Alaric could watch all day.

He can think anything he wants, but he really shouldn't be staring.

Alaric blinks twice and shakes his head, pulling the door closed as he steps back into the room.

"If that was the RA, we missed our chance to ask about getting rid of the desk," Rory points out, and Alaric's expression twists.

"We'll ask after the meeting." Because if one desk is gone, Alaric thinks the room might be livable. He never really thought about sharing space with this much stuff before. There are two guitars—one electric and one acoustic—and a bass, each with their own stand, as well as a full-sized keyboard that Rory claims is better than having a piano in the room. At least it has a headphone jack. Of course, Alaric can't complain because his own workout gear is taking up one corner of the room, mostly neatly stuffed into bags or stacked on shelves, but still taking up space.

"I'm not used to sharing a room with strangers," he admits.

A faint flush tinges Rory's cheeks. "I'm used to being crammed into tight spaces," he says. "We tour in a van. I share a room with my brother back home. I grew up on the road during the summer, so I'm used to sleeping in a puppy pile and waking up in different places. I don't mind it, if it's someone I know." He glances at Alaric, and Alaric offers a rueful smile because he can smell that faint trepidation again.

The way Rory lives sounds stifling, and it's almost a relief to realize that Rory's as wary as Alaric is of sharing space with each other. "We don't touch as much as rumor would have you think," Alaric says, because there are public ideas about what Clan is like, and Rory grins.

"I didn't think you did. I'm pretty sure no one hugs as much as my family. I'm sorry about that. You looked—you looked like Mom was torturing you, but now you see where Thorne gets his lack of spatial awareness when it comes to people." Rory touches the two guitars, his fingers lingering on the neck of the acoustic. He reaches for it, lifts it carefully. "Let's get to the meeting."

"You planning on breaking the ice with a song?" Alaric gestures at the guitar. He figures it's an identifying item for Rory, but Alaric's thing is football. And he can't exactly carry a football around without looking ridiculous. So he strips his shirt off quickly and digs through his things to find the T-shirt they gave him with his name and number on it, pulling that on instead.

"I'm planning on sitting with a guitar," Rory says with a little shrug. "It gives me something to do with my hands."

And something to hide behind, but Alaric won't fault him for that. They're still dancing around most topics, but instinct has Alaric liking Rory for all the things he doesn't say.

When they get down to the common room, it's already packed. Rory sinks into the last open chair, commenting quietly, "I don't mind if you want to share."

Alaric makes himself as comfortable as he can perched on the arm of the chair, his arms crossed and his knees and hip kept carefully away from touching Rory. There's a moment of tension, then he feels Rory relax, and the guitar bumps against him while Rory gets comfortable.

There are eighteen people, split evenly between women and men. The guy who knocked on their door clears his throat, then claps his hands to get attention. "I'm TJ Howell, and I'm your RA. This is Douglass Hall, second floor, which you already know, and every single one of you is a freshman. I'm a sophomore, and I'm in the School of Fine Arts, majoring in dance and performing arts. If you need anything, I'm here. Want or need to talk? My door is always open. Got locked out of your room? I can help with that. And lock your room when you're not in it, and when you're sleeping—this is not a joke. I hope we can trust everyone on this floor, and the building is supposed to be locked, but people are polite and hold doors open, and sometimes things disappear."

TJ walks as he talks, and Alaric tries to watch his hands and his mouth, not the way his feet move. Dance. That makes sense. It makes a lot of sense.

He'd be fast on the field, too, Alaric thinks, with quick steps.

TJ stops in front of Alaric, takes a step to one side so he's looking at everyone and not blocking Alaric's view. "There are some ground rules, and there's a poster right over there." He points to where it hangs just above the kitchen counter. "Rules about the kitchen, the bathrooms, food. Plenty of rules. But I want to bring one up now, because I think it's the most important." He takes a step back, spreads his hands, and looks around the room, and Alaric can see the way he meets the eyes of every single person here.

"Pine Hills is known for being one of the top one hundred most tolerant schools in the nation," TJ says solemnly. "We will not tolerate discrimination based on race, religion, sexuality, gender, Talent, or any other difference you can think of between people. Don't make assumptions about the person sitting next to you. Don't intrude on their privacy. No slurs. No hate. Be polite and do your damnedest to be accepting. If there's something you don't know or don't understand, learn. Remember that we all live together here." He goes silent, and Alaric feels the silence, feels the way everyone spends time processing TJ's statements.

"One more thing before we introduce ourselves and get to the food." TJ makes a face. "No displays of destructive Talent in ways that might cause a problem. This is subjective, of course, but let's put it this way: lighting a candle with a flame from your finger is okay, but starting a bonfire in the middle of your room—whether you can control it or not—is not allowed."

Alaric swears he hears Rory snort and mutter *Thorne*, but no one else seems to notice.

TJ starts the introductions with a repeat of his own information, and as they circle around the room, Alaric tries to match names to faces but only manages to catch a few. Pels and Nikita are two of the girls in the only triple on the floor—room 211, next door to his own room, but he entirely misses the name of the third girl in their room, and he has no idea what the names are of the girls in 215, on the other side of his room. He catches Jackson's name—but not which room he's in—mostly because he comments on playing basketball, and he's the only other athlete on the floor. Everything else is a blur, and Alaric takes advantage of the chance to get up and get pizza to regroup and take a break from sitting too close to everyone else.

"You don't like people?"

Alaric steps to the side, keeps the wall at his back as he puts space between himself and the man standing next to him. He has to look down; unlike Jackson and Rory, this new floor-mate is significantly shorter than him. "I don't hate people," he grumbles, "but I don't like crowds."

"Patrick," the guy says. "Call me Pat. And you're Alaric. You said you play football, right? I'll have to check out your stats later. I've never been into playing sports—too small for a lot of them, and I'm terrible at soccer—but I love watching them." Pat runs a hand over his bald head, blue eyes crinkling with his smile. The movement shows the ink that runs along the inside of his forearm, words in script that Alaric can't read from this angle and isn't rude enough to ask about. The tattoo matches the image already set forth by the gauges that stretch Pat's earlobes, and his tank top and loose shorts. "You any good?"

"I'm on a scholarship." Alaric bites his tongue, stopping himself from asking further questions. He wants to know how to catalog and place these people so his inner hound doesn't try to worry at the issue of who they are. He inhales, exhales slowly because questions invite questions, and he doesn't want to answer them. "Quarterback. I'll be second string, so I'll only see action when the starting QB is off the field. And during the scrimmage Friday, because it's orientation. We're doing an all-freshmen starting line."

Pat nods, opens his mouth to say something, when there's a *plink* of a guitar string, answered by another one. "Your roommate has found my roommate," Pat says, "or vice versa."

Jackson has pulled a chair over from somewhere and is sitting in it with a guitar, facing Rory, who is cross-legged in his own chair, his hair dropping forward as he plucks at the strings of his own acoustic. The guitars are mirror images, the necks facing in the same direction as the boys face each other, and it takes Alaric a moment to figure out that Rory must be playing left-handed. Jackson and Rory confer quietly, tuning their guitars for a moment before Jackson starts to play something and Rory laughs, low and vaguely embarrassed.

"Did you hope no one noticed?" Jackson asks. Alaric makes his way over to them slowly, curious about Rory's music.

Rory shakes his head. "I didn't think it'd be that easy, but I'm not going to go around telling everyone I'm in a band. I leave that to Thorne."

"Wait, you're that Rory Everett?" Pat ducks around, takes a good look at him. "You have three albums out already. 'Fired Up' is one of my favorites; it's on my skate mix."

Rory shifts what he's playing, and the few notes are almost familiar, like it's something Alaric's heard overplayed on the radio when Drea was listening. "Thorne wrote that one." He pauses, changes again to something a little slower but no less energetic. "This is one of mine."

It takes a moment, but Jackson manages to follow along, and a moment later, TJ is there and singing in a rich tenor that doesn't sound right for the song but is nice to listen to anyway. As Rory picks up tempo, Nikita starts banging out a rhythm on the table, and someone else starts singing along as well.

Maybe music to break the ice isn't a bad idea. It's put Rory dead center of the circle of people, but Alaric's not sure Rory actually notices; his focus is entirely on the music, his head down. Occasionally he lifts his gaze to check if Jackson's keeping up or so he can offer advice on how to improve a riff.

It gives Alaric a chance to step aside, get some more pizza, and feed the beast simmering under his skin. It gives him time to look at everyone, try to match scents to faces, because that's more important than names. He closes his eyes, listens to the beats of their hearts, lets himself assimilate this new background noise that he'll be living with for the rest of the year.

It's only day one. They still have a long way to go.

3

By the end of the first evening, Alaric's head is spinning. Some of his floor-mates are more open than others. He now knows that Pat is half Chinese and half Irish and grew up mostly in Cambridge, which isn't actually part of Boston. The third girl in the triple is Jennifer, and the two girls in 215 are Soledad and Winter. He also knows that Soledad is extremely flirta-tious and thinks nothing of taking a seat in a lap if it's available, whether it's offered or not, and doesn't really seem care if she's flirting with men or women. But she also doesn't seem to want to push it past flirtation and that somehow makes Alaric comfortable with her level of personal space inva-sion.

He has a long conversation with TJ about VIT, because TJ's sister is starting as a freshman there, and Alaric's best friend, Corbin, is a freshman as well. TJ offers to drive Alaric over if he wants to visit, but also explains that there's a shuttle bus that runs between the two schools and stops in the town as well.

Alaric escapes eventually. He knows they have to be up early for social activities in the morning; he's not sure how well he'll sleep now that there's someone else in his room. He pushes open the door and flicks on the light, turning it off a split second later when he catches the low breath and the uptick of Rory's heartbeat. "Oh, sorry. Didn't realize you'd come back."

He can't read the emotion that slides off of Rory's skin, but he hears the huff of sound when Rory turns over, faces him in the dark.

"There was a good time to slip out, so I figured I'd try to fall asleep be-fore you got back," Rory says.

"And I woke you up."

Rory snorts softly. "I've been here for a half hour, and I haven't fallen asleep yet, so no. It's fine."

Alaric closes and locks the door behind him, toes off his shoes, then pads through the darkness to his bureau. He doesn't need the light, although it does make things easier. It's not easy to shift just enough to let the hound's vision take over, but he can get at least partly there, see the large shapes around him and not trip over anything. He pulls out a pair of sleep pants and changes quickly in the dark.

"Would you rather be called Alaric, or Ric, or Al?"

He'd almost managed to forget about Rory, even though his soft breath is a part of the room's strange atmosphere now. Alaric stiffens slightly, then strips off his shirt because the room is heavy with the lingering remains of late-summer heat. He drops the shirt over the back of the remaining desk chair. "My twin calls me 'Ric' sometimes," he says. "Tonight's the first time anyone's called me Al." He shakes his head, the name unfamiliar to his tongue still. "Either Alaric or Ric's fine."

It's not fine. It's just a name, sure, but "Ric" seems like family to him. It's the name Drea uses, or the one…it's the one Corbin uses, and sometimes Orson. On the other hand, it's the one his father will never use. So maybe it is fine. Maybe this is a new space, new people, new name. "Ric's fine."

Another small huff, and he takes it as agreement; it's followed by the shiver of sheets and skin while Rory turns over. When Alaric glances over, Rory's a lump under the sheets, one foot sticking out, his back curved as he curls in on himself, away from Alaric.

Alaric climbs into his own bed, tugs the sheet up, and wraps himself up in it. It's past one, he thinks, so he lets himself drift, tries to find the sleep that seems to elude him. And he waits for Rory's breath to even out, waits for the way his heart will go even with slumber.

It doesn't happen.

"What's wrong?" Alaric grumbles, because maybe that's what's keeping him up. Maybe he can't sleep because there's someone else—a stranger—in his room and awake, and the beast in his heart won't let him let down his guard.

"You breathe wrong," Rory grumbles. He shifts again, the sound of a hand punching a pillow into shape. "I spent sixteen years sharing a room with one person, and after that I learned how to sleep when he wasn't there, and you just…you sound wrong. This whole place is wrong."

"But you travel all the time." Alaric is sure he's missing some part of this explanation. "You're always sleeping in different places."

"And Thorne's always there." Rory says it like it's obvious. "When I'm someplace strange, he's there, and he just—I know what he sounds like when he's breathing."

It's such a Clan statement that Alaric doesn't know how to respond at first. He stretches out, rolls over to face Rory through the darkness. "You listen to how he breathes? You know how your brother breathes?"

"Share a room for that long and you get to know everything about what it sounds like in the dark," Rory says quietly. "Like when I had bronchitis and Thorne panicked because I kept sounding like I was wheezing at night. Or when he snuck out and thought he could get away with sneaking back in hours later. It's easy to ignore the familiar things, because they're there all the time."

"I had to listen to everyone's heartbeats," Alaric admits. He shifts to lie on his back, one arm thrown back under his pillow as he stares at the ceiling. "I'm going to be living with people—and it's not all Clan, but some of us are more sensitive to it than others. Depends on what you're like. But my hound—I need to know scents and heartbeats. So I get it. If you were my friend Corbin, this'd be easy. But you smell wrong, and you sound wrong."

A low huff of a sigh, like the breath relaxes out of him. "Exactly," Rory says.

"It'll get easier," Alaric says, because it has to, right? They'll get used to each other, get comfortable with the new sounds and scents. He moves, cranes his head to look over when he hears a disgruntled sound. "What?"

"It took me—" Rory cuts off, pauses before he says, "Yeah, it'll be fine. It just takes time. And don't take this the wrong way, but if they didn't say that every freshman needs to live on campus, I wouldn't be here."

"I'd have an apartment with Drea if I could," Alaric says, and there's another soft sound of assent.

"I'm moving into one with Thorne next year." When Rory exhales this time, it's a little slower, a little closer to sleep.

Alaric turns away again and burrows under the covers. He wonders if Rory would be bothered to find a hound in the room in the morning, but as nice as it would be, it's not the right option. Alaric knows this, can almost hear Drea's voice in his mind reminding him "control" and that he can't let himself slip. So he lies there in the dark and hopes that eventually sleep will come.

4

WHEN ALARIC LEAVES to get ready for the game on Friday, TJ lets him know that the entire floor will be there to cheer him on. Not to mention that somehow TJ has managed to make friends with Drea during the three days since move-in, so Drea's floor from Davison will be joining Alaric's floor in the stands.

That means there will be sixty people sitting in one section, entirely focused on Alaric's part in the game. He can't let it get to him, not on a night where everything has to be about the football rather than worrying about what people think of him.

He's played in front of larger crowds. Fuck, he's played in front of his parents. This should be easy.

Alaric is in the locker room, in the middle of tugging his shirt down over his pads, when someone claps his shoulder on the way by. He growls and tugs the shirt down quickly, the snarl dying when he sees that it's Chris Stone, the first-string QB. The confidence that Chris projects should help, but Alaric still feels prickly and uncertain.

"What?" he asks, the one word sharper than he means it to be.

Chris straddles the bench opposite Alaric, moving someone's things out of the way to make space so he can sit. "You ready to start tonight? Coach says he's thinking you might start more often this season, depending on how you play in this scrimmage. He's impressed with your performance during practice."

"You don't want that," Alaric says, because why *would* Chris want it? He's the starter, and he's a junior. He's got two seasons left in the limelight and a chance to see if he could go pro. Because as far as Alaric knows, Chris isn't Talented, and if he's a human willing to play in a Blended league and who stands out as a starter, the pros have to be impressed.

"You're good," Chris says plainly. He reaches out, grips Alaric's wrist, and turns his hand palm up. Alaric stares at the dark fingers that wrap around his paler wrist, tries to ignore the heat of Chris's touch. "These are good hands. You can throw farther than I can, and you've got a good grip. I'm smaller and faster. You're tougher. We can learn from each other this season, and you are going to kick ass after I graduate. But you're not going to do shit if you don't play."

"I don't need to start to play."

"Neither do I." Chris spreads his hands. "Coach is going to make sure we both get our time in the game, Ric. It's just a question of who starts first. So take a deep breath and settle yourself, so you don't get the whole team on edge."

"I'm not on edge." It's a lie, and Alaric sits down, stares at his feet while he gets his shoes on.

Chris's laugh is a low rumble, and it's warm to Alaric's ears. It's a good sound, the kind that makes his hound whine and want to roll over, and fuck that, Alaric doesn't have time for this. He lifts his gaze, sets his jaw as he meets Chris's brown eyes which are lit with amusement.

"According to Bea, your nerves are a simmering volcano, just waiting to erupt," Chris tells him with a shake of his head that sets his locs swinging. "Her words, not mine. On the other hand, you're moving like you're tense, so she might be right. Let yourself relax. You need softer hands or you're going to fumble the second you get the snap."

"I won't."

"I know you won't. Because you'll get your head in the game before then." Chris pushes to his feet and steps over the bench in one motion. He grips Alaric's hand, tugs him in to thump a hand against his back. "Go out there and kick some ass, Herne."

Alaric's breath goes tight and for just a moment he squeezes Chris's hand too hard. He hears the small noise Chris makes and let's go quickly; he doesn't want to break anything. There's heat in his face, and he swallows as he looks away, ignores the fact that Chris lingers for a moment before he walks away.

Alaric liked it better when he was captain of his own team. He liked being the top of the pecking order on the team rather than the new guy who needs a pep talk before he goes on the field. Because he's fine. He is absolutely fine, and he's going to get out there and perform better than anyone expects. Fuck nerves, and fuck the beast. Fuck the way the hound is upset by the onslaught of change.

He can do this.

He lines up with the team, makes an entrance onto the field as a song plays; he doesn't even register what it is. He waits until his number and position are called, then moves out to join the line of starting players for the night. This is it, his first game starting at PHU, and everything he's been waiting for.

It's time to show them that the scholarship is money well spent.

PHU loses the coin flip, so Alaric has time on the sidelines to wait. He bounces on his toes, does little sprints to keep himself warm while he watches how the other team plays. He won't have to deal with their offense, but it's still good to know how they think, what kinds of plays they rely on. The defensive coach will have different ideas, but watching will still give him insight into the overall play style.

And frankly, in his opinion, they suck. The quarterback is slow and steady, preferring short, quick passes that get them nowhere when the PHU defense tackles the receiver, pushing him back. Alaric stops moving when they're on a fourth down and decide to punt, and special teams goes in.

It's time. He's about to be on.

The kick goes long, bouncing into the end zone for a touchback, and the refs bring the ball out to the 20-yard line. Alaric runs onto the field with the rest of the offensive starting line, everyone clapping shoulders and butts on the way by.

Focus.

They move into position, the play already set, and Alaric glances up after he settles into a crouch. This is the moment when time seems to stop, when he can look over the opposing team and try to read what they're going to do. He goes through the play, takes the snap and sinks back, arm up as he seeks out the receivers. He spots Jensen midway down the field and lets the ball fly.

He doesn't even see the hit that takes him down coming.

It's just on the edge of legal, and for a moment he wonders where the hell his defense was, why they didn't protect him from being hit. But he wasn't sacked, the ball left his hand in a valid pass, and while Jensen's on the ground, the refs are signaling a good catch.

The opposing player stands up, offers Alaric a hand. He clasps it automatically, sees the sudden swift grin from behind the mask of his opponent.

"So it's like that," the other guy whispers. Number 44, Marks by the name on his jersey. "Didn't know they let dogs on the field."

There's a swift rush of blood to Alaric's head, enough to make his ears ring and his body sway. He clenches his hands, refuses to listen to whatever Marks says next.

But he can't get away, can't get his fullback into position to block Marks. It's like Marks just walks right through, takes Alaric down every damned time until his head is spinning. He loses ground after being sacked, makes it up with a wobbly pass that just barely makes it into Jensen's hands for a first down.

And everyone's watching. He can hear the voices, hears Drea plain as day shouting his name, cheering for him. And Chris, standing by the sideline, yelling to him. Yelling at him. The advice and encouragement burns in his chest, because he's disappointing them. He is fucking this up and he can't get the ball down the field, and he needs to get it right.

He hunkers down at the line of scrimmage, calls the play on the third down, and waits for the snap from the center. As soon as he has the ball in his hand, he looks up, sees Marks coming toward him.

And he won't let him. He won't let Marks take this away from his team.

The hound bays in his heart, but it's the bear who burgeons forth. It's the bear that sends him lumbering into Marks, throwing him roughly to one side before he sinks back into humanity and rushes ahead, racing to the other end of the field.

He hears the whistle, sees the flag, and he skids to a stop.

The bear.

Fuck.

Alaric turns slowly, the ball dropping from nerveless fingers. The opposing team clusters around a fallen figure on the ground, the coach crouched over Marks as he holds up three fingers. There's a call for a stretcher, and Alaric dimly registers the penalty of aggravated unnecessary roughness. A hand touches his shoulder, and he blinks and looks at Dawson, nods as Dawson takes his place on the field.

He's numb as he walks off the field, yanks his helmet off before he even gets to the bench. He sinks down on the bench and looks out over the turf again, spots where Marks is on the stretcher, slowly being wheeled off.

"He's conscious; he's going to be fine." Chris settles next to Alaric on the bench, his helmet off as well. Brown eyes are soft and kind, careful as he nudges his knee into Alaric's. "Coach is going to want to talk to you about that."

"Yeah." Coach. Both coaches. Whatever governing bodies there are. Alaric knows there will be people looking for him and that this is bad. Possibly scholarship-ending levels of bad. A full-body shudder rolls through him, and he clasps his hands together, tries to keep the change from happening again.

He has control. He's better than this.

"Has that ever happened before?" Chris's voice is low, carefully even.

Alaric shakes his head. "Not like that." Not with the beast escaping. He's punched a guy. More than once, but always after being pushed, always after the fight has already broken out around him. Alaric has a temper, he knows this, but he's always managed to keep it at bay on the field. It's always been the only place where the beast was fully at rest and under control. Until now.

"Herne!" Assistant Coach Young calls out, points to the locker room.

Alaric rises slowly, ignores the way that Chris pats his butt to offer luck on the way by. There's nothing he can do now. Alaric will be lucky to still be on the team after the game is done. Better to face the music now with Young than to have to wait. It's barely happened and he's already ready for it to be over with.

5

ALARIC SLUMPS IN the chair behind Young's desk in the office that the coaches share. He spins it slightly back and forth, his toe pressed against the floor, his fingers digging into the arm of the chair. Left, right, left, right. It squeaks every time he goes left, groans a little going right; the sounds synchronize like the rise and fall of a song.

"Alaric."

His nostrils flare as he looks up. Coach Campbell is there, with Young behind him, and even though he can't see them, Alaric recognizes the scent and heartbeats of Drea and Rory in the hall. He presses his lips together thinly and stares at the wall above the door. "Have they made a ruling?"

"They need time to consider," Campbell says.

"This is the first time there's been a bear attack during a game," Young adds, and Alaric can catch the hint of amusement in his scent.

It's not funny.

"Fine," he says sharply. "I'll wait here." He pushes at the floor roughly with his toe, sends his chair spinning to the left, leaving his back to the door. The hound whispers in the back of his mind, and with a growl he spins to the right again, crosses his arms, and stares at the coaches.

"You're having a tantrum." He still can't see her, but Drea's voice is clear.

"I'm trying to maintain control," Alaric counters. "In case you didn't notice, I hurt someone."

"They'll review the tapes, determine all the factors, and make a ruling." Campbell leans on the corner of the desk, looks down at Alaric. "In the meantime, go back to your dorm and find a way to relax. I expect the decision will come tomorrow, and we'll probably have a small press conference."

Great. Just fucking great. "I can stay here."

"You're not in jail," Young points out. "And I have work to do and need my desk. You're fine, Herne, and you'll be more settled if you're in your own space. You're not the first Clan I've worked with."

"I'm the first to shift on the field in the middle of a game," Alaric snarls, his teeth dropping sharp as his lip curls. Campbell doesn't move, and Young only steps closer.

"We're still learning how to integrate Talent in Division 1 sports," Young says blandly. "At least you didn't light the field on fire like Halstead did in Seattle."

"No one got hurt then."

Silence at that, because it's true. Halstead may have killed off an entire field of grass, made it so they had to replace the turf and forfeit a game, but no one was hurt. Whereas Alaric may have been pissed off at Marks, but he hadn't wanted to hurt the guy. His beast apparently had different plans.

"You can't stay here." Campbell points to the door. "Your roommate's waiting, and the team is already gone so you don't have to deal with them. Just go back to your dorm and get a good night's sleep. I'll let you know as soon as we have a decision."

Fine. Alaric pushes to his feet, starts to head out, but hesitates at the door. "How bad do you think it's going to be?"

"One game suspension, minimum," Young says. "You showed Talent on the field, and you used it against another player in an offensive manner. That's an aggravated penalty at the very least. We won't know the rest until we know how Marks is."

Alaric's mouth is dry; he has no idea what happened. He has minimal memory of what he did, no coherent view of how he might have hurt Marks. All he knows is what he saw afterward, and that if it weren't serious, someone would already have given him more information. He nods once and backs out of the room, stopping when he comes up against Drea's hand at his back.

He closes his eyes and drinks in her scent, takes comfort from the closeness of Clan and twin.

"Do you have everything you need?" Drea asks.

He has to look at her when he shakes his head, and he can't avoid spotting Rory standing behind her, just out of reach and slightly hunched, arms crossed over his chest. He looks away and tries not to catch the scent of what Rory's feeling. He doesn't need more fear, more worry. He shakes his head quickly. "My bag's at my locker. I went into the office after I got changed. I couldn't stay in there."

"Makes sense." Rory's voice is steady when he speaks. "Want me to go in and get it for you?"

"I'll get it. If the team's gone, it doesn't matter if you come in too." He includes Drea in the gesture, loathe to leave his twin behind, and when he pushes open the door, she's right behind him as he goes inside.

He heads straight for the team space in the back. His bag lies where he left it against his locker, which hangs ajar. He tugs the door open, makes sure his equipment is stored properly, his helmet on the shelf, then closes it with quiet finality. That might have been his only game at PHU, and it wasn't more than a scrimmage.

Someone clears their throat; Chris is standing three lockers down, a towel wrapped around his waist.

"My sister's in here," Alaric says, and Chris laughs softly.

"She ducked out of sight as soon as she saw me, along with her boyfriend," Chris says. He tucks the towel a little tighter, and Alaric's gaze drops to his hips and the bright line that the white of the towel makes across his skin.

Think later. Don't stare now.

Alaric looks up slowly, meets Chris's eyes. "Don't think I'll be starting again any time soon," he says. "Dawson's not bad. Train him up and he'll be fine."

"Jeff Dawson's a decent player, but he's not you." Chris reaches into his locker and pulls out a shirt, tugs it over his head. "You'll be back, Ric. What did Coach say about the decision?"

Alaric shrugs. "Tomorrow, probably. Press conference." He should say more, but it's hard to find the words right now. All he can think is *disappointment*, and it rings in his ears louder than anything else.

Chris makes a small noise, turns his back, and drops his towel so he can pull on a pair of tight boxer briefs. By the time he turns around again,

Alaric's gaze is firmly on his face, and Alaric is holding onto his bag, ready to go.

"I'll be here for the press conference," Chris says easily. "All three captains will be here, and we'll have your back. So don't worry, Ric. Marks knew what he was signing up for in a Blended league."

"If it happened to you?" Alaric has to ask, because he doesn't know if Marks is Talented or not, but he's pretty damned sure he knows where Chris Stone lies on that scale.

"I wouldn't blame you," Chris says firmly. "Go get some rest. Do whatever you have to do to work those nerves out, Ric. I'm not going to say drink—you're in training. But spend time with friends, go get laid, whatever it takes. Unwind. The shoe will drop tomorrow, and we'll deal with it then, okay?"

No, it's not okay. Alaric's not sure it's going to be okay tomorrow, either, but he nods because that's what Chris expects, and he takes a step back.

Chris turns away to grab jeans from his locker, and Alaric takes that as a dismissal, heading quickly for the door and holding it open so that Rory and Drea can precede him into the hall.

"You could have corrected him," Rory grumbles.

"About what?" Alaric's confused, and Drea's laughter surprises him, as out of place as it seems.

"About Rory being my boyfriend. Mom and Dad would have absolute shit fits if I brought home a musician and said I'm dating him." She giggles so hard she starts snorting, and it's infectious enough that he laughs before he realizes what she's said. His gaze darts between the two of them, Drea still laughing and Rory rolling his eyes.

"I am not dating you just to piss your parents off," Rory tells her. "You're not my type."

"You're not my type either, cute as you are." She manages to land a kiss on his cheek and Alaric isn't even sure how, given that Rory's a solid foot taller than her. Then she links her hand with Alaric's and squeezes gently. "Let's get you back to your room and order a pizza or Chinese or something. So you can relax. Unless you'd rather take the rest of his advice."

Alaric can feel his cheeks heating up abruptly and wonders if it shows.

"No," he says curtly.

He takes a few steps, stutters to a stop when he almost walks into Rory, who falls back abruptly. Alaric's jaw goes tight, and he looks at the wall. "I'm not going to hurt you," he mutters, a snarl tearing at his throat.

"I didn't think you were." Rory doesn't move, standing only a few inches from Alaric, one hand slightly raised. "I just—" He turns his hand palm up, offers it, and Alaric has no idea why.

Alaric's brow furrows. "What?"

Rory's breath goes tight. "Will you let me touch you if I say it will help?" A small thin smile. "This isn't... I don't touch people like this all the time, not unless they're family or close friends. And you don't like to be touched, I get that. But this...it will help."

Alaric doubts that. He's already got Clan with him, and Drea's scent wraps around him like comfort, and if that's not enough he can't think what would be. But what does he have to lose? "Fine." He reaches out, bridges the distance between them and lets his fingers close around Rory's.

There's a second where nothing happens, then his anger melts away, the fury dropping into a soft buzz in his chest. Alaric tugs his hands free, presses them to his chest as the beast rises under his skin again, making him itch.

"Do you see?" Rory offers his hand again, and Alaric warily takes it, waits for the moment when the beast leaves him alone. "It's my innate Talent. Some people control fire. Some people call storms. Me, I make Talent stop." There's a faint flush on his cheeks, high bright points against pale skin, and Alaric just swallows because he can't find the words for what this feels like.

He's not sure if he likes it, but it's better for now.

"I could kiss you for this," Drea says, and Rory's scent goes sour.

"Please don't," he replies.

The door behind them opens, and Alaric freezes. He turns, his hand still tucked into Rory's; Chris stands in the doorway, his bag slung over one shoulder, attention fixed on Alaric. Chris cocks his head, and he looks them over, sweeping from Alaric to Rory to Drea, then he nods once and turns to walk away without speaking.

"This looks far more awkward than it is," Rory says, and Alaric winces.

"It doesn't matter." Alaric slowly takes his hand away, shoves both his hands in his pockets. "And thank you. It's…it helps. If you could—if you wouldn't mind…" He isn't quite sure what he's asking, but Rory nods anyway.

"Sure. We'll get food, watch a movie, and I'll…" Rory raises his hand and drops it.

Drea bumps Alaric with her shoulder. "Between him and me, we'll get you back on track." She tangles his fingers with his, and Alaric lets her because he can walk across campus holding his sister's hand. That's okay. "Don't worry, Alaric. Everything's going to be just fine."

Aggravated unnecessary roughness. A Talent-based penalty, and at minimum, a one game suspension. Alaric's not sure anything's going to be fine after this, but there's nothing he can do until the decision is handed down. "Of course, Drea," he mutters, and he follows when she tugs; Rory falls in behind them. "Everything's going to be perfect."

Excerpt from *When Magic Entered the World: Interviews With Lineage Talent,* by Pawel Szczek, © 2009

I was eighteen that summer. I didn't like gymnastics, but my youngest sister was obsessed with the sport. We were home alone, and she was watching the Junior Nationals on TV, while I was trying to read and hiding in the next room over so I could ignore her chatter.

Then she screamed, and I didn't know if it was a shriek of pleasure or a howl of terror. Lightning struck the rod at the top of the house, and thunder boomed all around us as it started pouring down rain that sheeted against our windows. Whatever it was that made her scream, it also had her calling down a storm from nowhere, and she was only eight years old.

She screamed my name—*Tammy! Tammy!*—and I ran into the living room where she was jumping up and down, pointing at the TV. There was a dark-skinned girl in a bright yellow leotard performing on the bars; it's funny how I remember exactly how she looked, her hair all tightly pinned in place on top of her head but fuzzing out around her face as she moved effortlessly from the lower bar to the top bar and started to do those big loops. She released the top bar and flew into the air. Something wasn't right, and I could see that she wasn't going to be able to catch the bar on the way down. The television went silent, as if everyone held their breath in horror, then the girl blinked out of existence.

One moment she was there, and the next she was gone. The announcer shouted, and I saw the girl falling from much higher, blinking in and out of existence before she caught the bar and swung around and around it. She dismounted after that, stuck a perfect landing and threw her arms up in the air while the cameras zoomed in on her shaky smile that didn't even come close to reaching her eyes.

The replay started again, and I muted the TV.

My sister was chattering, amazed at what she had just seen. The storm outside faded to a soft pitter-patter of rain, and I walked to the window, threw it open, and leaned out to feel the water over my fingertips. I touched it and sent it on its way, coaxed the clouds to disperse until the sky was as blue as it had been before our world was shaken.

Because I knew then that everything would be different. What I didn't know was what would happen next, and I wondered, would we finally be free to tell the world about our magic? Or would our neighbors come hunting witches and burn us at the stake?

NEW BEGINNINGS

6

ALARIC FOLLOWS RORY into the lecture hall. They pause in the back, Alaric's nostrils flaring, his expression twisting at the thick scent of too many people. He smells a buzz from the caffeine, a heavy overlay of chocolate, coffee, and tea above the other scents, muddled with sweet pastry and egg sandwiches. There's a touch to the back of his shoulder, and the scents fade.

Alaric glances at Rory. "I don't need your help." The cacophony of scents floods back in as Rory's hand falls away.

"You stopped dead, so I figured..." Rory stops, looks out over the lecture hall. "We should get seats. Front, back, or middle?"

There's really no good answer. "Not the middle," Alaric grumbles. If he can keep from being surrounded, the beast under his skin should be mollified at least somewhat. He spots Pat sitting at one end of a row with a dark-haired girl that Alaric doesn't recognize, their skateboards leaning up against the wall. Drea's in class as well, but she's dead center of the front row, and Alaric doesn't feel like being that close to the professor, nor that much in view of the rest of the class. He nudges Rory, points quietly toward Pat, and they head that way.

Pat glances up when they drop into the two seats behind him, a quick grin brightening his expression. "Hey. Ric, Rory, this is Sera."

"Hey." She turns slightly, one hand raised. It's covered in black ink, an intricate design that starts around her wrist and trickles across the back of her right hand like lace. Alaric just barely catches the glint of shine from her nose ring; his gaze narrows slightly, because he can smell more metal but doesn't see it, not at this angle. When she curls her fingers down, leaving only her middle finger raised, he makes an embarrassed sound.

"I don't like staring," she says.

"If I don't figure people out, it irritates the beast," Alaric tells her flatly.

"So you needed to figure out my tits?" She twists more, looks over her shoulder at him, one eyebrow raised. Now he can see a narrow silver bar through the edge of her eyebrow, and he spots a small cluster of five silver rings just at her temple.

"Piercings. Smelled the metal," Alaric says. "I never even noticed anything else." His voice is even. "I don't really give a fuck about your tits." If she's going to be blunt, he might as well be blunt right back.

She twists fully around now and reaches up to pat his cheek. "I think I like you," she says, then she slumps in her chair again, arms crossed and her back to Alaric.

He looks at Rory, because honestly, what just happened? Rory shrugs, and Alaric sighs.

There's a sound pricking at his ears, too low for anyone else to notice. Alaric rubs at his ear, spots Drea doing the same along with two people in the back. It lasts for only a moment before it cuts out, replaced by tapping against a microphone and squealing feedback that dies out as soon as the chatter goes silent.

"Sorry, sorry." The man standing next to the podium doesn't look old enough to be teaching. He's got sharp cheekbones but a slight roundness to the rest of his face that makes him seem young, and the buzzed haircut doesn't help. "But hey, now that I've got your attention, let's get this show on the road. I've got a hundred of you in this section, and another hundred and fifty in the Tuesday morning section, so if you don't pay attention you're going to get lost in the shuffle."

He claps his hands once, the sound reverberating in the room. "I'm Pawel Szczek. My name is not a sneeze, and I'm not Professor S. You will practice it, learn my name, and when you talk to me, you will use it. This is only polite, just like I will learn every one of your names, and I expect you to learn the names of every other student and professor you interact with regularly on this campus. They say that names have power, and while it's not true that knowing a true name can help you conjure a curse against a person, it does go a long way to making friends. So let's all say it once together: Szczek."

Alaric would feel more awkward repeating the name aloud like a five-year-old if it weren't for everyone else around him doing exactly the same thing. He has to admit, it doesn't sound a thing like it looks. He writes down *Szheck* in the corner of his notes to remind himself.

"Good. If you keep going past this class and get into one of my seminars, your reward is that you can call me Pawel, which is a hell of a lot easier to pronounce." Pawel reaches for a stylus and starts drawing on his laptop, the words projecting onto the screen behind him. "There are five TAs for this class, and each one will be teaching two recitation classes of twenty-five students each. If you don't already know, recitation is your chance to go over homework, ask questions, and seek clarification. It's not required that you attend recitation, but we highly recommend it. Which brings me to my next point: I don't care if you're Talented or not, you're here to learn. Don't think you know everything just because you grew up with magic, because you probably don't."

There's a small flash in the front row, and Pawel glances that way, then nods. He finishes writing on the screen, and Alaric copies down the five names and email addresses. "You already have your recitation on your schedule. Your TA will email you before the first session. I highly recommend that you at least try to get to that one."

Pawel sets the stylus down with a soft *thunk*. "Welcome to Introduction to Magical Studies. This is a gateway course. Without this, you cannot take more advanced courses in this major. Without this, you cannot declare either a major or a minor within this department. This is the class that almost everyone takes at some point or another. It is offered in the fall, in the spring, and in the summer. If you think you're in the wrong place, please feel free to consult with me. If you want to change sections, you're out of luck because Tuesday's already overfilled. If you think you're going to hate me as a professor, you might be right, but give it a few days. I'm an acquired taste."

Pawel grins, and Alaric grins back before he thinks about it. He scowls when he catches himself, busies himself copying down the remainder of the information about the TAs.

"Quick personal points about me. I have office hours; pay attention to them." Pawel leans against the front of the podium, crosses his arms. "I'm busy, and while I spend a lot of time on this campus, I have plenty of responsibility. I am the faculty advisor for the PHU Coven, and I am a faculty coach for the PHU taekwondo team. I am also a single parent." He gestures at where a young boy sits in one of the yellow chairs in the front, headphones in his ears, thoroughly absorbed in a game on his tablet. "Conor will be a guest here until his own school starts. My schedule revolves around classes, office hours, and him. Any questions?"

Pawel gestures at one of the raised hands in the back of the room, and he goes through answering a series of questions fired at him from students, all about the specifics of the class. Alaric doesn't care. He takes the syllabus that one of the TAs passes down the line of seats and looks that over instead, adding office hours into his calendar and signing up for the text notifications for both his specific recitation and the entire class.

"Books!" Pawel gestures and the remaining questioning hands around the room lower. "There are three of them. There will be selected periodic readings available in the library that I will expect you to review and return. We will also be watching two movies, selections from two modern television shows, and video of important events taken when Talent and the modern world have intertwined. There will be classes that begin early—they are noted on the syllabus. I'll bring donuts, you'll be on time. It's that simple. If you don't already have the books, get them. Your first readings are listed on the syllabus, and they are due on Wednesday morning; be prepared for discussion. In the meantime, let's do some introductions. If there is anyone in this room who is willing to acknowledge being Lineage Talent, please raise your hand."

Alaric sees the small twitch from his sister, several rows down and several seats away. He murmurs an assent under his breath, and together they raise their hands. Perhaps a quarter of the room, maybe less, have their hands up, including Rory, and the two Alaric had noticed wincing at the sound earlier.

"Good. Plenty of personal experience to draw on in our discussions." Pawel gestures and waits for their hands to lower. "Next, anyone who is willing to acknowledge being Emergent Talent, please raise your hand."

There are fewer this time, including the professor himself, all five TAs, and Sera.

"Thank you." Pawel slowly looks around the room, and as his gaze seems to fall on him, Alaric sinks a little lower into his seat. "The rest of you are either not Talented or unwilling to disclose, which is fine. One of the important things we will be talking about in this class is the intersection between Talent and the rest of humanity, and how the Emergence changed the world in all aspects of society. Can anyone tell me one way that you see the world as having changed in the last ten years?"

Rory glances at Alaric, and Alaric sinks even lower into his seat. Alaric can think of several ways. Like football. Like having the chance to play and blowing it all by causing an injury to another player. He stares down at his paper and makes a conscious decision to let this discussion go on without him. He's had enough of this particular topic in his day-to-day life lately.

7

"Alaric Herne, can I speak to you before you leave?" Pawel isn't looking at the students as he gathers up the papers on his desk, but Alaric is still pretty damned sure that the professor knows exactly who he is.

"You were dead silent. How'd you get in trouble already?" Pat asks. He stands up, hitching his skateboard under his arm, backpack hanging low on his back.

"Some people are talented like that." Sera nudges Pat, her own board hanging loose from her fingertips, almost scraping the floor. "We've got class in Hopper, let's get going."

Alaric shoves his things in his bag, pausing when his phone chimes.

Need me to stay?

Drea's hovering at one of the exits on the lower level, near the stage. He shakes his head and texts her back: *I'm fine.* He waits for her to head out, then realizes that Rory's apparently already gone as well.

Alaric makes his way to the front of the room, where Pawel waits at the podium. Class ended early, so there's time before the students for the next class will filter in. The empty room doesn't help the way Alaric's skin itches, the beast reacting to the tension of having to stay trapped here and to the idea of potential confrontation.

Pawel looks up as he approaches, and Alaric catches a swift scent of ozone around him, as if lightning's struck at the front of the class. Pawel neatly stacks his papers on top of his laptop, then gives Alaric his full attention when he speaks. "I mentioned that we'd be reviewing incidents where Talent and the world have intersected in memorable—or impactful—ways. I'd like to use video of the game."

Alaric appreciates the blunt speech, even if his breath is tight in chest.

"Thanks for the warning," he says.

"It's not just a warning." Pawel leans against the podium with one hip, cocks his head as he crosses his arms. He's an inch shorter than Alaric, a little slighter, but it doesn't make him seem any less intimidating. The bright, fresh scent increases, and Alaric's hound whines, wants him to step back. Instead Alaric swallows and stands his ground; Pawel seems to relax a little and the scent fades.

"Then what is it?"

"I'm asking permission." Pawel shrugs one shoulder, and Alaric isn't sure he believes him. "There are plenty of incidents I can use, places where Talent has come out unexpectedly, or has been used very purposefully in ways that the Talented never thought would impact those around them or themselves. Your incident has several advantages over others, however. For one, most of the freshmen in this class either attended the game or heard about it after. For another, there were two incidences of use within the game: one purposeful, and one accidental and reactive. It highlights both sides of the equation, as well as highlighting how the rules of the game have changed in order to protect the players in the Blended league."

"Sounds like you have it all thought out," Alaric mutters. "It's not like I'm going to say no because I'm worried people will find out. It was on the fucking news." He catches himself moments after the word is out. "Sorry."

Pawel laughs and looks past Alaric. He shakes his head. "My son has his headphones in, so it's not like you're corrupting young ears. Look, I'm going to blow more F-bombs during the year than you'd think any professor would. Most of them will be accidental, but there are some that are very much on purpose. I understand the reasons behind language, Alaric. We speak the way we do because it helps present emotion and tension, and it adds verbal clarity to the situation. I'm not going to ask you to temper your speech in class unless you are being offensive to another person. In this particular case, given your situation, I can't deny that the news was not on your side. That's another aspect we will discuss, because prejudice against Talent remains a problem even a decade after the Emergence and will continue to be a problem for a long time. So yes, I really am asking permission. While it's a fantastic choice to use for this class, I can find other options if you think it will be a problem."

"It won't be a problem." The words are tight, but Alaric forces them out. He needs to deal with this, and he needs to face it head on. "I have a three-game suspension, and I have to do mandatory anger management counseling, all because some asshole decided to use his Talent to antagonize me."

"And what kind of suspension did he get?" Pawel asks.

"One-game suspension, can't start for the first half of the season," Alaric tells him. He memorized Marks's sentence as much as his own, and it fucking burns that Marks gets off lighter than he does. Some people might argue that because Marks is a senior, it's worse for him, losing out on starting for most of his senior year. "It pisses me off," Alaric grumbles. "He did it on purpose, and I'm the one paying because he pushed me to the point where I shifted."

"There are arguments to be made in both directions." Pawel's tone is mild, and he holds up one hand. "I'm not going to say whether I agree or disagree with any argument, either. But be prepared that we will be looking at all aspects of this case, because Marks did act with full knowledge of what he was doing. And you did lose control, and in doing so, Marks was injured. On the other hand, you expressed immediate knowledge of what you had done, expressed regret, and left the field, whereas Marks hid his actions until they were proven during a review of records, and that's why the punishment wasn't handed out immediately." He pauses, gaze narrowing. "What are you intending to do for your anger management?"

Alaric shrugs. "Haven't talked to the coaches about it yet. I'm sure they've got something they want me to do. We've got practice today."

"I've got something I want you to think about, and I'll send it to your head coach as well." Pawel digs out his wallet and withdraws a card. On the front there is a silhouette of a figure kicking, and it says PHU TKD. On the back is Pawel's name, email, and multiple phone numbers. "Come by on Wednesday at 7 p.m. in the gym—we're in one of the exercise rooms upstairs. You're Clan; you're not going to be satisfied by yoga or tai chi. You need an active form of anger management, a way to channel your energy and find your center. I've known plenty of other Talents who've used tae-kwondo as an outlet for their energy, myself included, as well as my son. It's particularly helpful with Emergents who've never had to handle that kind of energy before, but if you're having control issues, I think it could help as well."

Fighting. Because that sounds like such a good idea to Alaric, using violence to make himself less angry. He shakes his head but tucks the card into his pocket. "Maybe."

There's a soft sound of someone walking in, and Alaric tenses for a moment before he recognizes Rory's scent. He turns before Rory clears his throat.

"I just wanted to ask Professor Szczek about Coven," Rory says quietly. "It's the only official club for Mages, and I'm interested in traditional ritual. Thorne participated his freshman year."

Pawel grins. "Thorne Baker? I remember him. He was…explosive, then he took a year off."

"Dad calls him a force of nature." Rory gestures with his right hand. "And he's back. He's my brother."

Pawel holds up his hand, one finger in a clear *hold that thought* gesture. His gaze falls on Alaric. "I want you to think about what we discussed and let me know by email what your decision is. Take some time and don't just say yes because you feel you have to. And if you want to talk to someone who's Talent-aware but isn't a therapist or your coach, feel free to come by my office any time I have office hours or send me an email to schedule an appointment. Also, don't forget what I said about Wednesday."

Rory throws him a curious look, but Alaric doesn't want to get back into that particular conversation, so he just nods once. "Fine, yes, I'll let you know." It's a statement that covers everything Pawel has said, and it gives him an escape. "See you later, Rory," he mutters, and heads out of the room.

8

WHEN ALARIC WALKS into the practice room in the gym for the first meeting of the taekwondo club, he's surprised to see how busy it is. They've opened an airwall, combining two rooms into one, and there are at least thirty people there. Some are standing awkwardly, like he is, around the edges of the room. Others are helping get mats out of the closet, spreading them out across the floor. Alaric spots Jackson, wearing the same kind of white pants as the people who seem to know what they're doing, along with a long-sleeved white top that looks hot in the late-summer heat.

Pawel directs Jackson to lay out one set of mats, and Jackson motions to Alaric when he sees him.

"Do you do taekwondo?" Jackson shows Alaric how to get the mats linked together like puzzle pieces, and they add a strip to the long line that covers most of the floor. Alaric shakes his head, and Jackson offers a reassuring grin. "I've been looking forward to working with the club. It was one of the things that drew me to PHU." He shrugs one shoulder. "That and the basketball scholarship."

"Figured I'd try it." Alaric feels like a fish out of water here. Everyone else seems skinnier. Quicker. Lighter on their feet. He's fought before, but it was brawling: fists and knees and wrestling on the ground. He glances at where a dark-skinned girl is bouncing lightly on her feet, tightly coiled springs of black hair in a cloud around her face, bouncing with her. She explodes forward, kicking at the targets that Pawel holds, three kicks in rapid succession before she finishes with a spinning kick that Alaric is pretty sure went as high as his own head. "Not sure it's for me," he mutters.

"You might be surprised. I started when I was a kid because I had behavior issues. Couldn't sit still," Jackson admits. "I had to stop for a while, but when I started again, I got my black belt. I had this and basketball, and I love them both."

Alaric's still watching the girl kick. It's like a dance, the way she moves, all compact energy and flowing motion. She almost seems to anticipate where Pawel is going to place the targets, footwork taking her easily from place to place, finding the target with her kick, then moving back out of range as he chases her down. There's a faint sheen of sweat on the back of her neck, just barely soaking the collar of a T-shirt that says *Kick with PHU* across the back.

She stops and turns, hands on her hips. She places her fingers to her lips and lets out a piercing whistle.

Everyone goes silent.

"Have a seat by the windows," she calls out. "Sit comfortably."

Alaric follows Jackson to a spot along the long wall of windows. They sit cross-legged with everyone else other than the girl and Professor Szczek. It gives Alaric a chance to take stock, notice the smaller details, like the black belt around Jackson's waist with his name on it and the brightly colored belts some of the others wear. There are T-shirts that say PHU or Pine Hills University, and there are T-shirts bearing names that Alaric has to assume are taekwondo schools. Or maybe they're something else entirely; he honestly has no idea.

The girl takes a moment to look over the group. Hands on her hips again, she faces the group and smiles slightly. Her T-shirt says *I get FIERCE to stay CALM* on the front, and Alaric's gaze shifts from that to Pawel, who is watching him in return.

"My name is Mac Palmer, and I'm the coach of the PHU taekwondo team," Mac announces. "I've been doing taekwondo since I was a kid, and I got my first-degree black belt when I was a teenager. I'm currently a third degree, and if you forget my name, you'll see it right here." She holds up her belt where her name is embroidered. "You'll call me Coach Palmer, or Miss Palmer. I'm not a Master yet—but Master Pawel is. Give him the respect that's due."

Pawel raises a hand, points to Mac. "Give me respect, yes, but remember that even though I outrank her, Mac's in charge. I'm just here as the faculty advisor. I've been kicking since I was four years old, and my dad enrolled me because I was a hyperactive little shit, and because I was small and easily bullied. I sometimes train with my son's taekwondo school, but my primary training is here, with all of you. Don't be intimidated by the kind of belt someone wears—we're all still learning, here."

Mac gives him a side-eye. "He likes to take charge more than he thinks," she says dryly. "But yes, I'm the primary coach. We meet on Wednesday, Friday, and Saturday, and you can join the club whether you've never done taekwondo before or if you've been doing it since you were four. I don't care if you have Talent or not, but if you want to compete, you must be purely human. Talk to me if you're interested in competition." She never quite stops moving, bouncing slightly on her toes as she speaks. "We're going to pair up, get ourselves warmed up, start working on some basics. If you've never done this before, pick a partner who's wearing uniform pants and a belt. The darker the color, the more experience they have. Newbies, pick a brown, red, or black belt if you can. Any final words?" She glances at Pawel.

"Just this." Pawel's expression is serious. "This is based on the tradition of martial arts, but it's also a sport. There will be forms, movements that you need to learn, but there will also be fighting. When you're working, don't think about how hard the techniques are. Don't hesitate. Don't overthink it. Commit to the kick. It's easier to do something when you give it all you have than it is to accomplish a goal if you're afraid. Be willing to go all-in. We're all here to help you. And everyone falls on their ass at some point, even the black belts. Pick yourself up, move on."

Jackson taps Alaric's shoulder, and Alaric nods in response; as Mac calls out for them to run, they start jogging around the room side by side. Mac leads them through warmups which are familiar enough from football— a mix of endurance, speed footwork, and flexibility. By the time they're claiming space on the mats to work together, Alaric can already feel the burn of hard work.

Jackson holds two paddles, and they start with simple kicks, working from the quick front kick to a rotating roundhouse kick, then the sharply falling axe kick. It's a simple set of drills, ten kicks on each side, switch partners, then repeat until Mac changes the drill. Alaric needs to pay attention long enough to figure out how to hold the paddles properly for each kick, but it surprises him how easy it is to get out of his own head. He can focus on the repetitive motion, the simple act of getting into position, then firing the kick, then chambering his foot back so he can repeat. When Pawel asks him to stop long enough to correct his stance and help him see how far he needs to rotate his hips for the correct strike, Alaric simply nods and tries again. And again, and again.

They drop the paddles after a time, and Alaric lines up behind Jackson, learning what a horseriding stance is. They move quickly through the simplest of hand techniques—a proper punch, several blocks, a knifehand strike. Again, it repeats, over and over, until the sharp sound of Mac counting reverberates in his mind, and Alaric simply throws the technique and forgets everything else.

When Mac calls a halt, he's surprised to realize that he's damp with sweat, his hair falling across his forehead. He pushes it back, rubs the sweat from his eyes, and grabs for his water bottle. "It's more of a workout than I expected," he mutters into the water.

Jackson laughs. "It's fighting. We have to be in top shape if we're going to go two minutes in the ring with someone else. Football isn't the only physical sport on this campus, Ric."

Alaric throws him a dark look. "It's not that. It's just not…it's not the same as football. I'm in shape."

"And you're going to hurt tomorrow." Somehow Mac is right there, by his elbow. She's small, he realizes, her head coming to the top of his shoulder. It doesn't make her seem any less dangerous. Her stance is light and ready, her body tense. Alaric catches the scent of a predator rolling off of her, and he bares his teeth when he smiles at her.

"Oh yeah, this hits completely different muscles than basketball." Jackson slides down onto the floor into a straddle that's not far from a split, then sits back so he can stretch. "Don't be surprised if you hurt like hell tomorrow, Ric."

He has no idea how to reply to that, so he simply shrugs. "That's fine. Not afraid of getting hurt."

"I'll show you some stretching methods that can help." Mac takes a few steps, glances back at Alaric. "Come with me. We're going to talk."

"Guess I'll see you back at the dorm." Alaric follows Mac into the hall where he spots TJ, Patrick, and Sera lingering at the other end. Sera's on her skateboard, balancing, fidgeting while TJ and Patrick talk. Mac takes up a spot against the wall opposite the room; it looks like she has to concentrate on relaxing, arms folding over her chest and the wall taking her weight, legs crossed at the ankles.

"Pawel told me he recommended that you try this," Mac says. "I just wanted you to know that I know where you're coming from."

Great. Fuck. Alaric growls, the corner of his lip lifting in a snarl. He doesn't need a babysitter. "I'm not going to hurt anyone."

"I didn't think you would." Her tone stays mild, her brown eyes calm. "And if you do lose control, I'm stronger than I look, and I know techniques that could drop you in your tracks. Or at least make you cry like a baby and beg for me to let you go. But that's not the point I wanted to make here."

Seems like she made it anyway. "Then what was?" Alaric grumbles.

"The point is, I get it." She meets his eyes. "Pawel's not wrong—this is a great way of learning to control your temper, control your Talent. He's been through it, and so have I. It's not an easy road, and this isn't the answer for everyone. But the repetition, the need to think through exactly how hard you hit a target—or a person—really does help. It's a level of control you're not going to get in football. But it's also a different level of control and respect that we'll be demanding from you, and we'll expect you to practice. So if you're not up for it, don't start."

"The fuck?" Alaric shakes his head, pulls back from her so he won't advance on her; he doesn't want to loom. "You think I'd walk away just because you expect me to practice? It's okay. I liked it. Wasn't bad working with Jackson."

"You'll work with different partners. Tall ones, short ones. You'll learn how to measure your strength so you don't overwhelm a smaller opponent." Mac fires each word like a bullet, and Alaric finds himself nodding along. "And in the end, we're here to help the non-Talented folks get to a point where they can compete. And we can't work toward competing ourselves, because there isn't a Blended league to allow Talent to compete in taekwondo yet. So you'll be stuck on the sidelines. Benched." Her smile is small and tight.

"That's fine." Another door farther down the hall opens, and people spill out, talking as they go. Jackson lingers for a moment, and Alaric waves slightly; Jackson turns and meets up with TJ and the others and they head downstairs. "I'm in," Alaric says firmly. "Where do I get the T-shirt and pants?"

"This T-shirt?" Mac pulls it out slightly, showing him the words.

I get FIERCE to stay CALM.

Alaric shrugs. "Sure. That one. Whatever shirts you have. I'm in." And maybe that particular shirt is dead-on, but it's not like Alaric can hide from his own reputation. That bear is going to follow him like a hulking shadow; he might as well show that he's making an effort to put it to rest.

9

THE SECOND TAEKWONDO class is as good as the first. Mac asks Alaric to stay when it's done, and waits for everyone to clear out, leaving the mats on the floor. Pawel lingers by the side, watching without saying a thing, while Mac shows Alaric the protective gear that they use when they fight. She helps him get the arm and shin protectors on, then laces him into a chest protector and hands him a helmet. He feels awkward, like the chest protector is too tight and restricts his breathing. The gear on his forearms seems to be in the wrong place, but he reminds himself that he won't be lowering his shoulder for a tackle here—he'll be blocking with his arm.

Mac leads him out to the center of the mats. "Pawel's the ref. He says stop, we stop. And this is just so you can get a feel for what it's like to kick an actual person. You need to know if this is something you're going to have to work on specifically, if it will trigger your change."

He rolls his eyes because no, it won't. But he also has no idea how hard to kick and doesn't want to damage Mac. In the end, they spend twenty minutes exchanging kicks, and Alaric knows exactly how much strength the slender woman has. She lands a head kick that makes his ears ring despite the helmet, and he shakes his head.

"Do you beat up every potential teammate?" he mutters, and Pawel laughs.

"Only the ones I'm worried about being able to bite my head off," Mac deadpans. When she grins, it's bright and shiny, her eyes creased in the corners. "I want you to do well, Alaric. You've got a lot of anger; I know what that feels like. And I know what it's like when it starts exploding out in all the wrong directions. Now go shower. We all reek when we take off the gear."

He isn't sure what to do with the gear as he takes it off, but Pawel gives him a backpack, shows him how to pack it up, and instructs him to take it back to his room and label each piece so he doesn't lose it. Alaric shoves it into his closet as soon as he gets back to the room, praying it doesn't smell as much as Mac threatened it might. But he probably does stink, so he strips quickly and wraps a towel around his waist before heading down the hall to the showers.

He hears people talking when he's walking back to his room. The door is slightly open, and Chris's voice is obvious. The other voice is familiar, but Alaric can't place it, and he isn't sure why they're in his room and why he doesn't hear Rory as well.

Alaric grips the edge of his towel with one hand, his basket of toiletries with the other. His shower shoes flap against the floor, and he sees the door pull open farther, then Thorne is standing there in his way.

"Didn't expect this," Thorne says cheerfully. His gaze lingers on Alaric's chest, then slowly drops to look him over. "But can't say I mind. You look good."

"You think all football players look good," Chris says, nudging Thorne out of the door.

"I think most athletes look good." Thorne shrugs. "Actually, I think most people look good, and the ones who think they don't just aren't seeing themselves in the right light. But Alaric here, he's a damned good example of an excellent specimen."

Alaric can feel the heat of his flush all over his chest and face, adding a red undertone to his tanned skin. "What are you doing here?"

"Believe it or not, I'm friends with him," Chris says dryly. "You get changed. We'll talk when you're wearing clothes."

"We could just wait here…" Thorne's voice trails off as Chris manhandles him through the door and into the hallway. "What? I won't look, if he doesn't want. Consent is important."

"You're ogling, and he's uncomfortable." Chris yanks the door shut, leaving Alaric standing in the middle of his own empty room.

The voices outside are muffled, but Alaric doesn't listen. He's not sure he wants to know what they're saying, although he catches something about freshman year, and something else about football, then he tunes out completely. He drops the towel, drags on clean clothes as quickly as he can. By the time he opens the door, Rory's there as well, slightly hunched as he ducks into the room, Thorne following after him.

"My house is throwing a party tonight," Chris explains. "Omega Pi Tau is mostly football players, although not everyone there is on the team. We always do something on the first Friday of the semester. First game's on Sunday, and we'll be spending part of Saturday on the bus. It's a good way to blow off steam before the real season starts."

Because that exhibition game was only a scrimmage. It didn't even count, and Alaric still managed to find a way to fuck things up. His gaze falls, and Chris catches him, squeezes his shoulder. "The team wants you there," he says quietly. "You took off after practice, and I didn't get the chance to tell you then. You're going to be at the games, even though you'll be on the bench. And you'll be playing when the suspension is over. So come over, spend some time with the team, and relax before the first game."

Relax before there are people watching him, staring at him, knowing that he's the one who fucked up. Alaric's breath is tight in his chest. Chris's fingers go a bit tighter on his shoulder. "Alaric?"

"Fine. I'll be there."

He doesn't mean to sound as blunt or dismissive as he does, and he winces when Chris abruptly drops the touch and steps away. "Good."

"And if getting laid is part of how you relax, there's nothing like a frat party to pick up girls," Thorne says with a ready grin. "Or boys, if that's your preference." Rory makes a choking noise, and Alaric feels the flush on his skin heat up all over again.

"I don't—" Alaric fails to find words.

"Leave off, Thorne." Chris slaps Thorne on the back hard enough to send him forward a step. "Let's go. I'm sure they'll make it over in their own time."

The door closes with a *thud* again, and Alaric looks over at Rory, who is leaning against his bunk, arms crossed tight over his chest.

"I feel like I've been run over by a truck," Alaric grumbles, and Rory snorts softly.

"A lot of people come out of encounters with Thorne feeling like that."
Rory unfolds himself carefully, picks up the discarded towel from the floor,
and tosses it over the back of a chair. "Are you going?"

If he goes, it's going to be uncomfortable. If he doesn't go, Alaric suspects
he'll offend the football team. He lifts one shoulder. "They're my teammates. I'm probably supposed to pledge the frat eventually."

"Do you want to?"

"Don't know. I'm not big on group houses. Never got much privacy at
home." Alaric pulls at his T-shirt, looks at it critically. He has no idea how
to dress for a frat party, and he doubts that movies or television shows are
at all accurate. "I should go. You going?"

"Thorne wants me to." Rory glances at the corner where his instruments
are stored. "It's not the kind of place where I can bring a guitar. At least not
when it's not an official gig."

"We'll go together. Have each other's backs."

It startles a laugh out of Rory. "It's not a fight."

"It's a social event." Which is worse, in so many respects. Alaric knows
what to do in a fight. He hates being in a social crowd, being expected to
make small talk, to know how to interact. "So let's go."

Once the decision's made, Alaric takes the time to switch into a different T-shirt, something that's a little nicer. He finds a blue thing that Drea
bought, then he texts Drea to tell her to meet him downstairs and they'll
walk over together. By the time Rory's done changing, there's a knock on
the door, and Soledad pushes it open without waiting for an answer.

"Drea says we're going to a party!" She links her arm through Rory's,
bumping him as they walk. "TJ's coming, and so are Jackson and Patrick.
Nikita's staying in—I don't even know why—and Pels is still at the library."
She shakes her head. "But Serina and Winter are coming, they'll meet us
downstairs."

It feels a little like they've gained an entourage, or maybe it's armor in
the form of people. As the group gathers just outside of Douglass, Alaric
counts heads and realizes that they're a small invasion force. He doubts this
was what Chris was looking for when he stopped in, but it makes Alaric
feel better. At least he knows he can stand these people and their familiar

scents. It'll help him get through the evening.

"And later, Drea and I are taking you with us to a sorority party," Soledad says.

Alaric meets Drea's gaze, and she nods as if to say *oh yes, we're going.* Maybe the evening isn't going to be as simple as Alaric thought.

10

THE PARTY IS just as bad as Alaric thought it would be, but also in some ways it's not nearly as awful as he'd worried. He fights with the keg to get a drink in a red cup and carries that and a can of soda back to the couch where Rory is sitting. As soon as he sits down, Soledad moves from the arm of the couch to his lap, one arm around his shoulders as she steals his cup for a gulp of beer. She passes it back and Alaric takes his own gulp; it's not good beer, and when Soledad reaches for his cup again, he lets it go easily. Two more girls come by, and Alaric doesn't catch their names, only that one of them is interested in his being a football player, and the other apparently recognizes Rory from some magazine article that was published that summer.

"It must be so *exciting* to be on tour," the girl gushes, and Rory pulls back a little.

"It's actually exhausting. And being in a van is cramped. And sweaty." Rory's smile looks forced, and Alaric can smell the tension in his bones. "Don't think it's romantic. It's actually a lot of hard work. Can you imagine what it would be like to be performing in front of people all the time?"

"I think it would be awesome." The girl pats Rory's arm, smile turning to a frown when he moves out of reach.

"I'm not interested," Rory says quietly, and the girl changes how she's sitting, drawing her feet up on the couch and taking up a smaller space between Rory and her friend. Her expression gentles as she gives him space.

"I'm not an asshole," she says, then shrugs one shoulder. "Okay, most of the time I'm not an asshole. And I try very hard to be less of an asshole when I'm drinking."

"Rory and I have very different views on sex."

Alaric blames the crowd for fucking with his senses, because he should have known Thorne was coming up behind him. He should have had some warning before there was a body leaning on the back of the couch, a face pressed close to his, and a voice whispering in his ear, breath hot on his skin. He grunts an acknowledgement, wincing when Soledad turns to see Thorne and gives a small shriek of joy.

"Want to join the pile?" she offers, patting the complete lack of space next to them, and Alaric struggles to take a deep breath.

"I think you've already buried Ric, and I don't want to intrude." Thorne drops one hand on Alaric's shoulder, fingers warm and light. "My advice to him was to relax by getting laid; if he doesn't find what he's looking for here, he knows where to find me."

"I'm not planning on getting laid tonight," Alaric manages to say, and Soledad pats his cheek.

"Neither am I. I am planning on remaining virginal as long as I can." She laughs at Alaric's expression and blows him a kiss. "Did you think I'm promiscuous just because I like to flirt?"

"I am." Thorne raises one hand. "Both flirty and somewhat promiscuous. No strings needed."

The conversation has gone beyond what Alaric's comfortable with. The girl next to him—Penny? Pansy? He can't remember what she said—is giving him a curious, thoughtful look, and the other unknown girl is still curled tight on the sofa, just outside of Rory's personal space. "Maybe we could stop talking about sex," Alaric says slowly. "Let's just assume there's no sex involved, and we can all flirt if you want. That's it." Not that Alaric even knows how to flirt. He just wants to stop any worry about someone coming on to him and expecting him to jump into bed.

"Any time you want to go out drinking and be my pretend protective boyfriend, I'm all in," Soledad tells him. She downs the rest of his drink in one gulp, then makes a face. "Sorry, finished your beer. I'll go get a refill and get you a new one at the same time." She shifts in his lap, about to climb off.

It's his chance, and Alaric shakes his head quickly, puts one hand on her hip to stop her. "You stay here. I'll bring back—" He counts heads quickly.

"Four—four?—beers. You need another soda, Rory?"

Rory's glance flashes between Thorne, Alaric, and Soledad, then stops when he gets to the other two girls. His eyes are wide, and he shakes his head. "I'm good."

Rory doesn't sound good, but he also motions like he figures Alaric is going to leave anyway, and Alaric takes that as permission to go.

As soon as Alaric stands, Thorne climbs over the back of the sofa and slides in to sit between the two unknown girls, opening his arms and offering his lap to Soledad. Rory's scent eases, and Alaric lingers just long enough to make sure that he seems okay. But then the conversation shifts focus from only Rory to Rory and Thorne and Phoenix Rising, and Alaric has a chance to make an escape.

He stops inside the kitchen to take a deep breath. He forgot Soledad's cup, but that doesn't matter. There's a leaning tower of red cups next to the keg, and now that Alaric has some idea how to operate the irritating temporary tap, it's easy to draw four cups. He tries to awkwardly carry all four, and when one of the other guys on his team—Dax—offers to help, Alaric shoves two of the cups at him. As he directs him to the sofa, Dax raises his eyebrows. "I don't think there's room on that for you."

"I don't mind." Alaric's not sure how he can deliver the beer and disappear once the guys have spotted him. "Look, you take these to them. I forgot one for me. Tall one's the only one not drinking." He tries to sound convincing, like the beer doesn't taste like piss.

"I've seen you with him." Dax juggles everything and manages to hold the four cups securely. "Boyfriend?"

Alaric stands his ground, manages to keep from flinching. He needs a slow breath before he shakes his head. "Roommate. Good friend already."

Dax nods. "It's good to make that kind of connection. Met my girlfriend during orientation a year ago and we clicked instantly." He raises the glasses. "I'll take those over. Go get yourself a drink. Don't overdo it; you might not be playing Sunday, but you'll still need a clear head."

Alaric inhales, tasting for vitriol on the breeze, but there's nothing other than friendly concern. He's not sure how to take that, and he steps backward, still watching, before he turns away and escapes back to the kitchen.

There is no way he's getting another cup of that swill for himself. He stands there with an empty cup in his hand and stares at the cabinets and fridge, wondering whether there's anything other than bad beer and soda. Fuck it, there's water; he can deal with that. It's not like he's going to be getting drunk anyway.

"Alaric."

He jerks back, twists the faucet roughly closed, the water sloshing in his cup as he turns around. "Chris. I just." He raises the glass.

"I'm not going to say anything if you're not drinking." Chris raises his hand to show that he's carrying a can of soda rather than anything alcoholic. "I'm not going to fault the guys for having something as long as it's not the night before a game, but I also don't blame anyone for not."

"It tastes like piss." Alaric bites his tongue as Chris's eyebrows go up. "We brew back at the community. I just can't convince myself to drink shit."

"You brew?" Chris sets his can on the counter, reaches back to pull his locs away from his face and twist them together, keeping them behind his shoulders. "My uncle used to, but it was strictly hands-off for us cousins."

Alaric snorts softly. "I grew up drinking beer. Most shapeshifters can't get drunk, so there's no point in holding off until we're twenty-one. It's just another drink to us, and we want it to taste good." He glances at the door; he can see a thin path out through the living room, including the sofa, where Dax is now perched at one end, a girl on his lap, and Thorne is in the middle with Soledad. Somehow there's a girl on Rory's lap, but she's talking to Thorne, and he doesn't get that strong whiff of anxiety from Rory. "I never brewed on my own, but it's just chemistry and cooking, if you've got the right equipment and a decent kitchen." He looks around. "This one would probably work."

"If you had the right equipment. Is it expensive?" Chris's dark-brown eyes are furrowed slightly, thoughtful. "I'm on scholarship; I don't have much in the way of spare money. But there are guys on the team who would buy into that, if you do the work." It smells like an honest offer, and Alaric nods slowly.

"It'd be another way to lower stress," he admits. He can get the recipes that the Clan uses, or at least the recipes that Orson started developing on his own. All it would take is one phone call. He should stay in touch better with Orson, and his father would be pleased that he's getting along with his brother and taking an interest in Clan ways. It might lower stress in more ways than one. He nods again. "There's a brew store back in Haverhill. We'd need a car, but I could show someone what to buy."

"We'll do that after we're back from the game, sometime in the next week or two," Chris says. He reaches out, grips Alaric's wrist lightly. "Hey. Don't flinch every time I mention the game. Has anyone on the team given you a hard time? I saw you with Dax earlier."

"They're fine." It's been easier than Alaric thought it would be. He knew they'd be fine on the field during practice, but here, with no coaches watching over them, he wasn't sure what to expect. "I'm fine." He lies the same way he's lied about things his whole life, his tone flat and gruff, no different than any other time. When Chris doesn't take his hand back, his attention still on Alaric as if he's trying to burrow inside of his head, Alaric jerks backward. "I'm fine," he repeats.

"You're tense, and you're worried. It's only a week into the semester and it looks like you've already got a lot going on." Chris's gaze flicks toward the door, and Alaric has no idea what he's talking about, why that seems to be a significant look.

"I haven't missed a practice or a class. I'm here. I've been to taekwondo twice, and I'll go tomorrow." Alaric shrugs one shoulder, because okay, maybe he does have a lot going on already. "Professor Szczek recommended it, and it's not bad."

"I know Mac—the coach. She's a junior, and we've had some classes together. She's older than the rest of us, here on some kind of GI bill. She's quiet most of the time, and incredibly focused, and she's good at what she does." Chris holds up one finger. "I might have tried kicking a few times because she tried to convince me I could do it. I can't. It's just not my thing. But if it helps you, that's good, and we'll support you when you compete."

"Can't compete." It seems logical to Alaric, but Chris gives him a quizzical look. "Talent," Alaric reminds him. "It's not Blended, so only humans can compete. You could."

"I could," Chris says, confirming Alaric's assumption that he's not

Talented. He glances at the door again, takes a step back as Pat comes sliding through, one hand up as if he can get Alaric's attention from a distance.

"I think Rory could use a rescue," Pat says quickly. "There's a drunk girl who seems to be very intent on kissing a famous musician, and Rory seems equally intent on not being kissed."

Alaric sifts through the scents, quickly finds one that matches Thorne and arousal that seems to be nowhere near the main room, whereas Rory is still on the same sofa and now reeks of tension. "What happened to Thorne?"

"A girl and a guy and they just left a little bit ago." Pat gestures between Alaric and the door. "Sera and I tried to intervene, but we figured you're bigger and you're Rory's friend, so..."

It's logical in its own way. "I'd better go."

Chris exhales, the sound tight in his throat. "There's a bus that goes to the away games, sometimes, with the pep band and supporters. If there's anyone that you want at the games, they could probably get a spot on the bus."

"Drea's not into football." She'll go when it's a home game, and she'll cheer louder than anyone there, but Alaric knows that there's not much that would get his twin on a bus to voluntarily travel for hours to get to a game.

"Or anyone else?" Chris offers, and Alaric shakes his head.

"I'm good. Besides, I'm not playing." Alaric pushes away from the counter, leaves his water behind. He raises one hand in silent goodbye as he leaves Chris in the kitchen. Then he makes his way through the crowd to see if he can do anything to help Rory without getting himself stuck with the girls instead.

11

ALARIC CAN HEAR Rory's low breath, slowed in the darkness but not yet long and drawn with sleep. The party has left Alaric's skin itchy, wanting something he's not sure how to define. "You smell better," he mutters, and he hears Rory huff a low laugh.

"Thanks, I think?" Rory rolls over, and Alaric tunes his sight just enough to see the shape of him, lying on his back, arms pillowed behind his head. "Did I smell bad before?"

"Anxious." Alaric lets out a rough breath, tries to work through everything in his head. "Uncomfortable. Sorry I didn't rescue you sooner."

"It's not your job, and that kind of attention comes with being on stage." There's a bitter taste to Rory's scent, mixed with a hint of frustration. "You'd think that the fact that they've never seen me close to anyone but my bandmates might make them think twice, but no. They all think they'll be the one, I guess."

"They hope." The words are right there, on the tip of Alaric's tongue, and he says them just because they've been said to him so many times. "Maybe someday one of them will be right."

Rory snorts. "I doubt it. Not like that, anyway." He rolls again, and Alaric hears the way his blankets slide over his body as he cocoons. "What about you?"

"It's complicated. Maybe I'll just pretend to be Soledad's boyfriend. Then I don't have to worry about any of it." Alaric scowls, because as much as he likes Soledad, that sounds like work and he's not sure he can manage it. "I'm not really boyfriend material. There's this whole...romance...thing. And I don't get it."

Another shift, and Rory is up on his elbow, looking over at him. "How do you mean?"

It's not an easy question to answer. Alaric opens his mouth, closes it again. "I don't understand relationships," he finally says slowly. "I mean, I get the non-romantic ones. I have family. I have a best friend." And that's just a whole different level of complicated and Alaric isn't ready to try to explain Corbin yet. "I'm interested in sex—what guy isn't, right?—but the things you're supposed to do...all that romance and flowers and just being the two of you forever, it doesn't make sense."

"You could take Thorne up on his offer." Rory lowers his head slowly to the pillow, stretches out. "He was serious, you know. Pure sex, no strings attached. If you're into guys, that is."

"Is he really as promiscuous as he acts?"

"Yes." It doesn't sound like Rory needs to think about it. "Thorne celebrates sex. He thinks it's something to be enjoyed, any time, anywhere, with whoever else is into it, and only if they're into it. It's not that he doesn't love people. I think sometimes he loves them all, at least a little. He's just not ashamed about desiring pleasure."

"What about you?" Alaric still hasn't answered Rory's unasked question, twisting and turning the conversation to give himself time to think it through.

Rory's silent for a long moment, and Alaric thinks maybe he's broken the conversation or that Rory's slipped off into sleep. But the low breaths are quicker than before, an edge of tension around them. "I think..." Rory's voice trails off, pausing again. "I think that if I ever have sex with someone, it would be a guy. But I just don't see it happening. Sex just isn't...I don't think about it all the time."

"I do." Alaric has honestly wondered if maybe there's something wrong with him, the amount he thinks about sex. "I see some guy's ass and it's like, I wonder what it looks like when he's undressed. What it would feel like. What his hands would be like on me. But it's just that. Just...sex."

"So guys, huh?"

Because of course that's the part that Rory held onto. "Yeah, guys," Alaric admits. At least Rory isn't horrified by his admission of feeling like an oversexed idiot most of the time. "Don't worry, I'm not staring at your ass."

"I don't care if you do, because you're not getting sex from me." Rory's words are muffled by a snort of laughter. "You should probably talk to Thorne about this. He wouldn't judge you, probably just offer you a hand job or something. But he'd be good about listening if you just want someone to talk to, too."

Alaric's cheeks heat up. "Fuck. No. I'm just...I don't want to talk to anyone about this."

"You're talking to me." The words are slow and soft, hesitance in the scent between them.

Alaric rolls over, looks across the space between their beds. "Yeah, well, I trust you. Talk to you more than I talk to Corbin, these days. Maybe I have two best friends."

Rory pushes up on his elbow again, and Alaric can see the seriousness of his expression in the dim light let in around the window shades. "I don't make friends easily, either. It's nice knowing someone outside the band."

As declarations go, it's lacking, but at the same time, Alaric's pretty damned sure he's found something here. That he has an unexpected friend, his first outside the Clan. And of course, Rory's a Mage. Alaric's father would have a shit fit if he knew.

Excerpt from *When Magic Entered the World: Interviews With Lineage Talent*, by Pawel Szczek, © 2009

It was different when I was growing up. Lineage Talents, especially Mages, tended to gather together. We took over neighborhoods in small towns or rows of townhouses in big cities. I grew up in the kind of rural town in Vermont where everyone knew everyone else, and you had to check to see if you were maybe cousins before dating in high school. And every single person there knew that my family was that strange family. Not because they knew we had magic, but because we were like a commune out on an old farm in the fringes of town.

It's more common for Clan to live that way, but we liked our space and being a little separate from the rest of town. We had a cluster of houses in a rural neighborhood that backed onto a huge tract of farmland. Everyone in our neighborhood shared in working the farm. Maybe half of our parents worked at home—growing food, making yarn and cloth and clothes, everything that was needed—and the other half worked in industry somewhere, traveling to the nearest city. We had technology, such as it was in the '80s, and we weren't completely withdrawn. The kids went to the local schools, and we were raised by committee. Everyone was Mom or Dad, and we knew that every adult was overseeing every child.

They say it takes a village to raise a child, and that's what we had. But it really worked for us. We had love all the time. We all had a support network, and a place where we could be ourselves without recrimination. I grew up believing in deity, in nature, in magic, in love, in life. It always seemed like everyone else—all the other kids at school—lacked something at home because they didn't have five moms and seven dads.

It wasn't literal. We knew who our biological parents were, and it wasn't some kind of group marriage. In fact, no one was married by law or traditional religion. But it was definitely not a typical home with one father, one mother, two-point-five children, and a dog.

My mom was a cat person actually. We had three cats, five rabbits, and a donkey.

Anyway, that's beside the point. We had our community, and it really worked. We learned magic and control at home, and we learned everything else at school. And we were pretty open about it—most of the town just thought we were weirdo new-age hippies and let it go at that.

Every once in a while, someone new would move out to our neighborhood. We didn't own every house, and things went on the market, and then a new family would be there. And we'd go over with cookies or brownies to welcome them, and it would always come out that they felt drawn there somehow. That maybe the dad felt comfortable, or the mom had a really good feeling about it, or the kids were just not settling in anywhere else, but here felt really right.

Because here's the thing no one talks about: there have *always* been Emergent Talents. Kenzie Davis was a very public Emergence. She was an event on live national television, and she catapulted the idea that magic was real into the minds of every single person in the country, and after that, in the world. And yes, there were more Emergent Talents every day after that. It's been constant since then, and now everyone knows what Talent is. Everyone probably knows someone Talented, unless they're hiding under a rock.

But there were Emergent Talents even back when I was a kid. Not as many, of course. It was rare, but it did happen, where someone would just suddenly be there in the midst of a non-Talent family, and they could twist words a special way, or make fire, or speak any language. Luce—my wife—is also a Lineage Mage, and her own natural Talent is sniffing out other Talents, which is handy since our husband is Emergent, and when we first met, he had no idea.

That's part of why we had communities. Because Lineage families knew that we needed to make spaces to bring in others when we found them. We knew we had to raise our children in the tradition of our Lineage, and we had to be ready to help any Emergent Talents that we met. We had our own networks, our own ways of finding families that had the right Lineage, to place an Emergent if they didn't fit in as well with the community that found them.

And we haven't always gotten along, that's true. Everything you've heard about Clan and Mages? For every Mage who gets along with someone who's Clan, I can point to ten others who hate each other. We've clashed in the past—ancient and recent—in big, showy, and deadly ways. And in the end, we're just different. Mages can hide in plain sight; it's easier to hide our magic than it is for them to leash the beast. We can fundamentally change and affect things—the environment or emotions—and that pricks at their skins. They were always at risk for exposing us to those who were human, and before the Emergence, we had no idea how that would go.

But despite that, now, we all band together. Because for the last few years the only people who've been able to help the Emergent Talents have been us, the Lineage families who have been here all along. We know how Talent works, and we want to keep the new folks safe.

We want to keep the world safe.

It's only been three years since Kenzie fell off the bars, and I think sometimes everyone forgets that the world didn't just change for the non-Talented, it changed for us, too. For the better, I hope. I know we're doing everything we can to help that happen. But the only thing we can do now is keep on going and do our best to stay on track. And welcome everyone to a world with magic in it.

RUSH

12

THE FIRST FEW weeks of the semester pass more quickly than Alaric expects, between classes, his schoolwork and exams, taekwondo, and football practices. He and Rory become adept at hanging out in the time between their responsibilities, and Alaric realizes that he's memorized his roommate's schedule as well as he's learned his own and Drea's. The first three games of the season pass quickly, then he's on the bus to Pennsylvania, riding five hours for a Saturday afternoon game, where after a brief substitution during the first half, Alaric starts the second half.

It feels good.

Tension rides his shoulders before the first time he goes in, but in the end, he's surprised at how easy it turns out to be. He swears that everyone's watching him, staring at him, waiting for him to fuck it all up again. But as soon as he receives the snap, his mind switches over, instinct running through his bones as easy as a shift. He passes more than he runs, because that gets past this particular defense. When a long bomb falls into Dax's hands like it was meant to be there and Dax crosses the goal line, Alaric feels a rush that he lets loose in a long, low howl that's echoed in the shouts of his teammates. He heads off the field to let special teams take over for the extra point, and Chris claps his shoulder and pulls him in for a rough back-slap of a hug before passing him on to the next teammate.

It feels really good.

The team rallies after that, the touchdown bringing them up enough that another touchdown and a field goal take them into the lead, and they win by two points. The energy in the locker room sets Alaric's blood singing, and knowing that he was a part of it leaves his head feeling like he's floating. He changes quickly, gathers up his gear, and gets onto the bus.

As soon as he's settled, he has his phone out, and he sends separate texts to both Drea and Rory saying only that they won and that he played half the game.

"We need to work together more during practice." Dax drops into the seat next to him, hip checking him lightly to make him move over. Dax is about the same height as him, his build a little narrower than Alaric's. He looks like a runner, wiry and fast, with big hands that are light when he handles the ball. "That was a sweet pass. Perfect placement, almost didn't think I'd get there in time."

"You're fast." Because it's that simple, and Alaric knew he had to trust his receiver to be there. "You pushed; you made it."

"Yeah, well, I had to push. It was this close to being overthrown." Dax holds his hands up, inches apart. "We should work together, get the rhythm down. You need to know just how far you can push me, and you need to figure out the right spot to hit."

"I never would've thrown it that far." Chris's voice comes from behind them. He leans over the back of the seat, elbows across the top, warm against Alaric's shoulders.

Alaric turns slightly to look at him, taking away that warm pressure. "So you think I threw it too far." It's not a question; he can see where his captain's going with this.

"Yes, but no." Chris waves his hand. "It's farther than I knew would work, but you still managed to hit the right spot. And by pushing it, you forced Dax to get away from the defenders who otherwise would've probably tackled as soon as he made the reception. So it worked, and it was a good decision. But you either overthrew, or you went on some instinct that we need to figure out how to exploit. Dax is right—we'll be working on this with all the receivers this week. If you're going to rely on a passing game, you need to know more about who you're passing the ball to."

"I can rush." Alaric's shoulders are tight, pulled between the blades, taut with the idea that he's being chastised. "I can play a running game. It just wasn't the right game to play today."

"Again, the right decision, and you were in charge of the game at that point," Chris says. His tone is firm, gentle. Decisive. Something curls up inside of Alaric, warm and comfortable at the way Chris speaks. This isn't anger, and it isn't praise, not exactly. But it's good.

"It almost didn't work." Alaric admits. "But you ran the ball more than passed, and that wasn't working either. Figured I have a good arm, might as well get it in the air."

Chris puts one hand on Alaric's shoulder, squeezes firmly. "You made the decision: own it."

Dax snorts, and Alaric's brow furrows. "What?"

"I just know what he's going to say."

Chris elbows Dax. "Shut up; let me give my fucking speech. He's going to hear it from Mac, too, I'm sure. You've seen the shirts by now."

"Shirts?" This isn't making any sense to Alaric.

"I may not have done taekwondo long, but this is one thing that Mac and Professor Szczek say often. And Mac says it to me still, even when she's not talking about actual kicking." Chris's voice goes low, serious. "When you're going for a tough kick, like a head-high kick, it's harder if you try to take it easy. It's harder to get your foot up that high, harder to get your body into position. So Mac told me, commit to the kick. Don't think about it, don't test the waters, just commit. Throw it like it's going to work, and it'll work. I know she's got at least three T-shirts that say it."

Now that he says it like that, Alaric's pretty sure he's seen those shirts. They seem to be Mac's favorites, along with *I kick to stay sane.*

"Point is, there's not a lot of time on the field, and when you're running the team, you need to be able to make a decision, commit to that decision, and execute it all in the few moments that you have. Don't hesitate. Don't just try. Do it," Chris says. "And afterward, whether it was the right or wrong decision, own it. Commit to it."

It's not as easy as that. Alaric's all too familiar with making the wrong decision or heading in the wrong direction. Or making a decision and having the beast come out. His lips press together. "Doesn't always work that way."

"Mistakes happen," Dax says. "Your throw is off. You zig left when you should've zagged right. Chris's point is that if you don't commit to the decision you make, it's always the wrong decision."

Alaric grunts, because it's clear that he's not going to win the argument.

"Enough game talk." Chris knocks into Alaric's shoulder, then Dax's. "Rush starts this week. You need to decide if you're going to rush OPT."

"Does everyone?" Alaric isn't sure if it's required or not. He's seen most of the team hanging out at the house in the last few weeks, but he isn't sure how many of them are brothers, and how many are just there because their friends are.

"Not everyone." Dax digs through the bag at his feet, pulls out headphones, and plugs them into his phone. "Maybe half the team are brothers at OPT, and then there are about six guys who don't play football. We have a cheerleader, and two guys from the basketball team, and three guys don't do sports at all."

"Eric plays ultimate frisbee."

Dax rolls his eyes at Chris. "School sports, then. Point is, you don't have to pledge if you don't want to, and don't think it's a captain's order that you need to rush."

"You also can come to the rush week events without actually rushing," Chris says. "If you say you're not interested, we just won't consider you when we're voting on pledges. That said, if you do rush, I think you'd be at home in OPT."

Alaric's gaze narrows; he's not sure what Chris means by that. He breathes in, trying to catch some hint in the scent in the air, but all he gets is stale sweat and dirty equipment, with that underlying tone of pleasure after the win that afternoon. "When do I have to decide by?"

"End of the week." Chris's eyes crinkle at the corner, the brown warm when he regards Alaric. "Just come to the events and sign the register by Friday if you're interested. We tap next Sunday."

"Tap?"

"Let you know if you're a pledge." Dax plugs the headphones into his ears, his voice a little louder when he speaks again. "You will be, if you want to be. You're being groomed as the future captain of the team. You've got two years to step up."

Chris swats the side of Dax's head, and Dax twists away, bringing one hand up between them. "Switch with me," Dax says, and Alaric stands up, shuffles into the aisle so that Dax can take the window seat. Dax ends up leaning against the window, his eyes closed.

Chris looks at Alaric. There's trepidation in his scent now, a sour scent of nerves. "You're good," Chris says quietly. "You'll make captain no matter what, eventually. You don't have to pledge to do it. But it's a good house, and unless you're planning on moving off campus, it's better than living in the dorms. More like an extended family than a series of disconnected rooms."

"Drea wouldn't be there." It's not an argument that Chris'll understand, but Alaric makes it anyway. He's still planning on getting an apartment with his twin next year. Clan's like that. "Do I have to live in the house?"

"We've got brothers that live all over. There's actually a place off campus that's like our second house," Chris admits. "Six guys who are OPT and two independents from the team. So yeah. You can live somewhere else."

Alaric's shoulders relax.

"First event's tomorrow night at the house."

Alaric nods slowly. "Fine. I'll be there for that." Because he can manage that much, feel it out, check if it's a place where he can see himself more permanently. There's a lot to get used to, a lot of noise and chaos and too many heartbeats and scents. But at the same time, he can see the comfort in it. "I'll think about the rest."

"Sounds good." Chris pulls away, and Alaric can feel him go. There's creaking behind him as Chris settles into the bench, and Alaric figures they've still got four more hours on the road. He might as well do what everyone else seems to be doing and get some sleep.

13

The Townhouse Dining Hall is huge, catering to all seven houses on Townhouse Row. By this point in the semester, groups have staked out different areas, and Alaric automatically heads to the set of tables where his floor sits. They've taken over a corner section large enough to fit everyone from Douglass second floor who has an early class on Monday, along with a few stragglers who pass through and visit. It's out of the way of the children that rush around from the family housing in Savoie but still close enough to everyone else that they can interact when they feel like it.

Alaric intersects Drea's path as she approaches, pausing when she waves to a table full of girls from the sorority that's in one of the townhouses. She grins at him. "I'm rushing," she says cheerfully. "SigPsiEp is my top choice."

"That's the one where you and Soledad keep trying to get me to go to parties." Alaric may not be all that interested in sororities in general, but he pays attention when his twin talks. "The one in Townhouse Row."

"The one two doors down from your team," Drea says, nodding. "I think at least one of the girls is dating a guy in OPT, and your taekwondo friend, Mac, is in SigPsiEp as well."

"She didn't strike me like the sorority type." Alaric says it just as he sits down, and Pat winces on the other side of the table while Jackson makes a low whistling sound.

"What makes you think sorority girls have a type?" Soledad leans across the table, her mouth twisted into a moue of irritation. "Do you think I'm the type? Drea? Winter? Pels?"

Alaric scans the table, wondering if invoking her name will summon his elusive floormate. "I don't know what type Pels is," he admits. "The hermit type. I never see her."

"She's an odd duck, but she's not a bad roommate. Better than Jennifer." Nikita ducks her head, gray eyes stormy. There's a rumble outside, and Soledad touches Nikita's arm. The fights in Nikita's triple are already legendary and have made for a historic amount of bad weather springing up during the arguments thanks to Nikita's weather witchery.

"No storms. I have to get all the way across campus for class," Soledad says quickly. "Make clouds over Jennifer's head later if you have to. I promise I won't tell TJ."

"I heard that," TJ calls from a table away.

"At least Nikita doesn't make it rain inside." Rory pushes at a piece of toast, most of his breakfast eaten already. "Stormy once made it pour inside a concert hall. She claimed it was too hot, and that triggered her Talent. I think it's because we were the tenth band in an all-day lineup, and no one was paying attention to their time slots. And all our gear was protected." He glances up. "Nothing got ruined. It all turned to steam before it hit the equipment. Thorne," he says, like that means something. From TJ's loud snort of laughter, it must make sense somehow.

Drea coughs into the resulting silence, and when Alaric glances at her, she smiles slightly. "Yes, I'm rushing SigPsiEp. I'll visit a few others, but they're my first choice. If I don't get a bid, I'm not sure I'm interested in any of the others. What about you?"

There's a lecture coming. Alaric pokes at his eggs with his fork and wonders how slowly he can eat without being late for class. "Went to the party at OPT last night."

"And…"

Alaric can feel the attention of everyone at his table. He shrugs one shoulder. "I know some of the guys. Wouldn't mind if any of my friends from Douglass wanted to rush, too."

"Fraternities are more Thorne's thing than mine," Rory admits. "I think he said he might rush, but he's not sure where would have him. He might go for one of the co-ed frats."

"Not interested, not this year anyway," Pat says, and Jackson echoes him quickly. They glance at each other, and Alaric frowns, wondering what he's missing between the lines there. He cocks his head, watching to see if there's anything he can figure out, but Pat's just fiddling with the skate deck he has across his knees, and Jackson's focused on eating. Drea elbows Alaric, and he turns his attention back to his eggs and hopes no one's noticed him staring.

"So you're rushing," she says quietly.

"Thinking about it," he corrects. He hasn't made up his mind, hasn't signed the register yet. He's pretty sure he'll get there, but he's going to go to every event this week. If he can't make it through an entire week being social with his team, then he won't make it through a year of living with them. "Might mean we'd still live apart next year."

"You don't like that." Drea's soft voice is concerned. "Alaric, this is when we're supposed to learn to live like humans do. Without Clan right there. Orson made it through four years at VIT, and he's in the middle of another year on his own. This is when we're forged. Be human. Learn to love what makes us Clan."

"Everyone says we'll miss it, and it won't feel stifling when we go back." Alaric leans a little closer to his sister, his words for her alone. "They say that being away from Clan will make us want to be with them again. I don't think that's worked for Orson."

"I think our brother hides it well," Drea tells him. "He has always loved being our father's son, loved knowing what he'll become. This is his only chance for freedom. You know he'll be better for it, and that he'll be a part of the community as soon as his last year is done."

He'd better. Alaric doesn't want to think about what his life will be like if his brother decides to turn his back on Clan and community and walk away. He grunts his acknowledgement, shovels the last of the eggs in his mouth, and chews instead of saying anything else.

"Hey."

Alaric sees the hand coming in from the edge of his vision, manages to get his own hand up to block before Mac can tap the side of his head. There's a grin in her voice as she says, "Good morning."

Alaric nudges out a chair with his foot, and Mac twists it around, sits on it backward. He realizes there are two other girls with her, and he stands up, offers his chair to one of them, and grabs a third for the last girl.

"Attentive." She's short, with a round face and a soft build. A strong smell of citrus lingers in the air around her. "But I don't need to sit down, even if Mac's already made herself comfortable. I need to get to class early this morning. I just wanted to check in with Drea and Soledad."

Drea's already out of her seat, leaning around Alaric to get a hug from the one girl. "This is Heather," Drea introduces her. "She's the social director at SigPsiEp, and she's running rush. Carolyn and Mac are both sisters there."

"Heather takes her job seriously," Mac says dryly. "I think she'd issue a personal invitation to every girl on campus if she could manage to do it without being late to class."

"Being social is serious business. Besides"—Heather claps her hands and spreads them out, and Alaric feels a faint buzz on his skin; he takes a step back, brows furrowing—"if everyone has fun, I feel better, and they all feel better, so it's a win/win situation." There's a fresh burst of citrus, and Alaric scowls at it.

"Empath."

"Alaric," Drea says softly. "No prejudice. Your best friend on campus is a Mage, remember?"

Alaric snorts, shakes his head. "I don't like how it feels." He has enough trouble with his own emotions; the idea that someone could manipulate him bothers him immensely.

"It's okay, I'm used to it." The citrus scent dims as Heather shrugs, her body language making her seem smaller. "I'm going to head to class, but Drea, Soledad, you'll be there tonight, right? And please, bring your friends. Everyone's welcome." Her smile is swift and sweet as she looks over the rest of the table, glancing to the tables beyond as well, where TJ and a few of the girls from the floor are watching. "SigPsiEp is the best house on campus."

"We're biased," Carolyn says, her voice rougher than Alaric expects. "But she's right."

"We'll be there," Soledad assures them. "Wouldn't miss it. Drea and I have *plans*."

Mac stands up, pushes her chair under the table. She leans in close to Alaric, pressing up on her toes as she speaks under her breath. "Between you and me, I hate rush. Feel free to stop by and distract me from the incredibly peppy games we'll be playing."

Alaric's eyebrows rise, because no, he is not going to a sorority rush party. There would be him and a few hundred girls going through the house over the course of a few hours and just...no. "I'll be at OPT," he says stiffly, and Mac sighs.

"Thought I could count on you, Ric." She crooks her finger, and Carolyn stands as well. The three girls head out together, and Alaric grabs one of the chairs, sinks back into it as they go.

"She's flirting with you," Jackson says. When Alaric gives him a dark look, Jackson spreads his hands. "She leaned in close, whispered something to you. She touched your arm, and I don't think you even noticed. Would it be such a shock to think she's into you?"

Alaric blinks twice. "Yes."

Pat coughs, and it sounds like laughter.

"I don't like rush," Alaric mutters, grabbing onto his coffee. "Rory, you ready to get to class?"

"I am ready to be done with breakfast." Rory shoves a yogurt cup in his bag, followed by an apple and a banana. "Let's go."

They make it out of the building before Rory clears his throat. "You don't have to rush if you don't want to. I'm going to a concert tonight over in Clifton Park with some of the guys. It's all standing-room only, and it's not sold out if you want to get a ticket and join us. The openers are a local band, and Jackson knew one of them in high school."

"My roommate is a pop star," Alaric reminds him, and Rory's cheeks flush. "And I'm not impressed by that, either."

"I'm glad. You'd be insufferable if you were actually impressed by me." Rory shoves his hands in his pockets, hunches forward a bit to walk faster. "I just figured you don't sound enthused by the idea of rushing, so maybe you could take a night off and come out with us."

Alaric isn't sure how to explain it. "I don't mind rushing," he says slowly. "I'm not sure I want to live in the house. And parties are overwhelming. And when I think about sorority rush, I'm with Mac—it sounds like a bunch of giggling and posturing, and things that smell like plastic. But it's the same with the guys, everyone trying to prove something. It reeks of nerves, and it makes my skin itch, makes the bear want to lumber out and push everyone out of the way. But it's good practice. Because I have to deal with people even if I hate it."

Because his father might actually be proud of this. He'd hate that he's dealing with humans and Mages, but he'd like it if Alaric got involved. If he did something that might someday show that he knows how to lead. That he can be like Orson, and not useless and only interested in some sport the Clan doesn't care about.

At least it'll teach Alaric how to handle crowds with more grace than he usually manages.

He's grateful that Rory drops the topic, doesn't push into the reasons why Alaric might choose a fraternity that he's not sure he wants. Alaric's not really interested in explaining.

14

IF ALARIC PRETENDS not to notice the large number of random guys coming through the house, rush parties aren't entirely awful. He finds a corner of the couch and settles in, a pitcher of something orange and ridiculously fruity on the table in front of him. Dax had set it down earlier, let him know it's not alcoholic, then disappeared into the crowd and left Alaric on his own.

He doesn't really mind being on his own.

He spends a few minutes talking to a couple of other freshmen from the team before they're drawn off into a game of beer pong. There's a guy who he vaguely knows from taekwondo, and they talk about the tournament coming up in October. Alaric can't compete, but he'll be there to cheer everyone on, and Mason's looking forward to his first time competing on the collegiate circuit. Alaric doesn't have to talk much after that, letting Mason go on about AAU competition and some kind of national championship down in Florida and how Mason's been kicking since he was seven years old.

It's not that Mason's being an asshole about it. He isn't bragging. He just obviously loves the sport, possibly even more than Mac, which is fucking impressive in Alaric's eyes. With his three weeks of experience, he doesn't understand half the things Mason is saying, but it still sounds interesting, and when Mason offers to send him links to videos of the gold medal rounds from the summer Olympics, Alaric trades phone numbers with him.

Chris and Dax show up with another pitcher—the liquid in this one a violent bright blue—and Chris takes Alaric's cup to refill it. Chris squeezes between Alaric and Mason on the couch, and Dax brackets Mason on the other side. There isn't quite room for four athletes, and Alaric puts his drink down, starts to stand.

"I wanted to talk to you about strategy," Chris says. "Since we're not drinking."

Alaric stops, lowers himself back to sitting. He grunts a small acknowledgement, takes a long sip, expression puckering at the sour taste. "What the fuck is this stuff?"

Dax laughs. "Sourberry Lily, at least according to Lewis, who gets to name the drinks since he mixes them. He claims it tastes like sweet poison, but it would be better if we added vodka."

"We're not adding vodka, not tonight. We're talking game," Chris points out.

Mason excuses himself, and the pressure on the couch eases enough for Alaric to relax and turn slightly to face Chris and Dax. "What kind of strategy?"

"This weekend we're playing at home against Cherry Hill." Chris drops the name, leaves it there in the silence.

Alaric's shoulders are tight, his fingers gripping his cup hard enough that it crinkles, almost spilling. He takes a long gulp and sets it down, careful not to slosh on the table. "Has anyone scouted them yet this year? Do we know the starting lineup?"

"Cal Thompson is number 47, and he's not a starter." Dax is the only one of them that's relaxed, his legs stretched out as he leans back, one arm along the back of the sofa, the other still holding his cup. "But they've been playing him regularly, like we've played you. He's gotten more time on the field than you, but he hasn't had a suspension so that's to be expected. His stats are good."

"One of the best defense players in the league last year," Alaric says slowly. He's played with Cal, but never really against him. He knows his techniques, but even more than that, he knows that Cal knows *him*. "He might be a problem."

"Between Thompson and Ruíz, it's going to be a tough game. Ruíz can run through almost anything." Dax sets his cup down, uses his hands to illustrate as he goes in depth on a play from a game last week. When Alaric frowns, Dax pulls out his phone and brings up the video, and Chris holds the phone while Alaric and Dax crowd in close to view it.

"Cal's good at interceptions," Alaric muses. "He's going to know how I throw."

"Maybe we run when he's on the field."

Alaric shakes his head, looks at Chris for confirmation of his instinct. "I don't think so," Alaric says slowly, watching Chris's reaction. "I think that's what Cal will expect me to do. We need to make sure we mix it up, keep him guessing."

Chris nods. "We'll go over the video, come up with ideas this week. It's never easy to see your old teammates on the opposite side of the field."

"It's not something I've dealt with before." Alaric shrugs, leans back out of Chris's personal space, and crosses his arms. "We had players from all over, and the ones who graduated scattered. It's going to come up again."

"But Thompson was your co-captain, so he's not just any player. Was he someone you knew growing up?" Chris grabs the remainder of the orange drink, mixes it with his blue, and tastes it, expression thoughtful.

"He was from somewhere past Saratoga. Somewhere rich." Alaric takes the cup when Chris offers it, tries a sip. It's sweeter now, not so violently sour, but it's still got an edge that offends his senses. He pushes it back at Chris and ignores the remains of his own partially crumpled, waiting cup. "Cal had a lot of money. A lot of the guys on the team did. They were from home schools and private schools, places that didn't care if you had Talent as long as you could pay for the equipment."

"You sound bitter," Chris says.

"Might be." It's hard to explain, and Alaric struggles to find the words when Chris has no background in Talent. "Cal was a Mage. Out of twenty guys on the team, maybe four weren't Talented, and I was the only Clan."

"It's different doing sports when your Talent is invisible and doesn't really impact the game." Dax isn't looking at them, and Alaric remembers that he's listed as *Talent: unknown* on the roster. "The league my school played in didn't care if you were Talented as long as it wasn't physical, so I've been playing since Pop Warner." He finally looks over at them. "Local. I grew up in Valiant, and I went to Wilson High. I could've gone to play in the Blended league, but I figured, since I was able to play in my own school, why bother taking up a spot someone else might need?"

"My school didn't approve," Alaric comments quietly. "Didn't matter whether you were Clan or something more…" He taps the side of his head. "They didn't care. Magic was magic, and they weren't having any of it."

"There was a Clan family in my town," Chris says slowly. "I went to school with the middle kid; his older sister graduated two years before me, and his younger sister started high school our senior year. He wanted to play lacrosse, and they wouldn't let him. He was too fast and too strong. And Massachusetts didn't have any kind of a Blended league. So we set up pick-up games because there were enough people who didn't care. Sometimes we'd play football; sometimes we'd play lacrosse. If the weather was bad, we went to the Y and played basketball."

"There was *a* Clan family in your town." Alaric can't assimilate the idea that there could be a single small family and nothing more. "Not a community."

"Not a community," Chris tells him. He offers his drink again, but Alaric brings a hand up to say no, and Chris drains the remainder of the cup. "Two parents, three kids, and his mom was pregnant again when we were in high school. She had the baby November of my freshman year, I think. I didn't really know how strange it was for Clan until I left for school and I took Professor Szczek's intro class. But I guess that's the point, right? There are a lot of traditions for Lineage Talent, but not every single person, or family, is alike. Everyone's got their idiosyncrasies."

That's something Alaric wishes his father would understand: that not every person in the Clan wants to be in the community and highly involved. That Alaric is conflicted about what he wants, that he both wants to be close to his twin but, at the same time, wants to be away from his home. "It's hard, when the traditions have been handed down for centuries." His voice is low, gruff.

"Even when it's only decades," Dax agrees. "I mean, it might be centuries, but I've never gone looking." His smile tilts, wry. "We've been living in the same house for so long that my great-uncle Dimitrios died there. His brother inherited, and my grandfather and my dad both grew up there."

"Wasn't your grandfather already old if he inherited from—?"

"*Great* is a simplistic term. It's easier to say than however many generations it actually was," Dax says dryly. "The Katsoulis family has been in Valiant for as long as VIT has been on the hill, and Dimitrios was one of the earlier members of the family."

"Corbin said VIT was founded in 1832, thirty years after Pine Hills." It's one of the random things Alaric remembers Corbin mentioning, along with the fact that VIT is situated on land that was once used for sheep farming while simultaneously noting that neither VIT nor PHU offers a degree in agriculture. That works for Alaric; he doesn't want a degree in farming, no matter how much it might please his father. His brother at least went for a degree in chemical engineering, while Alaric is still undecided.

"Then it's more than a century," Dax says with a shrug. "It doesn't surprise me. Oh, hey." He cuts off abruptly, grinning when a girl curls onto his lap. "I didn't know you were coming by tonight, Cass." He strokes his hand over her head, sliding down to tug at her long brown braid. "I've got rush."

"And I've got you." She presses one hand against his chest, and Alaric looks away, smelling the blend of perfume, musk, and want. "I just wanted to see you, and you've got rush all week. No one will miss you for an hour."

"Chris?" Dax's voice is questioning, dropped a little lower, and Alaric feels the heat of his own skin as he smells Dax's reaction to Cass's presence.

"Go, go." Chris shoves at Dax, pushing himself closer to Alaric. "Text me when it's safe to come back. This shit will be winding down soon anyway."

Cass stays wound around Dax, tall and lithe, her arm behind his back, hip pressed to his, body moving in concert with him as they walk away. Alaric remembers Dax mentioning meeting his girlfriend during orientation, and it looks like they've been together long enough that they are almost perfectly in sync. He swallows hard, tries to steady his breath. "They..." He fails to find words to explain it to someone who isn't Clan. "They reek," he finally mutters, grumbling under his breath when Chris laughs.

"I'm not surprised. And now I'm sexiled, because Dax is my roommate." Chris offers a rueful smile. "Like I said, this event is going to wind down soon, probably before Dax texts me. Cass's estimate of an hour is very conservative." He picks up the pitcher, makes a face before he puts it back down. "I'm sick of sweet drinks. Don't know what Lewis was thinking with this shit. Want to get out of here? I need something better than this." He hesitates a moment, adds, "Not alcoholic. I don't go to bars while underage. I'm not risking my scholarship."

Alaric had tensed, but he lets it go, nods slowly. "Sure. Fine. I'm not a fan of crowds, so getting out of here sounds good to me." He should probably ask where they're going, but he's willing to let Chris lead. Wherever they're going, it can't stink worse than here.

15

As THEY CROSS campus, Alaric figures they're heading out for coffee, so he's a little confused when he spots the sign for Teas Please hanging above a door. There's light music spilling out through the cracks around the door, and it's brightly lit. The voices are muffled, but it looks like the place is still busy despite it being late in the evening and the middle of rush. Chris pushes open the door and motions for Alaric to head inside.

Teas Please is a crash of styles: tables with clustered, mismatched chairs in some spaces, a few booths in the back, and a series of couches and chairs at the front. It looks old and eclectic, but Alaric can spot the almost-hidden power outlets so that the students can charge their laptops while they drink tea and eat sweet desserts.

"Is the kitchen still open?" Chris asks as the hostess leads them to a booth at the back, a corner space larger than they need with a wrap-around bench going almost three-quarters of the way around the table.

"Dessert only; all the meals are off the menu for the night," she says, dropping two menus on the table. "Any kind of tea is still available, and there's a specials list for the desserts tucked into the menu. Haven't run out of anything yet, as far as I know. Nate'll be over to take your order shortly."

"Sounds good." Chris slides into the booth from one side, and Alaric takes the other side. It's an awkwardly enough shaped table that sitting at the ends of the benches leaves them far apart, so they both slide closer to the center of the U so they won't have to talk too loudly.

The menu is long. There's a list of teas with more variety than Alaric can ever remember seeing in one place. White, green, black, rooibos, herbal—he's not even sure what some of them actually are. "What the hell is some of this stuff?" Cranberry white? Something that sounds burnt?

"Do you like tea at all? Maybe I should've asked, but I figure everyone likes either tea or dessert." Chris looks over the top of the menu. "We'll just share a pot of what I usually get. It's a good tea for studying, and not bad for late night. Greens have less caffeine."

A new voice interrupts. "Although if you like your sweets full of chocolate, that might be what ends up keeping you up at night." Two glasses of water thunk lightly onto the table, along with a pitcher.

Alaric glances up, thinks the guy standing there looks vaguely familiar, but he can't place the name on his name tag or his face with any kind of a location on campus.

"I'm Nate," the guys continues easily, "and I'll be your server tonight. First order of business—are you here in an exclusive way, or are you up for company?"

"…the hell?"

Nate grins at Alaric's gruff response. "We're busy tonight, and sometimes we go family style for our seating. Are you two up for company, or do you want to be alone?" Nate leans a little closer, one eyebrow up. "I could see it going either way, and honestly, if you're not here together, feel free to leave me a number. Either of you, if you're interested."

Alaric's positive that his cheeks must be flushed a deep, bright red. He picks up the menu, stares at it as if it holds the right answer, and tries to ignore the soft sound of apology from their server.

"We wouldn't mind company." Chris puts his menu on the table without even opening it. "It'd be better if it's someone we know, although I don't think there will be many OPT brothers or football players coming in tonight. Can you get us a pot of the jasmine ginger green and two cups? And what's the best dessert on the menu tonight?"

Nate tilts his head, clears his throat, and waits until Alaric looks up. "If you like chocolate, you want the flourless torte. It's our most popular menu item. Everyone wants the flourless torte, and most people say they can die happy after having it. If you prefer fruit, we've got an apple-cranberry crumble, made with locally sourced apples. We also have the best crêpes. Whatever you get, make sure you've got an appetite, or plan to share."

"I need time." Alaric bites the words out, takes a deep breath and lets it shudder through him as he stares at the specials list for desserts. Drea would like this place; he has to remember to tell her about the torte. And Corbin has a thing about apples, so it might be a good activity if Corbin visits campus. But Alaric can't decide what he wants with Nate standing right there, hovering over them, and Chris quietly watching.

"I'll be back with the tea."

Nate leaves, and Chris sits there for a long moment, arms folded on the table. Alaric can feel the weight of his gaze, and he grumbles under his breath, "What?"

"You don't like it when guys hit on you," Chris observes quietly.

"I don't like it when anyone hits on me," Alaric corrects.

"Then Thorne..." Chris doesn't finish the statement, and Alaric isn't sure where he was going with it. Alaric just shrugs in response.

"Thorne's Thorne," Alaric says, because he's figured out that much at least. He gets the feeling that Chris is waiting for more of an explanation, and the problem is, Alaric can't figure out how to put it into words, and he has no idea how to explain that Thorne doesn't bother him the way that others do. "I like my personal space." Thorne, at least, seems to get that Alaric's not interested.

Chris's gaze narrows thoughtfully. Alaric looks back at the menu—he's read it six times by now—and waits to see if Chris will continue to dig.

"Jasmine ginger green: one pot and two cups." Nate sets the pot down and slides one cup toward each of them. "And Becky's bringing over a group who say they know Alaric here." He nods at Alaric, then steps back, his pad of paper in his hand. "Did you decide what you want to eat?"

"Alaric!" Ravi comes up behind Nate, puts his hands on his shoulders and squeezes before he drops into the seat next to Alaric and pushes in, leaving space for Ekaterina. There's a girl Alaric doesn't know who also hugs Nate on the way by before taking the seat next to Chris, crowding the bench. Ravi leans on the table, holds out one hand to Chris. "Hey, I'm Ravi, this is Ekaterina and that's Priya. Ekaterina and I live on the same hall as Alaric. Sorry to crowd you guys."

"Luckily we lost two people on the way over, or it would've been worse," Ekaterina says. "You don't mind, do you, Alaric? Nate said you'd be okay with it."

"It's fine." Alaric has the edges of the menu tight in his fingers, and the plastic-covered cardboard compresses under his touch. "We just came from OPT, and it's rush. The couch there was more crowded."

It's only half a lie. On the couch, he was twisted slightly, facing Chris. Now he's pressed up against him, thigh to thigh, with Ravi against his other side. He's not sure how Ekaterina's taking up so much space, or maybe it's because Nate's sunk onto the seat, settled in next to Priya as he shows her something on the menu. Whatever it is, it almost seems like Chris is too close, and it makes Alaric's skin itch.

Chris shifts, puts a little space between them, but Alaric can still feel the heat from his body. Chris is looking past Priya, at Nate. "You planning on taking our order, or are you going to keep flirting?"

"She's not my type," Nate says with an easy grin. His mouth tilts up more on one side than the other, and Alaric realizes that one of Nate's eyes drifts inward. It does nothing to detract from the way his smile lights his eyes, though. The grin grows, like Nate knows Alaric is looking at him, and there's a twist in Alaric's gut.

"He's not really my type, either." Priya closes the menu, slides it toward Nate. "Besides, Nate lives on my floor. He knows I'd break his balls if he tried anything."

"True. You want the torte tonight?" Nate slips from the bench, pad of paper in hand again. Priya leaves the space next to her open, like she's expecting someone else to sit there now that Nate's gone.

"And the hazelnut black tea." Priya sits back, hands folded against her belly. "My usual. I'm predictable and boring, I know, but it tastes so *good*."

"Torte for me, too, because chocolate," Ekaterina decides.

"And me." Chris makes a face. "It doesn't exactly go with the tea, but ginger and chocolate won't be a terrible combination."

"Ooh, have you had the chocolate-covered ginger jellies from Merri-weather's around the corner?" Ekaterina makes a little, breathy sound, her eyes closing. "Heavenly. They've also got a salted caramel chew that's divine."

"I'm going to get jealous that you're cheating on my desserts with some other place," Nate says idly, tapping his pen against the pad of paper.

"Apple-cranberry special thing for me." Ravi times his interruption just as Ekaterina is going to shoot back another comment, and she pauses, mouth open, then rolls her eyes and sticks her tongue out at him. He lifts his arm, dropping it across her shoulder as she tucks herself close to his side.

Alaric has no idea when that happened, or if it's actually happening romantically or if maybe it's just one of those friend things. And he wonders how people deal with living on the same floor after they break up. Fuck, relationships are hard enough to understand without thinking about the post-romance fallout.

"Alaric?" Nate raises both eyebrows. "Are you getting something?"

Chris's knee presses against Alaric's under the table, and he bites back a grumble. What he's getting is hot. Uncomfortable. And he hasn't even tried the tea.

"Crêpe," he says, voice sharper than he means it to be. "Something with cheese and fruit."

"You like surprises." Nate smirks. "That'll be fun. How do you feel about nuts?"

Alaric's pretty sure there's an innuendo in there. He keeps his tone even as he replies, "No nuts."

Nate turns away to check for drink orders from Ravi and Ekaterina. Priya reaches past Chris, touches Alaric's hand where it rests on the table. He manages to keep from jerking it away, although he knows he moves enough for her to notice when she pulls her own hand back.

"Did I read that you're Clan?" she asks. "On the football page, your profile. My brother is starting with the Blended league this fall—he's fifteen and he's homeschooled down on Long Island. So I was reading about all our players, and you played in the same New York league that he's starting in now."

This is a simpler topic. Alaric nods. "I'm local," he says. "Out in Haverhill." His head cocks, brow furrowing as he looks at Priya, blinks twice. "You're not Clan."

"Can you smell other Clan?" Priya's smile is tightly polite. "There are Clan in India and throughout Asia, Alaric. Don't base your assumption on my heritage."

Alaric winces, ducks his head, the hound inside whining an apology.

"Most Clan I've known are geographically restricted." Chris looks at Priya when he talks, but his knee touches Alaric. "Professor Szczek does an entire unit on the geographical distribution and cultural heritage of the five primary branches of Lineage Talent. He doesn't go into it in depth in the introductory class, but there's a later class that delves further into the cultural differences between similar branches from different locations. I haven't taken it; it's restricted to Magical Studies majors."

"I've only spoken to Clan from the States and Canada," Alaric admits. "I know of Clan in South America, but I never thought about how widespread we actually are."

"Talent is worldwide," Chris says, his tone mimicking Szczek almost perfectly. "Both Lineage and Emergent. There is no country which is without Talent, and there are many cultures which have acknowledged Talent in day-to-day life all along."

"We're not Clan," Priya admits. "Healers. Always have been, as far back as we can trace our Lineage. But my brother is a giver of pain. The local schools were unwilling to have him on their grounds."

"I don't think the class went into this." Chris's brow furrows in confusion, and he looks between Alaric and Priya.

"In every Lineage, there are those who reap the benefits, and those few for whom the Talent can be a curse." Alaric's voice rumbles in his chest. He's close to cursed, close to the ones who are Clan without being given any of the gift. It's a familiar teaching, heard often over many years, and the words—far more formal than his own—slip from his tongue easily. "For the Healers, there are those who cause pain rather than heal it."

"And Raj doesn't have complete control," Priya admits. "He wears gloves when he plays. He doesn't want to hurt anyone."

Chris sits back, makes space between them again as Nate places tea for the others and desserts for everyone on the table. Nate winks when he drops extra forks right in front of Alaric. "Just in case anyone wants to share," he says.

The smell of the tea and chocolate overwhelms him. The chocolate itself is strong three times over, surrounding Alaric on all sides. It's thick and rich and cloying, and as soon as Chris breaks into the torte with his fork, the depth increases, a hint of cinnamon and coffee clinging to the edges. Alaric reaches for his cup of tea, raises it to his lips, and tastes the sweetness of jasmine mingled with the sharp bite of ginger, all wrapped around that thick, dark scent.

He can't even focus on his own crêpe.

"Do you want a bite?" Chris picks up a second fork, spears a hefty bite of chocolate, and offers it. Alaric shakes his head, puts one hand up. He can imagine how good it must be to someone who's human, who doesn't get overwhelmed by the strength of the scent, but for him it's more than he wants to taste.

"Don't need to. I can smell it." Alaric's voice is gruff, and he looks away, staring down at his own plate. He cuts into it, watches as blueberries and peaches spill across the plate. He smells some kind of sweet cheese mixed with vanilla, then the bright taste of the fruit as he takes a bite and lets it melt on his tongue. It can't cover the chocolate completely, but leaves it as a side note, a dark accompaniment to the bright/sweet/tart/tangy of his own dessert.

The crêpe is good.

It'd be better if his stomach weren't churning.

Chris talks to Priya, while Ravi and Ekaterina lean close to each other, their conversation quiet and private. Alaric's breath is tight in his chest, and he sets his fork down, lays both hands on the table as he inhales slowly, exhales even more slowly after that. He can feel the hound whining behind his eyes, feels the itch of his skin as he wants to transform, and he's not sure why. He has no idea why he wants to escape into another form, why he wants to crawl out of his skin and hide. He lets his eyes drift closed, raises his cup, and inhales the steam from his tea, focuses on the sharp ginger, tries not to think about the heat of Chris sitting too close on the bench.

Chris nudges his knee and Alaric flinches, eyes opening as he growls. Chris frowns, dark gaze serious. "You okay? You know, you can probably talk to Mac any time, if you need someone who really gets it. She's good like that. And she does get it."

Alaric's not sure Chris knows what "it" is, right now. Alaric's not sure if he even understands himself. But the sentiment is good and makes sense. "I know. We talked." Alaric's mouth feels too full of teeth. He shakes his head. "I'm fine. I just… Look, I need a break. Too many people. I'm not— I've never been social. Clan has our Clan gatherings, but being out with everyone else, it's just…it's not what I'm used to. I need to get out of here."

Alaric wishes he could read minds, wishes he could see past the all-too-serious look Chris is giving him. "I'm fine," Alaric says again, tone gruff, and Chris finally slides toward Priya. They both move to let him out of the center seat, and Alaric feels better as soon as he's standing.

Priya slides back onto the bench, but Chris lingers, gaze still narrowed. "Are you leaving?" Chris asks.

"Yeah. I'll be at the house again tomorrow." Because it's still rush, and Alaric is still going to attend every damned event. He'll get past this. Whatever the fuck this is.

Silence for a long moment, then Chris nods once. "See you then." He sits on the edge of the bench and nudges in, Priya's hand on his arm before Chris is even fully situated. Alaric turns away and leaves, pushing past Nate when he tries to ask if there's a problem, ignoring the hostess who calls out to him.

He's halfway down the block before he can identify the problem, before he can put it into any kind of words. His claws are out, tipped on his fingers, and his teeth feel thick. His heart is racing, his skin heated, and he knows he wants something. Needs something.

He could go home. It's possible that Rory's still out, that the dorm room will be open and he'll be alone. He could take care of things.

Or he could…he could talk to someone.

Alaric takes out his phone and it takes him five tries to type the words into a brand-new conversation to a number that he took without thinking he'd use it. They look stark and solid in the little space on the screen, and he feels his breath punch out when he presses send.

If you meant it, I need to get laid.

The text comes back quicker than he expects. *No strings attached.*

Something rushes out of Alaric, his shoulders losing tension, and he leans back against the wall. *No strings attached*, he agrees, because that's what he needs. No worries about friendships, or relationships, or how it'll fuck with things. No worries at all. Just…a chance to get past whatever this is fucking with his head and body right now.

He just wants to feel good.

When he gets an address, he doesn't let himself think about it again, only tucks his phone in his pocket and starts walking. No more thinking, not tonight.

16

By Wednesday, Alaric doesn't want to talk to Mac, but he does want to kick, hard and fast and for a very long time. He texts to find out if she'd mind starting early, and she agrees to meet him a half hour before class begins. They're on the mats as soon as the room is set, and she warms him up with running laps around the room and a hundred each of jumping jacks, sit-ups, and pushups. Then it's gear on, and they start to work.

She doesn't ask what's wrong or why he wants to work harder than usual, but she doesn't let him rest, either. Kicking keeps the itch at bay, lets him sink into the movement and just do it. Lets his mind settle. By the time Professor Szczek arrives, Alaric's out of breath and drenched with sweat, taking a two-minute break to let his heart rate slow while he drinks some water.

"Gear off." Mac gestures at the bags lining the wall across the room from where she's talking to Professor Szczek. "Get out a bag. Pawel's going to run the class through forms tonight, but I want to keep you working. Endurance drills will do you good."

He yanks off his sweaty gear, shoves it into his bag as neatly as he can manage, looping the ties from his chest protector up and out of the way so he won't trip over them. He grabs his water bottle for another long swallow, then drags one of the bags out to the corner of the mats.

Mac meets him there, drops into a fighting stance on one side of the bag. "We're going to work together today, and it's going to be about timing, strength, and speed. The drill is simple: right foot back for your stance. Punch, reverse punch, rear-leg roundhouse. Pull it back and reset. But we're going to be going at the exact same time on opposite sides of the bag, so we need to kick in sync, or the bag's going to move. You need to match my power, or the bag's going to move. And when I speed up, you need to speed up with me. Got it?"

It sounds simple enough; he nods and drops into his stance, ready to go.

He has to check his power; his punches are stronger than Mac's, and when he's not paying attention, the bag wobbles toward her. She clears her throat, and he tries harder to match the exact pace and power of her strikes. Two quick punches, then a little slower for the kick. Reset, pause, then repeat it. He sinks into the rhythm of it—one, two…three—and barely registers when she speeds up, pulling the kick out faster until it matches the cadence of the punches: one, two, three. Then she speeds up again, and it becomes a blur of motion. All he can do is focus on the technique, on the strikes, trying to keep in sync with her.

It's not an easy drill, and the faster they go, the more the strikes become a little *pop-pop* of asynchronous sound as he hits a beat behind her. The bag wavers, and he growls, feels his claws bite into his palms as he keeps his fingers curled in tight fists. The hound bays, begging to be released, and he forces it back, drives it down. He growls again under his breath, blows air out through his nose, and puffs of smoke whisper out, swirling into the air.

Mac stops, and Alaric stops one kick behind her, the bag tilting roughly before she catches it and shoves it back upright.

"Never seen that happen to anyone before," Mac says plainly, and Alaric doesn't have the words, so he simply grunts in reply. He's never seen anything like it either.

He sucks in breath, lets it out through his mouth, and can't see a thing. No condensation in the air. No smoke.

It couldn't have been smoke, must have just been condensation. That's what it had to be, from him being so overheated from working out.

Mac claps his shoulder, gently guides him to the window ledge that lines one side of the room. "Sit down. Drink. Rest. You need to catch your breath."

He sinks down, considers pouring the water over his head, but that would be a waste. He'll cool down better just by sitting for a bit. He drains the bottle, knows he has to refill it, but he doesn't want to walk to the bathroom. "Don't let that make you stop working with me," he says quietly.

"Won't happen again."

"It probably will. If it happened once, there's a reason." Mac sits next to him, takes off the bandana she has holding her hair back. She uses it to wipe the sweat from her face, then ties it neatly back in place. "But I'm not going to stop pushing you. Did it help?"

He huffs a sigh and nods. "Yeah. It did." It feels good to be exhausted, like his body's gone limp and boneless. There are other ways to achieve the same feeling, but this is one of the safest. Even if he'll probably use the other way, too, later on. "Thanks. Chris told me I should talk to you because you get it."

Mac snorts softly. "Yeah, well, Chris and I used to talk a lot back in freshman year, when I was fresh out of the military, and he was starting out as a very human QB going up against a hell of a lot of Talent in the league."

"You here on the GI bill?" Alaric swears he remembers someone mentioning that, but the swift, sharp scent of rising tension makes him think he shouldn't have mentioned it.

Mac sets her water bottle down on the ledge, then leans forward slowly until her elbows rest on her thighs, her hands loosely intertwined where they fall between her knees. Her back is hunched, tension lining her shoulders. Alaric leans forward as well, and she glances over at him with a tiny wry smile.

"Yeah," she says quietly, a hoarse note to her voice. "Things happened while I was deployed, and I broke." She taps the side of her head. "So I decided it was time for less military and more growing up normal for a while, and here I am. And it's not easy being here, because sometimes I remember the shit that broke me, which is not something I talk about much so consider yourself blessed with knowing the intimate details of my life without actually having any of the details. The thing is, PTSD sucks. It sucks like I imagine having a creature inside of you probably sucks sometimes, like there's this thing and it takes over and sometimes it comes out when you're least expecting it."

"So you do taekwondo."

Her laugh is a low snort. "I've been doing taekwondo since I was tiny. I used to compete, when I was really little, but that stopped, and well, now…" She shrugs, and he gets it.

"Talent." He doesn't need more than the one word.

She sits back up, grips his shoulder, and squeezes. "Here's the thing." Her voice is still low, just between them. "People are going to talk to you about breathing and control, and you're going to think they're nuts. And you're going to come here and try to kick the shit out of something until you feel like you're flying. But when it comes down to it—those people are actually right, and you're right, all at the same time. And you can get that here. You can channel it, and you can control it, and you can kick out the crazy. And you'll get there, Alaric. Give it time. It'll work."

"Because it worked for you?" It seems like the logical response, and he's confused when she laughs.

"Oh, hell no. I'm still a work in progress. But it's helping, and I'm getting there too," she admits. "Now get up. I want you to do your form."

She makes him do his white-belt form three times, slowly and carefully, with controlled power and sharp moves. Each kick and punch has to be precise, each stance sunk low, his breathing perfect. It's as hard to do that slowly as it is to kick quickly, and he's out of breath by the end. Professor Szczek is calling for everyone to gear up, and he finds himself pulling his sweaty gear back on to spar with the rest of the class.

He goes three rounds trying to be careful with other white belts before the groups are rearranged and Mac partners him with Jackson.

Jackson grins brightly. He raises on hand, waggles his fingers at Alaric in a *come and get me* gesture. "You're strong. I'm fast. This'll be good practice."

And it is. It gives Alaric one more chance to let loose, sparring until he's gasping and thirsty, and Jackson's leaning over, hands on his knees for a moment before he straightens up and puts his hands over his head and sucks in a deep breath.

"Fuck, I am out of shape. I need to work harder if I'm going to be ready for basketball in a couple months." Jackson stretches, groaning softly. "I should get my ass into the weight room, too. Do you go?"

"With the team." Alaric shrugs. "It's a new resource for me, had to make do with what we had at home or with the league before. I'll keep it up in the winter if you want to work together."

Rush

"I'll be with my team then. Spring. And we should run then, too, keep us both in shape." Jackson slaps Alaric's shoulder, turns him enough so he can untie the chest protector for him. "In the meantime, we've got this and those two making sure we stay fit." He pulls off his helmet, runs his fingers through his close-cropped, sweaty curls.

"Will you be competing?" Alaric can't, but he'll still support the teammates who can, and he's looking forward to the first competition.

Jackson nods. "Hell yeah. I'm sorry you can't. But is it helping? You spar like you're made for it. Does one of the—?" He cuts himself off, nose wrinkled. "Hell, I don't know how to say it. You have animal forms, right? Inside you? Does one of them like to fight?"

"Most of them like to fight," Alaric admits. "This is different, but it's the kind of thing I'm good at. I like the way it has more focus and discipline than a brawl."

"Then keep doing it, if it's working for you. I'll be your sparring partner any time you like." Jackson shoves his gear in the bag, makes a face as he goes to close it up. "And now I'm going to go piss off Patrick with my stinky gear, and he'll probably retaliate with something loud, then I'll have to get louder with my own music. Think TJ'll mind?"

Alaric winces, glad for once that Rory's music seems to be much quieter than either what Jackson plays or Patrick listens to. "I think you might want to just clean your gear and avoid the war," he says dryly.

It takes him a little longer to pack his own things, taking the time to wipe everything down with a towel soaked in bleach solution. He can't stand the smell of the astringent, but it helps dull the sweat to a point where he's pretty sure Rory can't smell it, even if Alaric still can. By the time he's ready to go, everyone else has put the mats away, and Professor Szczek is lingering, waiting to lock up.

"You did good today," Pawel says as Alaric passes by him on the way out.

Alaric's not sure if he agrees—the smoke still bothers him when he thinks about it, although it's possible it was some weird kind of fluke. But he accepts the praise with a nod and a mumbled "Thank you" because, good or not, he feels better than he did before practice started, and that's why he's here.

17

Somewhere in the back of his mind, Alaric knows it's a dream. He's flying, but his wings don't belong to his eagle. They're bigger, beating at the air with huge strokes, taking him higher than he's ever flown in the waking world.

As soon as he notices that—realizes it with a semi-conscious mind—it's too much for the dream. He falters, wings shrinking back on himself until the eagle bursts free and he hangs there for a moment, tiny in a huge sky. He flaps once, feels the world spin around him, and he's falling, crashing from eagle to hound, baying in frustration as the air rushes over him. He slips from hound back to eagle, then briefly becomes the bear before the lizard pushes through and his body strikes the ground, and he wakes with the air blown from his lungs. His body aches, and there's a haze in the room as he struggles for breath.

The door pushes open, and Alaric makes a small noise of irritation at the light spilling in from the hallway.

Rory closes the door behind him, sets his guitar in the stand, and drops his bag. "Hey. Sorry I woke you." The words are tight, the heat of anger coloring his scent.

" 't's okay." The words are rough, mumbled together into one stream of sound. Alaric coughs, trying to clear his throat. "What time is it? I got in late and decided to just pass out."

"Around three." Rory moves around in the darkness, stripping out of his jeans before climbing into his bed. "I was working on lyrics and lost track of time." He rolls over, fluffs his pillow with more force than seems necessary. "Thorne skipped out on a session, so I got lost in what I was doing. And had to do it all myself anyway."

Alaric's brain is still fuzzy, but he thinks he can put together what Rory's saying. "You were doing band things with Thorne? Or you were supposed to be?" Because he knows exactly where Thorne was for the second time that week, and it wasn't writing lyrics. Or at least he's pretty sure Thorne wasn't writing lyrics. Who knows what was going on inside his head.

"We got started after dinner, then Thorne got a text and took off early." Rory grumbles under his breath. "Some kind of emergency, I guess."

Alaric makes a strangled noise, rolls over, and buries his face in the pillow.

He hears the way Rory's breath stops, then a moment later, Rory sits up in his bed. "Did you see Thorne tonight?"

Fuck. Alaric refuses to say anything. Maybe Rory will think he's gone back to sleep.

"You have got to be kidding me." Rory leans off the bed, grabs his phone. The light's bright in the dark room. Fingers slide across the screen hard enough for Alaric to hear it, and he can't breathe through the irritation in Rory's scent.

Alaric rolls over enough so that he can speak somewhat clearly. "What are you doing?"

"Asking Thorne to please not have sex with my roommate." Rory huffs. "No, that's not it. It's your choice, and it's his choice, so whatever, but if Thorne's skipping out on something, he shouldn't lie about it," Rory mutters. "It's not you I'm angry at. I don't care who you have sex with. I actually don't care who he has sex with either. It's just—I live with you. And if he breaks your heart—and he will, because that's Thorne, and while someday he might want to settle into a committed relationship with one or several people, that's not who he is now—I still have to live with you. We're *friends*. And Thorne doesn't always think with the head that has his brain. Not to mention that sometimes Thorne forgets to filter his stories, and I really don't want to end up with a mental image of you that I can't forget because of what he said."

It's a barrage of words that leaves Alaric reeling, his skin hot enough that he feels like it should be shining brighter than the light of Rory's phone. "It's not a big deal," Alaric mutters. "He's not going to break my heart. You don't have to worry about it. It's just—"

"No." Rory cuts him off quickly, the tone pleading more than angry. "I really don't need the details. Please."

"I don't want to talk about the details. I didn't mean to tell you." Alaric thinks that's probably worse, if he could really wrap his head around any of this, but he's too sleep fogged. "I mean. It's private. It doesn't have anything to do with you and me." That still doesn't sound right, and Alaric tries one more time. "We're okay. Right?"

There's a *thud* as Rory falls back against the pillow and sighs. "Yeah. We're okay."

The light from the phone still shines, and Alaric can hear the sound of Rory's fingers tapping against the screen. But Rory's scent has eased, and Alaric lets the sound soothe him and drifts back into sleep.

He's in the sky again, his wings spread wide around him. Wings beat the air, and he pushes higher and higher, feeling the way the air drags against the claws that tip his wings. He roars, the sound rumbling through him, startling him into human form. He's tumbling down, spinning through the sky until he falls and wakes with a shout.

He's off the bed, lying on the floor beside his loft, and Rory's heart is hammering as hard as his own.

"Are you okay?"

"Fell off the fucking bed," Alaric grumbles. It's embarrassing, and he takes a moment to get his heart rate to slow down. He considers shifting shape and falling asleep on the floor, curled as the hound under his own damned bed, but that's not what he really wants.

He just wants to stop dreaming strange things that he's sure have something to do with the frustration still simmering under his skin. Thorne helped, but there's something lingering, something bothering Alaric that he can't get a handle on or exorcise.

"Nightmare?" Rory asks. "You were thrashing around before you fell."

"Second one tonight," Alaric admits. He hitches himself back into his bed, stretches out, and tries to get comfortable. He feels like the dream is still there, waiting for him, and when he closes his eyes, there's a rush of wind around his head as if he's taking off, flying away. He shakes awake, the bed moving beneath him.

"If you keep that up, I swear I'm going to sleep on you to keep you still," Rory grumbles. "It's been a long day, and I'm exhausted, and I still have work to finish before my 10 a.m. class. And I don't want to miss breakfast again."

"I don't fucking care if you do." There's a sharp noise, and Alaric goes over what Rory said and what he replied and can't make sense of it either. He whines softly under his breath, scrubs a hand over his face. "Sleep on me, whatever, I don't give a fuck. I just want to sleep, too, and I'm over the fucking nightmares. So whatever you want. I don't care."

He's not entirely surprised when Rory's bed shifts as Rory climbs down. Footsteps pad over to him, and Rory hesitates at the side of the bed. "Will it help?"

Alaric shrugs. "Don't know. It's what Drea would do." Or Corbin. Or anyone from home. It's a Clan thing, piling in together as if their animal sides can burrow through their skins and ground them in humanity.

"Fine." Rory hitches himself up, stretches out next to Alaric, one arm thrown across his body. There's a low noise, and Rory shoves at Alaric, who slides closer to the wall.

There isn't much space in the long, narrow twin bed, but they make it work. In the end, Rory sleeps half on top of Alaric, lanky body loose and limp in slumber. Alaric closes his eyes, lets himself drift in a space where scent is more than anything else, the weight of Rory's body welcome and comforting as his scent wraps around him. It's almost like Clan, and it grounds Alaric.

Images of wings fade away, and he slides into sleep peacefully. In the morning, he can't remember any more dreams.

18

ALARIC ONLY HAS to get through two more rush events before it's over. He's been at OPT every night, and though he likes the guys from his team and from the fraternity, he's tired of the crush of people. He's spent enough time on the couch that by Friday, when he hears his name, the response is, "in the usual spot." He expects to see Chris or Dax coming, or maybe one of the others, but it's Drea, looking out of place among all the guys.

She settles in on the couch, snuggles close to Alaric, and he drops an arm around her shoulder. He nuzzles the top of her head, sighs slightly when she rubs her cheek against his shoulder.

Clan.

He's missed this.

He doubts she's stopped by just to snuggle, though.

"What's your ulterior motive?" he rumbles softly, and she swats his chest.

"Who says I have one?" She shakes her head before she pulls back, lets space slide between them again. "For one, I missed you. We've barely seen each other this week, although I checked out that tea place you texted me about. I guess Trish goes there all the time—plays there when they want live music sometimes—and Serina has a crush on one of the waiters."

Serina, he's met, but Trish isn't a familiar name. "Trish?" It's bait, he knows, and he takes it anyway, catching the scent of her rising glee.

"One of the sisters, and I was thinking that since tonight's an open event, maybe you should come over and meet her. And see the rest of the sisters. Since you seem to have all this misplaced concern about me pledging a sorority." She tilts her head, and Alaric isn't fooled by her attempt at innocence. There's another part to the story, but he won't find it out by asking. He only ever finds things out too late, once Drea has him thoroughly embroiled in her plan.

"Fine. I'll go." He starts to push out of his seat, pausing when he spots Chris and Dax, each of them carrying two red cups. "I think I can go," he says slowly, not sure of the rules around rush. It's been a week, and he's been here every night. He's already been here for an hour, and he can't stay out late tonight anyway, not with a game on Saturday.

Chris's gaze shifts from Alaric to Drea. "You're not stuck here. You signed the register of potential pledges already, right?"

"Yeah." Alaric had done that after the first few days, decided he was pledging even if the social aspect made him uncomfortable. This is his team, for the most part, and he wants to try to be a part of that.

"I'm just taking him over to SigPsiEp for the evening." Drea wraps her arm around Alaric's, leans in close. "We haven't spent much time together, and I want him to see the girls I'm starting to think of as family." She cocks her head, chin slightly lifted as she settles her gaze on Chris and Dax. "Which means I'll be back to see what I think about all of you. Clan takes care of their own."

Alaric would protest that he can take care of himself, but he doesn't want to push her to more displays of overprotective siblinghood. "I'll stop back, if it's not too late," he says, and lets Drea tug him through the crowds and out the door.

They could go inside, through the basement that lies underneath all of Townhouse Row, but it's a nice night, so Alaric doesn't blame Drea for taking the outdoor route. They walk around the corner of the row, then back down the other side, past Douglass on their way to SigPsiEp, which is in the direct opposite corner from OPT.

Alaric's steps slow as he approaches the sorority. There's music spilling out, a fluffy pop sound that's thankfully not overwhelmingly loud. He can smell fruity drinks and hear the high pitch of excited female voices. He doesn't care about any of that. He digs his heels in, stops in front of the house as Drea tries to tug him toward it.

He wants to look at the bike parked right in front.

It has a recognizable logo, but he's never seen a motorcycle built quite like this. Or this color. It's low and sleek, the distance from the seat to the pedal made for long legs, the handlebars leaning back toward the rider. The frame looks light, the different parts painted either a shiny black or a gleaming, rich orange. The tank has an orange base, with scrollwork in black painted along the sleek edges.

"It's fucking gorgeous," Alaric breathes, and Drea chuckles.

"You can tell that to Trish when you get inside," she says. "And if you're nice, she might take you out on a ride. You still want one of those things?"

Anything Alaric could afford is never going to measure up to that bike. He's pretty damned sure it's custom built. "Hell yes," he growls, because someday he will reward himself with a damned good bike.

Drea starts by dragging him through the crowd, introducing him to girls on the way by. Serina he already knows, and he remembers Carolyn and Heather from breakfast the other day. He won't let her pull him past Trish when they meet, and spends a half hour listening intently to her speak in a soft Tennessee accent while she tells him about how she built the bike from junk parts. She worked with her uncles, who said she needed to know how to put it together and take it apart before she hit the road.

When she says, "I rode from California to Florida and back again on that bike before I came here," there's a low twist of jealousy that has him growling and Drea giggling. He wants that kind of freedom, and he wants that bike.

Drea tugs him away from Trish, and they continue on their rounds. There are more girls, but the names slip away from him after the first few, and he's content to realize that he's nothing more than Drea's twin here. He trails after her, nodding when he's introduced, only half listening to conversations as he indulges in the pleasure of just being close to his twin and Clan.

There's a touch to his shoulder, and he turns to see Mac behind him. "I didn't expect to see you here. Don't you have an event of your own?"

Drea's deep in conversation with—Alaric can't remember what her name is, but the conversation is something about biology and agriculture, and he's been lost since it began. He hooks his finger with Drea's and squeezes, a quiet signal to let her know that he's stepping away. Then he grabs his cup, motions for Mac to lead, and they head to a corner and take over an empty couch.

Seems like maybe Mac has a usual space of her own for parties.

She sits cross-legged at one end of the couch, facing Alaric as he takes over the other end. "Drea wanted me to meet some of her potential new sisters," Alaric admits. "Not that she's assuming she's going to get a bid. She's just hopeful."

"I like your sister," Mac says. "She's got a level head on her shoulders, and she's got a lot of good ideas about work in the community. She's also the kind of person that seems to get along with everyone. She knows how to talk to people."

"She got all the social skills," Alaric says dryly. It's not the first time the observation's been made; he's heard it since he was small.

"You're not antisocial," Mac says firmly. "You're cautious, and that's not a bad character trait. Remember, I've been places where being cautious could keep you alive."

Alaric doesn't think he's going to war. He hopes he's not going to war. He just wants to get through college and do something he loves afterward. He nods anyway, like that made more sense to him. "And you're cautious?"

"Sometimes. I used to be a daredevil." Mac's smile is wry, and she takes a long sip of her drink. "I didn't think I could get hurt. And then for a while I didn't actually care."

"Because of taekwondo?" Her brow furrows in confusion at his question, so Alaric clarifies, "Is that why you thought you couldn't be hurt?"

"That was part of it. I started really young because my father wanted me to stay in touch with my heritage, and Mom just wanted me to do something to tire me out."

Alaric's mouth opens, closes again, because he's pretty sure anything he says is going to come out very wrong. He feels his cheeks warm when Mac starts laughing, a low snort escaping.

"My dad's Black, my mom's Korean," Mac says. "My mom was adopted back in the '70s, and my grandparents wanted to make sure she knew her heritage. She learned the language, traveled to Korea before I was born, and she did taekwondo, too. My parents didn't immerse me as much. I learned some of the language, when my mom taught me, but mostly I just learned the sport. Sometimes I think my grandparents are disappointed in me for being so American." She takes another long drink, her tone thoughtful. "I'd actually like to go to Africa, someday, with my father and brother. We've dug into my father's ancestry, and while we weren't able to trace everything, we think that some of his family was taken from Senegal. It's possible we're wrong, but that's Dad's best guess. Records weren't exactly well-kept."

"Taken?" Alaric feels like he's sliding down into things he shouldn't ask, unsure of how to step.

Mac gives him a frank look. "Taken. As slaves. It's a fact of our family history—some of my ancestors were brought to Georgia from Africa during the late parts of the eighteenth century. My great-grandfather moved north in the 1940s, met my great-grandmother in New York, and they settled in Harlem. My dad grew up there, and he's living there now."

"Ah." Alaric looks at his drink, but it can't save him. "Don't have a fucking clue what to say to that."

"There's nothing really to say when you're presented with some of the worst of American history," Mac says dryly. She leans her head against the back of the couch, watching him. She curls her feet up, knees bent and feet on the couch. "But we can trade stories. I grew up on Long Island, then in Washington DC. You?"

"Here." Alaric makes a hand motion, shrugs a little. "Not exactly here, but about a half hour west of here. Where there's even more land and less people. It's pretty much farm country, but that's what Clan does. We find places, and we make our own communities, make our own towns sometimes. Live in the now, mostly, or in our own history. No one cares where anyone comes from, as long as they're Clan. If you're Clan, you're part of the community."

"You're lucky people don't expect more from you because of who you are," Mac says idly, draining the last of her cup, and Alaric wonders just how much she's had.

"Didn't say that," he replies, leaning forward to take the empty cup from her. "You don't usually talk this much. Maybe you should stop drinking."

"Maybe I should." She doesn't wobble when she stands, but Alaric catches a rush of uncertainty in her scent. He doesn't ask, just puts an arm around her waist, walks with her to the stairs, and heads up, ignoring the comments he can hear following in their wake.

Mac's got a single in the attic, one of three tiny rooms under the eaves. Alaric makes sure that she's settled safely in her room with a big glass of water before he leaves her behind. He has to duck to walk through the hallway between the three rooms, and he heads down the stairs carefully so he doesn't bump his head. He's about to keep going down the next flight of stairs, back to the party, when he hears Drea calling his name. He follows her heartbeat to a room on the second floor.

"Don't worry, I'm just leaving." Heather brushes by him on her way out, that citrusy scent trailing in her wake. He blinks as she goes, noting the crisp, sharp notes of her voice and the way her heart speeds up when she sees him.

He's not a big fan of Empaths, but he'd never kick someone out of where they live. He's the interloper here, and he feels guilty as she disappears down the stairs.

"Come on in." Drea pats the bed she's sitting on, and Alaric steps into the room slowly before he sinks down next to her, budging in close before he realizes that they're talking to someone else. Carolyn, the other girl from breakfast, who he saw in passing downstairs earlier in the evening. She offers a small smile and a wave.

"This is your room," Alaric says.

"Mine and Heather's." Carolyn has cards in her hands that she's idly shuffling as she sits. The bed is mostly made, the comforter pulled taut in the space between them. She sets the cards down, nudges the deck toward Alaric.

"Cut the deck." Drea's shoulder presses into his. "Carolyn gave me a tarot reading last night; she did them for all the prospects. I want her to do one for you."

And with that, the shoe drops. "This is why you brought me here."

"Just cut the deck and let her read for you."

"I'm not a Mage, not exactly. I'm not going to manipulate you somehow by doing this," Carolyn says, her hands curled together in her lap. "I just tell fortunes. And I happen to be very good at predictive Talent."

"Carolyn's also a twin," Drea says, like that's somehow going to impact his decision.

Alaric lifts the cards, holds the large deck in the palm of one hand. He's no stranger to tarot—he's met other readers, people who've dabbled, but none who've said flat-out that they have predictive Talent. "It's rare," he says. "Mostly Emergent."

"Does it matter?" Carolyn curls her fingers, motions at the cards. "If you don't want to do it, it's not going to hurt my feelings. When Drea asked me about it, I figured she might want it more than you."

"She usually does, and I usually give in. We're twins." Alaric shrugs, and Carolyn nods as if that makes perfect sense.

Alaric picks up the top third of the deck and sets it on the bed. He takes a few cards after that, then a few more, then another set, until he's finally placed them all neatly back in one stack. He hands her the set and sits back, waiting to hear what she has to say.

She lays out the cards in a pattern, murmuring under her breath as she goes. Alaric tries to listen, but he's not sure she's using recognizable words when she speaks. She runs her fingers over the cards, lightly touches each one, lifts them, looks at them closely, and her heartbeat remains perfectly even the entire time. Finally she sits back, her knees drawn up slightly as she sits cross-legged, her hands around her shins.

"You're going through a lot of change right now, which is to be expected. I mean, you're here. Some of it is about the connections you're making with other people—the possible relationships you might have. Some of it is about what you're learning, the messages you're getting from classes or from other people. But there's a lot of conflict around it. You don't know how to take all of it, and you're kind of frustrated and disgusted, and you don't know if that's because it's new or if it's a real feeling. That's something you're going to have to figure out: how you actually feel about things. Because it's all changing, and by the time you're done here, the entire world could be different for you."

She touches a card where there are five people walking through a gloomy landscape, the card upside down compared to the rest of the spread on the comforter. "You were in a place where everything was a mess. People disagreed with you; they didn't have the same belief in the future that you did. So you walked away from it and put yourself in this new space. And this place has the potential to make you transform. Change. Discover hidden or latent abilities, things you don't even have hints about yourself yet. And the thing is, you're scared of change. You're scared of all this chaos around you, and maybe a little indecisive because there's what's expected and what you want and maybe some other options. So you need to get over that, deal with the fact that maybe you'll embarrass yourself. It's okay. Just make a decision and go forward; you'll figure out whether it's the right one when you get there."

Alaric growls, and Carolyn pauses, glancing at him. "Don't shoot the messenger."

It makes his gut churn to hear this from her, from someone who doesn't know him at all. "Don't insult me," he grumbles. "I'm not indecisive."

Drea makes a noise; he refuses to look at her.

"So there's a guy." Carolyn lifts up a card to show him the image of a young man with a scorpion on his arm. "He's probably charming. He may bring you a message, and it's up to you to listen to the message. It might not be something he says so much as something he does, or something you learn from watching him. But keep in mind that there's a hidden sting if you're not careful; he could mean more trouble than he's worth. He's going to help you get past that indecisiveness, but he might also take you down the wrong path entirely."

Alaric doesn't necessarily believe in fortune telling, but that particular statement strikes a nerve he isn't ready to look at. "Go on," he mutters, gesturing at the cards. "What else?" He wants to get this over with, find out why Drea wanted him to sit through this. Because he knows there's a reason in her mind, he just isn't sure if she'll share that with him.

Carolyn sets the card down, says quietly, "I'm not insulting you. I'm just telling you what the cards say, okay? And this isn't some kind of *this is going to happen* predictive Talent. The cards are a path. They're one path. Maybe they're a warning, or maybe they help you see something that can help you find a new path. But I'm not laying out a future that's carved in stone. I'm giving you information."

He makes a noise, because he's not sure that matters. "Just tell me about it."

"You feel alienated." Her words drop like stones, and Drea's hand covers his as she leans into him with her full weight. Carolyn doesn't look up from the cards, just keeps talking, her voice careful and even. "There's a deep sorrow inside your heart, and you feel as if either you need to separate from those you love, or possibly that you are already separated and there's nothing you can do about it. Maybe both. You're grieving for that lost connection, but at the same time, you can't see a way past it."

Carolyn's fingers drift from the card with three swords to the one above it, bearing an image of two lovers surrounded by six overflowing cups. "Things may be bad, but the memories are good. You had a good childhood. You loved your family, and they loved you. And they don't see that things have changed. Maybe they think you're still the same person you were when you were six, I don't know, but they don't feel the same alienation you do. Or they don't want to see it."

There are only two cards left, and the man on the penultimate card has a piercing, sharp gaze, like a lion or a hawk. "I don't know if this is your hope or your fear, but you see leadership in your future. And maybe you're afraid of the dark side of it, where you can be domineering instead of merely dominant. Or maybe you don't want this at all; maybe this is part of the divide you feel. But you see it looming in some way. And the actual outcome isn't clear in any way, which is frustrating to me, too, let me tell you." She sweeps the cards back together, drops them on top of the rest of the deck, and slides them into a black silken bag.

"That's probably one of the most useless final outcome cards," she grumbles. "It's about making plans, and hope, and confidence, but it's also warning you about failure and quarreling. It doesn't really help in any way, it's more of a *watch out* sort of thing. Be aware that you might have hopes and dreams, but someone else important might disagree with you."

Alaric can't help the snort, because that's absolutely the truth. That's his life. He glances at Drea, who still leans close to him, her head tucked on his shoulder. "Was there a point to this?"

He feels the twitch of her head as she shrugs. "There was something in mine that made me think you needed to hear this. And I still think that."

Carolyn tugs the tie on the bag, sets it into the drawer of the table next to her bed. "Maybe you two should go talk."

In other words, get out of her room. Alaric can translate that one for himself. He stands, and Drea puts her hands on his shoulders. They don't need to speak for him to understand the request; he crouches slightly, lets her hitch herself up onto his back while he supports her.

He carries her piggyback down the stairs. It looks more playful than he feels, and she waves as he heads through the crowd and out the front door. The cool evening air is refreshing, and he lets her slide to the ground, find her own feet again.

"I am never going to be in a leadership position," Alaric says slowly.

"You hope you won't. That's a fear for you," Drea counters, the words quick enough that he knows he's found the crux of the issue in her mind. "What if you create a new community? One that thinks like you do."

"Break from home?" He can't imagine stepping out on his own, creating something new. "It wouldn't work."

She threads her fingers with his, leans in, and he cradles her against his chest. He feels her heart beat in time with his, twinned souls in two bodies. He bends his head, kisses the top of her hair.

"Whatever happens," she says softly, the words against his shoulder. "Whatever comes, I'm with you, Ric. Remember that."

He squeezes her gently. It's not something he could forget. But it's okay, because he's not going to lead anywhere she wouldn't follow. He's not good Clan. He's broken, and none of them will ever let him forget it.

19

It's the first home game since his suspension lifted. Alaric half expects to be booed when he enters the field, but he's treated just like the rest of the team. His shoulder blades itch, the hound baying under his skin as he warms up on the sidelines. They've switched up the lineup, trying to surprise the other team, that leaves Dax with Alaric, idly tossing the ball back and forth.

Alaric couldn't sit still if he tried.

His gaze is drawn back to the field over and over throughout the first quarter. Chris tries to keep the plays unexpected, but Cal Thompson is somehow just there every time. The first time Cal intercepts a short pass, Alaric's breath catches in his throat, wondering if Cal somehow just teleported across the field.

Alaric knows better, of course. Cal just moves that fast. It's why he's so good, and why they played well together. He groans softly, rubs at his face, and nods when he's warned that he'll be going in for the second quarter. They need to change something up if they're going to have a hope of winning this one.

He finally sits when Coach Campbell directs him to. He leans forward, elbows on his knees, and keeps an eye on Chris, watches the plays that he's running and tries to analyze their effectiveness. Chris will get to do this when Alaric goes in, might just leave Alaric in for a few plays before taking over again, long enough to get an outsider's view. It gives Alaric something to think about other than his ex-teammate out there on the field, winning the game for the opponent.

He watches Chris drop back like he's going to pass, then tuck the ball under his arm, cradled tight against his body. Chris fakes right, then swings left, darting forward through a chink in the defense. He makes it thirty yards before a defensive player barrels into him from the side, taking him down in a rough hit that flattens Chris against the ground.

He doesn't get up.

The opposing player calls out, and a whistle blows. Play stops.

Chris rolls onto his back, and even from the sidelines Alaric can smell tension and pain, something close to panic. It has him on his feet, two steps forward before Coach Young stops him with a hand on his chest.

"Helmet on," Coach Young says, and Alaric pulls it over his head, lets it drown out the sound. Coach Young's voice is muffled when he speaks next, leaning close to Alaric. "I'm going to need you to go in as soon as we've got Chris off the field."

The announcer's voice rumbles in the distance, thin and tinny. First down, no penalty, and number fourteen—Chris Stone—is on his feet and walking off the field. Walking is a euphemism for the way Chris has Coach Campbell's shoulder wedged under one arm and Dax under the other. Chris hops on one leg, the other hanging while he drags it slightly, a fresh wave of pained scent radiating outwards with every step.

It's slow going, but Chris makes it off the field without a stretcher. He passes close enough that Alaric makes a small noise, and sees when Chris glances at him. Then Coach Young is pushing at him, and Alaric takes the field with his team, and the game is his.

Alaric manages to keep from bleeding more points until halftime. In the locker room, he's drawn into a discussion of how the coaches want to change up play, what they want him to try to see if they can get past Cal's defense. Alaric tries to ask how Chris is—what happened—but the questions are pushed off, and then they're heading back onto the field to play the second half.

He's distracted. His mind is on his teammate, and Cal can tell. Alaric spots the small smirk, and it digs at him, irritation settling in his chest with cold flames. Alaric growls, and he pushes past Cal, keeps the beast in check as he runs, rushing for twenty-two yards.

They make their way down the field by inches. Dax's fingers are perfect and light, letting Alaric aim the ball in unexpected directions, trusting that

Dax will somehow be there, somehow elude Cal's interception. It almost works until it doesn't, and suddenly Cal is running down the field with the ball, making it halfway to the goal. Alaric wonders if they can possibly pull this out, if there's any way to save the game.

There isn't.

The game ends on the thirty-one yard line with a failed field goal attempt. They're down by two in the end, and Alaric couldn't manage to get the ball to the goal. He gets through the post-game in a haze, vaguely aware of the other team around him, of his own teammates talking to him. They have to walk back to the locker rooms side by side with their opponents, and Cal is somehow next to him, helmet tucked under his arm.

Alaric blinks. "Good game," he rumbles; it's the right thing to say.

"Took the words out of my mouth. You're playing better than you were," Cal tells him, and Alaric can't think how he could mean that, because he lost. And last year, when they were still in high school, he never lost. "PHU's going to be the one to beat next year, once you've found your rhythm with the team."

A whine builds to a growl, frustration filling Alaric's mouth with angry teeth. He lets the growl slip loose, low and controlled, vibrating in his chest.

Cal takes a step to the side; he keeps pace with Alaric but puts space between them.

It feels good to make him wary.

"I need to go with my team." It's a dismissal. They used to be friends, but Alaric doesn't want to deal with Cal now. He doesn't want to think about all the ways he failed on that field, all the ways he should have been an advantage instead. No one on his team knows Cal better, and Alaric still couldn't get past him enough to win.

Cal closes the distance briefly, claps Alaric on the shoulder before he moves off toward the guest locker room. Alaric ducks into his team's room quickly, moves through his teammates to get to his own locker and start shucking his gear. There's no sign of Chris although the room reeks of pain and tension.

He makes himself move at a normal pace: shower off, towel his hair dry, pull on clean clothes. He tugs the henley down, does up his jeans. He can still feel the beast riding under his skin, his heart thudding with the need to do something to make up for how much he's done wrong today.

At the least he needs to apologize to Chris.

The team drifts out, most heading back to OPT. Alaric calls out that he'll meet them there, but he lingers in the locker room. In the absence of his noisy team, he can hear the voices murmuring in the small back room: fragments of conversation about ice and painkillers. He pushes through the door to where Chris sits on a cot, his knee heavily wrapped in ice.

"Shit." It's probably not the right thing to say, but it's the first thing out of Alaric's mouth. He glances at the coaches, shrugs one shoulder in apology for the language. As if it's not something they all say every damned day.

"Pretty much," Chris agrees. "General consensus is that at minimum, it's a sprain, and at worst, I blew my knee out and I need surgery."

The words are a punch to the gut, stealing Alaric's breath away. "Fuck."

The corner of Chris's mouth quirks up, almost smiling. "I have an MRI scheduled for Monday; they can't get me in with the specialist until then, and they don't want anyone else to have a chance to screw it up beforehand. So I'm on crutches and icing until then, and the only painkillers I have are acetaminophen and ibuprofen."

"That fucking sucks." Alaric manages an entire sentence. And that's a shit-ton of ice Chris has around his knee, wrapped semi-securely with a bandage. "You want me to help you get back to the house?" It's the least Alaric can do after he fucked up any chance of them winning the game.

"That wouldn't be a bad idea. If I'm able to get out of here?" Chris glances at the two coaches. Campbell motions, and Young leaves the room. Campbell grabs the pair of crutches, holds them out.

"If you think you can make it, then go, but it's a long walk and you might be better off waiting for Public Safety to get here and give you a lift."

"He has a point." Alaric's never had to deal with crutches, but they don't look comfortable. "We can wait."

"Fine." Chris slumps back against the wall. "We'll wait. You don't need to hover over us like a watchdog. Alaric will help me get out to the car when Public Safety gets here."

Coach Campbell pauses next to Alaric, grasps his shoulder for a moment. "You played well today. That was a tough game, but you ran the team well. I knew you were a good choice for PHU."

It's easier to hear from him than from Cal. Alaric just nods, mutters, "Thanks," and he means it even if he's not sure yet that he believes that he's as good as they think.

When the door closes behind coach, Chris says quietly, "You're going to be fine starting. You have Dawson for backup, and I'll be back in a few weeks. Nothing popped, it just hurts like hell, so it's probably a sprain. Which means I'm going to be doing PT for a while to get back in shape while you play my games."

"You won't know that until the MRI." Alaric gives him a dark look. "You're human. You need to heal."

"I'm human, and I'll need a few weeks to heal, but that doesn't mean I won't be at training." Chris pushes himself to sitting upright again. "We'll go over the tapes, figure out what worked and what didn't work against Cal. You're getting a rhythm with Dax, but you need to figure out how to work with our entire offensive line. This just means you're going to get there sooner rather than later."

They're nice words. Easy to believe, if Alaric lets himself. He grunts, makes a low noise like he agrees in case that's what Chris is waiting for. He's about to say something when his phone starts singing, some fluffy pop song about not caring what the world thinks, and he frowns as he digs his hand into his pocket to fish it out and answer. "Yeah, Drea? Did I miss a text? I'm waiting to help Chris…" His voice trails off as he hears her breath, tight and shivering on each exhalation, and his chest goes tight. "What's wrong?"

The cot shifts and there's a groan, but then Chris is behind him, the heat of his body contrasting with the stark chill where the ice on his knee rests behind Alaric's leg.

Drea doesn't answer at first, her breath choked on a sob. "We have to go home," she whispers. "Mom called. We have to go home."

He can hear the rapid-fire beat of her heart, hear the anxiety that twists her into knots of tension. "Why, Drea? What happened?"

"It's Orson." His gut churns at the sound of his brother's name, at the way Drea sobs. "We have to go home."

114

Excerpt from *When Magic Entered the World: Interviews With Lineage Talent*, by Pawel Szczek, © 2009

I don't know what you think you're going to get out of this. I'm not giving away Clan secrets. Not that we have any secrets, none that would interest a Mage. Emergent, aren't you? You reek like one, too much power to hold inside that frail body. Unnatural.

We keep to ourselves mostly, out here. Always have. Made our way west and found ourselves space. Fit into the world as it was; didn't want to interfere with the people already here. Made our peace back then, kept it best we could.

You want to know how things changed, though. When that girl did magic in front of the world.

We've grown since then. Used to be about three hundred of us in Easton, and now there's upwards of five hundred. Not everyone's Clan; I remember when one family drove in, their baby in the shape of a lion club. Didn't know what to do and asked us to put him back the way he belonged.

They didn't much like it when we explained that the lion was part of who he was, now. They adapted, though. She teaches at the school; she's good with the ones who are more comfortable with their animal side. Her boy's started kindergarten, and she runs a play group after school. Helps a lot, I think, to let them just run. Or fly. Or move in whatever form it is they take.

You know how it works; don't try to tell me you don't. Every Clan person has a way of changing. Sometimes it runs in a family, but not always. Knew a man who had a way with birds once, and his kids tended toward rodents, every single one of them. Funny bit was that his wife could take any mammal form, but she preferred the big cats. Ever seen a lion lying down with an eagle tucked in her ruff, and three voles under her chin? You Mages don't know what it's like.

Clan's taken the worst of it, in the media. We were right to stay out of the way as much as we could. Magic can be stopped. Oh, sometimes it leaks out, like that scent of ozone you're giving off, but you can usually keep it inside. Clan doesn't work that way. We're beasts at heart, and the beast will come out when it needs to.

And people are afraid of that. Rightfully so, sometimes, I suppose. Takes teaching and work to keep the beast at bay. Clan children start learning young. Someone coming into their heritage when they're a teen or already an adult? Recipe for disaster.

I was called in after the disaster in Springfield in '07. It's not easy to talk down the press when they've just seen a mountain lion rip three people apart. No matter that the victims were robbing someone at gun point. No matter that the mountain lion was a terrified teenage boy. Press never gave him a chance.

Good thing he disappeared from the holding cell, isn't it? Can't really stop a mouse.

We take them all in, good or bad. We're Clan, and we stay together, whatever that means. And we'll do it without you. It's your kind that brought this on us, your kind that changed the world. Haven't got any proof of it, but I'm as sure as I know my name's Theodore Lent. A Mage did this.

Everything bad that happens, we can always trace it back to the Mages. And it's always Clan that takes the fall.

HOMECOMING

20

ALARIC TEXTS RORY from the Public Safety car, and together they manage to get Chris up the stairs to their floor. As Alaric helps Chris sit in the one chair they have left in the room, he mutters, "You didn't have to come. This has to fucking hurt."

"It's cold, and yeah, it aches, but you look like shit just went sideways," Chris says. "Like I said, I'll stick with you until I know you're all right." He pauses and adds, "With me out, you're the heart of the team. Have to make sure you're good."

It's a lie, and Alaric has no idea why.

There's a hiccup in the hall, and Alaric pushes past Rory, yanks the door open, and pulls Drea in, cradling her head against his chest. He can feel her tears, the way her body shakes with sobs. Her scent is distraught, heavy with salt, and it tears at him until his breath shudders in his chest, and he swallows a sob of his own.

He would cry just because she is, without even knowing the details. She's his twin.

Soledad edges into the room, holding a box of tissues in one hand and a small trash can in the other. She smiles wanly, her eyes rimmed in red, as she moves past.

Drea's hands clutch at Alaric's shirt, tiny claws tipping her fingers. Drea never loses control, and seeing her beast manifest… Alaric looks up, uncertain, glancing from Chris to Rory.

Rory holds up one hand, and Alaric nods. As soon as Rory touches her neck, Drea shudders, the claws receding. "I'm okay," she whispers, but she's not. She's not okay. Alaric can smell the depths of her despair, her fear, her uncertainty. He can feel the way she's still shaking even though the beast has withdrawn for the moment.

"What happened?" he asks cautiously. "What happened to Orson?"

Drea untangles herself from Alaric, pushes Rory's hand away. Her cheeks are puffy from tears, her eyes a bright, bright red. Soledad offers a handful of tissues, and Drea takes them. She blows her nose noisily and drops the waste into the bin Soledad offers as if this has somehow already become routine.

"Mom called." Drea hiccups, breathes in, and holds that breath to steady herself. Rory offers his hand again, and she shakes her head, points at Alaric as if to say he'll need Rory next. "I'll be okay now. I promise. It's just— Orson's dead, Alaric. He's dead."

That's not possible.

Alaric takes a step backward, his hound coming out before he hits the ground. He howls his fury, baying at the impossibility of his brother being gone. There are footsteps in the hall, voices as Rory and Soledad rush out. Alaric howls his grief again, long and low, ending in a piteous whine. He takes a shuddering breath and drags himself back to humanity. He's bent over, his forehead touching the tile, cold and grounding. He curls his hand into a fist, feels the bite of claws against his palm. He huffs out a breath and sees a curl of smoke.

"Fuck."

"How?" Chris's voice is low and even, carefully controlled even though his heart is racing. Alaric can smell the pain on his skin, the tension that twists his scent sour. Alaric closes his eyes; he doesn't dare move yet, doesn't dare try to interact. He doesn't mind if Chris is his voice.

"I don't know yet, not everything. Mom called, told me he'd been found, and—" Drea's phone rings, the gentle tones of John Denver a sharp contrast with the screaming inside Alaric's mind. "I need to get this."

She answers with a quick, "Mom, hi, wait a minute." She pushes out the door, says curtly, "We're fine. Rory, go back in. No one's breaking anything." The door bangs against the frame in her wake, before Rory comes through it cautiously.

"TJ wanted to make sure no one's exploding," he says quietly. "Soledad's gone with him to explain what she knows."

Alaric sits back on his heels, shoves his hair out of his face. He's pushed the beast back inside, but he can feel it wrapped around his heart, squeezing with every beat. "I need to go home."

"I'll go with you," Rory says. He's hunched, his arms wrapped around himself, shoulders curved. "I can't even imagine losing Thorne. You need someone—"

"You can't," Alaric snaps. Rory flinches back at Alaric's sharp tone, and Alaric's breath shudders, hiccups on the backlash in his scent. "It's not that. It's just…" Alaric shakes his head. "I'm not angry at you. I'm not… I don't… please stop smelling like prey, it isn't helping."

"You're a Mage." Chris is the only one who still sounds calm. Every breath is careful around the stutter of his heart. Alaric can hear the underlying tension, even if Chris won't show it. "You can't just walk into a Clan compound, not now, not when they're grieving."

"I know you want to help, Rory," Alaric says softly. "My father would tear you apart." Possibly literally.

"I get it." Rory's scent eases, and he unwinds himself in order to show his hands carefully. "Do you need help?"

Alaric wants to say no. He doesn't want to look weak; his beast insists that he has to stay strong now. But he can feel the simmering anger, can feel the way he teeters on the edge of control. He drops his head forward, his hands on his knees. "Yeah."

The scent of curiosity pricks at his nose, but Alaric refuses to look up. He can feel Rory moving behind him, and he sits up enough to make it easier for Rory's hands to fall on his shoulders. There's a moment of tension, then everything bleeds away and he's left blissfully free of his beast. He groans softly, and there's a low cough.

"Do you need me to leave?" Chris's voice is dry, but something twists sour in his scent. Resignation.

"It's not like that," Rory says sharply. "I'm making his Talent stop. It helps."

Silence for a moment before Chris asks, "So he's human right now?"

"Not exactly, but he's as good as human," Rory says quietly. "This is not something I advertise. Keep it between us." When he lets go and steps back, the beast returns in a frantic rush, but Alaric can hold it at bay. He has control.

"Understood." A scrape of wheels against the floor, and the chair slides closer. Alaric sees Chris's leg first, his knee still wrapped in melting ice. There's a slow drip, a trail of water across the floor. Alaric focuses on it, watches as another droplet forms and slides down, plinking against the tile. Chris's voice is still soft. "What do you need, Alaric?"

"I need to get home." If he concentrates, he can almost hear Drea's conversation, but she's stepped far enough away from the door that it's muted. Indistinct. There's still a note of horror in every sentence that comes through clearly, and Alaric shivers at her tone. "I need to get home as soon as possible."

"I have a car here."

Alaric looks up sharply, and Chris spreads his hands. "I'm a junior. I've had a car here since last year. I can give you a ride home."

Alaric's gaze falls to Chris's knee. "You can't drive."

A small snort of dry laughter. "I'm assuming you have a license. I don't mind if you drive my car. I'm just going with you, since it is my car."

"What about your appointment?" Alaric shakes his head, because it's impossible. He can't bring someone home, not now, not someone who looks like prey. Chris doesn't smell like it, doesn't smell *weak*, but he can't move. With emotions high, it might be disastrous.

"The appointment is for Monday afternoon, and if you're not coming back before then, you and your family can help get me and the car back tomorrow night or Monday morning, before you go home again. You'll want to talk to the school on Monday anyway and make sure that professors are aware that you're missing classes." It all sounds reasonable when Chris says it, enough so that Alaric nods once before he catches himself.

The door opens, and Drea lets herself back in, sinks back against the door as soon as it's closed. She still has her phone cradled in her hand; Alaric's phone buzzes a moment later. He pulls it out, sees a picture of Orson grinning at the camera. He's sitting with two people that Alaric doesn't recognize, his arm around the girl, the guy leaning in close with a beer held toward the camera. Orson looks happy and relaxed.

"He sent me that last week," Drea says.

"Last thing he sent me was a file full of recipes." Alaric had promised to call as soon as he had a chance to go over the collection of Orson's private notes, to talk about which beer he wanted to brew first. Orson was going to try to meet up with him in Haverhill once football season was over, help Alaric pick out the equipment he needed from the brew store.

Alaric's phone cracks; at the touch to his arm he lets it go and Chris pulls it away. "Do you need Rory again?" Chris asks, sitting back upright. He winces before his jaw sets and the calm returns to his expression.

Alaric shakes his head. "I'm fine. That was—I've broken things before without it being a lack of control." He glances down; it looks like the damage is a small, spidering crack near the top of the screen, and a bigger crack in the case. The phone will still work.

"Then pack a bag," Chris says. "I'll call Dax and have him bring the car over, and we can go over to Drea's dorm to get her things after that."

"What?" Drea still has her phone cradled in her hands.

"You're using my car to get home," Chris says. "Since it's my car, I'm coming with you."

Rory goes to Alaric's closet, pulls out a bag. He grabs for things, sniffing at them in a way that makes Alaric wrinkle his nose. "What are you doing?"

"Making sure it's clean and doesn't smell like... is it true that some Clan can smell Mages?" Rory asks, a shirt in one hand, a pair of Alaric's jeans in the other.

Alaric glances at Drea, who shrugs. "It's not so much that we can smell Mages," Alaric says slowly. "But magic sometimes has a scent, like lightning or storms. Professor Szczek reeks," he admits.

"Professor Szczek has more magic than most Lineage Mages, and he's had it since before the Emergence." Rory shoves the clothes into the bag, grabs for more. "At Coven, he was telling us about all the things that happened when he was a kid, before he had any idea he could control it or that there even was real magic to control. But Emergent Mages can be like that sometimes, especially when no one knows what's going on. Anyway." He shoves in a handful of underwear and zips the bag closed.

"Me touching it shouldn't be enough, and that's all definitely clean.

Smells like soap, still, like it's fresh from the laundry," Rory says. "And it doesn't smell like me or Thorne."

Thorne? Oh, fuck… Alaric's jaw goes tight, and he doesn't look at Rory or Chris. There's a small, choked sound, and he goes to Drea's side, pulls her in close, presses a kiss to her temple. She angles her phone so he can see it.

It's an article from the local news out of Albany: *Ritual Leaves Three Dead in Midway.* There are no pictures, but the article clearly states that the location was an apartment belonging to Orson Herne and Salvatore Pagliazzi. "Orson wouldn't," Alaric murmurs.

"This is going to kill Mom, and Dad will be furious," Drea whispers.

"What?" There's nothing but concern in Rory's scent as he holds out Alaric's bag.

Alaric drops the bag by the door. "I'll come back for it. After we get Chris down the stairs."

"They found some kind of a symbol. They think he was doing a ritual," Drea murmurs, still scrolling through the article. "The police are asking anyone with information to come forward."

"If it's magical, they'll probably talk to Professor Szczek," Rory says.

"You definitely can't come with us now." Alaric smells that Rory's upset, the scent of worry swirling around him, tangling him up. He growls low in his throat and yanks Rory closer, wraps his arms around him and hugs him hard. He holds on a moment too long, just this side of bone-crushing, waiting for the moment when he feels the tension slip from Rory's bones. "Dad doesn't like Mages to begin with, and this—this is going to set things over the edge. He'll tell the police to stop looking into it. He'll deal with it on his own."

Rory's gaze narrows. "That's stupid. We can help."

"You're a Mage."

"That's my point."

Chris stands, wobbling on his crutches, and wedges a hand between them. "Don't start fighting now."

"Text me," Rory says, and Alaric grumbles in return. Of course he'll text Rory. "And send me the symbols," Rory continues. "Or I'll get them from Professor Szczek. Because the police aren't going to just let murder go because your father says so."

Alaric snorts, and Drea says dryly, "You've never lived in a Clan town before, have you? He's got his influence. And Clan likes to keep their business private."

It's not something Alaric agrees with, but there's a lot he and his father don't see eye to eye on. "We'd better go if we want to get in by dinner," he mutters. He wraps an arm around Chris, wedges his shoulder under Chris's, and motions for Drea to take the crutches. The stairs aren't going to be any easier to get down than they were to climb in the first place.

21

It's NOT A long drive out to Haverhill, although the rolling hills and farmland make it seem longer. They pass through Unity and into Valiant, and from there it's all countryside for a half hour until the first few communities of Haverhill come into view.

Alaric drives carefully, his hands loose on the steering wheel, not wanting to leave imprints of his fingers on Chris's car. The inside of the car smells like worry and exhaustion and grief, and he keeps checking the rearview mirror to make sure Drea's okay in the back seat. She's curled sideways, her feet on the seat, pressed back into the corner by the driver's side door. It's almost as if she doesn't want him to see her face. His hound whines in his heart, worried about his twin.

Chris has the passenger seat pushed as far back as it can go and reclined so he can keep his knee as straight as possible. Alaric can smell the pain, and it crawls under his skin, makes him want to get out and run instead of driving home. "You should have taken something," he mutters as they drive through the outskirts of Haverhill.

"I'm fine. It's not like I haven't gotten hurt before." Chris readjusts the fresh ice he'd gotten just before they headed out, makes sure it's wrapped tightly to keep it in place on his knee. "It's a sprain, Ric. You don't have to mother me."

Drea snorts softly, and Alaric scowls. "I'm not *mothering* you."

Chris makes a low noise, leans back. "It's fine. I'm just saying you don't need to worry so much. I'm human, and I'm breakable, but I'm not going to fall apart here. I'm stronger than you think."

"And I still need to practically carry you into the house," Alaric says curtly. "So you're weak in my family's eyes. Be ready to deal with it."

"Maybe we should've gotten a wheelchair," Drea muses. "It would've made it easier. Except your room's on the second floor, and while there are guest suites on the first floor, there is no way in hell Dad's putting up a human there. Broken or not." She tilts her head. "Sorry, Chris. Dad is…he's Clan. I don't know how to put it any better than that. We are a ridiculously insular community. If you think there are some people who have difficulty stepping out of the 1950s, sometimes it feels like Clan wants to go back even further. We have our own rules, our own ways of doing things."

"Which is why you thought it was so weird that we had a single Clan family in our town," Chris says, and Alaric nods.

"Exactly." He has to slow down as he approaches the school. There are always kids on bikes here, both human and Clan, riding into town to spend their free time having fun. As insular as Clan is, they also believe in free range for their children, and the humans don't argue as long as they're not participating in organized sports or causing trouble.

There are more cars than he expects, and there's a blare of an air horn, lights somewhere behind the school. Alaric makes a face. "Football game tonight," he mutters. "We suck, if you're wondering. Even for humans."

"I am going to pretend you didn't just imply that non-Talented people suck at playing football," Chris teases. He knocks his knuckles against Alaric's shoulder, and Alaric grunts and goes silent. "It's a big school. I thought you were homeschooled."

Alaric makes a face. "I was part of a homeschool-league football team. Most of the guys were homeschooled. I attended this—it's the town school. All grades from kindergarten on up. Maybe fifty kids per grade, total, so that's what…?"

"It was around 600 kids total, give or take, depending on whether it was a good year for babies or not," Drea completes his thought. "We were actually one of the larger classes; there were seventy-five us of when we graduated. Our cousin's kindergarten class only has thirty. There was one class four years before us that had only twenty kids, and they were almost all Clan. It was a weird year."

Orson's class.

Alaric licks his lips, feels his throat go tight.

"Is Clan the only Talent in town?" Chris asks, like there's no tension to break. Or maybe he knows he's breaking it. "There wouldn't be any Mages around."

"No Lineage Mages. Maybe some Emergent folks," Alaric says. He speeds back up as they pass the school, and not long past that is the one light in town, where he turns left onto Rural Route 572. "It's not like we invited them out for Gathers."

"We're about five minutes out now." Drea leans between the two seats, points down the road. "See that sign on the right? That's Herne Way, and it goes into the compound."

Alaric turns, and he feels something settle into his bones at the familiarity of home. As good as it's been to get away, there is something right about coming home, about being back on Clan land. It's as if their Talent has soaked into it over the centuries, as if it knows him and welcomes him.

There are houses along the way, set back from the road. It's a circuitous route, showing off the land owned by their Clan, the establishment that they've built, the community that they share. Every once in a while, Alaric catches a curious scent, spots someone running alongside the road, then another swinging through the trees, both more beast than human. It's only what he'd expect.

The road opens up at the end into a parking lot, large and wide. There are already cars there, and bikes, and two horses in a small corral, grazing contentedly. The house seems larger than Alaric remembers, looming wide and tall across one end of the lot.

"That's your house."

It's not a question, more a flat, confused statement, and Alaric nods. He climbs out as the door to the house opens, and he lifts his hand in silent greeting. He helps Drea get out, and she calls out to one of their younger cousins to come help take all the bags in. There's a rush of relief in the air that quickly shifts to confusion as Alaric walks around to the other side of the car and opens the door.

Tension rises in the air, and Alaric's cousin rushes off with the bags, disappearing into the house with a yell. Alaric knows that everyone will hear quickly that he's brought a guest, and that he'll be judged.

He leans in, offers a shoulder to Chris and one of the crutches for his other arm. He helps him out of the car carefully, steadies him as they turn to face Alaric's parents.

"This is not the time for bringing a guest." His father's voice reverberates inside of Alaric, nearly sending him to his knees with the need to bare his throat, give in to the stronger beast.

Instead, Alaric growls, pushes forward with slow steps, and holds his ground. "It's his car," he grates out.

His mother touches his father's shoulder, takes his hand.

Anger is hot and sour, and it chokes Alaric with every breath. Drea moves through the thick air as easily as she always does, placing herself between Alaric and their parents. "Mom, Dad, this is Chris Stone. He's on the football team with Alaric. He would have driven us here, but he was injured in the game today, so he came along for the ride since it's his car. It's thanks to him that we were able to get here this fast without needing to get a ride with someone else."

"Corbin managed to do it without bringing a guest," his father growls. Alaric's breath hitches, and his grip flexes around Chris's waist, but he holds his tongue.

Drea turns to Chris. "Chris, these are our parents, Alia and Theobald Herne. We welcome you to our home and grant you safety within Clan walls."

Alaric smirks as his father growls at Drea's formal welcome.

"Get inside," Theobald orders, and stalks away.

Alia rushes forward as soon as he's gone, pulls Drea into a hug, rubbing her cheek along Drea's. She pauses when they're done, her head tilted slightly as she regards Alaric. "My son," she says quietly.

He extracts himself from under Chris's arm so he can get the second crutch out of the car and offer it to Chris. Chris is left to wobble awkwardly until he gets the crutches planted securely, fresh pain suffusing his scent as Alaric steps away.

Alaric lets his mother pull him in, lets himself take comfort in his family and Clan, and tries to give what comfort he can. He kisses her temple, murmurs wordless sounds that are meant to reassure. He feels her hiccup, smells the grief that lies under the outer shield of tension. "We're here," he reassures her.

Alia steps back, pats his chest, then frames his face briefly with her hands. "That you are," she says quietly. "And you'll have to go back soon enough, so we'll have of you what we can while you're here." Her gaze shifts past him, looks to where Drea still stands with Chris. "Your friend is as welcome as we can make him. These are trying times, Alaric, and the Clan has already gathered. This is no place for a human."

"At least he's not a Mage," Drea says softly, and Alia goes tense.

"You would never," Alia says, voice hardening.

Alaric licks his lips. "Of course." It's a lie, but it's enough to mollify her, to get past this moment. He can guess how many people are already here, that the Hall is full of Clan waiting to convene, and that this is not the time for a confrontation. "I'm going to take Chris upstairs, get his things settled. We'll be down in the Hall shortly."

"Your father will not be pleased."

Alaric smiles tightly, gets his shoulder under Chris's again. "My father can go f—"

Drea tugs on Chris's other side, and Chris catches his breath in pain. "Let's get upstairs, Ric," Drea says quickly. "It's going to take time, and we probably need to get Chris fresh ice."

Alia motions for them to move by. As they enter the house slowly, Alaric is aware of movement in the Hall, of the way the teenagers and younger children dart out, curious, and watch from corners as they go by. A cat stands under a wolf, a bird perched on the wolf's back. A small lizard scuttles out of the way, just before a family of ducks waddle past.

Chris blinks. "Are those...?"

"All of them are Clan, yes," Drea says. "If you happen to spot a big orange cat, that might be just a cat. We have three of them. But we also have a lot of people who can take that form, too, so sometimes it's hard to tell which it is."

It takes time to get up the stairs, wrestling with every step. By the time they reach the second floor, the world closes in around them. Where the first floor is open as it welcomes newcomers to the Hall, the second floor is the primary living space. It is the family kitchens, and the communal bath is just off the side. The door stands open, and the air smells wet and fruity, as if someone were in there not long ago; Alaric wonders which of their family it was. Drea turns to walk down the long hall that leads to their rooms, and when they reach Alaric's door, she carefully hands Chris back his crutches.

"I'll go get ice. You make sure Chris is settled. Because they'll pitch a fit if you try to bring him down to the Gather," she says quietly. "I won't be long."

Alaric can't think of the last time there was someone in his room who wasn't either family or as good as such. He pushes open the door and helps Chris in, settles him in the heavy, overstuffed chair that sits near his bookshelves. He carefully ignores the low grunt of pain, just offers an ottoman and helps Chris get his foot up to ease his knee. "Drea'll be back with ice soon."

"I was standing right there, Ric. I heard." Chris pushes himself so he's sitting more upright, twists to look around. "I heard all of it. The fact that your father hated me on sight, and your mother wasn't much better. Most of your cousins were lurking around spying on us."

"We're not all related," Alaric corrects him. "There are a couple hundred of us, total, here in the compound, not counting the few folks who've grown up and moved on. Families like to stick together, but some folks move to other compounds or start places of their own. Isn't easy to move out into a new space these days; the country's too built up."

"I know what you said about Clan—I know what Pawel said in class—but I don't think I really expected this." Chris sinks back into the chair with a low groan.

"Clan's Clan," Alaric says quietly. He drags over his desk chair and sits on it backward, leaning his elbows on the back. "Nothing quite like it. Smallest town you'll ever get, right inside another small town. Pretty much self-sufficient for a lot of things. We've got plumbers and carpenters, anything you might need to do with your hands. Some folks work outside the compound, bring in money. Some folks stay here. Orson was going to come back and build it up, change how we did things. Modernize us."

"How'd your father feel about that?"

Alaric gives Chris a sharp look at his dry tone. "Good. He wanted Orson to be comfortable here. To be the one who took over this home, who ran the Hall and called the Gathers. He wanted Orson to lead."

Chris goes silent at that, and his gaze drifts away, lingering on a far corner of the room. "Why do you have a spinning wheel?"

Alaric can feel heat in his cheeks. "It's one of the things I do. We raise sheep here, and my mother sheers them and cards the wool. I spin it, and I weave. That's my wheel, and my loom." He twists the chair back and forth, digs his toe against the floor to keep the chair from rolling. "Started when I was young, because it helped keep the hound calm. Mom and Drea both knit and crochet. I knit, too, but I like weaving better. Something about the rhythm of it feels good."

Chris's gaze falls to Alaric's foot. "You don't like being here," he says quietly.

Alaric licks his lips, tries to find the best way to say it when he knows someone might be listening from a distance. "Don't exactly get along well with my parents," he replies, voice low and gruff. "But Orson was my brother, and that's different. My father—he has a lot of expectations, and I've never been good at living up to them."

"You did all that." Chris points to the shelf of trophies, and Alaric barks out a laugh.

"Football means nothing to Clan," he says sharply. "Football does nothing for Clan. Worth here is measured in what we bring to our home, and that," Alaric jabs a finger at the wheel and the loom. "That's what I bring. That's what I'm good for. That and whatever I major in, whatever skill I bring home. Football doesn't matter at all."

"It matters to you."

There's a scent underlying Chris's words that Alaric can't tease out. He smells a hint of worry, but the pain overrides everything else, too strong to let Alaric figure out the rest. He shakes his head as the door opens and Drea comes in with a bucket of ice. She glances over curiously as Alaric says, "That doesn't matter to Clan, and it's never mattered to my father." He takes the bucket from Drea and carefully starts unwrapping the ice around

Chris's knee. "Let's get you rewrapped so you're not dripping on the floor."

It's not going to do much to help Chris, but it shifts the focus away from Alaric. It gives him something to do with his hands, a way to stop fidgeting against the anxiety that's always rising when he's home. He can't fight with his family this time, and he can't escape. He just has to weather it and get through.

22

His father meets Alaric at the door to the Hall. He stands in the opening, arms crossed, shoulders stiff and set. Waves of disapproval roll off of Theobald, but Alaric manages to stand his ground, keep his hound from bowing down and baring his throat.

"Humans don't belong at a Clan Gather," Theobald says firmly. "Take him back to your room. He can wait there."

"I'm not locking him in my room while I'm here," Alaric responds, tone dry. He steps forward, moving into Theobald's personal space. He's got two inches on his father, and he uses them, glaring down at him, refusing to give way. "He's my friend, he's my teammate, and he's not planning on stealing secrets. He's just going to sit quietly with me and Drea. So either let us in, or I'm going back to campus now."

"Theo." Alia's voice is a murmur, her hand gentle on her husband's shoulder. A low rumble vibrates in Theobald's chest, shivers through the air around them, but he gives way and steps back, making space for Alaric and Chris to pass through.

Chris is on his crutches, moving slowly with every hop, his leg swinging along, knee stiff. Alaric nudges him carefully, and they change direction to join Drea. There are clusters of chairs set up around the edges of the Hall, many already filled. Drea's sitting with three other teenagers, all seniors this year in the high school. Alaric greets them by rote, helps Chris settle into one of the chairs as soon as introductions are complete. There are no chairs left in this cluster, and he's just trying to decide whether he should bother to get one when he hears his name shouted.

It's embarrassing how his heart skips, the way it thuds at the sound of Corbin's voice. A low whine slips free, and he turns around in time for

Corbin to wrap his arms around him, pull him in, and hold on tightly. It's all too easy to fall into the embrace, to sink into the sense of friend and family that Corbin brings. Alaric holds on, fingers tangling and twisting in the back of Corbin's shirt. Alaric's head bows, and Corbin slides his hands into the strands of Alaric's hair and holds on.

At the sound of a dry cough, Alaric jerks backward, lets go of Corbin. Alaric rubs a hand across his face, tries to dry the tears that have sprung up. There's a low growl, and Alaric takes another step, puts distance between himself and Corbin, Chris, Drea—separates himself from everyone nearby.

His father smiles thinly. "Let's begin."

"You need to get out of here." Corbin wraps his hand around Alaric's upper arm, fingers pressing tight. "Your dad can speak for ages; Drea will come get us when he reaches the part we need to be here for."

Alaric shouldn't follow Corbin. He shouldn't leave Chris sitting with Drea, surrounded by Clan, and he shouldn't walk out while his father is speaking. He can feel the eyes on him, the back of his neck prickling under the weight of numerous gazes. But he goes where Corbin leads, ending up in the grand foyer of the house, just outside the heavy main doors of the Hall.

Corbin puts his hands against Alaric's chest, pushes him toward the stairs. "Sit," he says, and Alaric does. Corbin takes up his space one stair above Alaric, his knee pressed comfortably against Alaric's side. "You look like shit."

"You sound surprised," Alaric mutters.

"Not at all." Corbin leans forward, elbows on his knees. "He was as good as my brother too, Ric. I'm just better at putting a bright, shiny face on it." He knocks his knee into Alaric. "Someone has to be the smiley one in this relationship. I'm the sugar, you're the lemon."

"Fuck you."

"You wish." Corbin leans back again, elbows on the stair above him, legs stretched out next to Alaric. "This is so fucked up, Ric. I keep thinking about it, how it doesn't seem real."

"How'd you get back here so fast?" Alaric's looking for anything to think about, anything other than the reminder that Orson is dead. Or the heat of Corbin's leg leaning against his side. He curls tighter, and Corbin's knee knocks into him hard.

"Don't retreat," Corbin snaps. "Drea needs you. Your mom needs you. And even though he won't admit it, fucking Theobald Herne needs you."

Alaric straightens, looks at the door. "Keep your voice down."

"I'm the golden boy. They'll blame you for my bad attitude; they always do."

Alaric would be hurt by Corbin's words, but he can hear the sarcasm, can smell the cynicism under the words. Everything he says is true, and he knows it's not Corbin's fault. They've always been a team, friends practically since birth. And somehow all they have is the roles Clan gave them. "You didn't answer my question."

"Amy Sanderson's doing graduate work at VIT. My department, actually, so I'm hoping to get in on her research next semester. What's Clan for if you can't pull a few strings?" Corbin's smile is sharp, and Alaric's reminded of the birds of prey he prefers to become. "By the time I texted Drea to let her know that Amy and I were coming, she said you were already on the road with some human. Did you even see my text?"

"I was driving." Alaric forgot about his phone. He pulls it out now, sees a half-dozen missed messages that must have come in sometime in the last hour or so. He scrolls through them quickly, deleting the one from Corbin since he's right here. He opens one from TJ, makes a mental note to talk to him later. The one from Dax is also to Chris—they'll deal with that later. He pauses on the one from Rory: *You get in okay? Let me know if you need anything.*

Corbin leans against Alaric's back, cheek pressed to cheek. "Who's Rory? Girl or guy?"

"Guy." Alaric realizes his mistake as soon as he says it, and he digs an elbow into Corbin's shin to encourage him to move back. "Roommate." He lowers his voice. "Mage."

"Huh. Really?" Corbin draws breath, interest in his scent. He tenses, and Alaric's positive that he's going to say something, but the heavy door to the Hall opens, and Corbin exhales instead, breath whispering against Alaric's ear. A soft huff as Corbin sees Drea and Chris standing there. "So, who *is* the human?" Corbin whispers.

"Teammate. Starting QB. Came back in his car."

The door thuds softly shut, and Drea calls out, "Get your ass down here, bird boy, and say hello like you mean it. Don't let my brother monopolize you, asshole." She's grinning, and Corbin's on his feet before she finishes speaking.

Corbin squeezes Alaric's shoulder on the way by. "Later, we are having a conversation where you answer with more than one- or two-word descriptors." He jumps, flapping raven wings in Alaric's face before flying down to coalesce into human again in front of Drea. It's showy and ridiculous, and it's all Corbin.

Alaric stands more slowly, meets Chris's gaze for just a moment before Chris looks at the pair next to him. Corbin and Drea are of a height, wrapped in a fond hug, and Alaric can smell contentedness from a distance. Tension spills away, and Drea sighs, relaxing against Corbin.

He leaves his fingerprints in the railing before he forces himself to let go and walk down the few stairs to join them.

Drea ends up with Corbin's arm slung over her shoulder, her own arm around his back. She pats his chest. "This pretentious idiot is Corbin, and he's been our best friend forever. If VIT let him have a car, you'd have already met him."

"Or if freshman could have a car at PHU, you could drive to visit me," Corbin points out. "Or there's a shuttle bus. We could meet in the middle. Get food. Shop. But no, no, last I heard you two were too busy. Something about football, and fraternities and parties and sororities and was that taekwondo? When the hell do you two take classes?"

"Shut up."

Alaric loves the way Drea is at ease, body relaxed for the first time since she called him. The tension is coming back to Alaric, his spine straight, arms crossed.

"And your human?" Corbin asks, and Alaric growls.

"He's not a pet," he grumbles. "This is Chris. Captain of the football team, and a friend. We drove his car back here."

"Impressive, walking into the Clan's den." Corbin turns to Drea, kisses her cheek. "Did you come out to be social, or is Theobald chomping at the bit to get on to the important bits and needs all his ducklings in a row?"

"The only duck here is you." Drea sighs as she disentangles herself. "But yes, that's the point. Alaric, you need to get back inside. Dad's winding up the formal greetings and calling of names, which means we're going to get started soon."

It's silent when Drea pushes the door open, and they walk in. Corbin brackets Chris on the other side, offers an arm, and they make their way across the floor to the chairs where Alia stands waiting at the head of the room. A fourth chair is hastily brought and placed to the right of the others, and Chris takes it gratefully.

Alaric and Drea sit with their mother, and Corbin stands nearby, by Alaric's right hand. It's a quiet statement of position, and Alaric appreciates it. No matter what anyone thinks, Corbin has always been on his side.

"You've seen the news," Theobald says bluntly. "You've seen the pictures. The paraphernalia. The sigil. Orson was found in the company of his roommate, clearly mid-ritual. Both had self-inflicted wounds that should not have been deep enough to injure, yet both were bled out. There was no indication that any other person was involved in the ritual. And yes, Salvatore was a Mage."

Alaric flinches; Corbin's hand falls to his shoulder, squeezing.

He closes his eyes, tries to separate out the swift rumble of replies. The old unrest. The wars. The last time a Mage came to Haverhill, the last altercation more than thirty years past that nearly resulted in the Clan being exposed long before the Emergence. He curls his hands into fists, bites his tongue against his immediate response that Clan is not blameless. Clan is not innocent.

This is neither the time nor the place.

"What are you going to do?" One voice rises above the rest—Emmanuel Walker, patriarch of one of the few families as old as the Hernes. One of the few families who could claim leadership of this compound if the Hernes were to be found unfit.

Alaric's claws prick skin. Drea's nostrils flare and she glances at him, and Alaric forces the beast to back down. He huffs out a breath, a faint wisp of smoke curling around him.

"We're going to tell the police to let it go," Theobald says flatly. "Orson's body will not be carved up in the name of modern science—they know nothing about Clan physiology, nor can they recognize the effects of magic upon it. They can investigate the site—we can't do anything for that. But we will have Orson returned to us, to be interred next Sunday."

"And after that?" Emmanuel stands, and Alaric smells pain as his son stands near to support him. He has no idea how old Emmanuel actually is, only that he was alive when Alaric's grandfather presided over the Clan of Haverhill.

Alia touches Theobald, and he leans down, listens to her whisper before he straightens again. His expression twists sour as he states, "My children will return to their education and will have their year apart after it is done, as Orson was given and as is tradition. After that, Alaric will be expected to return to the compound as my second."

No.

No.

Alaric tries to stand; Corbin's hand is a heavy weight holding him in place. Corbin leans in, hisses, "Shut up and stay still, for once."

The words of the Gather have impact now, flung at Theobald and striking Alaric as he sits in their way. *Incompetent. Unfit. Impossible.* Alaric shudders and holds his ground, sits straighter and sets his jaw, biting down hard. He swallows his hound, holds back the bear that wants to barrel into the crowd and toss them aside until they listen to reason. He wants to take wing and let the eagle fly away.

"This is not a point for discussion," Theobald thunders, and the dissenters shrink back. Alaric stays as straight as he can, refusing to cow before his father. He catches a faint scent of approval from his mother. "Elders remain. Everyone else leave."

"Now we can go." Drea captures one of Alaric's hands as Corbin grabs his arm and yanks him up. Drea whisks away Chris's crutches, and both Corbin and Alaric get an arm under Chris, almost lifting him.

"Let's get out of here before he changes his mind." Corbin casts a quick glance back at where the elders are convening with Theobald, then he angles them toward one of the side doors to the Hall. It's a quicker escape, but a farther walk to the stairs, and right now, Alaric doesn't care. He'd pick Chris up and piggy-back him if he thought it would get them out of there faster.

"My room," Alaric says, and they move as one group, working together to get away from the rest of the Clan and into the peace and quiet of Alaric's retreat.

23

COMPARED TO THE dorm room, Alaric's room is spacious. He has his desk and his reading nook, and the separate space by the window with his loom and wheel.

And of course, the bed.

Corbin doesn't ask, just collapses backward on Alaric's bed, scooting up to leave plenty of space as Drea joins him. Alaric swallows hard, glances from the bed to Chris.

"Clan," Alaric says, because that explains everything.

Chris hobbles forward on the crutches, rotates carefully to turn his back to the bed. He hesitates at the edge, and Corbin moves behind him while Alaric takes the crutches.

"Ease back," Corbin says, his hands firmly on Chris's back. "Alaric, asshole, get back over here and get his arm. Help him."

It takes both of them to help Chris get situated on the bed, lying down finally, his head pillowed on Drea's shin and his knee resting on a small pile of pillows. Chris closes his eyes, lets his hands fall to the side. "It feels good to not be standing or sitting."

"Alaric's a terrible host. He probably should've let you lie down while he went down to the Gather." Corbin knocks into Alaric, grabs his shoulder, and drags him onto the bed. Alaric goes with the movement, grunting when he finds himself lying next to Chris, Corbin tangled with him. Drea's fingers drift through Alaric's hair. It's comforting. It helps, a little, distracting him from the fact that Chris is close enough that Alaric can feel the heat of his body.

"I wanted to go," Chris admits. "I can't help if I don't know what's going on, and how things are here is not what I expected from class."

"Class?" Corbin snorts. "Every Clan community is different, and every Clan community has its secrets. You're not going to learn about our traditions in some class."

"Magical studies," Alaric reminds him, and Corbin nods.

"Oh yeah, I forgot PHU has that for a major. That what you're doing?" Corbin pokes Chris's side, and Chris idly swats at him, his hand landing on Alaric's chest momentarily. Alaric freezes, and Chris pulls away.

"No, but I took the intro class that just about everyone takes, and I liked Pawel, so I took one of his seminars in comparative Talent," Chris says. His hand falls back against his own chest, and he looks up at Drea. "What do you think of him so far? I'd ask Ric, but he's biased."

" 'm not biased," Alaric mutters.

"He also coaches taekwondo," Drea points out to Corbin. "Which I'm sure you've already heard about from Ric. And I like Professor Szczek. I've read ahead in some of the books for the intro course, and he's not offensive. He's done his research, and he's catalogued everything: Clan, Mages, all of the five primary Talents as well as their single-ability sub-classes, and even some of the legends. I might take another one of his courses, but it'll be hard to squeeze in with biochem."

"You could be an engineer," Corbin points out. "I get one elective per year. Not semester, year. It sucks."

"And that would be why I'm not an engineer," Drea points out with a smile. "Although I think you might have sucked Ric into your sad, scary world."

Alaric shrugs one shoulder when they all look at him. "Maybe. Civil." Corbin pokes him, and Alaric knows that's a silent statement on his one-word answers, but he doesn't have more words in him. Not right now.

There's a sharp knock on the door, and Alaric freezes, pushing to sit up and only lying back when Corbin shoves him down. "Yeah?"

His mother nudges open the door, her smile tight as she sees them tangled in a pile on the bed. "The decision is official," Alia says quietly. "The burial will be next Sunday, once we have his body. Preparations will be completed this week, and you are not expected to be here until the weekend. The grave will be dug on Saturday."

"And the investigation?" Corbin asks.

There's a rush of tension in the room, thick enough to choke Alaric. He curls his hand into a tight fist, doesn't look at his mother.

"There won't be one," she says, tone clipped. "The case was made, and it was denied. The mundane officials have no place interfering in Clan tragedy. They will be informed. Further investigation will only encourage those who murdered Orson and potentially incite violence. In the interest of the Treaty, we will let this go."

"You're going to just—" Corbin cuts off as Drea places a hand over his mouth, drags him backward.

Alaric smells salt in the air; even from a distance he tastes the tears that roll down his mother's cheeks. He sits up slowly, careful not to disturb Chris. "I understand," he says solemnly. "Drea and I will be back Friday night."

Alia's scent eases. "Thank you." She hesitates, her gaze falling to Chris. "Your father has stated that the human is not welcome at dinner tonight. Please forgive my husband; we have taken a grave blow, and he grieves."

"It's okay," Chris says softly. "I'm sorry that my presence brings added stress to your home."

"Thank you." Alia nods, backing out and closing the door.

Chris falls back against the bed with a low groan, one hand over his eyes. "I'm making this worse for you. Sorry. I just—"

"—wanted to help." Drea kisses his cheek. "You're a good friend, and a good fraternity brother. We'll keep you, even if our parents don't want you. Alaric sucks at making friends, and he seems to like you; that means you're worth it."

"Not the first thing I've done that pisses off my father," Alaric grumbles. "I'm the child he'd like to forget."

"He just named you heir," Corbin reminds him quietly. "For what it's worth, and if it goes through."

"That's because he doesn't have Orson." Alaric grits his teeth, closes his eyes, and refuses to look at any of them. He can smell the concern from Drea and curiosity from Chris. "I'm the worst choice he could make, you know that. He'd be better off with Drea."

"Gee, thanks. As if I'd want that role in this misogynistic hellhole." Drea's mutter is low. Alaric's not sure anyone else can hear her.

"Why are you the worst choice?"

Of course Chris asks, bald and right there in the open. And there are so many fucking reasons, so many things his father wouldn't approve of, but the big one...the worst of it...

"What did you learn in Pawel's classes about Clan abilities?" Drea asks. She nudges Chris over, his bad leg somehow ending up thrown across Alaric, tangled with Corbin. Alaric is the center of a sandwich, with Drea draped across Chris's back so she can see him as well.

Alaric can't decide if this is the worst place to be or the best. It's warm and strangely comforting. Corbin is pressed close against him, his scent achingly familiar. And Chris's hand is hot where it rests on Alaric's chest, sending heat through his body.

He can feel the rumble when Chris speaks. "That it's something like Magical Talents, but instead of a family of weather witches, you can get a family of cats."

"That's the gist," Corbin agrees. "You get some Clan where the innate ability is very specific. Like cats. Or others where it's more general—Drea can turn into any kind of a mammal."

"I've never tried to turn into a whale," she says idly. "I've never really been anywhere with a big enough body of water. But you get the point. I can be anything from a vole to a moose. But most people have a specific subset, like rodents or felines."

"I'm birds," Corbin says. "All birds, not just the predators, although I prefer those. Ravens, in particular, but I like owls. Sparrows are good for spying."

Alaric can feel the heat under his skin as they speak. Chris's fingers are tapping thoughtfully against Alaric's chest, and Alaric wants to grab his hand, move him away. But he doesn't want to bring attention to himself, nor can he handle their proximity.

"So what does that have to do with Alaric being a bad choice to...what, lead the Clan? Is that like being Governor?" Chris asks.

"Human terms," Corbin says dismissively.

"It means I'm broken," Alaric growls. "Not only do I have shit control—which you already know—I can't shift correctly."

"I've seen you become a bear," Chris says dryly. "Very abruptly, very smoothly. It seemed to me like you could shift just fine."

"I have four forms." Alaric bites the words off as if they could poison him just by being on his tongue. "Bear. Hound. Eagle. Lizard. That's it. Nothing else. I'm barely fit to be Clan."

"He's almost like a single-line Talent," Drea says, tone low. "Like the people who can only do one form of magic and can't do ritual, or the shapeshifters with only one form. He's more like a weak Emergent, rather than being the strength and heart of our Clan."

"Orson could be any mammal, and he specialized in the big cats and canines. Predatory." Alaric falls silent, breathes deep. "I'm broken. And that's not going to change."

"You can't learn—?"

"If I could, don't you think I would've?" Alaric snarls. He feels sharp teeth fill his mouth, bright claws tip his fingers. He rolls away from Chris, pushing Corbin out of the way so he can get off the bed. "Drea, fix his bandage. He probably needs more ice. I'll go get it."

Alaric takes his time in the kitchen. He grabs one of the stock pots and puts a trash bag in it, then fills that with ice. He pauses before leaving so he can send two texts.

One goes to Rory: *There's not going to be an investigation and my father hates Chris.*

The other goes to Mac: *I'm so tense I can barely breathe.*

He adds *don't call me* after that to both of them, not wanting to deal with an actual conversation. It's easier to put words down in type, to take his time and string them together into sentences and have them make sense. When he has to answer immediately, they tangle in his mouth, tie themselves to the tip of his tongue and trip him with every breath.

He picks up the pot and heads back to his room.

Everyone's rearranged.

Chris is sitting propped up against the wall, his knee unwrapped and up on two pillows. He has an arm over Drea's shoulder as she curls in close, and Corbin kneels facing him as they talk. Corbin looks over as Alaric comes in, waves emphatically at the door until Alaric closes it behind himself. He sets the pot to one side, figures he'll deal with the ice in a bit.

"We've been talking about the investigation," Corbin says.

"Because there will be one, even if Dad doesn't let the police look into it," Drea says quietly. "And it's not going to be pretty."

"That's retaliation," Corbin replies.

"He has to investigate enough to figure out who to retaliate against," Drea retorts. "And you know he's not going to be exactly subtle about it. Everything Mom said about not risking the Treaty? Flat-out lie, and you know it. You know what Dad's like."

Alaric's phone pings, and he looks at the text from Rory. *Guess it's a good thing I didn't come. He would've hated me more. Can you get me the police report? Information on the symbol? I can see what I can find out. I know you want to know what happened.*

Alaric pauses with his thumbs on the keyboard, looks at Drea. "What do I tell Rory?"

"Boyfriend?" Corbin asks, eyes alight with mischief, as if Alaric didn't explain Rory an hour ago.

"Roommate," Drea and Alaric answer in chorus. Alaric flushes, and Drea rolls her eyes.

"He wants the police report. You know they won't talk to Szczek if the investigation is stopped." Alaric sits on the bed, and Corbin peers over his shoulder, makes a small huff of sound. Alaric puts his hand on Corbin's face and pushes him away. "He's a Mage," he reminds Corbin, in case he forgot that as well.

"I'd rather that you have a Mage for a roommate than a boyfriend," Corbin says quickly, and Alaric feels the blood rush to his face.

" 'm not dating anyone," he mumbles as he types. *We'll get what we can before we come back. I don't know if they'll give it to us. We might have to figure out some way to do it.*

His phone pings right away. *Okay. Let me know if you need anything. And Thorne says to let him know if you need anything, too. Please don't tell me if you do.*

Oh God.

Corbin's draped across his back, looking over his shoulder, nose close to Alaric's skin. It doesn't matter. Alaric knows that Corbin doesn't have the same ability to pick out scents that he does, that he's looking for other things. Little hints in his clothes. Tiny traces left behind that a bird might spot. But Alaric still feels the heat under his own skin as he hurries to type back. *Don't worry. Not going to say a word about that.*

"About what?" Corbin asks, and Alaric bites his tongue, trapping a low growl.

Chris's eyes go wide. "Ric."

Alaric inhales roughly, pushes at Corbin again. "Go sit down, and leave it alone."

"We are going to talk," Corbin tells him. "And you are going to tell me everything you haven't said about your roommate, and about whoever Thorne is, and everything else you've been leaving out of every single brief conversation we've had since school started. Because I know you, Ric, and if you bottle that up, you're going to explode. Again."

"Already did," Alaric growls.

"Yeah, and that was when you were pushed," Corbin points out. "I care about you, remember that. I've known you forever, and if you can't talk to me, who can you talk to? Or maybe you've decided that it's different now."

"This isn't about you." Alaric's hands clench. "Corbin, not now. Just…not now. Not this weekend. Not here. Not in front—" He stops abruptly, winces because it's obvious what he was about to say.

"That's our cue to leave." Drea slides off the bed, wraps an arm around Corbin's waist, and pulls him toward the door. "Corbin, you and I are going to see what information we can get from the folks who stayed to hear what my father had to say. You know the rumor mill is running, and we're going to glean what we can before the flow of gossip stops. Then we'll try to separate hyperbole from what might be facts. And while we're at it, I am going to bawl on your shoulder and you are going to comfort me, so let's go get some tissues." She lets go of him and shoves. "Out, Corbin. Now."

The door slams behind them, and Alaric stands in the middle of his room, his phone still held loosely in one hand. He can't quite look at Chris, so he looks down at the phone, opens the message stream with Mac to see what she's replied.

I heard what happened. Death sucks. It really sucks, and I've been there, and I know there is nothing I can say that's going to make this in any way better. Are you with someone?

It's funny how easy and normal her words are, like she really does get it. It's matter-of-fact. Simple. Alaric makes his way to the bed, sits down on the edge, and cradles the phone in his hands. "It's Mac," he says aloud, and it's refreshing how Chris doesn't try to look over his shoulder.

Yeah, my sister and best friend are home, too, and Chris is here. I just feel like I'm going to explode.

There's a pause, his phone signaling that Mac has started typing, that she's stopped several times, before the message comes through.

Go run through your forms. If that doesn't work, kick a tree. I'm not joking. If you think your feet can handle it, kick it barefoot. And if that doesn't work, use your Talent. But do something that gets you out of your head.

There's a brief pause, then another message comes through.

And when you're done, let them help you. You're not an island, Alaric. You've got family and friends. I'm assuming your sister and best friend won't hurt you, and I know Chris wouldn't. He's a good guy, and he's got a good shoulder. I may have cried on it a few times myself.

Alaric snorts softly. "Mac says I should trust you."

"Mac's right. If you think I'm going tell the team you're weak because you're mourning your brother's death, you're wrong." Chris's voice is low, firm. "You want to talk to me, talk. You want to be silent, that's fine too. Do what you've got to do. But if there's something that would help, then fine, I'm here." A small hesitation, and Alaric hears the uptick in his heartbeat. "I didn't just come along because it's my car. I'm your friend, Ric, at least I hope that's what you think. We're teammates."

Lie.

Chris smells like guilt. He smells like anxiety, wary and worried. Alaric has no idea why, but he's certain that the words themselves aren't wrong, even if something in what Chris has said is a lie. He nods once and taps out a single word to Mac before he puts the phone down: *Thanks.*

"So?" Chris leans forward, gets a hand on Alaric's shoulder. The movement has to hurt—Alaric can smell pain surrounding him still—but Chris holds the position and squeezes slightly. "What next?"

"Mac thinks I should kick a tree." Alaric snorts softly. "Which I could probably do until I bleed, and my mother would fuss, and my father would think I'm fucked up, again. It might help."

"It sounds painful," Chris says dryly. "And I think it would be good if one of us could walk. Just in case we need to go anywhere, since I'm stuck on crutches."

"Yeah." Alaric looks over at the window, at the few clouds in the sky beyond. "There's still some light left in the day. I'm going out for a flight, and I'll be back with dinner for us later."

"You don't need to miss your family dinner just because—" Chris stops when Alaric growls.

"I'm not eating with my father if he refuses to be a decent host," Alaric rumbles. "I'll bring dinner up when I get back. It'll save you the walk down to the dining room."

"First floor?"

Alaric shakes his head. "It might be downstairs, but I think this'll be in the family dining room at the far end of this floor, and that's bad enough. This place is huge. We have wings to support visiting Clan communities, and plenty of space so the entire Clan can sleep here if they need to. Which we do, sometimes. It's Clan. We're meant to be close."

"Is that why your bed's big enough to fit four comfortably?" Chris pats the empty space next to his hip. "I thought it was going to be crowded when Drea and Corbin piled on, but we all fit."

"We're used to fitting ourselves into it. For some reason they like my room better than their rooms." Alaric shrugs one shoulder; it's never bothered him, and he likes that his room smells like them. "Are you going to be okay here on your own?"

"I'll be fine." Chris leans back again, grunts a little as he lets the wall take his weight. He waves at the window. "Go on and fly. I'll be here when you get back."

There's weight to the words, and Alaric wonders at it, wonders what

Chris is saying that Alaric can't hear or smell. He leaves his phone on the nightstand, yanks open the window. He jumps a little as he takes the form of his eagle, flapping to keep himself aloft. It's one quick pump of his wings and he's through the window, into the air. The sky calls to him, safe out here above his home, and for a little while, Alaric leaves everything else behind.

24

ALARIC ENTERS THE dining room with Corbin and Drea. He avoids looking at his father, simply goes to the buffet where each of them takes a plate,
and Alaric takes two. They talk as they go, piling all four plates high with
plenty of food—three plates overfull with dinner, and one with a selection
from the dessert table. When they head for the exit again, Theobald rises
from the table, stops only at Alia's touch to his arm.

Alaric takes a deep breath as soon as they're in the hallway outside.
"Thanks," he says.

"Until you learn how to give yourself multiple arms, or bother to steal
one of those rolling trays from the kitchen, you're going to need help carrying this much food." Corbin raises his plate, offers to take the one Drea is
carrying. "Why don't you go back in and make nice with your parents; I'll
help Alaric deliver this to his room, and we'll be back soon."

"I'm not going back," Alaric states, not sure if they're paying attention.

Drea walks down the hall. "Come on. The sooner we get Alaric to his
room, the sooner we'll be back. You aren't escaping this, Corbin. Let Alaric
make his statement."

"I'm not making a statement." All Alaric wants to do is eat in peace, and
if he eats in his room, he won't have to deal with elder Clan at dinner staring at him. Besides, it's not right to leave a guest on his own.

Corbin makes a dissatisfied noise. "It's a statement. Even if you don't
mean for it to be. I'm just not sure exactly how everyone will take it. Remember, they'll be watching you, now."

"Can't think why. There's no point in waiting for me to fuck up; I've
already done that." Alaric shakes his head. "Sure I'll do it again, several
times, before I'm back here. Fuck if I even know what I'm going to do when

I get back."

"Thought you were considering being a CivE, like me." Corbin darts ahead, pulls the door open to Alaric's room, and holds it for Drea and Alaric. "Your father would be thrilled if you're an engineer. Any kind of engineer."

"Still not sure that's what I want." Alaric sets both plates down on his desk, grabs a tray table that he has tucked in his closet, and opens it next to the bed. He glances at Chris, expression darkening before he looks back at Corbin. "I'm in the School of Engineering right now. I'm taking the intro courses every engineer has to take. I'll figure it out."

Corbin sets down his plate while Drea hands hers directly to Chris. "I'm not trying to pressure you. I'm just pointing out that if you want to smooth things out, declaring your major would be one way to do it. Orson was a ChemE, and he had plans. He was going to bring in alternative energy sources, and he had the electrical background to help redesign the community. You know they'll be looking to see what grand plans you have."

"I don't have any," Alaric grinds out, teeth gritted closed. "I want to play fucking football. You know this. I want to have a few years where I get to live my own fucking life without someone looking over my shoulder. And right now, I'm not even allowed to grieve for my brother because I'm already being hoisted up onto his pedestal, and people are staring at me, saying I don't belong there."

Drea catches Corbin's hand, tugs him back a step. "Come on. We should get to dinner."

Corbin shakes her off. "Yeah. We should go make sure your father's not pissed off that his son is hiding from his responsibility."

"You know that if he hadn't said that, Chris couldn't—"

"I know that Clan is Clan," Corbin says firmly. "And maybe Alaric should remember that."

"I'm aware." Alaric crosses his arms, stands his ground, and watches as they leave. The *thud* of the door leaves him shaking, breath shuddering in his throat. He hunches forward, sinks down to sit on the edge of the bed. Elbows propped on his knees, head in his hands, he tries to breathe deeply. "I am so fucked."

"Do you want to talk about it?"

He'd been so wrapped up in his argument with family that he'd almost forgotten Chris was in the room. His voice comes as a surprise, and Alaric flinches at the sound. He shakes his head. "Not really. We brought dinner."

"You brought a lot of dinner," Chris says dryly. "I don't know how much you think I eat, but it all does look good."

"I went flying." It makes sense as an explanation to Alaric, and apparently Chris accepts it as well. Alaric helps Chris move to the edge of the bed so he can use the tray table for his plate, then grabs his desk chair and rolls it over. He has to move the dessert plate to the nightstand, but it all sort of fits and they can both be mostly comfortable.

"Somehow I didn't imagine visiting your house and ending up with a table for two," Chris comments quietly, tearing off a piece of buttered bread.

Alaric blinks down at the table, looks across at Chris. "It's all I had."

Chris looks like he's fighting back a smile, his scent amused. "It's fine, Alaric. Thank you for bringing me dinner, and I'm sorry I'm causing you problems with your family."

"Imagine if Rory had come." It's all too easy for Alaric to bring to mind, especially with what happened to Orson. His expression twists sour, and he focuses on dragging bread through the gravy on his plate, soaking it up. "My father is buried in the old ways. Clan is Clan, and that's best. None of us knew Orson had a Mage for a roommate."

"Do they know your roommate's a Mage?" Chris points out, and Alaric shrugs.

"Haven't gone out of my way to tell anyone but Drea, and now Corbin." It'll get out now, Alaric's sure of that, since it seems like Corbin can't seem to keep his mouth shut. "My roommate's a Mage. I'm training with a Mage, and other Talents. We've got just about everything on the team."

"And there's Thorne." Chris reaches for the third plate, takes a slab of roast from it, and puts it on the plate in front of him. He cuts it carefully into pieces before he takes a bite.

Alaric chews and swallows, waits for Chris to elaborate, but the silence stretches on. "What about Thorne?" Alaric finally asks, voice tight.

"Thorne's a good guy," Chris says slowly. "He's fun. He likes people. He likes people a lot, in fact, and he's always good to them. But he's never serious about anyone."

Alaric's heart thuds in his chest. "Why do you think I'd want him to be serious?"

"Rory thinks you're going to smell like him."

"So? We're friends." Alaric stabs a meatball, cuts it with his fork before shoving half of it in his mouth. It's too much all at once, and he chews, frustrated.

Chris licks his lips. "Thorne doesn't do relationships," he says bluntly. "And I love him like a brother, but I don't want to see him fucking with your head." He huffs a breath. "Scratch that—I've seen Thorne have relationships, but they aren't traditional. I just don't want to see you get hurt."

Alaric's gaze narrows. "What makes you think I'm looking for a relationship? And what makes you think it'd be with Thorne? And why do you get to have a say in it?"

"I don't," Chris admits. "I'll stop prying." There's no excuse tacked on, no extra words. Just the apology and done. Alaric tries to tease out meaning from the scents in the air, but he can't pick out anything that can help him.

"Thorne isn't going to hurt me," he mutters. "We just…I just…I'm not looking for anything. So it's fine. It's not going to fuck with my head, and it's not going to fuck with the game. 'm fine."

The corner of Chris's mouth quirks up, and Alaric can't think what he's done to make Chris smell pleased. "Don't be afraid to tell him when he's being an ass." His tone is lighter.

"Still not a relationship," Alaric grumbles. There's less tension in the air now, and he can keep his words light as well. "And you're kind of a dick for pushing me about it. Just like Corbin's a dick for helping put the thought in your head." Because Alaric's pretty sure that Chris might have left it alone if Corbin hadn't managed to bring up Thorne as well.

Chris pauses, looks up. "Two years ago, Thorne and I lived on the same hall. I was there when he started the bonfire in his room, actually. I know you heard about that—the RAs love to use that story as a cautionary tale. He started the bonfire to impress someone. This girl Kara, you probably haven't met her, and it isn't really important anyway. What's important is that he and I had been hooking up, and I hadn't thought about what it meant until right then. And I realized that to Thorne, hooking up is hooking up. And that's fine, as long as he's clear about it. We weren't clear, and I'd started to think maybe it was something else."

Alaric parses through the story. He sees the lesson he's supposed to get out of it but has no idea how to address it without getting into a conversation he's not interested in having. "So you're gay," he says, wincing inwardly because that's the same damned thing Rory did to him.

Chris rolls his eyes. "Yeah, I'm gay. Thanks for missing the point of the story."

"No, I got it." There's no good way to respond to it, no easy way to repeat, again, that Alaric doesn't care whether Thorne wants more than a hookup or not. "Thanks for telling me. And you don't need to worry. I knew what I was getting into, and it's pretty much all I was looking for."

Chris nods, points with his fork. "I guess he's not really the kind of guy you're going to bring home to meet the parents."

Alaric snorts loudly, takes a drink to try to swallow the laugh. He thinks about Thorne standing there, palms cupped full of fire as he makes it take shapes to entertain the Clan children. "My father might have a heart attack, and I definitely don't want that."

"Because then you'd have to step into his shoes?" The tension's gone from Chris's voice, the question simple and curious. "I still don't understand—why are things so different here?"

"Clan's Clan." Alaric's said it a number of times, but he can see that the point isn't made by the phrase. "We're not part of normal human society, not the way Mages are. We've got our own community and our own ways. It's like we said before, a small town within a town, and that comes with our own traditions, our own leaders." He gives Chris a moment to accept that before he tacks on the most important part. "Remember, we're not human, Chris. We're as animal as we are people, most days. Some of us more than others."

He pokes at the remainder of his meatball, shoves it in his mouth, and chews quickly. "There was an elder I knew—Corbin's great-grandfather, actually—who spent most of his time as a magpie toward the end. Even when he was in his human form, he sunbathed, and he roosted, and he anted." At Chris's confused look, Alaric makes a face. "He applied ants to his plumage. Which wasn't actually feathered at the time. When someone who's Clan's mind starts to go, it isn't pretty," he says softly. "Someday that might be Corbin."

"And someday you might get old and lie around waiting for your belly to be rubbed," Chris says. "So you need different rules. Because of your animalistic side."

"Exactly. We have control issues, and we've always had to hide," Alaric says. "Even after the Emergence... At first, we thought it'd be better. And it was, for a bit. We went from being that weird commune just outside of town to being the kids who could turn into things. We did it at lunch, just to show off. I was eight when the Emergence happened, and it was like we were suddenly free to be ourselves everywhere. Like we didn't have to hide."

"Until?" Chris asks, and Alaric wonders how easy it is to hear the *until* in his voice.

"Until someone lost control," Alaric says quietly. "No one died, but two kids were hurt. It's a small town; everyone knew what happened. Everyone knows everyone here. There was no lying, no hiding, not anymore. My father thought about taking Clan children out of the school, thought about teaching them within our community. But we'd gone to the school on purpose. We'd wanted to get that education, to step into the world outside of our own. We have to hide, yes, but we also have to live in the world. And we have to bring it back to the community, bring modern advances back. We have to grow. Everyone has a part to play, a role to fill. And we couldn't do that if we never left home."

"So you had to be careful."

"So we had to be careful." Alaric's appetite feels flat, and he sets aside his plate unfinished. "We were restricted from sports. We were kept apart at lunch, which was fine—we tended to group together as it was. And in the places where things had changed—where Clan had started to join in town events, and where non-Clan had been invited to our community—those doors slammed closed. We were eleven when we separated again. We'd managed three years of peace, and we had just started to discover what we could have if we were part of the normal world, before it ended."

"Enough time for you to really discover football." Chris's foot nudges Alaric's under the table, and Alaric smiles ruefully.

"Yeah. The Blended league started, and I took advantage of that," Alaric says with a small shrug. "Corbin tried to date a human girl once, when we were fifteen. That ended with her father standing on the edge of Clan property with a gun, threatening him. No less than seven ravens and four wolves followed her father home, made sure he left us alone without hurting him. So we keep to ourselves, and we keep to the old ways. My father's convinced more than ever that it's right."

Chris's toe rests against Alaric's ankle. Chris taps him once, waits for Alaric to look up. "And you? What do you think?"

"I think it keeps us safe," Alaric says slowly, "but I don't know that it's good for us. I don't think it's healthy. And even though we go out for our education, spend time in the human world, I don't think it's enough. I think we come back here, and we stagnate, and we keep to the old ways and we don't grow."

Chris tilts his head, considers Alaric. He licks his lips, and Alaric fights not to stare at the path of his tongue. "For what it's worth," Chris says, "I think it sounds like you'd make a good leader."

Alaric laughs dryly. "Not to them. Not to anyone here. Not for Clan."

Chris makes a small noise, nudges Alaric's plate closer to him again. "You were flying earlier, and you said you need to eat. So eat."

Alaric's stomach is still in tight knots, twisted up from too many things to let him unwind it. "If the Treaty's failing, this is going to be a mess," he mutters. "If a Mage killed Orson…there's been violence before. But I can't think why one would."

"Could it be someone from another Clan community?" Chris asks. "Could someone be trying to get you to fight an enemy that isn't real?"

"It doesn't work like that." Alaric shakes his head, a low growl under his breath. "Clan's Clan, Chris. We don't fight against each other."

"But you don't always like each other," Chris reminds him. "What about the people who don't agree with your father's decision? What could they do?"

"Not this. They wouldn't attack the community like this." Alaric can't deny that people are going to be angry, but this isn't how Clan fights Clan. It'd be brutal and bloody, yes, but it wouldn't be covert. Clan's blunt, open. Challenges happen, and they're violent, but then they're done. Everyone knows what's on the table when a challenge occurs, and everyone's in agreement about the outcome.

He fully expects to be challenged, and he's thankful that the bear is strong enough to handle most threats. He may not have diversity in his forms, but he does have strength.

"So you think there might be a war? What would that look like to the rest of us?" Chris polishes off the remainder of the food on his plate, pushes it away, and leans his elbows on the small table. It brings him almost too close to Alaric, lets Alaric feel the heat from his body.

Alaric draws back, crosses his arms. "You haven't noticed when it's happened before, but it'd be different now. There are more Clan and more Mages since the Emergence. I think if something goes wrong, if it turns violent, it'll be noticed by the mundane police. It'll be obvious, and humans'll get dragged into it. And I think it could go wrong for all of us. Who's going to trust Talent again if we start a war?"

Chris presses his lips thinly together. "But do you think it'll happen?"

"Hoping it doesn't," Alaric says flatly. "My father was one of the Clan who helped negotiate the current Treaty. Hoping he upholds that, but I don't know if I trust him to do that. Not when it's Orson. Family makes everything different."

It's a simplification, but it's the best he can do. And it's why he wants to figure out what's going on rather than following his father down a dark path.

Alaric has always had issues with his family, but this is the first time that he realizes that he doesn't trust his father, and he's not sure he ever really has.

25

DREA AND CORBIN stop by after dinner, and they all end up sprawled on the bed, watching a movie on the TV affixed to Alaric's wall. Alaric is torn, his beast calmed by Drea and Corbin staying close to him, his skin prickling where he's pressed up against Chris's hip. Chris smells content and doesn't seem to mind that Corbin sits on his other side, leaning across Chris to talk to Alaric or periodically throwing popcorn into Drea's mouth. And Drea is draped across them all, curled in Alaric's lap, cradled against his chest, her legs stretched over Chris and Corbin.

After a time, Alaric feels as if their scents merge, as if Chris takes on the scent of family as much as Drea and Corbin do. It's just being here, in this familiar space. It's the way he's the only thing different in this room, so Alaric's mind assimilates it, slots it into place as if he belongs. Alaric understands how it works, lets it happen because it settles the hound in his heart, lets him take ease in the evening.

Drea wrinkles her nose, presses a hand to Alaric's chest. "Did you bring any painkiller?" she asks, and Chris winces.

Alaric can smell the pain, a sour scent that's growing stronger. "C'mon, Drea, off." He helps Drea get off the bed without putting any more pressure on Chris's knee. "Think it's time for him to sleep."

"Good meeting you." Corbin offers a hand, and Chris takes it, pulls Corbin in for a backslap. Corbin grins. "Not bad for a human." He glances at Alaric, and for a horrifying moment, Alaric thinks he's going to say something else. Instead Corbin crosses to Alaric and yanks him into a hug, holding on tight. "We'll do something tomorrow before you go back," he murmurs. "I'm still expecting you to talk to me."

"Right." Alaric lets Corbin take his weight for a moment, knowing that he can handle it despite his slighter build. By the time he straightens, Drea is there to pull Corbin away so that she can claim her own hug. She kisses Alaric's cheek, and they leave.

The room is quiet save for the hum of the television.

"Could you grab my bag? I've got something in there." Chris reaches in when Alaric hands it to him, pulls out some over-the-counter painkiller. "It'll take the edge off, anyway. Should let me get some rest."

Some rest.

In the bed.

Alaric hands Chris the glass of water. "You need help getting to the bathroom?" He'll deal with the bed later. Chris won't question it if Alaric sits in the chair and does something for a while before he's ready for sleep.

Chris takes the pills sets the glass on the nightstand. He digs through the bag to pull out a pair of sweats, then drops the bag onto the floor next to the bed. "Just give me the crutches; I can manage on my own if you give me directions. I hate the things, but like I said, this isn't my first injury. It isn't even the first time I haven't been allowed to put weight on one foot. Sprained my ankle hard during my freshman year; I was out for a month with that one."

Alaric makes a small noise of affirmation. It grates on him to let Chris struggle to stand alone, but when he steps closer, Chris holds up a hand and motions him to get back, out of the way.

"I'm fine," Chris insists, even though his heartbeat and scent say he's not.

Alaric changes while Chris is out of the room, pulling on flannel pants and a spare T-shirt from his drawer. He settles into the overstuffed chair, puts his feet up on the ottoman while he pulls out a knitting project he left behind when he went to school. He could be reading—any one of these books would be a good comfort reread—but he needs something to do with his hands. He'd rather spin, but there's no wool in his basket and the wheel makes too much noise. The loom would be even worse, between the sound of the shuttle slipping between the threads of the warp and the low *thump* as he taps the weft into place. He doesn't want to keep Chris from sleeping, and he hopes that the soft slide of wood on wood from his knitting needles won't bother him.

Chris makes his way back in slowly, and Alaric is deep in the pattern of the current row. He glances up, jaw tight, but Chris just turns away and closes the door. He crosses to the bed with a careful *thump-thump* of the crutches on the floor, heavily swinging his weight with every step. When he reaches the bed, he settles with a groan, sitting for only a moment before managing to work his way up to lying in the middle, half on top of the covers.

"Fuck, that hurts," Chris mutters.

"I can smell it." Alaric makes a face. "Not that I'm sniffing at you."

"Don't care right now." Chris cranes his head. "What're you doing?"

Alaric lifts the needles, the soft gray-and-lavender yarn knit into about three inches of a semi-intricate pattern. "Scarf," he says quietly. "For my grandmother. Mother's mother," he clarifies. "She gets cold easy these days, and she likes anything soft. She's more cat than anything else."

"Mm." Chris stretches, arms pillowed behind his bed, back arching as he shifts his weight. "Are you going to tell me that Clan don't sleep like the rest of us do?"

"Hm?" Alaric stops, one needle through a loop, right in the middle of the stitch. "What do you mean?"

"You're knitting instead of sleeping," Chris says slowly. "Shouldn't you get some rest? It sounds like Corbin's planning on dragging you somewhere tomorrow—not in my car, by the way, unless we're all going. And I'd place a bet there will be more family drama that you need to be fully rested for before you leave here."

Alaric focuses on the stitch, trying to remember where he is in the pattern. He wraps the yarn around, slides the stitch over, and then stops and lowers it. He stares at the needles in his lap. "I'm fine. I'll sleep when I'm ready to sleep. Plenty of room on the floor, and I'm comfortable here right now."

"You're not sleeping on the floor." Chris's voice goes low and firm. "You spent half the day sitting on the damned bed with all of us. It's big enough to fit four and still have room leftover. And if you're uncomfortable sharing space with me while we sleep, just shift into another form and curl up on the foot of it. I don't care."

Chris cares. There's a sour lemon note, a frustrated, irritable, almost angry twist to his scent. Anger at himself, Alaric thinks, not at Alaric. His jaw is tight because Chris isn't Clan and he isn't family, no matter what his scent implied while they were all together. "I'm not uncomfortable." There's a part of Alaric that wants to fall into the comfort of sharing a bed, that wants to call Corbin and Drea back so that there's family here, so it becomes Clan rather than just him and Chris. He glances at the foot of the bed, where the comforter is tangled and Chris's bad leg rests on top of it instead of under it. He makes a disgruntled noise and sets the scarf aside. He pushes himself to standing and stalks over.

It takes careful, gentle work to get the covers set right without hurting Chris more, but Alaric manages it. He glares at Chris, considers his options.

"C'mon," Chris says sleepily, and Alaric closes his eyes.

He lets the hound take over, leaps onto the foot of the bed, and turns around twice before finding his space and curling up. He takes care not to lean on the bad leg, but rests his head on Chris's good shin.

Chris falls asleep far faster than Alaric expects, the pain in his scent easing as his breath becomes slow. It shivers under Alaric's skin, his heart beating in time with every inhalation. It's a confusing sensation. He whines softly, nuzzles Chris's leg, and Chris mutters in his sleep, turning over.

Alaric can't sleep.

He's careful as he belly-crawls to the edge of the bed and leaps down to the floor before transforming back to himself. He searches for his phone in the dark, takes it to the end of the bed, and sits on the floor where the light won't reach Chris's eyes and wake him up.

You up?

The return text is quick. *Yeah. Just finished up with a song-writing session with Thorne, who is shockingly on track tonight. He's gone out to a party now and I just got home.*

Alaric huffs softly at the screen. *Productive night?*

Yeah. What's up?

A smile twists Alaric's mouth. I *want to say Chris breathes funny, but he doesn't. And it doesn't matter, because I still can't sleep.* He wonders if Rory will really understand it, but he figures he might. He seems to understand a lot of things that Alaric thinks of as Clan-specific.

Oh. How are things other than Chris not breathing funny?

Alaric rests his arms on his knees, lets his head fall forward. He has no idea how to explain his father, his family, his grief and confusion and, on top of everything, Corbin. It all needs more than a few words at a time typed awkwardly with his thumbs. *Tense*, he finally says. *I'll be back at PHU tomorrow night. Have to return next weekend for the funeral. Need to be home again in time to dig the grave.*

Dig the grave? You have to dig the grave for your brother? Doesn't the cemetery have a back hoe for that?

The response comes so quickly that Alaric can imagine the confused expression on Rory's face, the way he'd twist around to look at Alaric, brows furrowed. He swallows a snort of laughter that's inappropriate given the conversation. *Clan tradition. Family always digs the grave. Who needs a back hoe when you've got a bear?* Or his father, who can shift into the biggest fucking wolf that Alaric's ever seen. He remembers the fury of his father digging his grandfather's grave four years ago, the way dirt flew. *I think tomorrow I'll try to get to the police station. See what information we can get for you. And I'm going to stop by the brew store.*

Brew store?

It has to seem odd, going shopping on the way home from a family emergency. *Seems like a good way to mourn him, using his recipes. Make a good dark brew. He had this chocolate thing he really liked. Dark enough that it felt like it should stand up on its own.*

Gross.

Alaric catches himself before he laughs out loud. *Good beer tastes better than bad beer*, he points out, but it's a familiar argument, and he knows he isn't going to sway Rory's opinion. Not that he needs to. *Just figured it'd be like doing something with him, even though he's gone.*

There's a hesitation this time, minutes ticking by before the response comes. *Were you close?*

Alaric can see why he asks. Rory never goes a day—hardly goes an hour—without mentioning Thorne. The two are thick as thieves. Absolutely different, but almost codependent in some ways. While Rory's his own person, Thorne often shows up where he is, and it seems as if Rory simply expects him to be there.

And Alaric's barely mentioned Orson before.

Sometimes, he says, and he leaves it at that. There's a snuffling sound, and Chris shifts his weight, somehow managing to roll over. Alaric goes tense at the rush of pain in the air, ears pricked for more sound, but Chris's breath remains even and calm. He's still asleep. *I should probably try to sleep.*

His phone vibrates in his hand. *Whatever you're feeling right now—good or bad—it's still valid.*

You sound like a self-help article. Alaric snorts fondly.

You really should get to know my extended family. Dad's from a hippie commune. We may have picked up a few habits along the way.

Alaric smiles at the phone, his fingers touching the screen. *Thanks. It's a mess. I'll tell you about it when I get back.*

I'll be here.

Alaric locks the phone and dims the screen before he sets it on the nightstand. He slips into the hound's skin and leaps back up onto the bed. Chris is lying on only half of it, curled toward the side, and there's more space next to him than there is at the foot. With a heavy sigh, Alaric stretches out beside him, back-to-back, and lets himself relax.

He breathes in when Chris does, exhales at the same time, and within a few breaths, he's asleep as well.

Dreamwalkers aren't like other Talents. No, I get it, you've heard that a lot. But I want you to think about it, about what I mean. How long have you been doing these interviews? A year? And in all that time, have you found another Dreamwalker to talk to?

That's what I meant.

It's rare to find us while we're sane.

Sanity is a relative term when it comes to Dreamwalkers. In my grandfather's time—maybe even in my mother's time—it was simply accepted that any Dreamwalker lived half in this world and half in the next. Everyone knew that a Dreamwalker might be walking somewhere else at any moment, that the dream is real to them. It's all too easy to lose track of the boundaries between the dream and the real, especially if you don't have someone to anchor you in the real world while you're young, teach you how to manage your Talent.

That's not easy. There's something about our genetics that makes us harder to manage. If you put two Dreamwalkers in a room, their Talent will twist up together, create knots of dreamlands that they can't escape. The Talent isn't additive, it's multiplicative. An active Dreamwalker cannot raise a Dreamwalker child; they'd both be lost.

So survival of the fittest changed the way our Lineage works. It's very rare to have a Dreamwalker descend directly. Usually there's a grandparent, or maybe a great aunt. Someone two or three generations past.

We have to keep track of our families, of our children and grandchildren and their children beyond. We have to know our lineage, and we have to know where we go, who we marry, where our children go. Sometimes we fail.

Psychosis was once a typical diagnosis for a Dreamwalker. Even in my grandfather's time, before the days of ancestry websites, where you can build your family tree and track it back for generations. My grandfather traveled the world, searching for Dreamwalkers who had been placed in asylums and institutions, buried within the dreamworld because there was no one who could help them find their way back. They needed help to learn the borders between the waking and the dream. He helped some, and in the modern age, we try to keep track. We build our databases, we seek people out who may not even know that they have Talent in their blood, and we bring them to someone who can teach.

Everyone of Dreamwalker blood takes the name of the lineage.

Even without showing the Talent, they have the ability to bear a Dreamwalker. They can learn the ways and help teach a child, keep them anchored. They can take in Emergent Dreamwalkers, who are a pure nightmare that have come since the Emergence. People who slide into what seems to be psychosis so rapidly, and so hard, and in some cases, have the capability to take others with them.

Dreamwalkers have a light side and a dark side; those who can control dreams are dangerous to others until they learn control. Two Dreamwalkers, with their Talent multiplying, can create a dream-scape so lifelike it spreads through reality, confuses everyone around them. It takes over the waking world.

Unlike other Talents, we don't gather in communities. We put space between ourselves, communicate over modern technology now. It's easier than it used to be, when a Dreamwalker family could be isolated completely by distance.

We have stories that we tell, legends that we pass from parent to child, continuing down the line. We have signs that we watch for whenever a child is born, things that we do. And we always ensure that if a Dreamwalker bears a Dreamwalker, they are raised by some-one else.

I was given to my mother's second cousin, and even then, my mother was drawn to my dreams. We spoke almost every night de-spite living at opposite ends of the country. No one believed me when I told them what I dreamed, and I learned to stop talking about it. Even in our own community, no one is quite sure what is possible, what is dream and what is real.

It helped, in a way. I learned to identify the dreamscape, tell when my world was manipulated by my mind rather than by those around me.

The thing is, with everything we know about being Dreamwalkers now, there is much more that we still have to learn. I was twenty-one when the Emergence happened, and three days later one of my room-mates fell into a nightmare and never returned. My mother's boss slipped into psychosis.

Dreams are deadly, terrifying, seductive things. The Emergence took away the safeguards our lineage had created. Dreamwalkers Emerged near others, and we realized that we no longer could keep control. And all too often, the dreams would win.

It's safer to be among other Talents, for me. When I'm among hu-mans, I'm afraid that any one of them could Emerge at any time, and I might drag them into the dream with me.

CORBIN

26

THE BED IS warm, comfortable in the way that it only is when someone else is sleeping with him. No one is on top of him, which isn't usual when Alaric sleeps at home, but he can feel the press of another body behind him, heating him from head to toe. Alaric stretches slowly, not wanting to awaken even though light spills into the room around the shades. He slowly loosens his grip on the blanket and two pillows that he has clutched in his arms, as if they were a person to hold onto.

He rolls onto his back, slides his leg along the person behind him, and stops dead at the swift, sour scent of pain. Fuck. "Sorry," he mutters.

He's home, but that's not Corbin or Drea. That's Chris. In his bed, pressed up against him. Moving now, stretching slightly as if he's testing his limbs.

"Pretty sure that there's nothing that'll make this not hurt," Chris says with a heavy sigh. He stays curled on his side, his back still to Alaric. "I'll have to figure out how to move eventually. But I think I'm taking something for the pain before I even get out of bed."

Alaric inhales, exhales slowly. Chris can't hear his heartbeat, can't smell the anxiety that must surround him. Can't smell the musk of a typical morning, either.

"I'll get it." Alaric pushes himself to sitting, shoves the blankets into his lap. He has to reach past Chris and tries to do it as carefully as he can, wincing when his knee pushes against Chris's back. He grabs the bottle of painkiller and the glass of water still sitting there from the night before. "Think you can sit up?"

Chris wedges his hands against the bed, pushes himself to sitting, and drags himself back until he's propped against the wall. He has a cocoon of blankets wrapped around himself, his bad knee stretched out and the other knee bent. He takes out double the usual dose and throws the pills in his mouth, washing them down with a long swig of water. He lets his head fall back against the wall with a *thunk* that makes Alaric wince.

"I was hoping sleep would help," Chris grumbles.

"Everything else has probably tightened up, making it worse." Alaric knows how much he aches after a hard hit, figures it has to be worse for a human. "If you were back at school, you could see the trainer, have him work on you. Or a Healer. They might not be able to fix it, but they could take your pain. Like Priya." He remembers the girl from Teas Please; he's bumped into her on campus since, and they've talked about her brother and football again.

Chris runs his hand down his side, digging the palm into his hip and thigh. "I can work on it myself." He twists, trying to get a better angle, and Alaric watches the path of his hand over the muscle.

He can smell the pain and the frustration, thick and rank in the air, strong enough that it almost covers the musk. His fingers itch, and he reaches out, stopping himself and pulling his hand back. " 'm not a massage therapist, but I could dig into that for you."

"It'd help," Chris admits. "Hang on, I can make this easier for you." He huffs as he grabs the pillows, rolls onto his stomach, and holds one pillow under his chest. His head hangs over the edge, and he shoves the other pillow under the problem side. "I can feel it in the IT band. If you can work any of that out, it'll help. I'll work the groin muscle myself, later. After I've had a hot shower to loosen up."

The groin muscle. Right. Alaric doesn't want to touch any of those thoughts, so he simply grunts in reply. He kneels on the bed, tries not to look at the way the pillow has propped Chris's ass up. He bites his tongue, focuses as he gets his hands on Chris's hip and digs into the muscles with his thumbs.

Chris groans, and Alaric's thankful that he still has a blanket wrapped around his lower half.

"Feels good," Chris mutters, as Alaric keeps working.

"Not as good as it'd be with the trainer." And Alaric's pretty sure the trainer wouldn't be wondering other things, thinking things that Alaric really doesn't want to think. Not now. Probably not ever, not if he wants to keep being friends with Chris.

He needs to get back to school and be distracted. Soon.

"Don't sell yourself short. You have good hands." Another low groan, and Alaric feels the muscle go a bit looser under his touch.

"I—" Alaric cuts off as the door bangs open. He jerks away from Chris, his face heated, hands itching. "Corbin."

Chris huffs out a sigh, pulls the pillow out from under his hip and lets it fall on the floor while he relaxes back against the bed.

"Are we interrupting something?" Corbin grins as he pushes a cart into the room. "We thought you'd want breakfast, and your dad is still muttering to everyone about how you brought home a human—like he's a stray dog you want to adopt or something—so Drea and I figured we'd bring the buffet to you."

"You aren't interrupting anything."

"Are you sure?" Corbin waits until Drea's in the room, then nudges the door shut. He pushes the cart next to the table still sitting by the bed, and while she sets a basket on the table, he brings over the overstuffed chair. "Because it looked like—"

"Muscle cramp," Alaric says curtly.

"We brought breakfast." Drea speaks before Corbin can get another word in. Chris makes a muffled sound that Alaric thinks might be *thank you* but isn't comprehensible even with Alaric's hearing. "The basket's filled with cider donuts and cornbread muffins, fresh from the oven. We've got coffee and fresh cream. Apples and pears that were picked yesterday. Hard-boiled eggs."

"From your hens, right?" Chris lifts his head to ask.

"You're catching on to the theme," Drea says cheerily. "Butter was churned Thursday. The jams are from last summer—we've still got one or two jars of each of last year's batches to finish off, so Mom insists we're taking these back with us after we open them. And of course, there's bacon."

Alaric snorts; some things never change. "There's always bacon."

"We do go through a lot of bacon." Corbin looks at the bed, raises an eyebrow before pointedly taking a seat on the arm of the overstuffed chair, leaving the chair itself for Drea. "Were you planning on sleeping in, or are we getting up and doing things today?"

Alaric reaches down to the lower shelf of the kitchen cart and picks up a jar of strawberry-rhubarb jam. "This stuff's better than anything else you'll get." He nudges Chris. "C'mon. You'll never eat better than a Clan breakfast."

"And this one's light. If it had been a real Gather, there'd be steak and omelets and potatoes. Greens in the summer." Drea makes a happy little noise. "Harvest is the best time of year around here."

"As long as there's bacon." Corbin gestures with a piece of it, then pops it in his mouth. "You eat meat, right, Chris?"

There's an edge to his voice, but when Alaric skewers Corbin with a look, his expression is entirely innocent.

"The smoked sausage is still curing, or I would've brought that. Alaric loves sausage," Corbin says idly, and Alaric kicks him under the table.

"Plans," Drea says, rapping her knuckles against the table. "We need to make—" She cuts off, turns to face the door just as there's a knock and it pushes open. "Mom. Hi."

"Good morning." Alia's eyes are rimmed in red. "Andrea, Alaric—are you planning on returning to school tonight?"

Alaric glances at Chris. "We have to get the car back, so we should leave. But I think we've got some things to do in town, first."

Chris pushes himself roughly to sitting, rolls over, and manages to bend his good leg and drag himself to the edge of the bed. He shoves his hair back, rubs his eyes. "Thank you for your hospitality, but I need to get back."

Alia nods, but her attention is on Drea and Alaric. "You'll return," she says quietly, and it's half commanding, half pleading.

"We promised, so yes, we'll be back Friday night. I don't know how we're getting here yet. I just need to let the coaches know, so someone can sub for me in Saturday's game," Alaric says.

"The game doesn't matter," Alia snaps, and Alaric feels the hound's growl inside his chest. He flexes his hand, stops mid-motion when Chris's knee butts up against his.

"It's an obligation." Alaric's voice is tight. "My family comes first, yes, but it's still an obligation and I am not letting the team down. I will be here to dig Orson's grave."

Alia seems to deflate, shrinking smaller than Alaric has ever seen her while remaining fully human. "Thank you." A long, slow breath, then she shows a thin smile. "What are your plans for today?"

"We were just going to talk about that," Drea says. "Part of the plan will probably be taking over the communal bath to get Chris cleaned up."

"I probably reek," Chris says ruefully, and Corbin nods.

"You do, and I can't even smell you the same way they can," Corbin tells him, voice low.

"I've got some things Orson gave me, places I need to go pick some stuff up." Alaric keeps his voice carefully even. "Am I needed here?"

Alia's voice is just as neutral, her scent giving nothing away. "It would be best if you were to see your father before you leave. Alone, please, as it's Clan business."

"Corbin's my right—"

"Alone," she repeats, and Alaric grunts. It's as close as he'll get to a confirmation, and her expression softens. "He doesn't resent you for being here when Orson's gone," she says softly, and it feels like a kick in the gut.

Alaric flinches when she closes the door, leaves them. The only sound is the soft *clink* of Drea putting a knife on her plate. Alaric whines, and Drea reaches across the table, brushes his hair across his forehead.

The air is thick with discomfort, pain, and sweat. Alaric wrinkles his nose, lets out a shuddering breath as he looks at Chris. "You really do stink," he says, his voice as steady as he can make it.

"What was that about a communal bath? Because I'm not sure I—"

"We're Clan," Corbin interrupts him. "None of us care about nudity. I mean, half the time, most of us aren't even human. If it would make you more comfortable, we'll shift after we get you in there."

"Maybe I shouldn't join you." Drea peels the shell from a hardboiled egg. "I'll just take a quick shower today."

"I can shower." Chris is curt, the words sharp. His scent is still uncomfortable. "It'll hurt, but once I'm in, I don't exactly need to move around."

"You'll still need help getting in and out."

"I can do it on my own." Chris's jaw is set tightly as he looks across the table at Corbin. "I don't need your help or anyone else's. I told Ric, this isn't the first time I've been on crutches. The knee sucks, but I can manage. Just show me where the shower is, give me a couple of towels, and I'll be fine."

"Don't." Alaric holds up a hand when it seems like Corbin's going to try to be helpful again. "Let him be stubborn. Don't try to force him into Clan habits. He's not Clan."

Corbin sits back, smirks slightly as he pops a piece of cornbread muffin into his mouth. "Exactly."

He's acting like Alaric just proved a point, and Alaric has no idea what it was.

Chris shifts, and the bed dips; Alaric sinks into the gravitational well created by Chris's body, ends up with their thighs pressed together. He tries to focus on the food instead of the people, twisting the jar of strawberry-rhubarb jam open and inhaling the fresh, sweet scent. He puts a large swath of it on a muffin along with the butter, then offers both to Chris. "Don't know what I'll do with this back in the dorm, so we might as well eat as much as we can now," Alaric points out. "It's the best jam we've got."

"Alaric's a complete idiot for anything strawberry rhubarb," Drea says. "I'm all about the blueberries, and Corbin's a bird, so it's all blackberries and raspberries for him, although he's got a thing for apple pie. Orson mostly liked the fall fruits, like apples and pears."

"He sent me instructions on making hard cider as well as beer," Alaric says slowly, piling his plate high with eggs and bacon and slices of apple. "And the spices to buy for mulling cider. Said it's his own blend, nothing's better than that."

"Did you get that pumpkin beer from him?" Corbin asks. "Because that's the best thing he's ever made."

"The coffee beer," Drea counters. "C'mon, coffee, bourbon, and vanilla? You know that one's best."

Chris's arm presses against Alaric's, and he glances over to find Chris too close, watching him. Alaric raises an eyebrow, and Chris murmurs, "You going to be all right with your dad?"

It's not something he wants to think about. Alaric shrugs. "Don't really have a choice, do I?"

"You always have a choice." Chris pulls away, reaches for more bacon for his own plate. "Drea, can I have some of that creamer for my coffee?"

She passes the ceramic pot across, and for a moment it's like going back in time to being a child. Alaric can see the thin crack at the top where the pot broke when he knocked it off the table, remembers his father yelling because he'd been careless with his hound's wagging tail.

He remembers Orson telling him that it was okay, that it didn't matter that Alaric didn't have control. That he'd learn eventually, that he'd be useful. That the pot was just a thing and didn't matter. Alaric and Orson didn't always see eye to eye, but he took that moment to heart because Alaric was only six, and Orson seemed so much older at ten.

And Orson had made that pot for their mother, along with a lopsided sugar pot that always stays on the kitchen table.

Alaric takes the pot back carefully from Chris, sets it in the middle of the rolling tray so it can't get knocked off. He sees Drea's small smile at the action and knows she's probably remembering the same thing he is.

"So we're going to the brew store," Drea says. "In honor of Orson. We're buying equipment, and Alaric's going to start brewing. And after that, Midway?"

Corbin shakes his head. "Midway's too far. It'd take too long to go all the way out there, then come back here so I can get in Amy's car and you guys can head back to PHU. Speaking of, I'll get Amy to give you guys a ride back here on Friday, so you don't have to worry about it." He glances at Chris, and Alaric's skin bristles. "It should be Clan-only next weekend."

"I get the point," Chris says. "And I'm thinking I shouldn't use the communal bath because you might try to drown me."

"I don't not like you," Corbin tells him. "But I really don't like the stress you're causing, or the fact that you're a reminder to Theobald Herne that his son's a problem. He doesn't need any more excuses to have it in for Alaric."

Alaric huffs. "Believe it or not, Corbin's trying to protect me," he mutters. It's misplaced; Alaric doesn't need the protection, and he doesn't want it. He wants to make his place in the Clan in his own way, and if that includes bringing human friends and football to the community, then he'll do that.

Drea coughs, and Alaric looks at her. "Then we go to Midway on our way home," she says plainly. "Even if it's out of the way. By then we'll come up with some kind of a plan."

"Maybe he'll say something when we talk," Alaric muses. "Maybe he'll give me an idea what he's planning, whether he's going to break the Treaty right away or if he's investigating on his own."

"Maybe he doesn't even know yet. He's still grieving."

Alaric knocks his sister's foot under the table, presses his ankle against hers. She's putting on a good face, but he sees how the skin around her eyes is swollen, how the whites are more pink than white. "I know," he says. "We all are."

"We're going to figure this out," Corbin says. "And we're not going to war. Not this time." He bites off a piece of bacon with a snap. "Not ever."

Chris's knee presses against Alaric's, and he's sure it's meant to be reassuring. But it isn't, not with all the uncertainty hanging over their heads. Not with Orson gone, and Alaric's role changing.

And certainly not with the possibility of war.

27

THE MEETING WITH his father doesn't go badly. Of course, it doesn't go well, either, and Alaric is left feeling as if he's a disappointment once again. They go over a long list of things that Alaric needs to keep in mind, Gathers that he's expected to attend in the future. His duties as Theobald's heir. Alaric manages to remain civil the entire time, as does Theobald, but Alaric notes that they avoid all topics related to what he's doing at PHU and the friend he brought home. When Theobald asks if Alaric is avoiding Mages on campus, Alaric simply grunts rather than saying yes or no.

He can understand that his father is wary after what happened with Orson, but Alaric still doesn't believe that Orson was doing any form of ritual. He also doesn't think that Mages are the problem. As much as he understands the history between Clan and Mage, he doesn't see the same impact going forward, now that the world has changed.

The problem with tradition is that it takes time to overcome. And Clan are still afraid to be seen in public, to be known for what they are. Alaric isn't sure his father will ever be able to move past his upbringing.

The thing is, while the meeting doesn't go badly, it does go for a long time, and it leaves Alaric feeling drained and broken. He feels like he has secrets piling on top of secrets, and they are all necessary to keep the peace in his home. He pushes into his room, smells spice and soap before he sees Chris reclining in the overstuffed chair, his foot propped on the ottoman. Alaric grunts rather than say anything, words fled for the moment, and grabs clothes before he stalks down the hall to the bathroom.

There's no time left for a good, long soak today; it has to be a quick job of getting cleaned up. Then he dresses in the too-small space because he's not going to change in front of Chris. The locker room is one thing; the space where they shared a bed is something else entirely. He takes long enough that he's still running a comb through his hair when he hears Corbin call out, "We're getting Chris down the stairs, and we've got the keys. You're driving. Get your ass in gear, Alaric."

Alaric sets the comb down, leans on the edge of the sink, and stares at his reflection. He pushes at his hair, tries to get it to lie flat. It's too long now, and it's starting to reach the point where it will grow out into soft waves if he lets it get much longer. He grumbles at himself, carefully hangs up the towels, and heads back to his room.

By the time he gets his shoes on and makes it downstairs, the front door is open and Chris's car is pulled up in front of the steps. There's a wolf curled in the front hall, her nose tucked under the head of a doe, both with their heads cocked curiously, and Alaric waves quietly to them. Corbin jumps out of the car, leaves the door open and the car running. "When I get a car next year, it might be old, but it'll be interesting. None of this dull sedan crap for me."

"Corbin's not getting a car next year, so let him dream," Drea says. "He's been talking about this mythical sports car—something classic, he says— since he was fifteen. He's just jealous you actually have a car, Chris."

"Don't tell all my secrets." Corbin raises a hand. "Get down here and help out, Ric."

It's starting to feel normal to wedge his arm under Chris's shoulder, to rest his hand on his back while he helps lift him. Chris feels unbalanced, resting against Corbin's shorter height on the other side, and they take a moment to let him steady himself before handing him his crutches. Alaric stands nearby to help him again when they get to the stairs, and it seems easier after that to let Chris lean on him all the way to the car while Drea carries the crutches. They find a rhythm just in time to get Chris into the passenger seat, before Corbin and Drea take over the back seat and leave Alaric to drive.

It feels like it should be awkward, but it's not.

Drea leans between the seats. "Do you have a list? Because I'm thinking that making more than one batch is the best way to honor Orson's memory."

"Pumpkin ale," Corbin says, and Drea smacks him.

"Hard cider," Drea counters. "It's made with apple juice, right? If you park on Hammond, we can walk down the street and pick up apple juice and anything else from the normal grocery while you two go the brew store."

"Depends on if we have enough money to get all the equipment," Alaric says, glancing at Chris. "We took up a collection from the guys, between the house and the team."

"I've got about $750 on the card," Chris admits. "The guys were pretty into the idea, and Mac threw in a few bucks as well on the condition that we set something aside for her. So we'll do our best. I'm not setting up a kegerator for this, though. We're just brewing and bottling."

"Might need a small keg for the cider—can't make it sweet unless you carbonate outside the bottle, and a dry cider is painful to drink." Alaric makes a face. "Orson bottled the first batch he made, and it was fine to mix with something else, but none of us wanted to touch it straight."

"I'll kick in the cost of the keg and the tap." Corbin's tone is light, but Alaric knows where that money's coming from. He glances in the mirror, and Corbin meets his gaze there. "What? It's not like I can afford the car anyway. Like Drea said, I've been talking about it since I was fifteen. Might as well spend some of the money on a fantastic wake for Orson instead."

Alaric smiles slightly, reaches back with one hand for Corbin to squeeze it. "Thanks."

He pulls into one of the diagonal on-street spaces, midway between the two stores.

"We'll meet you at Hanson's," Drea says, checking her wallet. "How much apple juice do I need, and is there anything else?"

Alaric pulls out his phone, looks through the recipes Orson sent. He highlights the important parts and sends it as a text to Drea and Corbin. "Get me some crackers, too. You know the kind I like."

Drea huffs, laughing softly. She leans between the two seats and kisses his cheek. "You won't need to store the jam anywhere. It'll be gone before next weekend. You know Mom'd send you home with as many jars as you want, right? You can get your whole floor hooked on strawberry-rhubarb jam on crackers."

"No peanut butter?" Chris asks, and it makes Drea and Corbin laugh.

Alaric rolls his eyes. "This is why I shouldn't bring anyone home," he mutters. "You wonder why I don't invite you to PHU, Corbin? When you and Drea team up, all my childish secrets come out."

"We love you and all your odd habits, and you put up with ours." Drea squeezes his shoulder, then pushes her door open. "It'll probably take us less time, so give us the keys. We'll put everything in the car when we get back so we're not hauling it around."

Alaric checks with Chris first, and after his nod, hands over the keys. It takes some time for them to all get out, to get Chris balanced on the crutches. Chris waits while Drea presses the button to lock the car, then he slowly starts swinging along on the crutches down the sidewalk.

"Lead the way."

It's a slow path to Hanson's with Chris on crutches. Alaric pulls the door open before Chris gets there, holds it while he carefully swings through.

"Alaric!"

"Jimmy." Alaric nods, a small smile tilting his lips. "You've heard?"

Jimmy's expression twists, dark eyes furrowed. "Yeah, we've heard. My prayers are with your family. Good folks, didn't deserve that."

Corbin would say that Jimmy and the rest of the Hanson family only like them because Clan likes to drink. Alaric would rather believe that not every human in Haverhill is afraid. Of course, he might be wrong.

He takes out his phone again, sets it on the countertop. "I need to buy some equipment and enough supplies to make and bottle a few batches. We're on a budget, though."

"Well, then, why don't you give me the equipment list, and I'll get a total for you on that while you two look around, figure out what you're planning to brew. You going with grains or extracts?" Jimmy pulls a box from a stack of starter kits, sets it near the counter, and starts a price list.

Chris wanders away while Alaric goes over the details. Alaric's attention keeps sliding to where Chris is in the back of the store, balanced on his crutches, wavering slightly back and forth as he stands. Once Jimmy decides that he's got what he needs from Alaric, at least for now, Alaric heads over to where Chris is standing in front of a rack filled with cans of fruit.

"Wine," Alaric says. "My father makes it, sometimes, but he grows his own grapes. I don't think it's any good. I'd rather drink our beer."

"There are some beers with fruit in them. Did your brother make any of those?" Chris gestures with one crutch. "I've had a peach beer, and a cherry wheat. And there's this beer that always tastes like grapefruit, but I don't think it's actually got any in it."

"Orson didn't really want fruity beers; at least, he didn't tell me about any. Although there's the pumpkin ale that Corbin likes." Alaric closes his eyes, mentally scrolls through his emails to try to remember. "Orson made a fall spice one, it was supposed to taste like caramel apples. But there wasn't any apple in it, just some extracts."

Chris nods, expression thoughtful. "Corbin said that we're having a wake for Orson, doing this."

"I guess. In a way." Alaric shifts his weight, and somehow Chris ends up closer to him. Chris leans, and his shoulder presses against Alaric's, warm and solid. "Orson and I had a complicated relationship. We were brothers, but we were different. This…" Alaric gestures at a nearby wall of different bottle options. "This was something we were talking about. Something we were both interested in, both going to do. He wasn't looking at me like I was a problem. We both just wanted good beer."

"I can't imagine losing one of my brothers." Chris shakes his head. "We're all pretty damned close."

"We weren't. Not like you mean." It's easy to admit their faults because the cracks had always been there, although maybe it's harder now than it used to be. Harder because it's never going to change. "Orson knew I was broken, and I was supposed to be his second. When he was the head of our Clan. He always knew what he wanted to do, how he wanted to change things, and I didn't. Sometimes he was patient with me, sometimes he wasn't. He and Drea were a lot more alike."

"You don't seem like you're much like Corbin, and you're close with him," Chris says, and Alaric smiles ruefully.

"We've been close since we were born. Corbin doesn't treat me like I'm wrong," Alaric says. "He's just Corbin, and I'm just Alaric. He's always been in my corner even when other people weren't. And I'll be in his. He's my right hand. No matter what I do in the community, I know Corbin will be with me." He doesn't know how to explain that friendship, how it's always just been that way. Alaric grew apart from some people, but never Corbin, even though there's distance between them while they're at different schools. "Even if my father likes him better. Corbin can't do anything wrong in his eyes." A small smile tilts Alaric's mouth. "We used that sometimes."

"Oh?" Chris nudges him with his elbow.

Alaric shrugs. "When we were younger. We'd do something my father wouldn't approve of, and as soon as Corbin said it was his idea, everything turned out fine. He had to speak up, or else I'd take the blame. I was always to blame."

"I don't understand your family," Chris says quietly. "Why would they work so hard to alienate you, and then your father brings you back in now?"

Alaric glances sideways at him. "Because he doesn't have anyone else. I honestly think that my father always hoped I'd leave, except now he needs to find a way to keep me there. It's not *me* he really wants, Chris. It's the son he doesn't have."

The chime on the door rings out, and Chris shifts slightly, straightening up to lean more heavily on his crutches. Alaric catches the sweet, sharp scent of curiosity as Corbin comes in, finds them, and joins them.

Corbin slings one arm around Alaric's waist, pats his chest with his other hand. "Are we done buying out the store or are you still making decisions? Because you're staring at wine making equipment and a shit-ton of bottles, and I'm not sure if that's going to help you."

Alaric shakes Corbin off, laughing as he untangles himself. "Should I ask what you did with my sister?"

"I think she's adding things to your order." Corbin turns Alaric to look toward where Drea has a box on the counter, some kind of kit that Alaric can't read from here. "If you want any control over what you're going to make, you might want to get involved."

Alaric glances at Drea, then back to Chris. "Pick out some bottles," he suggests to Chris. "Decide whether you want the twelve-ounce ones that we have to cap, or the larger ones that have their own reusable caps. Then make this asshole carry the boxes for you. He's slight but strong, and he has two working legs. Make him work." Alaric lightly punches Corbin's shoulder and walks away.

Alaric calls out to Jimmy as he goes, looking up the two recipes he's decided on to start. Drea's already paying for the kit she has on the counter, a prepared set of extracts for a simple lager. Alaric lists out ingredients for two more brews: one made with extracts and one from grains that he asks Jimmy to crack. He ends up adding another set of base equipment to the list as well, once he checks the total so far, along with a bottle capper and a few bags of caps. Just in case they need them.

And he sits and chats with Drea while Jimmy gets things together, very carefully not trying to listen in on Chris and Corbin. Because he knows it really doesn't take that long to decide on which type of bottle to choose. At least he doesn't smell any anger, and there's no shouting. As long as his best friend and his team captain don't start fighting, that's the best Alaric can hope for at the moment.

28

"So, THIS IS a new thing." Corbin sits on the lowest branch of a maple tree, his back against the trunk and bare feet propped on the branch. Alaric's working through his form below the tree; Corbin picks off a yellow leaf and drops it on his head. "It doesn't look like much fun."

Alaric huffs, focusing on what he's doing, trying to remember the right moves in the right sequence. He exhales on every move, a small sound as he punches, steps, kicks. When he reaches the end, he yells his kihap and exhales slowly. He circles back to ready position, facing the tree as he had when he started, then finally relaxes. "It's a form, Corbin. It's for training, not fighting."

"It looks boring." Corbin crawls along the branch, ends up lying on his stomach, one hand reaching down. "That's what you're doing for control? I thought you said you were fighting. Not that you said much. You never text me."

"You could text me, too," Alaric points out. "You talk to Drea."

"She talks back." Another leaf floats down. "Before we left for school, I could get around that tough-guy won't-communicate thing you have going on by pinning you down until you talked to me. Can't do that when I'm at VIT and you're at PHU."

"You picked VIT." Alaric considers the tree, the roughness of the bark. He drops into a stance and throws a careful roundhouse, not striking with any speed or power. Unsurprisingly, it hurts, scraping across the top of his foot. He makes a face and steps back.

"Are you holding that against me?"

Alaric glances up. "I don't hold it against you. I'm just pointing out that you made the choice to go to VIT instead of PHU. So don't get pissed off at

184

me that you can't come into my room any time you want and bother me."

"I'm not pissed off. I'm frustrated." Corbin swings down from the branch, drops lightly in front of Alaric. "I feel like you're shutting me out. The first time I heard about the bear was on the news. You didn't tell me anything until after I texted you because I'd seen the report. Your roommate's a Mage and you barely tell me about it. Drea told me you're pledging a fraternity, not you. And then there's Thorne."

Alaric presses his lips together and kicks the tree trunk again, harder this time. He grunts at the pain. "Thorne's none of your business."

"You might not want to destroy your foot right before you have to drive," Corbin points out dryly. "Isn't this supposed to be a productive channel for your inner beast? Breaking bones is not productive."

"I'm not going to break anything." Alaric changes his stance, gives himself more room, and does a side kick this time, liking the way it feels on the bottom of his foot. More force, less pain. Leaves shake down around them. "And I'm not talking about my sex life with you."

"Which implies that you have one." Corbin grins. "Good for you."

Alaric gives him a dark look. "Why the fuck do you care, anyway? It's not like you were interested in me."

"Ah, that." Corbin circles around Alaric, leans against the tree, and blocks him from attacking it again. "I've been wondering—is that why you're avoiding me? Did I fuck up our entire friendship because I wasn't interested in you?"

Alaric's jaw goes tight. He closes his eyes, inhales roughly. "No," he says curtly. "I couldn't give a fuck who you're interested in."

"When you say it like that, I can't figure out if I should be relieved or insulted." Corbin slides down to sit on the ground, pats the space next to him. The trunk is wide enough that Alaric can sit and lean back against it as well, shoulder to shoulder with Corbin.

"I don't want to talk about it with anyone," Alaric mutters. "I don't know how to talk about it. It's personal."

"So your boyfriend's a Mage," Corbin says idly. "After everything that's happened with Orson, is that going to change?"

"He's not my boyfriend, and I don't think Rory and Thorne can stop being Mages," Alaric says dryly. "Corbin, it's just sex. And I'm pretty sure you don't need or want the details about me and some guy, so leave it. If you come to PHU to visit, you'll meet Thorne. He'll flirt with you, you'll say you're straight, he'll probably say it's a pity, and you'll both move on. That's what he's like."

Corbin tilts his head back, and Alaric echoes the motion, looks up through the canopy of half-changed maple leaves, a mix of gold and green above them.

"You know, it's weird, isn't it?" Corbin says slowly. "That we know different people now, I mean. That there are these people who are important in your life, and I don't know them. And I have these people in my life at VIT, and you have no idea who they are."

Alaric grunts, twitching at the idea that there are people that Corbin counts as friends that he doesn't know. "Fine. Talk. Tell me about your people."

Corbin looks over, rolls his eyes. "I'll talk about mine if you talk about yours." He ends up looking into the tree again. "I probably know Mages. I don't know. VIT is Talent-friendly, but we don't talk about it much. Not everyone is out in the open. It's not as common as at PHU, and everyone just lives and lets live. Unless you're in sports, because then it's on the web page and everyone knows. Well, and the girl who flies. She builds sets at the theater, and she doesn't need a ladder, which is handy."

"The theater." Alaric pokes at the opening Corbin leaves for him, feels Corbin shrug in response.

"I've been building sets for the fall show. I like building." Corbin raises his hands, and Alaric can see the callouses that have always been there.

"It's why you picked civil engineering," Alaric replies, because he's always known that. Corbin knew where he was going, knew what the plan was. Alaric just followed along until he realized that maybe it was the wrong direction for him. And that's why he's still undeclared. "So, theater?"

"I'm not going to act. Couldn't get up on stage in front of everyone."

Alaric snorts. "Bet you could."

Corbin nudges him with an elbow. "Maybe, but I don't want to. I want to do the behind-the-scenes stuff. I'm having fun, and I like the people. It's like finding a family. Which is nice, because the rest of the world isn't like Clan, and I miss you guys."

"More people are than you think," Alaric says before he thinks better of it. "Drea's got her sorority. I've got OPT and the team and my friends." He doesn't mention the way Rory's climbed into his bed twice, after Alaric's had nightmares.

"There's this girl, Karen," Corbin says. "Not the one who flies. One of the actresses. A sophomore, always wears black. She has this presence, like the kind of woman that when she walks in a room, everyone turns to look. She speaks, everyone listens." A small smile tilts one corner of Corbin's mouth as he leans his head back again. "She gets shit done, and she seems like she'd be all sharp edges, but she's actually the queen of the puppy pile. Her words for it. She'll walk in the room and be like *break time for anyone ready for a puppy pile* and then she'll go flop on the cushions in the corner. Some of us join her, and it's like Clan only most of them are human. No expectations. It's good. Grounding."

"We're not the only ones who find comfort in touch," Alaric mutters. "We just do it more instinctively."

"Mm." Corbin huffs a sigh, and Alaric looks over at him. "What?"

"You expect me to talk about my sex life, but you're not telling me about you," Alaric points out. "So who is she?"

Corbin laughs, small and tight. He licks his lips, and Alaric can hear the lie in his heart, smell it in his scent. "There isn't anyone."

Alaric lets him have the lie, lets him get away without elaborating. "If there ever is, you know you can tell me," he says, and Corbin makes a small noise of assent.

Alaric closes his eyes, listens to the sound of Corbin's breath, relaxes into the familiarity of it. He knows that there are things that still need to be done, that they need to get on the road as soon as Drea's done whatever she went to do, but he's not ready to move yet. Not when he can have this one moment of feeling like he's truly come home.

"This is how it is now," Corbin says quietly. "Going different directions, not quite coming back the same way we were when we left. But we'll be back eventually, right? We're coming home someday."

There isn't a choice anymore, not for Alaric. He grunts softly, feels the way Corbin relaxes against him for a moment. Then Corbin jumps up, tugs Alaric to face him. Corbin grins, places his palms against Alaric's cheeks, and leans in, smacking him loudly on the lips. "You are still my best friend," Corbin says firmly. "My best friend, and my brother, and I am only a short distance away in Valiant. We should get together. Don't be a stranger."

"You're an asshole," Alaric says, and Corbin squishes his cheeks giving him one more loud, smacking kiss.

"I love you too." Corbin pushes himself to his feet, pauses when he's standing. "I think Chris was looking for you, but he's gone back inside. You done getting your head back together?"

"I'll be ready when Drea's ready, if you want to let her know." Alaric makes no move to get up, fishing his phone out of his pocket instead.

"Tell her yourself."

Alaric shows the phone. "I've got one more thing to do, then I will. Drea can come get me if they're in a hurry."

He waits until Corbin walks away before he sends a text to Rory. *Do you sometimes wonder if you've changed, or if someone else has?*

The response is surprisingly quick. *Not really, no. But I don't have a lot of close friends, either, other than my brother and the band. And for all that Thorne seems like he's really erratic, he's actually pretty predictable.*

Alaric can see that. The more he gets to know Thorne, the more he understands him and relies on that predictability. *I'm not close to very many people either. I don't like that my best friend feels different. That I feel different. He still smells the same, breathes the same. But we're not what we were.*

People change. It's a short reply, and Alaric frowns at the phone in his hand, because of course people change. But it's not *helpful.*

My father doesn't, he types in return. *Never thought Corbin and I would. Not like this. It's weird.*

Give it time, Rory sends back. *You'll change, he'll change, but if you're friends, you'll still be friends after it's done. Thorne and I were weird for a while when he went away, but he's still him and I'm still me, and we're still brothers. And we're still just as close as we were before he left for school. So give it time.*

Yeah. Alaric sends back his agreement in one word, then shoves his phone in his pocket and pushes to his feet. The door opens, and Drea calls his name, so he raises one hand to silently say that he's coming.

It's time to get back to PHU.

29

IT'S BEEN TEN minutes since they left Midway, and Drea is somehow already asleep in the back seat. Chris carefully undoes the flap of the manilla envelope from the police station, slides the papers out. "That was much easier than I expected."

"She said I looked like a sad puppy," Alaric grumbles. "Don't think she realized I could hear her talking to the woman down in records."

"If the case hadn't been labeled 'closed' thanks to your dad, it would've been a lot harder, I think. She felt bad for you, and we took advantage of it. For a good reason." Chris flips through the papers, stopping on one which shows the symbol that was found. Alaric tries not to think about what that symbol is on when he sees the picture out of the corner of his eye.

Chris sets the paper on his lap, takes out his phone, and snaps a picture. "I'm sending this to Thorne, telling him to send it to Rory. They'll get it to Pawel."

Alaric gestures, and Chris obligingly turns back to the first page of the packet. "What else does it say?" Alaric doesn't want the details, doesn't want to think about the gruesome facts of his brother's death. But he needs to know more, needs to see some way toward figuring this out before his father takes it into his own hands.

"According to their neighbors, all three who died were living there even though only Orson and Salvatore were on the lease." Chris pauses to read, and Alaric wants to tell him to hurry up. "There are several neighbor witness accounts, and I'm not reading them all carefully right now." Chris flips past the pages. "The girl was Dionne LaRoche, and she was Emergent. Salvatore was a Lineage Mage—his parents came to claim the body. Dionne's body disappeared before her family could get there."

"What?" Alaric's fingers go tight on the steering wheel. He hears something crunch, and Chris reaches over, wraps his fingers around Alaric's wrist until Alaric looses his grip.

"Don't break my car," Chris says. "I won't be able to replace it if you break it, and I can't afford to fix it, either."

"What do you mean 'her body disappeared'?" Alaric clarifies. He focuses on the road in front of him, on keeping his grip loose and relaxed. "She's not dead?"

Chris flips to the last page. "No, she's dead. According to this account, mid-autopsy her body started vibrating, and it literally shook to dust. Her Talent was that she was fast, and the theory is that after her death, whatever tethered her atoms to each other fell apart, and she vibrated into nothingness."

"Emergent Talents are different." Alaric knows how to classify the traditional Lineage Talents. He knows how to handle a Healer or a Mage. But this is something else, something that might affect things in ways he doesn't understand. "So if there was a ritual, it was all the guy. But her Talent could've affected it."

"Salvatore Pagliazzi," Chris confirms. "Orson's official roommate. Apparently Dionne was there all the time. Some neighbors thought she was dating Orson, others thought that she was dating Salvatore."

"Don't think it really matters. She was there; she had some influence on it." Alaric didn't know Dionne or Salvatore, and he wishes he had. He wishes he'd heard something from Orson about these roommates so he'd have context. "Like I said, we weren't close. Don't think he talked to Drea about his life, either, so either he wasn't involved with her or he didn't want it getting back to our father."

"Having met your father, I wouldn't be surprised by that," Chris says dryly. "Your family and community aren't exactly approving of cross-Talent friendships. Or romances."

Alaric's still trying to reconcile what Corbin said about his friends at VIT with the way he reacted to Chris's presence in the community. "I think it depends on who you talk to. And context." His voice is low.

Chris glances over. "Your father hated me. And your best friend resented me. I think. I'm still not sure."

"Corbin doesn't hate you." Alaric presses his lips together. "He's trying to protect me. Thinks if I don't bring home people that make matters worse, my father might like me. I don't think it works like that." He looks at the mirror, where he can see Drea sleeping peacefully in the back. "And it's not that my father doesn't like me. He loves me, I guess. He'd kill for me, if he had to. Like he would for Orson, which is what worries me. But he doesn't approve of me."

"Mind if I ask a personal question?" Chris is looking out the front, his expression quiet.

"Probably, but go ahead." Alaric echoes the same posture, not wanting to lose his focus while driving.

"Was there ever anything more between you and Corbin? I saw the two of you—" Chris cuts off before he finishes, and Alaric frowns, trying to figure out what he meant to say.

It hits him, then, what Corbin had said while they were talking outside. *I think Chris was looking for you.* "That wasn't what it looked like. Never was." Alaric rubs at his eyes. "It was Corbin being Corbin. A friend thing. Not an actual kiss." He laughs a little. "See, I tried. Once. I figured that we already had this thing. We were already close, and he's fucking attractive—you have to see that, right? So during the summer I kissed him. And it was a bad idea, because Corbin's about as straight as it gets."

"Which is why he kissed you now?" Chris sounds confused, and Alaric can't blame him.

"It's complicated."

"Try me."

Alaric tries. "So there's this thing with me, Drea, and Corbin from when we were kids. It started when we were maybe ten or eleven. Orson had a girlfriend, and we kept stumbling into the places where they went to make out. So we made fun of him, because that's what kids do. Corbin started it. One of us would hold the other's face, lean in real slow, and then do this noisy, smacking kiss. Obnoxious. Pissed Orson off, and he got better at hiding. But it became a thing for us. And Corbin still does it, just because we're friends."

"But that's not what you did over the summer," Chris says, and it isn't really a question.

Alaric shakes his head. "That's not what I did over the summer. We've been best friends since we were born. Grew up together, spent half our time in the same places, sometimes in the same rooms or beds. We are Clan and family, and he's almost as much a part of me as Drea is. And like I said, he's attractive, and I like guys, and I figured that if I like Corbin, it'd be okay. We already had a relationship, so I didn't need to worry about fucking it up. It would be easy, and we'd kiss and do whatever else happened after that, and life would go on. Best friends with sex. So I tried kissing him without it being a joke, and it didn't work."

"I'm sorry."

Alaric laughs at that. "Don't be. I'm not hurt. I was pretty fucked up about it when I thought I'd screwed up our friendship, and I guess Corbin's been thinking that too. But we're good. We're still friends. Still brothers."

"So you never really wanted to be more than friends?"

Alaric looks over at Chris. "Why do you care?"

"I'm trying to figure out why he's so against me," Chris says plainly. "But fine, we can go with overprotective."

Alaric huffs and tries to figure out where he got the explanation wrong. "No, I never wanted to be more than friends. I figured we already *were* friends, so sex wouldn't fuck with that. I wouldn't have to figure out dating and whatever else it is two guys are supposed to do that isn't sex."

"And that's why you like Thorne." Chris sounds like he's finally got it. "You're aromantic."

"I'm what?" Alaric jerks on the steering wheel, hears another creak and carefully loosens his grip.

"Aromantic," Chris repeats. "Sex and romantic interest have nothing to do with each other. Most people do both at the same time, but some people have no interest in one or the other. Or very little interest. I suppose since there are demisexual people, there could be demiromantic people."

Alaric opens his mouth, closes it again, and shakes his head. It's all words to him, even if the definition resonates.

Chris's voice lowers. "It might be something you want to read about when we get back. It might make you feel more comfortable about not wanting a relationship."

"It's not about not wanting one. Not exactly." Alaric's failing at explaining, and he huffs, shaking his head. "I'll read about it," he concedes. It's something to think about, anyway. "Thanks."

Chris nods, crosses his arms, and leans the seat back another notch as he closes his eyes. They're only twenty minutes from PHU, but it looks like Chris is getting ready for a nap. Alaric shifts his gaze back to the road, and it's a surprise when Chris's voice comes, soft and low.

"You don't have to try so hard, Alaric," Chris murmurs. "Just be you."

It's all well and good for Chris to say that. The problem is, most days, Alaric isn't sure what's him and what's expectations.

He has no idea how to just be himself.

Excerpt from *When Magic Entered the World: Interviews With Lineage Talent*, by Pawel Szczek, © 2009

I hear you've been going around talking to all sorts of Lineage Talent, and I bet I'm the oldest person you've spoken to. One hundred and fifty-seven years old, and proud of every damned one of them. Ah, no, don't make that face; I'm telling the truth. Just because you haven't seen a thing before is no reason to disbelieve.

I was four years old when my family joined a wagon train west. All Lineage families in the train. Five Mage, five Clan, and yes, I see you there with the questions in your eyes. Clan and Mages don't get along often, but we've had our times when we've followed paths in the same direction. The East Coast was filling up, so we sought space of our own. We agreed to work together, to make our homesteads near each other and to protect each other along the way. It took all of us to safely ford the Mississippi; can't even think how the non-magical folk did it. But we found our space, and we settled here in Kansas, and this is where I grew up.

It wasn't easy. We weren't the only ones here.

I don't mean the indigenous folk. We lived with them in peace as best we could; what other settlers did to them was horrible. We didn't want to take their land, only share spaces. We didn't mind sharing what we had with others. We respected them. They had their ways, and we had ours, and the Clan had theirs. We found ways to fit in around each other.

Other settlers were another story, but they stuck to themselves, made settlements that curled in on themselves. They didn't trust the open land and they didn't trust us, so we stayed far from them.

I don't mean them.

I mean the Deathstalkers.

Everyone says they're a legend, but I know they're real. They exist, and they were certainly in Kansas in the 1800s. We settled in 1856. I remember seeing the shadows out of the corner of my eyes. I remember talking to other Talented folks and the members of the nearby Cheyenne folk, and they saw them too.

I don't mean the paingivers—Healers who give pain as easily as they take it. And I don't mean the Dreamwalkers, either. One Emerged in the township fifty miles south of us, and they came to us and the Cheyenne, begging us to take her and her nightmares. We did, of course.

But she wasn't a Deathstalker.

Look hard enough, you'll find the legends. Talent who live in the darkness and slip from shadow to shadow to steal souls in the night. They're hungry for our kind, thirsty for the power our souls give them. They can bide a time on humans, but they need Talent to survive.

Strife serves them, too, and the plains were a land of great strife. They fed on the pain of war.

I married when I was seventeen and bore my first child when I was nineteen. I bore a dozen babes, and of them I lost three to the shadows. Not long after my third child—my first daughter—was born, I went to look in on my three young ones at night. I had left them with a candle burning nearby, and it guttered in the corner, nearly out. My eldest lay on the bed, his thumb tucked in his mouth, and his brother lay in the trundle below. My infant was in the cradle, and it rocked gently, creaking in the corner farthest from the candle. The creaking stopped as I walked in, and a breeze nearly blew the candle out. I turned to look, worried that my daughter was restless, and I saw the face in the shadows.

I stared at it, and it stared back at me. I looked down and saw a shadowy hand on my daughter's chest, saw the moment that the fingers curled and her soul was sucked free.

I screamed for my husband, but there was nothing we could do, nothing that could save her. We lit every candle we had, made the room bright as if the sun were shining, but our daughter was already gone.

I grieved, but life went on. I kept light in our house constantly, but the shadows still crept in and stole two more children from me. I was lucky; there were some houses where entire families died, simply gone in the night. The humans blamed everything from witchcraft to deviltry; they had no idea what stalked their town.

When I was thirty-five, the deaths ended. The Deathstalkers moved on, and we found our own form of peace.

That was well over a hundred years ago, and yet here I am. My great-granddaughter Susie—don't ask how many "greats" that actually is, young man, I think I'm entitled to lose track of the years after all this time—she often wonders what keeps me alive. I've watched her mother die, and her mother's mother before that. I've seen every one of my children pass on from old age. I'm thankful that my family line helps me, keeps me with them.

I know why I'm here, young Mage.

From the age of nineteen to the age of thirty-five, I had a dozen children. I lost my third, my seventh, and my eighth. The last two children I bore were twins, tiny little things, and I knew the Deathstalkers would come. I sat in that room and I waited for them, candle burning, night after night. And when they came, I looked them in the eye and told them that they couldn't have my twins.

I felt a cold touch against my forehead as a shadow fell across my eyes. When I could see again, my twins were safe and the shadows were gone.

And so were the Deathstalkers.

I wonder sometimes if they marked me that night, if Death won't come for me. I wonder if I'll see the end of this world, if I'll still be standing waiting for Death because I once told it no.

My great-granddaughter says it could never be that simple.

I'm one hundred and fifty-seven years old. I've had a lot of time to think about how I got here. I don't have any better complicated ideas, so the simplest one might be the truth.

ANGER MANAGEMENT

30

WHERE ARE YOU?

Alaric picks up his phone, thumbs it open so he can respond to Rory's text. He's sitting on the floor of the waiting room, his laptop open on the coffee table, books spread out beside it. He's been staring at the same problem for his Intro to Engineering class for the last twenty minutes, and it doesn't make any more sense now than it did when he started.

Chris's MRI. Dax had class. I'm just doing homework. Figured I'd take him. Hate engineering right now.

I would hate engineering all the time, Rory replies. *Why do you do it if you hate it?*

Alaric's jaw clenches. He can hear his father's voice in his head, same way he's heard it ever since the declaration Saturday. *Have to*, he texts back. *Clan.*

There's silence for a long time. Long enough that Alaric picks up his book again, starts poking at the homework problem. He finally makes headway, manages to get through the first of the set and started on the second. It's been thirty minutes since they wheeled Chris away, and Alaric's starting to wonder how long this is going to take.

His phone chimes, and he glances over, figuring Rory's finally gotten around to responding.

Wednesday's going to be the day. Sorry for the short notice.

Professor Szczek. Alaric picks up the phone, his hand shaking. *The day for...the video?*

And discussion, yes. I meant to talk to you after class, but another student claimed my attention, and you were gone by the time we were done. Wednesday's current events and ethics discussion will use the game as an example.

Alaric supposes he should have guessed based on the reading for home-work. He'd noticed that the first of the selected readings from *The Ethics of Talent* was online for this class, but he hadn't paid attention to what it was about.

Fuck.

If you need to miss the class on Wednesday, it won't be marked against you.

Alaric stares at the message on his phone, growls softly because he won't take the easy way out. It's just a shit week to deal with this. He pinches the bridge of his nose, breathes in for a count of five and out for a count of ten.

I'll be fine, he finally texts back, then turns the phone to silent and flips it over so he can't see the screen. He buries himself in his homework, forcing himself through the remaining problems. He writes equations in careful script, checks them twice to make sure they're correct. He might hate his class, but it distracts him at least, keeps his mind from spinning around from Orson to Szczek's class and back to Orson again. The problem is, twenty minutes later when the work is complete, he's still sitting in the waiting room and there's no sign of Chris.

He shoves his books back into his bag and leaves it lying there on the chair. He heads to the window, ignores the sensation that everyone in the waiting room is staring at him, listening to his conversation.

The woman behind the plexiglass looks up with a small, tired smile. "Yes?"

Alaric clears his throat. "My friend went back for an MRI about an hour ago. Thought it was going to be quick, but he's…" He ends with a shrug, because it's obvious he's not back. He glances at the clock, frowns. "We're missing practice."

"The big Black guy with the knee?" she asks easily. "He's still waiting. We had an accident come in, and everyone from radiology's been tied up unex-pectedly. It might be another hour at least." When Alaric doesn't move, she nods at the seats. "Might as well get comfortable. There's a coffee station in the next room over, free for folks who are waiting."

Alaric doesn't want coffee. He doesn't want anything that's going to add to the sensation of being trapped in this underground office, waiting for something that was never supposed to take this long. Chris had talked about previous MRIs, getting in, getting out, getting it over with. They'd both figured that Alaric would be on time for practice, and it's obvious now that that's not going to happen.

He slumps back in his seat, pulls out his phone again. There are notifications, but he ignores them in favor of starting a new conversation with the coaches to let them know where he is, then another one with Dax that just says *you owe me*.

"Do you play for Pine Hills?" The elderly lady sitting two chairs down leans toward him, her voice low and kind. "My son went there years ago, still goes to see the team play if he's in town and it's a home game. He loves to watch football. He tried to get them to start a hockey team once."

"Everyone tries to get them to start up a hockey team," Alaric rumbles softly. He glances over at her, wary of the unexpected intrusion. "Yeah. Quarterback. Our starter got injured last game." He jerks his head at the door.

She nods understandingly. "My son was a running back. Long time ago, though, before the Blended league. He supports it."

"So do I." It's the understatement of the century, but Alaric says it with a straight face.

She laughs softly. "Well, of course you do. It's the same for him. He's a doctor now, you see. Seemed like the best way to use his Talent. Have to remind him sometimes that we're not miracle workers, just a bit different. Still, he tries. There's no miracle cure for cancer, not even our hands."

He wonders if it's obvious—*why* it's obvious—to her that he's Clan, or at least some kind of Talent. He nods at her words, not sure how to respond, and picks up his phone again as if it's vibrated. He shows it to her—there are still two unread notifications in his messages—and she smiles slightly.

"I understand. I hope your friend is well."

As she sits back in her seat and ignores him, it occurs to Alaric that he never asked why she was here. That the polite thing to do would be to ask who she was waiting for and then wish her luck or wish wellbeing for them.

Alaric's never been good at figuring out the polite thing to say before it's too late. He mutters under his breath, tamps down on the irritation at himself, and looks at the phone.

Pawel's message is short—*Let me know if anything changes*—and Alaric chooses to ignore it.

Rory's finally responded. *Just looked at our Magical Studies homework on LMS. He's got a reading online, and it's talking about the ethics of being a Talent in a field working with the non-Talented. And it specifically references the Blended leagues. Does that mean Wednesday we'll be watching the video from the game?*

Alaric stares at the phone, his fingers light against the screen. He starts several messages, then erases them before he hits "Send." After he's done that three or four times, another message comes through from Rory: *You okay?*

Alaric huffs a sigh. *Yeah, I'm okay. And yeah, we're watching the video and discussing it with the reading. It'll be fine. It's not like the whole campus doesn't already know it was me.*

He's thankful about how little fallout there has been. The team's been nothing but supportive. A few people said something to him—that that's why Clan shouldn't be allowed in Blended leagues—but not many.

Overall, he's gotten off easy. Maybe this is going to be his punishment.

He glances at the clock. It's been ninety minutes now, and there's still no sign of Chris. He glances back at the window again. He shouldn't go ask again this soon, but it's tempting. The window slides open as he stares at it, and the woman behind waves at him, then crooks her finger to get his attention.

He sets down his phone carefully, gets up to walk over.

"Your friend's heading in shortly," she says quietly. "Just finishing up one more ahead of him, then it's his turn. Figure on another thirty minutes or so for that, then another thirty for the radiologist to get a look at the results and have a consult. He'll be back out here not long after unless something shows that means he needs either a closer look or some other kind of treatment."

Alaric nods once. "Thanks."

He sinks back into his seat and tugs out his laptop. He connects to the guest Wi-Fi in the hospital, then logs into the LMS system back on campus. He looks through the updates for magical studies and decides that he can read it later. He doesn't want to be stuck here when he's reading something that he knows is going to feel like it's pointing fingers at him.

Instead, he switches over to his freshman lit class. He and Drea picked one focusing specifically on women writers of the 20th century. Drea loves it, and Alaric doesn't hate it; he's not fond of the writing assignments. They have two a week at least, and he might as well see if he can get this one finished, looking at themes in Atwood's *The Handmaid's Tale*, before Chris comes back. He glances over the requirements for the essay, then digs out his copy of the book. The red tabs are ones he placed, and the blue ones are from Drea. They exchange ideas by marking passages in each others' books, suggestions of passages to reread. He settles in to do just that, and slowly starts outlining, then filling in, his essay.

He finishes a draft and shares the document with Drea. They exchange papers to proofread and edit, the same way they've handled their writing assignments since seventh grade. It's as done as it'll get for now.

The only thing he has left is the reading for magical studies. He goes back to it on LMS, takes a look at the heading, then closes it again. He shuts the laptop down entirely, watches as it turns off instead of going to sleep. It feels more final than just walking away from the assignment, and he's not sure he'll pick it up again to read before Wednesday. He should, he knows, so he can argue his side of things from a logical, ethical viewpoint.

Or he could stay quiet. Might be safest. He doesn't need the class to get the opportunity to see the bear in person.

Something pricks at the edge of his hearing, and he looks up, nostrils flaring. The scent is tired, pained, pleased, and it's getting closer. He hears the thud of Chris's heart, ramped up from exertion, and beneath that, the steady *click-thud* of his gait on crutches.

Alaric shoves his laptop into his bag and is on his feet, ready to go, before the door opens.

"Are you sure you don't want the chair?" the nurse offers as Chris passes by him. Chris turns, waves.

"It's not my first time on crutches, and the brace makes it easier. I really don't want the chair," Chris says dryly. "I really hate that chair."

"Makes you feel helpless," Alaric says, and Chris turns to grin at him.

"Exactly." Chris knocks against the heavy brace that wraps his leg from mid-thigh to mid-calf. "And with this, I'm not entirely helpless anymore, and I want to enjoy it."

Alaric raises an eyebrow. "You're still not driving."

"I'm still not driving," Chris agrees. He swings forward a couple of steps, waits for Alaric to join him. "But I'm allowed to put some weight on it, so I can brace myself. And the good news is that it's only a sprain."

Alaric gets the door, waits for Chris to make it through before closing it again. It's slow going down the hall, but Alaric paces himself, shortens his stride to match the swing of the crutches as they head for the elevator.

"So no surgery," Alaric says quietly.

"No surgery," Chris confirms. "I'm out for four weeks minimum, and I start PT in two weeks. They'll evaluate, tell me if I'm ready to start practice and play again once I hit the four-week point or if I need more physical therapy." There's a tight set to Chris's jaw. "I'll be fine by then. I'm good at PT."

"Don't overdo it," Alaric tells him, and he catches the rush of irritation in Chris's scent.

"That's the whole point of being good at PT." Chris swings along faster, using the crutches to make longer strides. He wobbles when he gets to the elevator, punches the button. "You push just hard enough, but not so hard that you re-injure yourself. You do everything they say: every stretch, every exercise, all at the times they tell you to. You have to be perfect. That's the only thing that gets you back on the field."

The elevator doors open, and Chris gets himself in, leans against the wall inside. He breathes in deep, and Alaric tastes pain thick in the air.

"Sorry," Chris mutters. "It was a long wait, and it hurts like fuck right now. I've got a prescription for some good painkillers, if you don't mind swinging by the pharmacy. I hate that I have to take them, but I know it'll help. Sorry to keep asking you to do things. We missed practice."

"Yeah, well, I got my homework done." Alaric shrugs. He stands there with his arms crossed, hands tucked back against himself. He wishes he were a Healer, so he could reach out and take the pain away with a touch. As it is, he feels useless.

"Come to dinner at the house tonight," Chris suggests. "We'll feed you." When Alaric hesitates, Chris looks away. "You can invite Rory, if you want. Unless you've got plans with someone else."

"I don't have plans. I'm supposed to be doing the homework I already finished." He knows what Rory would say to the idea of dinner at OPT. "We'll go get dinner. Get you settled."

Chris looks over at him, gaze dropping to take in the tight stance. "You okay?"

Alaric's jaw twitches. "No. Why?"

"Did something else happen?"

The elevator stops, and someone puts a hand in front of the door, waits for them to come out and make room for the rolling bed going in. Chris stands in the hall, chooses a direction, and heads that way.

The pause gives Alaric time to think. Time to decide if he feels like unloading on someone else, if he feels like talking about what else is going on in his life. He bites his lip, huffs a sigh. "Just a tough week," he mutters.

It's true. Chris's injury, Orson's death, and now Szczek's class. Alaric's skin itches, feels like if he digs his claws in, it might peel away, and he has no idea what lies beneath. He wants to get out, to run, to fly, to hit things and to be hit in return. He needs something, and he can't say what it is.

He doesn't have words for this; he's not sure that anyone would.

Dinner at the house is going to have to suffice. He doesn't really have anything else to do.

31

DREA WAITS AT the door to the lecture hall before magical studies. She doesn't say a thing, just brackets Alaric on his other side as he and Rory walk into the hall. They head to their usual seats off to one side, and Drea joins them rather than taking her usual place in the front.

Pat and Sera are already there, backpacks, skateboards, and jackets spread out across the row in front of them and the row behind them, creating a buffer zone around their space. Alaric feels heat in his face as he nods to them, words caught in his throat. He follows Rory into the row, slumps down in his seat with Drea on his other side. When he closes his eyes, he inhales the concern of his friends and the comfort of Clan close by. He exhales slowly, brings up the mini-desk, and sets the reading on top of it along with his notebook.

He finally read the material late at night, curled on his bed and leaning against Rory while Rory slept, crashed out in Alaric's space. Alaric read through it twice, then carefully highlighted the points he knew they would discuss. He doesn't intend to say anything, but he knows he should have it in front of him.

He refuses to let anxiety over the particular topic keep him from class.

Pawel walks in, and the lights dim in the room, then flash bright, then dim again. Alaric blinks, and the lights go out, only a thin line around the back of the room staying lit. The students shuffle quickly to their seats and go mostly silent.

"You've all done the reading," Pawel says, "so we're going to start with a video this morning. When we start our discussion, I expect respectful language. Use your sources. Back up your arguments. One of the most important tenets of philosophy is the argument: you cannot make a cohesive case without substantiation. *Because* is not a reason."

He starts the projector, and it hums loudly. Alaric winces, rubs at his ear, and Pawel leans down to adjust dials on the podium until the hum slides into the background.

"This video is from a local event. It will cover the event itself and several instances of press coverage after the event. Please hold all comments until the video is complete—it's about fifteen minutes long. Afterward, raise your hands. This isn't going to be a shouting match." Pawel pauses the video just as the PHU football field shows on the screen. "The topic for discussion revolves around the material you read last night: the ethical implications of mixed Talent and non-Talent groups in a physical activity such as athletics. Do not stray from the topic; you will be marked based on your participation and argument today."

It's strange seeing the game from the outside perspective. As the team comes into focus, Drea nudges Alaric's shoulder, offers a hand. He places his hand on hers, palm to palm, and winds their fingers together. The video isn't a close up; he can't see how Marks is talking to him constantly, can't see the antagonism. But he sees the moment when he changes, when there's suddenly a bear on the field ploughing through Marks and throwing him aside like a stuffed toy. He sees the bear stop yards down the field, sees his own body coalesce back into being, heaving with struggling breath. He sees himself turn, hears the call from the announcers, and the video shifts.

He tunes out the press conferences, lets the sound of Young's voice wash over him without actually taking in the words. He lived through the event; he knows the results. He knows now that Marks is an Empath, and that he used that to rile Alaric on the field. To dig under his skin until the beast burst out.

He knows that Marks had an impact on what happened, but in the end, he knows it was still his own fault. Alaric was the one with no control.

He blinks as the video ends and the lights go back on, sees a sea of hands in the air, waiting. Pawel motions for the hands to be lowered. "I'm sure you all have things to say, but in the interest of at least starting out on point, let's begin with a question: what responsibility does a Talented player have to his teammates and to those on other teams when playing in a Blended league?"

Hands shoot up, including Sera's. Pawel points in her direction, and Alaric feels the weight of heavy gazes turned toward them.

"When in a Blended environment, a Talent is bound to control their ability, particularly when it would affect either those around them or the outcome of whatever they attempt to do," Sera says, her voice dry and bored. "Not every Talent on the team has an effect on the game, but those who do are supposed to not use them during play."

"Good definition," Pawel says. "In the light of that definition, who is at fault here?"

Alaric whines under his breath, slides down in his seat and tries to breathe evenly.

There are too many hands in the air, and Pawel motions for them to lower it again. "Let's make it a poll," Pawel says. "There are four choices: Alaric Herne, Derek Marks, both, or neither. Show of hands for Alaric Herne."

Alaric doesn't choose an option, keeps his arms tightly crossed against his chest once Drea withdraws her hand. Rory and Drea both raise their hands for Marks; Sera raises her hand for both, and Pat for neither. He'd be relieved at how many hands he sees for Marks and both as options, if it weren't for the sheer number who seem to blame Alaric alone.

"Time to defend your position. Folks who chose Alaric, raise your hands again." Pawel gestures at a girl sitting in the middle of the room. "Dana, why?"

"He's dangerous," she says flatly. "Look at what he did to Marks."

"Back it up," Pawel tells her. "Yes, he's dangerous. So am I, as a black belt and as an Emergent Mage. I also know humans who could kick my ass and could probably throw him across the room despite his size; sorry, Alaric. So back it up."

Dana opens her mouth, closes it again, frowning. "He's dangerous because he's out of control. He changed in the middle of the game, so he's the one at fault. He's supposed to maintain control when working in an environment with human competitors."

"And with other Talents," Pawel reminds her. "Marks is Talent, not human. But the question is, does his loss of control put the responsibility on him? Evan, you raised your hand for Marks."

"Marks instigated it." Alaric recognizes Evan as one of the other Clan in the class, and now he catches the glance that Evan throws him. "Alaric's Clan. Anyone knows that we have a temper."

Pawel raises his eyebrows. "Does that excuse the outburst?"

"It means that Marks shouldn't have poked at him. Or anyone," Evan adds as an afterthought. "It's not fair for an Empath to manipulate emotions on the field. They can change the course of the game by injecting unexpected emotion that doesn't belong there. They can make a person inexplicably sad or angry."

"Do you think Derek Marks expected the reaction Alaric had?" Pawel asks. "Parvati?"

"I think he thought he was poking a person and didn't realize he'd get a bear," Parvati says, leaning back in her seat. She tucks her hair behind her ear, gestures with her pen. "They were both at fault. Derek Marks shouldn't have poked. He probably went after others in the game as well—Empaths are subtle, and it could've been going on for a long time without anyone noticing—but Alaric's the only one who reacted. But at the same time, Alaric Herne should have been able to keep control. Someone could've gotten hurt far worse than Marks did. Part of being a Talent anywhere is knowing how your ability affects those around you and being sure not to damage them."

"Do you think every Talent spends all of their time thinking about how they'll impact the world around them, or do you think they spend their time just trying to live their life?" Pawel asks, and Parvati frowns.

"They probably just want to live their life," she says slowly. "But what if they have a dangerous Talent?"

Alaric's skin itches. He flexes his hands, claws tipping his fingers. Rory nudges him, lays a hand on Alaric's forearm, and he feels it all seep away. He closes his eyes and breathes deeply, counting each breath.

"That's one of the things we'll be talking about for the next several sessions," Pawel says. "In the last decade, questions have constantly arisen about the use of Talent in everyday situations. The first Emergence was in the middle of a national gymnastics competition, and the question was raised: was Kenzie as good as she was because she had used Talent prior to that moment, or was that a unique moment? How could we allow Talents to continue competing without invalidating the humans that they compete against or with? How does Talent affect life in the working world? This isn't just about the football field. Imagine an Empath in the government, arguing for new policy, or as a salesperson, convincing you to buy a product. Healers often become EMTs or doctors; is this a good practice? And the military. Think about Talent in the military."

Silence aside from the scratch of pens.

"The world has changed in the last decade, and it's still changing," Pawel says. "We are still trying to figure out how it works, and one of the things that everyone forgets is that Talent has been here all along. When Kenzie Davis teleported to save herself from a fall, that was the first time Talent was televised—nationally and internationally. After that, the number of Emergent Talents increased dramatically, and that thrust the concept of Talent into the public eye. But there have been Mages, Clan, and Healers living among us all this time. They've worked with us, played with us. They've competed with and against us. The difference is, we know now. And there are questions. Rules. And these rules are still being designed as we go forward, as we learn more." He taps the lectern; everyone looks up.

"I will be adding an assignment to LMS this afternoon, due Sunday by midnight. I want you to pick a choice that was *not* your instinctive answer today, and I want you to defend it. Include other known uses of Talent in sports to back up your argument. In addition, think about what could be done to prevent something like this from occurring again, or explain to me why you don't think it needs to be prevented. Think outside the box. Don't treat it as human versus Talent. See if you can explain to me why neither of them would be at fault for this." Pawel clicks off the projector, waves at the door. "It's ten minutes early, but go. We're done. Discuss in your recitation session if you want, but keep it polite. I'm looking forward to your essays."

Alaric closes his eyes again, listens to the squeak of desks being slid back into their storage space, the thud of footsteps on the stairs. He opens his eyes when Drea touches his shoulder. "You okay?" she asks, and he realizes that Pat and Sera are lingering as well, waiting for him.

He stands slowly, and Pat tucks his board under his arm while Sera lets hers dangle from her fingertips. Rory nudges him, and Alaric nods. He licks his lips, nods again to Drea. "Yeah, 'm fine," he says quietly. "Wasn't actually as bad as I thought. Don't know what I'm going to write for the essay." He looks over at Pat. "Why'd you say neither of us was responsible?"

"Your beast is a part of you, right?" Pat asks. "And I'm willing to bet that being an Empath and feeling someone else's emotions is just as instinctive for Marks. He's an asshole—I'm not going to deny that. But neither of you is human, and treating you by human rules is stupid. The problem is, for most of us, we don't really have another way of looking at what you do. It's still Talent versus humans, and maybe that's not what it really needs to be. So Marks is guilty of being an asshole, and you're guilty of getting pissed off. But neither of you is at fault for being Talent. And when it comes down to it, that's what you were being punished for."

"Clan's Clan," Rory says, and Alaric can taste the amusement in the air as he repeats the same thing Alaric always says.

Alaric growls, but there's no heat, and it makes Rory laugh softly.

"It's an interesting way to look at it," Drea says.

"Things are still changing." Pat pushes out of the row and into the aisle, starts up the stairs. Sera swings her board, waves to someone at the top of the stairs, and heads up at a faster pace.

"C'mon, Pat," she calls out, and Pat moves faster to catch up.

"Are you really okay?" Rory asks softly. He holds out one hand in offering, and Alaric nudges it back.

"I'm good." He looks past Rory, raises one hand to Pawel, who's at the lectern, watching them. "It's over and done. I'm going to be fine."

Something's still there, pricking under his skin, but he can ignore it. He's got taekwondo after dinner, and he'll kick himself back to sanity.

"Alaric." Rory reaches out, catches Alaric's wrist before he can get through the door.

They're at the top of the stairs in the lecture hall. Drea's already out in the hall catching up to one of her sorority sisters, and Alaric knows she won't miss him. He turns slowly, looks back down at where Pawel still watches them from the podium, then to Rory. "Yeah?"

"Almost forgot. We should check in with Professor Szczek about the symbol," Rory says quietly, and the reminder is like a knife in the gut.

Alaric inhales roughly, holds the breath as he nods. "Could've thought of it before we were almost gone," he mutters as they both head back down. By the time they get there, Pawel's got his laptop packed up, and he stands with his papers in his arms, waiting for them.

Students trickle in at the top of the hall for the next class. Pawel glances at them, then motions toward a door at the side of the dais. "Let's go out in the hall. Do you have another class to get to?"

Technically, yes, but at this moment Alaric doesn't care so he shakes his head. "I've got time."

They step out into a long hall that Alaric didn't even know existed. "What is this?"

"Access space behind the lecture halls." Pawel sets his things down on what looks like a lab bench across from the door. "I think it also used to be a lab space, but that was long before I was a student here." He pokes the air nozzle on the wall. "These aren't live anymore. I know, because I tested them ten years ago. Just in case you were wondering."

"I wasn't," Alaric says.

"We wanted to know if you'd found anything about the symbol," Rory says. "I know you haven't had much time to look into it, but I figured you'd be more likely to recognize it than I would."

"Not yet." Pawel pulls a notebook out of his bag, opens it to a page where there are several copies of the symbol. "I've been working with it, trying to get a feel for what energy it has, but I can't get anything out of it. If I had to make a guess, I'd say it's not magical at all."

"Impossible, since Orson's dead and they're saying a Mage ritual killed him," Alaric grumbles. "It means something. The question is what? And why would Orson be involved in a ritual?"

"You're friends with a Mage," Pawel reminds him gently. "If you can get past the gut instinct reaction most Clan have to Mages, then so could he."

"It's not gut instinct; there are reasons," Alaric says. "If Orson broke the Treaty, he had good reason."

"I never really..." Rory's voice trails off, and he shrugs. "I've heard about the Treaty, but it was never a big thing for us. We were told to be wary of

Clan because Clan don't like Mages. Thorne's always been fascinated by Clan because we couldn't really get near any. I mean, Thorne pretty much likes everyone, and he figured Clan would be the same for him. But we also knew that there have been Mage villages that have lost people to Clan."

"And vice versa," Alaric says curtly. "The Treaty's against interference. You don't expose us, we don't hurt you. Clan don't like getting involved in magic and ritual. Orson might be friends with a Mage, but he wouldn't do a ritual. The two are different things. Just like I'm not showing up for your Coven."

"But you're willing to look into this." Pawel taps the notebook and the symbol. "What if Orson ran into the symbol, and he thought it was magical, so he got his friend involved looking into it? Something might have spiraled out of control there."

"The girl was fast. She could've accelerated anything that happened. Even accidentally." It all sounds too easy, and it doesn't explain what happened. How could it have gotten out of control before Orson had a chance to fix anything? "Still don't know what the symbol is."

"If it is magical, my grandparents might have something," Rory suggests. "They've got this commune up near Burlington—maybe three hours north of here. And they have a library. It's the biggest library I've ever seen for magic. Stormy's been there once, and she spent the entire time in there, including sleeping on the window seat instead of in the guest room they gave her. If there's even the smallest bit of ritual knowledge about that symbol, they might have a book on it. The catch is finding it. There isn't exactly a searchable online index for it. There isn't even really a card catalog."

"Is there a librarian in their commune?" Pawel has his phone out, is sifting through something on the screen. "If you give me a name, I'd be happy to contact them, see if I can spend some time out there one weekend."

"Or I could set it up, and you could come as my guest." Rory glances at Alaric, says slowly, "You too. I know Clan and Mages don't get along, but you'd be with me. It'd be safe."

Not like visiting Alaric's home; the unspoken statement is clear. He presses his mouth in a thin line, licks his lips. "Yeah. Sure," Alaric says. "When are you thinking?"

"You have the funeral this weekend." Rory scrolls through his calendar. "What about next weekend? It's a holiday on Monday, no classes."

"Two home games," Alaric points out. "We can't leave until after the game on Sunday afternoon." If he's even back on campus by then. He doesn't want to think about how Theobald could change everything, could refuse to let Alaric return to school. He knows that his mother has already intervened, and that she's insisted that he should have his time apart. But Theobald might decide to say differently.

"Fine. We'll go out Sunday afternoon, come back late on Monday. It won't be a lot of time, but we could at least get started." Rory makes a note in his calendar, and a moment later Alaric's and Pawel's phones ping with an invitation. He glances sideways at Alaric, hesitates before asking, "How many people should I tell my grandmother to expect?"

"I don't have a lot of room in my car, and I'm bringing Conor," Pawel says distractedly. "So don't plan on inviting anyone else." He jabs at something on his phone. "Susan Brooks," he announces. "Allison Baker, and Rowan Baker. And um, David Pierson."

Rory lowers his phone. "Rowan's my dad," he says slowly. "Allison's my grandmother. So's Susan."

"I actually spoke to them, seven years ago," Pawel explains. He turns his phone to face Rory, the contact showing a dark-haired woman with round features and a pleasant smile. "I went up to Burlington and toured a commune, and I interviewed four different Mages. One of them grew up there but wasn't living there anymore, and the other three were still working the commune. I remember thinking how much like Clan they were, very different from most of the other Mages I'd spoken to at that point." He goes through his contacts, stops on another one; Alaric recognizes one of the men who dropped Rory off at the start of the year. "Baker. I can see the resemblance now, but it didn't even occur to me when I met Thorne. Your brother looks like him."

Rory has a wry smile. "I read that interview. I wondered if it was Dad, but you don't attribute any of them."

"I promised anonymity in the book," Pawel tells him, setting his phone down on the lab bench. "I was twenty-one, and I was working on my thesis and writing what would become one of the first published works talking to Lineage Talent. Most of them didn't want to be identified. Some of them were younger, like me—at least one was a student here at the time. I've kept in touch with some but not others. I haven't been back to the commune since," he admits. "But I've still got their contact information."

"If you want to set it up, that's fine," Rory says. "I'll email my grand-mothers, let them know that you'll be contacting them, and that Alaric and I will be coming with you."

"Perfect." Pawel picks up the phone, shoves it in his pocket before he shoulders his bag. "Alaric, are you okay? Class didn't get too out of hand. And you don't need to do the essay."

A soft growl, low in his throat. "I'll do the essay," Alaric grumbles. "Wouldn't be fair if I didn't. And 'm fine. Wasn't bad. Wasn't great, either." He shrugs one shoulder. "Plenty of folks still think Clan shouldn't be in sports."

"People don't realize that Talent have been there all along," Pawel says easily. "Just not as public as you are now."

Alaric bites his tongue, simply nods. He's got something to say about Clan being different than other Talents, but first, he wonders just how many people Pawel's taught in his class. "How long've you been teaching this?" he asks, and Pawel stops, one step down the hallway, about to walk away.

"I graduated a year early," Pawel says. "I pushed through a Masters and PhD-level thesis shortly after that, with enough psychology and philoso-phy classes to get that degree two years later. Far too early, according to most people. I started teaching this class while I was still working on my graduate degree, and the department opened as soon as I graduated. At that point, we were five years after the Emergence, and I was the only expert willing to start classes on the subject. It's still a young subject. Technically, I was the first to get my degree from the department, before it even existed."

Alaric stands his ground, one hand tightly fisted by his side. "You've been studying this for ten years, since you think it started," he says quietly. "You know a lot, but you don't know everything. Going out, interviewing people, that doesn't teach you everything about how Clan works. About how Talent works. You're the closest thing they have to an expert, but that doesn't mean you know where we were before the Emergence. Clan didn't mix. So no, we haven't been there all along. Not in sports. Not in public. Not in places where we could lose control and hurt someone. This is new for us, too, and we know they're scared. It makes a difference."

Pawel tilts his head, fingers tapping against his strap. "Sounds to me like you're going to have an interesting essay," he says, and Alaric's jaw goes tight. "If there's something I don't know, tell me," Pawel continues. "This is a changing field, and I may be the closest thing to an expert, but I'm also still learning. It's only been ten years, Alaric. I remember what it was like before, and so do you. So does everyone here. If there's something I should be teaching, and you think it'll help, then teach me. I'm not stupid enough to think that I know more than the students who've actually lived in Lineage families. I'm trying to bridge the distance between two worlds that merged unexpectedly, and I happen to be a part of that merging line. If you think you can help, then help."

Alaric's breath is rough and ragged, and when he blinks, he can feel the beasts under his skin. Rory's fingers brush against his hand in a question, and Alaric tugs his hand away, crosses his arms. "Fine," he says curtly.

"You planning on being at taekwondo tonight?" Pawel asks, and it's a clear shift in subject.

Alaric takes a step back, nods once, jaw still tight.

"Good. Mac's going to be busy working with the kids getting ready for the tournament, but we'll make sure you get enough time to find your center." Pawel turns to walk away. "I'll see you tonight, Alaric."

"Hey." Rory's voice is soft. "Are you sure you don't need—?"

"I'll be fine." Alaric fights to keep the growl out of his voice. " 'm going to get some coffee. Tea. Something. If you want to join me." He realizes that he's not sure where to go to get out of this space behind the lecture halls and, with a grumble, starts heading in the same direction Pawel went.

"Let's get off campus," Rory agrees, and Alaric translates that to the thought that he needs to get out of his head.

Rory's right, Alaric knows. He needs to relax. Calm down. Find a way to breathe around the beast.

32

THE FIRST TAEKWONDO tournament of the season is in just under three weeks. Not everyone will be competing—anyone with Talent isn't allowed—but everyone in the club is working hard to help the competitors prepare.

Pawel takes over for the start of practice, splitting them into groups to work on their forms. He runs them through their forms over and over, until Alaric has sweat in his eyes just from trying to keep his moves sharp and strength high. His form is simple—a series of steps, blocks, and a few punches and kicks—but it lets him focus on each move, perfecting it. Losing himself in the repetitive motion.

When Mac calls out to gear up, Alaric grins. This is what he needs tonight: to be able to let go. He catches Jackson's eye, and they gear up together, then set up at one end of the room. They bow when told to and shake hands, then fall into ready position with a shout.

It's long rounds tonight, a solid two minutes with a one minute breather before the next. Alaric loves sparring with Jackson. He has to stay moving, get out of the way because Jackson has long legs with good reach and isn't afraid to use his advantage. Alaric ducks back, tries to remember to circle so he doesn't just keep going backward until he bumps into someone else. Alaric uses his own speed to dart forward, trying to get inside Jackson's reach so he can get him hard with a roundhouse kick.

Somewhere in the middle of the first round, he feels the tension start to let go. It becomes a series of kick and move, move and kick. The round ends, and they bow, and Jackson tilts his helmet back and rubs across his face.

"Keep your hands up," Jackson says, gesturing for emphasis. "You may be able to take the kick, but it's still worth points. Don't let me score just because you don't care if you get hit."

Alaric grunts once and nods, glancing across at Mac where she weaves between the groups, offering advice.

"Grab a new partner!" Mac calls out, and everyone moves.

Alaric finds himself with Mason next. Mason's shorter, but he's fast and not worried about throwing spin kicks. Alaric tries to overpower him, but Mason comes in tight with a series of spins and lands two head kicks in swift succession. It leaves Alaric's ears ringing, and when he tries to shake it off, Mason punches him in the chest, then darts backward, shaking his hand.

"Ow," Mason grumbles. "That's like hitting a wall."

Alaric grins and closes in again, kicking Mason in the chest with two strikes solidly enough that he hears the air whoosh out.

"Shake it off, Mason!" Mac yells out, and Mason exhales roughly.

He comes back in for a roundhouse, and Alaric ducks to the side, but it's the wrong direction. Mason fakes the kick, using it to jump and bring his other foot up, which means Alaric moves right into the kick. It goes across his cheek, and his face hurts from the impact.

It feels good.

Alaric growls softly, air puffing out in a soft cloud around him as he circles Mason, blocks the kicks that come at him. He spins, too slow to hit Mason with his back kick, but the technique is good. He's learning, even if he feels like a lumbering bear.

"Time!" Mac walks over to them. "Mason, good job keeping going. Alaric's got a strong strike, and if you can take that, you'll be able to handle anything. Ric, tone it down. If you hit some of the other belts like that, they're going to fold." She raises one hand, calls out, "Mannie! Come over here, I want you to partner Ric next round."

At this point, they all know each other. Alaric's worked with Manuela before. She's a freshman and a green belt; she'd started training in her senior year of high school and decided to continue in college. She's also smaller than Alaric by over a foot. She grins up at him, bows sharply. "Ready?"

Mac checks her watch, calls out to bow and shake hands. Alaric tries to think through what he needs to do differently, both to use his height as an advantage and to avoid kicking Mannie across the room.

Mac yells to start, and Mannie doesn't give him the chance to think. She darts in tight, too close for him to be able to strike her with a kick, and lands two quick kicks on his chest and a third at kidney level. He steps to the side, trying to open up the distance enough that he can act, and she follows him with a spin hook that lands hard against his chest and a roundhouse that catches his hip.

She's not giving him a chance to breathe.

He starts blocking, lets her run into his punch so that she bounces off of it, and he's able to get a kick on her. She shouts and laughs, then circles back in tight, forcing him onto the defense. He can't think; he can only defend, and it's easy to get lost in the motion. He circles and blocks, tries to get away, but she's like a gnat buzzing in close, her kicks a constant irritant.

He huffs, and smoke puffs around him. Mannie spins, her foot coming up as he leans in to punch, and she nails him in the face. He reels back, teeth aching, a growl shuddering out in a fresh billow of smoke. He lurches forward, not thinking as he swings for her, but Mannie's not there.

"Time!" Mac yells, and she's somewhere by the windows, her arm around Mannie's shoulder. Alaric has no idea how they got there, wonders if he lost time in the fugue of not quite shifting. Mac leans in to whisper something to Mannie, and Mannie heads off to find a new partner. Mac stalks over to grab Alaric's wrist. "Come with me."

Alaric hesitates, and Mac tightens her hold. "You have claws," she says quietly, "and I don't want you hurting anyone, so come with me. We're going to take some time out."

Alaric grumbles, but he follows her to the corner of the room. She pulls a fresh water bottle out of her gear bag and passes it to him, then sits on the windowsill to drink her own. Alaric closes his eyes and downs most of the water in one long swallow.

Pawel starts the sparring again, and the room is loud with echoing *thumps* of feet against gear and shouted kihaps. It's familiar, and it makes Alaric itch to be back on the mat, losing himself in it. He leans forward, and Mac touches his shoulder.

"Not tonight," she says quietly. "Working out might be good for you, but I don't think you should be sparring right now."

He curls his lip, snarls at her, but she just stares at him. Her hand slides from his shoulder to his forearm, rests there as a warm weight. He looks at it, remembering what Jackson said when she'd touched him at breakfast, and his brow furrows. "Are you interested in me?" Her fingers tighten, and he has to explain. "I'm not going to be interested whether you are or you aren't; doesn't have anything to do with you. Jackson's thought you were flirting with me."

"I think that's because Jackson's interested in you," Mac deadpans, but there's a sorrow underlining her scent. "And no, I'm not flirting with you. I'm just trying to treat you like Clan. Physical closeness and comfort are a good thing between friends, right?"

There's no lie in her words. Her heart rate is steady despite the sour grief in her scent. Whatever's upset her, it isn't his words. He shifts, drops an arm across her shoulders, and tugs her in, curls her head against his chest. It's not comfortable with their gear still on, but he lightly strokes her back while her breath shudders. "Yeah, it is," he murmurs. "Still trying to learn what humans mean when they do it, though. 's different."

"It's different depending on the person, too. Some people just are like that—they touch everyone. Some people have meaning behind it, and it could be friendly or sexual." Mac's words are a murmur against his chest protector. She huffs a small sigh, and he feels the shrug of her body before she pushes back. She tucks a stray curl under her bandana. "You don't have to worry about me coming on to you. Or anyone. I'm not in a place where I'd even want a relationship."

The sour notes of her scent multiply, then slowly fade as she turns away, grabs another water bottle from her bag, and tosses it to him.

The sparring ends, and people start taking up the mats. Alaric thinks about asking them to leave some out, asking if he could work on a bag, but the pricking under his skin is gone now. Dissipated. Instead, he shrugs out of his gear and drops it next to his bag before he drinks down his second bottle of water.

"Thanks," he says quietly, and Mac taps him in the chest.

"Anytime," she says. "Sometimes it's nice to let someone hold you up, right?"

"Hey, Ric!" Jackson's got his bag over his shoulder, his gear already off. Alaric's nostrils flare as he takes in the scent of sweat and stale gear, stronger now that they've all stopped working. Jackson gestures at the door to the hall, where Alaric can see the shadows of people waiting outside. "A bunch of us are heading to Teas Please to rehydrate. You want to come with us?"

Jackson scrubs a hand through his hair, tilts his head, and regards Alaric, waiting. There's a scent of nerves in the air, mixed with sweat, and Alaric scowls. "Before showering? We reek."

"It wouldn't be the first time I've gone there straight from practice, and no one's kicked me out yet," Jackson admits. "You should come with us. I'll treat." A quick smile. "You can pay me back by dragging me out during basketball season."

Alaric's jaw tightens. Mac smells amused, her lips pressed tightly together as she turns away. He looks at his gear that stills needs to get cleaned and bagged, then back at Jackson. "I don't..." He shrugs. "I've got to get cleaned up."

"We'll be in the hall for a bit anyway. We're still waiting on a few people. Just come out when you're ready if you want to join us." Jackson claps him on the shoulder, squeezes before he walks away.

Mac snickers. "Like I said," she says, voice low, "Jackson's interested. *That* was asking you out."

Alaric grumbles, "It's a group thing. Not a date." He grabs one of the bleach wipes from the canister on the windowsill and starts cleaning his gear more roughly than it needs or deserves. "Does everyone see potential relationships everywhere?"

"I overheard him talking to Sera and Trish at the house," Mac admits. "I'm not seeing things, but he's not sure you'll be interested so he'll drop it if you brush him off. Or you could tell him flat out that you don't want a date, but you'll join for the group. You should get out with your friends. You probably need it."

He grunts in response and bags his gear. His phone buzzes, and he thumbs it open to find a message from Rory.

Jackson says he struck out.

Alaric looks to the door, sees Rory standing just outside. Rory lifts one hand, waves, and Alaric can see familiar faces beyond as well. He hears Thorne talking to Chris.

I'll come with you guys, he types back. *You have to help me figure out how to tell Jackson it's not a date.*

Mac snorts. "Let me guess, Rory's texting you. I see him with his phone there."

"How do I tell Jackson it's not a date if I go with them?"

Mac tilts her head, makes a face. "Well, there's the blunt option. Or not sitting with him when you get there. Or you'll come up with something. Or if he asks again, tell him you're not interested."

There's a heavy weight on his shoulders at the idea that his friendship with Jackson could be in jeopardy because Alaric has no idea how to handle this. "You coming with us?" he asks, and Mac shakes her head.

"I want a night in. And since I hear Sera out there, that means she's not hanging out with Trish, which means the house'll be a little quieter." Mac shoulders her bag. "I'll see you here on Friday. If you want to train another time, just let me know, okay? If I can help, I will."

She still smells like grief, rank and sour. Alaric reaches out without thinking, tugs her close and tucks her against his chest again, his chin on top of her head. He nuzzles her hair, leaving his scent behind, and holds on until he feels her relax a little.

"Clan gives the best hugs," she murmurs against him. "Noted for future reference." She brings her hands up, nudges him lightly. "Now go out. Have fun. Relax."

33

THEY WALK OVER to Teas Please in a large group. Chris hitches along on his crutches next to Alaric, insisting he's fine now that he's got the brace for his knee. Thorne walks on Chris's other side, talking animatedly about something from a class earlier in the day. Rory brackets Alaric, his hands in his pockets, shoulders slightly hunched although Alaric can smell a sweet, pleased scent, and there's a small smile lifting his lips.

Sera and Pat roll ahead of the crowd on their skateboards, periodically riding them up onto the curb, then popping off. TJ, Jackson, and Nikita take up the middle space, not quite able to keep up with Sera and Pat but not falling back as far as Alaric's group with Chris.

"I thought you didn't like crowds," Alaric says quietly to Rory, bumping his arm.

Rory shrugs. "Thorne and I were hanging out, and Chris stopped by, then TJ asked if we wanted to come along so we figured, why not? I didn't realize it'd be such a large group, but I like everyone. It's not like a party where I'm wondering when the next stranger is going to recognize me." He glances over at his brother. "Plus, Thorne's not drunk and wandering off. If anyone attracts attention tonight, it'll be him."

"Planning on flirting, if there's someone to flirt with, but I won't be ditching my brother," Thorne says with a grin. He knocks his elbow into Chris. "Besides, someone's got to make sure this guy gets back to his house without tripping over his own feet."

Chris tilts his head, mock glares at Thorne. "I'm not the one who slid down the stairs on the way out of the dorm," he points out, and Alaric bites back a laugh at Thorne's chagrined look.

"He did," Rory confirms. "Slid down the last few steps and pinwheeled.

Managed to stay standing at least."

Pat's holding the door when they get to Teas Please, his loosely gripped board hanging down from his other hand. "Just go straight back. Nate's already taken everyone to the big table."

Alaric's fingers flex, and Chris knocks into him on the way by. "You okay?" Chris asks, and Alaric nods once.

" 'm fine," he mutters. "I'll be fine."

"I'm going to sit on the one end," Chris tells him. "Sit next to me, and if you have to get out, I'll let you out. Hopefully you won't feel as trapped."

Nikita's already at the end of the table, in the middle of the U-shaped bench. Jackson and TJ sit on either side, with Sera next to TJ, and Pat takes the place left next to Sera. Thorne slides in beside Jackson, and Rory goes in next, leaving space for Alaric and Chris.

It's tighter than the last time he sat here, but this time, Alaric can breathe better. He's close enough to Rory to feel the heat of his body, smell his familiar scent. And on his other side, Chris is slightly twisted, his hip wedged against Alaric's, and his heat is familiar now as well. Alaric closes his eyes, inhales, and lets it out slowly.

"No chocolate for you, right?" Nate says, and Alaric realizes he's waiting for a reply. "And no nuts." Nate's grin tilts, and Thorne snorts.

Alaric realizes he has no idea what he wants, and he looks from Chris to Rory for help. "What're you getting?" he asks.

"Thorne and I are sharing one of the crêpes," Rory tells him. "Raspberry cream cheese."

"There's an apple-crumble sundae I was thinking of getting," Chris says. "How big is that, Nate?"

Nate holds his hands apart, fingers circled. "Bowl's about this big around, with a solid four-by-four piece of crumble in the bottom, two scoops of vanilla, and a scoop of dulce de leche ice cream, hard caramel crumbles, and some caramel syrup—all homemade, in house. Easily enough for two if you don't want to tackle it on your own. I can bring two spoons. And it goes well with your favorite ginger tea."

"I definitely want the tea," Chris says. "Ric? Want to keep me from eating more sugar than I should?"

Alaric picks up the menu without opening it, hands it to Nate. "Sure. Yeah. We'll share."

"Tea?"

"Ginger."

"And that's everyone." Nate looks around the table. "I'll be back with the drinks shortly, and the desserts soon after that."

"Isn't there some sort of rule about TAs not being social with the kids on their floor?" Chris leans in close, shoulder touching Alaric's as he murmurs softly. "I think I see yours out with your floormates more often than not."

Alaric shrugs, because it's not a rule that really matters to him. "He doesn't play favorites. Nikita's the worst offender for Talent indoors, and she's already paid fines for it because of damages. Think it's okay as long as he's not getting us alcohol—can't anyway, he's not old enough—and he's not dating any of us. Pretty sure he's not dating anyone, anyway."

"Would you know?" Chris smells amused, and Alaric nudges him, scowling.

"Probably not." Alaric glances down the table to where Thorne's deep in conversation with Jackson, leaning in with their heads close together. He frowns slightly because Thorne's barely said a word to him.

"Do not have the conversation you're thinking about across me," Rory says.

"I'm not thinking anything."

"You're staring." Chris bumps his knee against Alaric's. "You good?"

He's tense. There's an itch under his skin that taekwondo didn't scratch. But it's been there since they got the news about Orson, and Alaric is pretty sure it'll still be there after they bury him on the weekend. He's already been to Thorne's place once since the weekend, and he's kicked at taekwondo, and he's been through football practice. Nothing's worked.

He doesn't have a good way to answer, so he shrugs one shoulder and says again, "I'll be fine." He closes his eyes and crosses his arms, leaning back against the high leather back of the booth. Rory tilts toward him on one side, and Chris is hip to hip on his other side. When he inhales, he tastes their scent on the air, and it steadies him. "Let me know when dessert gets here."

The conversation flows over Alaric, and he lets it go. He smells when the tea arrives, the fresh, sharp scent of ginger in front of him. He doesn't need to drink it right away, waits with his eyes still closed and listens to Chris talk to Pat and Sera about the best decks and wheels, things Chris might want to get for his little brother for Christmas this year. TJ's talking about a dance class, and it slowly falls into an in-depth conversation with Thorne and Rory about music and the possibilities of a composition to use for a project in the latter half of the year.

He opens his eyes when something cold plinks on his forehead, slides down his nose. He reaches up to brush it away and finds cold water there as another droplet falls.

"Nik." TJ's voice, low and urgent as he has a hand on Nikita's shoulders, shakes her until she blinks.

Her eyes focus slowly, pupils constricting as she blinks again. There's a soft breeze as a dark cloud above them dissipates, and the droplets stop. "I…" She stops, looking around the table. "I think I fell asleep."

"And almost started a rainstorm indoors," Jackson says dryly. TJ still has a hand on her shoulder, squeezing as he looks worried.

Nikita ducks her head. "Sorry. I just…I haven't been sleeping. Stress is getting to me, and I keep having nightmares. So I wake up, and Jennifer wakes up, and she yells at me, and I yell at her, and no one gets any decent sleep except Pels, who can apparently sleep through the apocalypse."

"Are you starting storms every time you fall asleep? That's not a good sign," TJ says quietly. "There's a therapist on campus who works with Talented students to try to help them if schoolwork and stress are making it hard to stay in control."

"I haven't been out of control since I was eight," Nikita protests. "I'm not losing control. I'm just tired. And no, I'm not making it rain in the lecture halls. Only when I'm fighting with Jennifer. And sometimes when I get nightmares, although that's rare."

"You were having a nightmare here?" TJ's voice is soothing, a rich, low tenor. Alaric's pretty sure that TJ's not Talented, but moments like this make him wonder.

Nikita shakes her head. "Not that I'm aware of, but I might not remember. I just kind of dozed off. You guys are warm. I'm squeezed in. It's comfortable here." Her smile quirks wry. "Sorry, I'm not exactly great company. And you guys thought you were rescuing me."

"You were about to have another fight with Jennifer," Pat points out. "Maybe we were rescuing her."

A spoon is set down in front of Alaric, and Nate smiles when he glances up. Nate moves efficiently, passing out desserts and plates to everyone without intruding upon the conversation. Chris nudges the bowl so it sits between them, sweet ice cream melting atop warm apples. When Chris motions, Alaric digs in first, takes a big spoonful, and lets it melt on his tongue.

He makes a low noise. Orson would've loved this.

"Or you could do taekwondo, like Alaric."

He looks up at the sound of his name, takes a moment to realize that it was Jackson. He frowns, tilts his head. "What?"

"TJ suggested therapy again. Jackson suggested kicking things and smelling like sweaty gear," Nikita says. "Is that why you do it? Instead of therapy?"

Alaric stops with his spoon dug into the apples and leaves it there. When Chris glances at him, he makes a motion to tell Chris to go ahead and keep eating. His stomach twists uncomfortably. "Pretty much," he admits. "Yeah. Anger management. Keep control. Not always sure it helps."

It didn't help tonight, not after class or after Orson, not after everything.

"Started after the game," he says, since he figures everyone will know what that means.

"How are you feeling after class today?" Pat asks. Sera stares at him for a moment, then shifts her gaze to a point beyond his head. Alaric's used to the way she never quite seems to pay close attention.

Sera huffs quietly. "Someone started a discussion online about the class. Should I delete it?"

That twist grows tighter. "Bad?" Alaric asks.

"It's not good," she says dryly. "Bunch of dickheads who think they can make themselves bigger by tearing someone else down. It's sad that there are still idiots who think like this. I didn't think they were allowed to take the class."

"Anyone can take the class, they just can't use bigoted language during lecture," Rory says. "And if they try using it in their essays, I'm pretty sure Professor Szczek won't grade favorably."

"There are some people who don't even think the major should be offered here," Thorne adds. When Alaric looks at him, brow furrowed, Thorne spreads his hands. "PHU is great, and people are open-minded, but not everyone here is perfect. There are still people around who don't like Talent, or certain kinds of Talents. Who are afraid."

"If they bothered to learn how to handle themselves, there wouldn't be anything to fear," Chris says firmly. "Talents are like anyone else. There's good. There's bad. There are people with tempers and people who are calm. You aren't different just because you have magic."

The pricking under his skin is getting worse. A part of Alaric wants to get up and move, and a part of him is fine right where he is, where Chris and Rory seem to have somehow gotten closer to him. There's a palm resting at the bottom of his back, an elbow touching his. Grounding.

Thorne glances at Rory, and Rory tilts his head, then nods.

"We're going to a concert tomorrow," Rory says. "Not backstage, nothing to do with business. It's a standing-room-only place; should be good. We met the guys once," he admits, "when we did a big indoor concert. Same place where Stormy rained indoors."

"High-energy band," Thorne says.

"Already going," Jackson tells him. "Pat, Sera, Trish, me, and TJ are squeezing into TJ's car. How are you guys getting there?"

"Probably an Uber," Thorne says. "Didn't really plan that far in advance. Why didn't I bring a car again?"

"Because we have an equipment van, and you don't have an actual, useful car," Rory reminds him dryly. "And our van only fits four people and a shit-ton of equipment. Plus it smells like stale beer. Which is disgusting."

"Dax is going." Chris has his phone out, fingers moving across the screen. "He's got his mom's car for the night so he and Cass can get there. I was thinking about tagging along with them. Think Drea might want to go, Ric?" His thumb hovers over the screen as he waits for an answer.

The shift in conversation is so abrupt, Alaric has no idea what's expected. He has no idea who this band is or why he would even care, but he's pretty sure that Drea would enjoy any concert, so he nods once. Chris touches the screen of his phone, then does something else, and it pings.

"All set. Rory, Thorne, meet us at the locker rooms tomorrow after practice, and Dax'll pick us up to head over. His mom drives a minivan, so we can seat seven as long as we don't mind being squished a bit. Obviously, you and Drea are coming with us, too," Chris tells Alaric.

"Oh." The conversation is shifting away, moving to something to do with the band itself, a discussion of the music. Apparently they have good songs to skate to, and Sera's dancing quietly while still seated on the bench, like she's already listening to music. "We don't have tickets."

"Just bought them." Chris's elbow presses against Alaric's, and he gestures toward the bowl again. He waits until Alaric takes a spoonful and closes his eyes, letting the flavors coat his mouth.

"You've had a bad week," Chris says quietly. "Maybe you just need to get out of your head for the night. You and Drea both. If Corbin has a way to get there, he could meet us. VIT isn't that much farther out. We're out of space in the van, or I'd suggest having Dax pick him up."

Alaric tries to imagine Corbin with all of his friends from PHU, and even after talking about it with him, he just can't place Corbin here. "No, it's fine," he says, and he takes another bite of the apples, feels the tension slowly seep away until it simmers in the background. "I'll see Corbin on the weekend anyway. Maybe getting out tomorrow will help."

34

"ALARIC, HAVE YOU got a moment?" Coach Campbell calls from his office.

Most of the guys are out of the showers, and half of them are already dressed and gone. Alaric's moving slowly, arranging things in his locker after a quiet conversation with Dawson about the upcoming game. Chris is sitting on a nearby bench, his bad leg stuck out straight from the brace.

"I'm good," Dawson says and claps Alaric's shoulder before he walks away.

Alaric raises one hand to the coach and grunts an affirmative. He yanks his shirt over his head, runs his fingers through his hair in an attempt to get it to lie flat. By the time he's heading for the office, another crowd is leaving, and Alaric breathes a little more easily.

"I saw you talking to Dawson." Campbell gestures at the chair, and Alaric drops into it, arms crossed. Coach Young is sitting on the edge of the desk, quietly watching while Coach Campbell stands.

Alaric nods. "Went over all the plays. Chris and I watched tapes with him earlier this week, talked about options. Chris'll talk to him again tomorrow."

"And you worked with him during practice today."

Alaric has no idea what Coach is getting at, why he's pushing at this. "Yeah. He's ready for the game. He'll be fine. I'd be here, but I can't."

"Because you have something Clan-related." Campbell's voice is flat. "Alaric, Robbie and I have been talking, and we think you might want to spend some time with Bea. Your attention's been scattered, and she can feel that you're still dealing with *something*. If you don't want to talk to us, then talk to her."

"No." His arms cross tight against his chest. "I don't work with

Empaths."

"This isn't negotiable," Coach Young says quietly. "We need you to work with the team, Alaric, and right now your head isn't with us. And we can't let you lose control on the field again. We can't risk it."

"I thought you trusted me," Alaric growls, pushing to his feet. "I'm not going to lose control. I need to go home. I need to deal with Clan business."

"If you aren't going to talk to us about why—"

"It's personal!" Alaric roars, voice echoing back at him from the walls of the small office. "It's none of your business."

He shoves through the door. The sound of it bouncing off the lockers when it opens too quickly feels good, hammering like a hardened heartbeat. He's made it to his locker and is yanking his things out when the door to the locker room opens. He smells citrus, and his nostrils flare, the growl louder now.

"Ric," Chris is right next to him, balancing on one crutch, one hand on his shoulder.

"She shouldn't be here," Alaric grumbles, gaze fixed on where Heather is walking straight through the locker room, heading for Bea's office.

Heather pauses, turns slowly. In the background, Alaric sees the door to Bea's office open, smells when the other Empath enters the locker room as well. It's sharp and sweet and sour in his nose, and he feels the prick of their regard under his skin.

"Alaric." Heather's voice washes over him gently, soothingly, and he bristles.

"Don't."

"I talked to Drea, and I just thought that I'd meet with Bea to—"

"To what?" Alaric snarls. "Tell her that I'm out of control? Tell her that I can't handle my emotions? Tell her that I'm a danger to my team?"

"To tell her that you're grieving, since you won't do it yourself!" Heather snaps, and the citrus scent pricks at his nose.

He shakes his head, rubs at his face. "I'm fine," he says tightly. "I don't need your help, and I don't need hers. I don't need counseling."

"What you need is to grieve and not bottle everything up," Heather says quietly. She glances at Bea, and it's Bea who steps closer to him.

"Alaric." Her eyes are so kind. Too kind, drawing him in until he has to look away. The calm she exudes twists in his chest; he knows that it doesn't come from him. She reaches for him, and he steps back, slamming his locker door closed.

"My brother died," he bites out. "My brother died, and we're burying him on Friday, and that's why I'm going home. That's my personal business. Are you satisfied?" The last is to Heather, a low snarl with too many teeth filling his mouth.

He hears the sound of Chris's phone pinging, sees him tapping quickly on the screen. He doesn't have time for that; his entire attention is fixed on Heather's face, trying to read something beyond the rising scent of emotional control.

"You need to talk to someone," Heather says. "Drea's worried."

It feels like his brain is boiling, like anger is bubbling like lava until it explodes out in a rush. "I don't need to talk to anyone!" Alaric lashes out, punches into the nearest locker, feels the heat leave him. He steps back, stares at the melted, crumpled hole in the locker next to his. He shakes his hand, feeling cooler already, and turns slowly to look at everyone else.

Chris still has his phone in his hand, leaning heavily on the one crutch while he types. He slowly lowers the phone, expression almost blank as he looks over, but Alaric can smell the hint of fear.

Bea stands with the coaches and has her hand on Heather's wrist, bringing her closer to them. They're as far as they can get from Alaric and still be in the locker room. Heather is wide-eyed, gaze dropping as soon as Alaric looks at her. Bea's lips are pressed thinly together, and Coach Campbell stands with his arms crossed.

Coach Young looks sympathetic and smells worried.

Alaric slumps to sit on the bench. "I don't want to go to counseling," he mutters. "I don't want to talk about it to an Empath or to a human. You're not going to understand what it's like. You aren't Clan."

"We can't risk you exploding like that on the field," Campbell says quietly.

"Won't explode if you don't keep lighting the fucking fuse," Alaric mutters in response. He smells a quick wave of regret, and snorts because of course the Empath figures it out after the fact. "I don't like Empaths trying to mess with my head," he says. "I'll deal with it, and I'll be fine after this weekend. I promise. And if I'm not, bench me. I'll deserve it."

If he's benched, his father might get his wish. Alaric needs a scholarship in order to attend PHU, and unlike Orson, he's not going to get one based on academics. If football becomes an impossibility, Alaric's out of options. He gets his elbows on his knees, lets his head fall forward into his hands. It's easier to stare at the floor than to look at anyone else right now.

"Ric's been using other methods to manage his control and anger," Chris reminds them. Alaric swallows hard, tries not to think about what happened at taekwondo last night. He's pretty sure it's a good thing he won't have another practice until after the burial.

"And a bunch of us are heading out tonight, over to the concert hall in Clifton Park," Chris continues. "Rory and Thorne are meeting us here, and Dax is getting a van to drive us over. It's a chance to get out and relax." He pauses long enough to let them absorb it, then points out, "They'll be here soon. We should get going so we're on time."

There's a soft emphasis on Rory's name, and Alaric grunts softly to let Chris know he heard it. He doesn't want to be dependent on Rory's Talent to help him regain control, but he'd rather have that than anything else right now.

"I'll be here any time you want to talk," Bea says quietly. "And if you want to talk to someone who's not an Empath, I can arrange that, too. Heather." Her tone sharpens. "Let's talk in my office."

When Alaric finally looks up, Bea and Heather are retreating and Campbell is gone, but Young is several steps closer. As Alaric watches, Coach Young approaches, takes a seat straddling the opposite end of the bench.

"I'm sorry about your brother," Young says quietly. "Between that and the difficulties of coming from Clan to PHU, you've had a rough semester. I know you say you don't want to talk to Bea, but you need to find something. You need to find a way to let this out safely, because another explosion like that"—he nods at the locker—"might be more than we can explain to the administration. I'm not threatening you, Alaric. I know what it's like to feel as if everything's uprooted and unraveling around you. We'll do what we can to help, if you let us."

Alaric's jaw is tight as he stares at him, meets his eyes until Young drops his gaze first. Alaric makes a low noise. "I just need this weekend and I'll be fine," he says. "Clan takes care of Clan. I'll be stable by the time I get back."

"Except for your sister, you can't bring your Clan back with you," Young reminds him. "And I know Clan doesn't approve of you playing." He pats the bench. "You need to learn to be stable in the human world as well. You'll get there. But I meant what I said before: finding a way through is non-negotiable. If you can't work with the team's Empath, we need to find something, Alaric. So think about it this weekend."

"Thorne and Rory are outside," Chris says. Young stands, takes a step back to give Alaric room.

Alaric stands more slowly, tries not to look at the ruined locker door. He tugs his own locker open, pulls out his bag, and makes sure the rest of his gear is tucked inside before he closes it. He shoulders the bag, motions to Chris. "I'm ready to go."

They make it to the door before Chris speaks quietly. "You know, Drea's worried about you."

Alaric makes a low noise because of course he knows that. "I'm worried about her, too," he mutters. "But we handle things differently. She wants to talk to people. I'm good on my own. I just need you all to stop poking at me."

Chris's hand falls on his shoulder, squeezes for a moment before he lets go. "Then let's go have fun tonight."

35

Dax pulls up to the curb outside the club so he can let everyone but Cass out before he parks the minivan. Chris balances on his crutches, Drea leaning in against his shoulder as she raises her phone and snaps a selfie of the two of them together. Rory stands next to Alaric, his fingers lightly brushing against Alaric's wrist. It's not much of a touch, but it's enough to settle the beast under his skin, keep it from simmering back to the surface. After the week he's had, and in this kind of a crowd, it would be easy to lose control.

Thorne slides between Alaric and Rory, hands his phone over Rory's shoulder. "Picture," he says, and Rory holds the phone out to take the snap. Thorne takes it back and sends the picture off somewhere—Twitter or Instagram or maybe both—then tucks his phone away.

There's a shout, and Alaric spots Sera and Trish striding ahead of Pat, Jackson, and TJ. It seems strange to see Sera and Pat without their skateboards. Trish waves, and the groups converge, standing in a knot just outside of the long line waiting to get into the venue once the doors open.

Thorne looks from the line, to Chris, to the entrance. There are two doors—one with a line that stretches along the front of the building and turns the corner out of sight, and one with no line. Someone walks up to the door with no line, but after their ticket is reviewed, they're sent to the other line.

"Probably for VIP tickets," Chris says, turning on his crutches to head to the end of the line. Thorne snakes one hand out, catches Chris's shoulder.

"And some of us happen to be able to pull VIP strings," Thorne says. "We can get you in so you don't have to stand on the crutches for an hour, and we can get Rory out of the crowd so he doesn't have to worry about being bombarded with selfie requests."

Trish tugs on the hem of her T-shirt, which says *Folk This*. "I'll come with you, Thorne." As she turns away, her hair swings, and Alaric can see ink that seems to extend the cut-off image of a guitar on the back of her shirt onto her skin, the headstock across the back of her neck.

They speak to the guy at the door for a few minutes, then Thorne waves them over. Dax and Cass join them, and they crowd around the entrance. There are whispers from those waiting, even one shout that has Thorne waving in acknowledgement. Thorne gathers their group together, and Alaric ends up sandwiched between Chris and Rory, his arms around their waists, as the security guard snaps a picture, then waves them inside.

"Sometimes it's nice to use our influence for the forces of good," Trish says, leaning on Thorne cheek to cheek.

"I am actually in shock that they knew you," Thorne says, and Trish sticks her tongue out.

"You realize that not everyone who plays here is pop-punk or screamo," she says dryly. "I actually played here once. It was a folk night out, and we kept going until no one had a voice left to sing. I wrote a song onstage that night. Top that."

Thorne bows low before her. "I will offer my shoulders in penance," he says. "Once the show starts, if you want to get above the crowd."

"Accepted." Trish grabs Thorne's hand and drags him to the front of the room.

There aren't many people inside yet, but the space against the stage is already starting to fill up with the people who have VIP tickets. Dax glances at Chris, and as soon as Chris waves him off, Dax and Cass are gone. Jackson, TJ, Pat, and Sera don't even stick around long enough to ask, squeezing in at the front, jockeying for position. TJ bends down and hoists Pat onto his shoulders, setting his feet in a wide base and shouting as Pat pumps the air. They don't stay like that long before Pat slides back down, but Alaric can smell the rising excitement and enthusiasm.

"So..." Drea's voice trails off, and she bounces a little. "I talked to Corbin and tried to get him here, but he's got an exam tomorrow. Some kind of brutal introductory engineering thing, and he said he's having a tough time focusing, so he figured he should stay in and study."

"And he thinks we're wrong for going out to do something fun this week," Alaric mutters, because he could see Corbin going either way. He's been on the receiving end of Corbin trying to drag him out and distracting him with frivolous things. But this is also an incredibly human place to be, and they're mourning.

"Of course he doesn't," Drea says, but Alaric doesn't entirely believe her. Her voice is too flat, her posture too careful.

Alaric reaches out, tugs her into a hug. He presses his face against her cheek, does his best not to flinch as people start to move around them, the main door finally opened. He inhales her scent, squeezes her gently. "Go have fun with everyone. I'm going to stick back here," he says, giving her a gentle nudge toward the front.

Drea turns, walking backward with her arms outstretched. "Rory? Chris?"

Chris raises one crutch, shakes his head. Rory actually takes a step back. "No," Rory says. "Nope. I'm fine. I can see from here, and I don't feel like ending up in a space where someone could decide to squeeze my ass and call it accidental because we're squished like sardines."

"You say that like it's happened," Chris says.

"More than once," Rory mutters.

"Go," Alaric says, and Drea turns and bounces off to join the others at the front.

Someone bumps into Alaric, pushing him closer to Chris, and Alaric reaches out to steady Chris. Alaric growls softly, and Rory gets a hand on his forearm, wrapping fingers carefully around his wrist as the beast abates.

Sour tension fills the air.

Alaric huffs. "I'm going to be fine," he grumbles, nudges Rory's fingers from his wrist. "I don't think you want to spend the entire time trying to leach my Talent. But we should move out of the middle unless Chris wants to get run over."

"You'd think that people would be able to avoid a big Black guy." Chris shrugs, gesturing with a crutch. "Not to mention the shiny silvery things under my arms. But apparently I'm invisible."

"People get stupid in clubs." Rory points, and they manage to slip through the crowd to a spot across from the bar where chairs line the wall. Chris leans his crutches against the wall, sliding them between two chairs and apologizing to the woman sitting down as he does so.

It looks like this is where all the parents sit when they bring the younger teens to the show. And there are a lot of teens there already. Their shrieks rise above everyone else, a sharp pitch that bites at Alaric's hearing.

"They'll only get stupider when the drinking starts." Rory makes a face. "Not the kids, obviously. They'll scream like that the whole time. But the older people. I'm not drinking."

"Thorne's not—"

"Thorne will find alcohol," Rory says sagely. "Thorne has found his way around age limits since we were fifteen. And if you want something, since we weren't carded at the door, and you aren't wearing these"—he holds up his hands, displaying the black X across the back of each of them—"you'll be able to get whatever you want. They don't card on the inside."

Alaric's not so sure about that, but he figures he'll give it a try. He takes the money Chris passes him, threads his way through the crowd, and a few minutes later returns with two beers for himself and Chris, and a bottle of water for Rory.

The lights flicker and go out, and screams erupt. Everything smells like anticipation mixed with alcohol, with an underlying thread of arousal. At the front of the crowd, people sit on shoulders. Alaric recognizes Cass, Trish, Sera, and Pat, but he can't see whose shoulders they're riding. A guitarist comes out on stage, slides up to the microphone, and when he shouts the distortion makes Alaric's ears ring.

Rory touches him, holds out what looks like four globs of clear wax. He hands two to Chris, and Alaric watches what they do, molding the wax and shoving it into their ears.

The worst of the sound recedes, muffled by the plugs, and Alaric is able to ignore the distortion. He feels the beat in his feet and starts tapping, and Rory sways next to him. Rory leans over, yells by Alaric's ear, "This is just the opening band," and Alaric nods.

He yells back, "I can hear you without yelling," and it feels strange to speak so loudly in such a crowd. Rory grins at him, taps the earplugs, then turns his attention back to the show.

Chris leans into Alaric, and Alaric ends up with one arm around his waist, offering him a shoulder so he doesn't have to keep weight on the one knee. The music is infectious even though Alaric has no idea what the words are. The sound keeps him moving, and Chris and Rory both move with him.

The first set is short, and Alaric finishes off his beer at about the same time as the band winds down. He winds his way back to the bar for another, as well as three bottles of water so they don't get dehydrated. When he gets back, Chris is in conversation with a line of older women who are sitting in the chairs. He has one hand on the wall, using it to lean, but he straightens as soon as he sees Alaric.

"There is no way I could carry that without spilling it," Chris admits. There's music playing between sets, and the background noise is still loud.

Alaric looks around for Rory, his nostrils flaring, but he doesn't smell nerves. His gaze narrows, then he finally spots him, on a raised platform off to one side, deep in conversation with three other people. Rory is gesturing at something on the floor, then the stage, then someone else points to the pit where security seems to be standing next to the stage. Rory shakes his head and points again at the floor, and the others nod.

By the time Rory makes it back to them, the other band is starting up, and Alaric is almost done with his second beer and thinking about a third. Rory gives the empty glass a dubious look. "I know you said you can't get drunk easily, but should you be drinking that much when you still have classes tomorrow?"

"I don't think it's going to affect anything," Alaric says.

"I'm done after this one." Chris raises the glass and knocks it back. "That's about all I should drink with the meds—don't give me that look, Rory, I haven't taken any since this morning, but I do want to take one before I sleep tonight. I know my limits."

"Plenty of people have known their limits and been wrong," Rory mutters. "Remember where I grew up."

Chris hands the glass to Alaric, who stashes it under one of the chairs along with his own. Chris doesn't seem unsteady, but he seems looser. Calmer and easier, like the alcohol's taken the edge off. When he leans close, Alaric's arm goes around him again, giving him some stability. Chris's body is hot against him, and Rory presses close on Alaric's other side, jumping as a new song starts up. They all end up bouncing on their toes, Chris hopping on his one good leg, and Alaric realizes that Rory is singing along with whatever the song is.

When he tries to listen for it, he picks out Drea's voice as well, and TJ's smooth tenor. Trish's voice is a husky alto, while Sera and Pat seem gleefully off-pitch. Chris is silent, but his fingers are warm, moving slightly against Alaric's side where he holds on.

It feels good after that, sinking into the almost familiar sounds and very familiar scents. Alaric lets himself taste the air around him, the way it feels like Clan as they get packed closer and closer together. Chris's arm ends up loose across Alaric's shoulders, and Rory's enthusiasm is bright and joyous.

At the point when Thorne climbs the front of the stage during the main set, Rory cups his mouth and yells out. Thorne pulls up Sera, Drea, Trish, and Cass, and there's a moment's pause while the musicians catch their breath and everyone gets introduced.

Someone brings out a guitar for Trish, who laughs as she checks to make sure she's in tune with everyone else. There's a quiet conversation off mic, then she starts to pick out notes. A moment later the drums come in along with the band's guitarist, then Thorne leans in close to the lead singer and harmonizes with him as they sing. The rest of the girls dance on stage, flirting with the band members and having a good time, and all Alaric can taste is joy.

Rory sings along, fingers moving like he's tapping out the tune on a keyboard, and even Chris hums under his breath as he dances in place.

It's infectious, and it's good, and for the first time in a week, the knot in Alaric's chest truly eases.

36

ALARIC MANAGES TO stay at ease until Friday, when he gets into Amy Sanderson's car to go home. He slides into the back seat with Drea, and his stomach twists at the thought of being trapped. He can't ignore where they're going and why. Just going home would be bad enough, but this. This…

Corbin turns around from the front passenger seat, but Alaric doesn't want to talk. Not now. He raises one hand and turns away, leaning his head against the cool glass of the window. His phone is on silent. He's cut off.

"We had a late night," Drea says quietly, her hand lightly touching the nape of Alaric's neck.

"Yeah, I saw the pictures all over the internet," Corbin says dryly. "Drea mentioned who your roommate is, and I followed him and his brother on Instagram. You guys looked like you had fun."

"Drea asked you to come," Alaric mutters. "You didn't. You don't get to argue about not meeting my friends."

He can't see him, but he can feel the way Corbin tenses and knows exactly what he looks like with his lips pressed tightly shut.

"If you were there, you could've gotten me on your shoulders. We ran out of guys to hoist us up," Drea says, her tone forcedly light.

"But you did go on stage," Corbin points out. Drea makes a small noise, and he keeps going. "You were hanging out with famous people. Someone posted a video and tagged Thorne. It looked like you were having fun."

"And you were stalking us," Drea retorts. "Next time just be there. It's easier. And yes, I'm pissed off at you now because you're acting like an ass. So turn around, face front, and leave Alaric alone. Stop acting like a sulky child."

Something thumps, and Alaric imagines that she shoves at Corbin, pushing him until he turns away.

The car slows, and Amy's voice is sharp. "All of you stop it unless you want to get out and run or fly home, because I'm sure a thirty-mile race will do you good right about now. If you're planning on staying in my car, be civil."

Alaric lets his eyes close, tries to ignore the music that pounds inside the small space when Corbin turns the radio up. The song is vaguely familiar, and when Drea starts singing along, he isn't sure if it's something he heard last night or maybe one of Rory and Thorne's songs. He mutters under his breath, pulls his hood over his ears, and pretends it actually helps block out the sound.

As soon as they get home and Amy stops the car, Alaric pushes the door open and stumbles out. He doesn't wait for Corbin or Drea, storming up the steps and pausing only long enough to hug his mother. He extracts himself from her grasp before Corbin and Drea can get there and heads upstairs to leave his hoodie behind on the bed before he leaves with wings via the window.

It feels good to let the eagle take over and fly, circling above the land. He takes his time on the way to the graveyard, where his father waits by a partially dug grave. Theobald lies on the ground as a giant wolf with his paws folded and head raised, and nostrils flare as he sniffs the air.

Alaric lands and returns from eagle to human, kneeling on the ground, and Theobald growls. Alaric scowls at him. "I know," he says. He should be better at this, able to go smoothly from one animal form to the next. He should be consistent, staying within one context, but he's not. He's bird, mammal, reptile all at once. Alaric is who he is, and no amount of desire can change that. He closes his eyes, lets the bear slip under his skin, and roars in his frustration.

Theobald huffs and leaps into the grave, and Alaric follows suit.

Alaric manages a few handfuls of dirt with the bear's paws before he pulls back and stops, lets himself fall back into his humanity, sitting against the edge of the grave.

Theobald barks sharply, but Alaric shakes his head. There's a shovel near-by; not everyone has a form that digs, but everyone is welcome to help bury a lost son. Alaric heaves himself out of the grave to take that up instead, then hops back in the hole. He strips off his shirt, throws it to one side, and begins to dig.

This. This is what he needs, the sweat and ache of a brutal workout with a purpose. He pushes himself, throwing shovelfuls of dirt out of the grave almost as fast as his father digs with his huge paws. He tosses it out, then digs again, pushing deep, taking up a little more soil each time.

This is where Orson will rest.

This is where it all ends, where he'll lay his brother down for the last time. This is where they will leave Orson behind, where he'll go without returning.

Alaric growls under his breath and digs again, the muscles in his back burning from exertion.

"Give me the shovel."

Corbin sits cross-legged on the edge of the grave. Theobald ignores him, keeps digging, and Alaric tries to do the same.

"I said give me the shovel." Corbin slides into the grave, and Theobald leaps out, stands with feet splayed and head low, growling. Corbin ignores Theobald as easily as he always has, his attention solely on Alaric.

Alaric doesn't stop.

"Hey." Corbin reaches for the shovel, ducks back when Alaric swats at him. "I have just as much right to bury Orson as you do. He was like a brother to me. You have paws. What am I supposed to do, peck at the dirt?"

"He was *my* brother," Alaric growls, voice low and rough in his throat. He pitches the dirt over the side, and Theobald shakes his head, ducks away from the edge. Alaric pushes the shovel as deep as it goes, uses his foot to plant it farther in, then leans on the handle like a lever. His brain supplies the physics of it, seeing it like an engineering problem, and tears prick at the corners of his eyes.

Fuck this. Just fuck it.

"And you're mine." Corbin grabs Alaric's arm, holding on when Alaric tries to throw him off. Corbin crowds close, backing him up against the side of the grave. It's much deeper now than when Alaric began, the edge smacking Alaric between his shoulder blades. Corbin gives him no room to move, bracing him there with his slighter form, hips wedged against Alaric, hands planted in the dirt to either side of his shoulders. "You're my brother, and I'm going to do this for you," Corbin says, voice low.

"It's not the same."

"Fuck you, Alaric. It is the same. Because how do you think I'd feel if this grave was for you?" Corbin shoves at Alaric, but there's no place for him to go.

Alaric shoves back, sends Corbin stumbling to the other side of the narrow hole. Corbin straightens up, a glint in his eyes, and Alaric attacks again, throwing a hefty punch. Corbin ducks under his arm, grabs him, and twists his wrist until his arm is behind his back, bound and painful as Corbin pushes Alaric face-first into the side of the grave. Corbin's weight is heavy against Alaric's back, and Alaric is ashamed of how good it feels.

Theobald growls a warning, deep and low. Corbin doesn't let go, just tugs on Alaric's arm until the ache in his shoulder is brutal.

"I know you want to punish yourself," Corbin whispers, breath warm against Alaric's cheek. Alaric is all too aware of the way his father's ears prick, wolf's senses probably hearing everything. "I know you want it to hurt. I know you, Alaric, and I will not let you dig this grave for yourself along with Orson."

Alaric pushes backward with his hips, but Corbin twists his wrist until Alaric howls from the pain. He bows his head against the dirt; tears prick the corners of his eyes, and he jerks ineffectively at another growl from Theobald.

"You can't bring him back," Corbin says softly.

And Alaric can't replace Orson, either. Alaric can never be what Orson was. He can't be perfect. He can't get along with his father. He can't be the heir that he's supposed to be.

There is nothing that will ever make him good enough. Make him Clan enough.

"It should be me," Alaric growls under his breath, and he lets the change wash over him.

It's quick enough that the eagle slips from Corbin's grasp, wings flapping in Corbin's face as he pushes upward. Corbin stands in the grave and doesn't follow, while Theobald howls in anger.

Alaric isn't going to go back down.

He circles long enough to see Corbin take up the shovel and dig. Theobald leaps back into the hole and uses his huge paws to make space. They work together, Theobald loosening the dirt while Corbin throws it, shovelful by shovelful, out of the grave.

Alaric wheels in a large circle and flies away.

He stays in the air until his body aches, until he knows he needs to become human again to eat and rest. He flies in through his still-open window, shrugs back into his hoodie and pulls it close around him. When he inhales, he smells remnants of his life at PHU lingering in the fabric. Rory, Thorne, Chris… He holds the air in his lungs for as long as he can before he has to set it free.

There's a plate on his nightstand with cookies that are still warm from the oven, and another plate loaded with grapes, orange wedges, and slices of freshly made mozzarella. Alaric gratefully eats as he pulls out his phone and skims through his messages.

He has one from Chris that simply says *you doing okay?* Alaric almost skims past it, but he opens it and looks at the space waiting for a reply.

No, he types. *But I will be. I'll be at OPT for dinner on Sunday, if that's okay.*

The reply comes quickly. *Brothers are always welcome, even when you don't live here. See you then.*

It's a relief that Chris doesn't say *text if you need me* or any other reminder that he's waiting for Alaric to talk to him. It's a relief that he mostly lets him be to grieve.

He skips the texts from Thorne, and the notifications on his Twitter that he's been mentioned a few hundred times. Social media has never been important, and right now he really doesn't want to deal with it. He checks his grades—an A- on the essay for magical studies; he'll take that, considering the amount he ranted. He brings up the text stream from Rory last, stares down at it like it'll somehow answer itself.

How's it going?

Alaric touches the words, huffs a sigh. *It's crap, but I've dug as much of the grave as I'm going to. I'm done.*

Dots appear and disappear like Rory's typing and erasing over and over. The text finally chimes.

Do you want to talk about it?

Alaric almost sets the phone down, but he types out his response slowly, carefully instead.

Not really, no.

Then he drops it on the table and picks up the plate. The plate goes on top of the phone. He knows it's there, will be able to hear it chime when someone tries to reach him. But out of sight is out of mind, and that's what he needs right now.

Excerpt from *When Magic Entered the World: Interviews With Lineage Talent,* by Pawel Szczek, © 2009

We buried my grandfather the other night.

He was old, and it was a life well lived. I'm still in mourning, yes, but we celebrated his life as we placed him in the ground. No, it's not a death ritual. Not really. Or perhaps it is; I've never thought of it that way.

He was a part of the community. Not just our Talent community, but the greater town around him. This is a small town—maybe a few thousand people total, and several hundred of us are Talented. Before the Emergence, everyone in town knew that if they wanted to talk to someone, they should come see Grandpa.

Everyone my age knew him as Grandpa. Before that he was just Ron. I'm sure there are other Rons in town, but if you said, "I think it's time for me to talk to Ron," folks knew exactly who you meant.

They used to just think he had a way about him, but of course, now they know he was an Empath. My mom's trying to step into his shoes, but it's not the same. She's not the same. The one who seems to be most likely to inherit his position in town is my little sister, Veronica.

We call her Ronnie.

I'm getting off point.

When we buried my grandfather, the whole town came out. We had viewings for three nights, and church suppers afterward each of those nights. Big potlucks in the basement of the church, where everyone stayed and talked until the wee hours. We shared memories of him, shared pictures and mementos. We talked to each other, opening up the way he would've wanted us to.

The service was lovely. The pastor spoke for him, and Ronnie got up to say a few words too. We had another dinner after that, and we stayed for hours. When the time finally came, the family left with the elders, but the rest stayed with the folk of the town.

The burial was private.

We're a mixed community: Empaths, Telepaths, and Weather Witches. Grandpa was an Empath, of course, and so am I. We intermarry at times, so the lines get a bit mixed. And we've blended our traditions over time; it makes no sense to keep ourselves apart and never has.

There are two elders for each. Max was Grandpa's partner, and my mom is now elder with him. Peony and Poppy are the Telepath elders, and Bridget and Samuel are the Weather Witches' elders. So it was the six of them, plus my aunts and uncles, my sister, and all our cousins. And we stood there graveside, and we waited for Grandpa's casket to be lowered.

It was a simple pine casket. There was a different, more elaborate, one for the viewing, but when we buried him, he was wrapped in a shroud and encased in pine, and that's it. We want him to go back to the earth.

Bridget and Samuel brought the rain down as we each took a moment to say our own private wishes for Grandpa's passage. Ronnie took longest, and when she was done, we all felt lighter, as if she'd brought something of him back with her words. As if he were with us, helping us let him go.

You asked about ceremony, and I suppose this is it. It's been this way for as long as I can remember, and my mom's told stories of burials when she was a child that were the same.

After the grave was filled, we each brought a plant, just something small. It's always seasonal. In the spring and summer we bring flowers, and in the fall we bring bulbs that will bloom in the spring. In the winter we plant evergreens. We brought flowers this time, and we planted them in the wet soil, then we stood back. We ringed the grave and clasped hands, and Peony and Poppy reached out to us all and brought us together, touching minds. Mom and Max helped us touch hearts, and we stood there in the rain, and we sang Grandpa's favorite song to him one last time.

I felt Ronnie clearly in the link. I felt her love and her life, and the joy she had in knowing that there was still so much life left in all of us.

And I swear I felt Grandpa there with us as well, like a kiss on the cheek and the smell of peppermint candy canes.

We were drenched from the rain when it was done. We sat by the grave and stayed for another hour; none of us were quite ready to let the feeling go.

But when we were done, we knew it was a good thing. That Grandpa had let go and moved on. And that he wanted us to do the same.

We'll still celebrate his life every day. And I know that we'll all go to his grave; we'll still talk to him when we need him. And he'll be there for us, just as he always has been.

GRIEF

37

ALARIC REFUSES TO be there when Orson's body is placed in the casket. He refuses to look into the open casket during the hour of visitation in the morning, refuses to go near it until the lid is closed and latched shut, ready to be carried. He takes his place on the front right in silence, jaw tight as he wraps his hand around the handle and lifts.

There are eight pallbearers. Theobald is in the front on the left side, with Drea in the spot behind him. When Theobald tried to convince her to stay with her mother, Drea refused. Alaric knows better than to argue with his sister, and he only glances at her now to make sure she's holding up. She nods at him, then glances at where Corbin stands behind him. The final four posts are held by sons of elders in the community, all of an age with Orson.

The air smells like salt and sour rage, and Alaric's beast writhes under his skin.

His mother stands before them as a mountain lion. She growls low in her throat, and sound rises from all who are present. When Alia begins walking, the pallbearers follow.

The procession is a part of the ceremony. A time to reflect. To commune. To let go. Alaric is well aware of Corbin's scent behind him and of the tears that stream down Drea's cheeks. Theobald's breath is rough, and the casket shudders slightly where he holds it. None of them walk evenly. None of them are without pain.

But they move on because it's the only thing they can do.

It's a short flight or run from the house to the cemetery, but it's an hour of walking while carrying the casket. There are moments where Drea hesitates, hitches it up a bit to shift her hold, but she pushes through, as strong as any of the rest of them. By the time they reach the graveside, Alaric's hand is numb and his shoulder aches. The pallbearers move to lower the casket into the grave, then step away.

His mother takes human form, motions quietly for Alaric and Drea to join her, while Theobald stands by the grave marker that has already been placed.

"We gather to send one of our Clan back to the earth, to nourish the land and renew our world. We gather to bury Orson Herne," Theobald says slowly. His voice cracks on Orson's name, but no one dares comment. Alia's arm slips around Alaric's waist, and he drops an arm over her shoulder, cradling his mother close and kissing the top of her head.

Alaric lets his gaze fall to the ground, staring at the casket rather than listening to Theobald speak. There are formal words to be said, and none of them encompass what's in Alaric's heart right now.

I wish I'd been a better brother.

I wish I were better Clan.

I wish I knew what you were doing.

I wish we'd talked about our lives.

I wish we'd actually known each other.

"...my decision is final." Theobald's words end on a solemn note, solid and ringing in the air.

Alaric looks at him, stands with his mother as his jaw goes tight, head tilting slightly. He swallows hard.

"My son, Alaric Herne, has four years at Pine Hills to complete, then his year of exploration," Theobald says. "I have heard your complaints and your concerns. I have listened to every argument, and I have reviewed every option. My decision stands: at the end of his time away, Alaric will return to be my right hand, and when I am ready to step aside, he will take my place."

Silence.

Alaric has no idea what to expect, and while silence respects Orson's passing, it doesn't feel like a ringing endorsement from his Clan. He casts his eyes at the mound of dirt by the side of Orson's grave, and Theobald nods. Alaric steps forward, digs his hands into the dirt, and spills it onto

Orson's casket. Then he lets the hound slip from his skin, and he crouches down by the side of the grave, waiting patiently.

Every single member of the community spills dirt onto Orson's grave. Everyone murmurs something to him on the way by, and Alaric hears every goodbye. Orson was well-respected, loved. No one seems to believe that he would walk into magic willingly. There's anger lingering in the air after they leave, even when only Theobald and Alaric are left.

Theobald crouches by the mound of dirt, shoves one hand deep into it while his other rests on Alaric's ruff. "Goodbye," he murmurs, and tosses the dirt far out, letting it rain down across the casket. Then he lets the wolf take him, and together he and Alaric use their paws to quickly push the rest of the soil into the grave.

Someone will come out later to tamp it down properly and to plant grass seed. But this part is for the family, and for once, Theobald is silent as he and Alaric work together. When they're done, they lope at an easy pace back to the house, parting ways as soon as they get inside.

There's no time for the long soak Alaric wants to take, only for a quick shower to get rid of the dirt clinging to his skin after he's human again. He stands under the steaming hot water, lets it pound over his head for only a few minutes, and pretends that it drowns out the voices of all the Clan in the Hall below.

He dresses quickly after he's done. When he emerges from the bathroom, Corbin is waiting, leaning against the opposite wall, arms crossed. He falls into step next to Alaric, reaches up to run his fingers through Alaric's damp hair. "You still need to get it cut," Corbin says. "Or if you want to stop off in my room, I could spike it for you."

Alaric rolls his eyes. "No. It's bad enough that it's too long and starting to curl. I'm not going to style it."

Corbin shrugs, knocks his shoulder into Alaric's. He doesn't say anything else, just sticks close as they head for the stairs and downstairs. When Alaric hesitates a few steps from the bottom, Corbin does as well, one hand on Alaric's back.

"You don't have to stay long," Corbin says quietly.

"Drea's already in there." It's not a question. Corbin nods, and Alaric takes another step down, Corbin echoing the motion. "So I have to go in," Alaric continues. "My father expects me."

He has to do what's expected. What's right. And he has to be there for his mother and his sister.

"Are you okay?"

Alaric turns toward Corbin, confused by the rising concern in his scent. Corbin presses the back of his hand to Alaric's cheek, frowns as he pulls back. "You're hot," Corbin tells him.

"Feel hot," Alaric admits. He touches his own face, but he can't feel it. It's under his skin, like a fire raging to get out. "It's just..." He waves at his chest, trusting Corbin to understand. It doesn't seem to set Corbin at ease, and Alaric fights for words. "It'll be fine. 'm going to bathe after this." All he can think about is sinking down into the cool water, losing himself in the bliss of floating there quietly.

"One hour," Corbin says. "One hour, then I'm dragging you and Drea out of there, and anyone wanting to say *I'm sorry* can come say it in the bath."

Alaric gives him a dubious look. "I don't want to take the funeral to the baths."

"You know what I mean." Corbin shoves him gently. "Come on then, let's go deal with the crowd so we can get out of here sooner and cool you down."

Having Corbin by his side makes the wake easier. Corbin never moves more than a foot away, always close enough that if Alaric glances over, Corbin can slide back, press his shoulder to Alaric's. It's like going back in time, the way the community treats them as a unit, always together. Corbin chats easily while Alaric accepts hugs, feels the press of a cheek against his, the rush of sympathetic scent. Clan touches, and normally that would be good, but each press of fingers leaves him itching. Burning.

When Alaric shies away from his aunt, Corbin grips his arm tightly. "Maybe it's time for us to make an exit," Corbin murmurs. "You're fidgeting every time someone comes near you. It isn't the words they're saying; you're doing fine with words for once. Why can't you stand to be touched?"

"Let's go," Alaric agrees rather than trying to answer. They turn together, and Theobald is waiting for them, arms crossed and expression stern. "I need to go," Alaric says.

"To run away and fly?" Theobald says dryly. "A leader doesn't run, Alaric. A leader stays and faces his issues. You'll lose respect the second you take to the air."

"He's grieving," Corbin snaps. "He lost his brother. Alaric's not a machine."

"I'll come back." Alaric rubs at his forearm, digging into it with his fingernails as if he can peel his skin off, free the heat, and let it escape into the room. "I've had a hundred people offer me sympathy, and I can't do it anymore. Drea's already gone."

"She's resting upstairs." The words are tight, as if Theobald doesn't want to admit them. "Drea is different."

"She's my twin. We're more alike than you think, and we are your children. The ones you have left." It's a brutal dig, and Theobald snarls at Alaric's words. Alaric holds his ground, grips Corbin's wrist. "Corbin, you go check on Drea. I'll be up when I get back. We should take care of her. Make sure she's okay."

"Do not go fly." Theobald's voice is low and dark, and Alaric stops after a step, turns back to face him.

"I'm still free for four and a half more years," Alaric says quietly. "Unless you want to find out what happens when I lose my temper here, let me go. You're still leader. If it's so important to show how a leader acts, then do that. Lead. I have time, and a lot to learn, since you never wanted me in the first place. It's going to take me time to catch up to who Orson was, and I know you think I'll never make it. Hard to get started when I'm faced with that. And right now—right now I just want to mourn my brother and take care of my sister. So I'm going to go fly, and then I'll be with Drea."

Theobald's lip curls, his teeth bright and sharp, and Alaric feels the flare of anger under his skin. Alaric bares his teeth in a snarl. Claws tip his hands as he snarls back, then turns and stalks from the room.

38

"Fuck." Alaric sinks down to his knees in the soft dirt, bows his head. "I don't know how to do this, Orson. I don't know how to be who he wants me to be." When he shifts, some of the dirt moves with him. He's a mess again by the time he manages to turn so he can lean back against the stone. "I get the feeling you didn't really know, either. You were just better at pretending than I am."

He pushes his fingers into the dirt. "You got it all right. You were good Clan. A good son. You actually wanted to be an engineer, and you didn't want to play football. Mom still doesn't understand it. She thinks I should stop. That it doesn't matter. But it's important to me."

He leans his head back, draws his knees up. "You knew that part, though. I remember you coming to see my games when you could. Thanks for that. I know we weren't close, but I knew you had my back. I knew you'd be there if I needed you." His breath goes tight in his chest. "I should've been there for you."

His breath whooshes out. "Football's my life. Not my entire life. I've got classes—I hate Intro to Engineering. It's so fucking hard, and it's not what I want to do. Don't know what I want to do, just that I'm pretty sure it's not that. 's not music, either. That's my roommate. And his brother. My— Fuck, Orson. Never told you I'm gay, did I? Should've. Should've talked about a lot of shit. Can't really now. Well, I can talk. Maybe you're even listening, don't fucking know. But you aren't going to talk back."

Alaric pulls out his phone, brings up Twitter because he doesn't have any other pictures. "This is Rory, my roommate. He's one of my best friends now. He's a Mage, but he's more like Clan. Half the time he sleeps in my bed. And this one, this is his brother, Thorne. We're, uh—" Even knowing that Orson's gone—that he's not really saying this to a person—Alaric hesitates. The heat under his skin is steadier now, burning him from the inside out. "We're fucking," he finally says. " 's all it is, really. All I want it to be." He feels like it needs a clarification, like he has to keep explaining it every time it comes up.

"Chris says I'm aromantic. Looked it up," Alaric admits. "Kind of fits. I don't feel like I need to fall in love." It's not exactly a lie, but it's not exactly the right way to say it, either. Frowning, he tries to find the words. "Sex is good. Relationships don't make sense to me. Too much shit to fuck up. People get confused about sex, right? They think it's something big. It's just two people getting off." He pauses, looking up and shaking his head. "You'd think that'd make it easier for me, right? If I don't give a shit about love, then I just find people to get physical with. Like Thorne. He's honest about it. Everyone else—they think it's going to be something more. And I don't know how to be that for them. Don't know how to do all the romantic dating shit. Don't really think I want to. I just want to be friends, and fuck. Is that such a bad thing?"

He laughs dryly. "Don't know why I'm asking you this now. Couldn't have asked it before. We didn't talk about this at all. You had a Mage for a roommate, and you were sleeping with some quicksilver girl, or he was, or maybe you both were, I don't know. People do that. Rory and Thorne have two dads and a mom, and they all seem fine with it. Maybe that's what you did. I don't know because you never told me.

"Can't really blame you for us not being close. I didn't make it easy, either." Alaric knows his faults well; for all his frustration right now, he's glad that Orson respected his limits. "You were good to me that way. You didn't push me. I appreciate that. But now...it feels strange. Like my brother is gone, and I'm finding out he's a stranger, all at the same time."

He thumbs through his messages, and brings up the text stream with Rory. *I'm sitting on Orson's grave talking to air*, he types.

"We're going to find out what happened," Alaric says, his voice low. "We're going to visit Rory's family so we can figure out what that symbol was. You were fucking with something big, Orson, and it killed you."

He can almost hear Orson admonishing him: *don't let it kill you, too, little brother.*

"It won't," he says softly. "Not gonna let it. We know how dangerous it is going in, so we know to protect ourselves. Wish you'd known."

His phone chimes, and he glances down to see Rory's response.

Want to talk to me instead?

Alaric huffs a sigh, presses the button to call Rory. "Hey," he says as soon as the ringing stops, and he puts the phone on speaker. "Now you can talk to Orson with me."

"Hey, Alaric. Hey, Orson." There's a twang in the background. "I was just working on a song."

"With Thorne?"

Rory snorts. "No, he's actually got classwork tonight. It's a Saturday night, and my brother is studying. Go figure. He claims he's going to finish and go out and get drunk later, so watch his Twitter if you want to know more. I'm not going to be there to take his phone away, and he loves to drunk Tweet."

"Is that why you don't drink?" Alaric asks, and he can imagine Rory's shrug in the moment of silence that follows.

"Someone has to be sober," Rory finally says. "And I'm the youngest. And I don't like losing control. I don't like losing control at all."

"Mm." Alaric tilts the phone toward the grave marker. "So, Rory, this is my brother, Orson, that we're talking to. And Orson, this is my roommate, Rory. He's a Mage, and he's in a band with his brother. Apparently they're famous. I was supposed to know who they were, and I still don't, but the music's decent."

"Want me to play the song I was working on?" Rory asks, and there are a few notes in the background, picked out on the guitar.

"Yeah." Alaric says.

He closes his eyes, lets the music wash over him as if he were sitting in his room at PHU. But he's also sharing this with Orson finally, letting his brother see a part of him outside of Clan, outside of home. Maybe if they'd done this before, Orson wouldn't be in the ground now. Maybe they could've changed something.

It's too late for "maybe" to make a difference.

39

THE BATHS ARE one of the few things that Alaric misses about home. He sinks into the water, slides all the way down and off the bench until his head goes under, and he floats there, breath held until his lungs are ready to burst. He surfaces and shakes his head, pushes the water out of his eyes.

Something pokes his shin under water; he glances at Corbin. "What?"

"Better?"

"Some," Alaric admits. His skin is cooler, and the water feels good against the heat that's left. Drea's hand touches his under the water, and he curls his fingers into hers, holding on. He manages to get himself situated on the bench, leans his head back against the warm stone. "I can't deal with all these people."

"You can't deal with them at normal times." Drea squeezes his hand. "I don't think anyone can really expect you to handle them now."

"How am I supposed to take his place?" Alaric doesn't bother clarifying whether he means Orson or Theobald. Probably both. No, definitely both.

"What did you do when you left?" Corbin asks. He's poking at the water, creating little waves that lap across the surface to Alaric, just like he used to when they were small.

Alaric smiles slightly, pushes the water back hard enough that the wave splashes and falls. Just like he always used to. "Flew out to Orson's grave," he admits. "Talked to him for a while, then I talked to Rory." Corbin's scent goes swiftly sour, and Alaric adds, "You should meet him. Rory. The two of you should meet."

"I don't—"

"Alaric's right," Drea interrupts him. "Don't be an asshole, Corbin. I know it's your natural state, and that's why you and Alaric are perfect for each other, but you need to deal with this. You both do. Grow up."

Corbin slides down out of view, under the water. Alaric counts and reaches thirty before Corbin surfaces again. When Corbin shakes his head, water droplets fly everywhere, and his hair is no longer carefully spiked.

"I still hate this," Corbin mutters.

"So do I." Everything's changing, and Alaric's tired of it. Tired of feeling as if there's nothing standing still in his life, as if the only things he can cling to are moving with him. "You're still my brother, Corbin. Just as much as always. I can have two best friends."

"But it's *you*," Corbin complains. "You don't even like people."

Alaric snorts because it's true. "You're going to hate Rory," he says slowly. "Because he's everything about me that drives you nuts. And you're everything that drives him nuts. But you're both important to me, and I'm not cutting either of you out of my life, okay?"

"What about your pet human?" Corbin asks, tone sharp.

Alaric kicks out without thinking, toe thunking against Corbin's thigh. "Don't call him that. Chris is a friend, and he's my captain, and he's a good guy. I have friends. Deal with it."

Corbin is jealous. Alaric knows this, can smell it coming off of him in thick waves. He can smell nerves, and he remembers what Corbin asked, whether he'd fucked everything up by saying no. Alaric huffs a sigh, swears under his breath, and lifts his left arm. "Just get over here, asshole."

Drea lifts Alaric's right arm, tucks herself in close to his side. "Does this mean you two are going to stop arguing, and I can cry now?" She shudders, sniffling loudly.

"Not like you need to wait for permission," he murmurs, kissing the top of her head.

"This isn't going to work, because she's not the only one that needs to cry," Corbin says. He climbs over Alaric's lap, slides down between them. And somehow Alaric slips from the bench to end up sitting on the bottom of the bath with his head barely above water, cradled against Corbin's thigh, Corbin's fingers in his hair.

He can hear Drea's muffled sobs, taste the salt in the air. He's surrounded by familiar scent and the soft lap of water against his skin. His face is buried against Corbin's skin. Corbin tugs slightly, and Alaric shudders, a low sob breaking free. As Corbin's fingers gentle, stroking across his neck, Alaric breaks and finally lets go.

He cries until his eyes ache, as hot as his skin felt earlier. He ducks underwater to cool his face, surfaces to find Corbin wrapped around Drea, cradling her close, his cheek pressed to hers. Alaric clears his throat; Drea slips away, pushes through the water to where he is, and hugs him hard.

Alaric rubs his cheek against hers. "I'm going back to my room," he says softly. "Think I'm done with the bath. Want to find out how the game went today without me or Chris in it. Dawson's not a bad player." But he's not a great player, either. Alaric doesn't have high hopes for it having been a win.

"Do you want company later?" Drea asks.

"Yeah, but no." Alaric shrugs when Corbin gives him a side-eyed look. "I feel better, but I still don't feel right. And you don't need a furnace burning you up or someone waking you. Will you be okay without me?" He doesn't want to abandon his twin, but at the same time, he doesn't think he'll be good for her right now, either.

"I'll be fine, and if I'm not, we'll come bother you, right?" Drea kisses his temple, rubs her cheek along his. "And if you need us, we'll be in my room. You can come in any time."

"We're here if you need us," Corbin says.

Alaric knows it's the truth. He climbs out of the bath, wraps a towel around his waist loosely, and pads back to his room. He leaves a wet path in the hall; it's not the first time he's done it, and he doesn't really care about cleaning up. He closes the door after himself and yanks on a pair of sweats before he climbs into bed and pulls out his phone.

There's a text from Dax that says simply *ow ow ow ow ow* and another from Chris saying *10-3, we lost.*

Alaric leans back against the wall, bends his knees comfortably, and lets his heels dig into the bed. He presses the button to dial Chris and waits while it rings. "What happened to Dax?" he asks when Chris picks up. He can hear a party in the background, the sound fading as Chris must be moving through the house. No, that's a door, and he hears wind. "Are you outside?"

"It's not that cold out, and Cass is 'taking care' of Dax in our room," Chris says dryly, and Alaric can hear the quotes in his words. "He bruised a rib—went down under a pile and caught an elbow in the chest. It hurts like hell, but he'll be fine. Just shook the air out of him when it happened. Cass is busy doting on him. Playing nurse."

Alaric can imagine, unfortunately. "I don't need details."

Chris laughs softly. "Yeah, well, neither do I. So I'm not going upstairs for a while." He pauses, asks, "How are you doing?"

"I don't want to talk about it," Alaric admits, but the words still come out. "We buried him. I flipped out during the Gather after the funeral. And I spent some time in the bath with Drea and Corbin." He hesitates, not sure how it'll sound but curious how Chris takes it. "I went out to talk to Orson for a while. Called Rory, and he played him this song he's working on."

"Did it help?" It's funny how a smile changes the sound of words, and Alaric can hear it clearly in Chris's voice.

"Yeah," he admits. "It did. I told Orson some stuff I should've said a long time ago." He falls silent after that, and it stretches between them.

Chris lets it go for a little while, picking up the conversation after a few moments when Alaric doesn't. "And now we got started talking about it. Sorry. So. The game."

"The game," Alaric echoes, relieved by the change of subject. "How'd it go, other than Dax going down?"

"Dax took the hit in the fourth period, and that pretty much spelled the end of the end," Chris tells him. "We were already floundering. Dawson couldn't punch through their defense. He tried to get it in the air, but after three interceptions, Coach switched him to a running game. But Dawson's not enough of a runner, either. The problem was their defense. They were just that good at knowing where the ball was going."

"Teleporters?" Alaric asks, not entirely serious with the question.

Chris laughs. "Just normal people, unless someone's predictive and doesn't need cards." Chris stops, and Alaric can imagine the curious expression. "Does that exist? People who can tell the future immediately?"

"Maybe? I've never met one. But Lineage Talents who are predictive tend to use cards or dreams, and nothing's ever exact. You could dream about the game beforehand, but we'd probably be gazelles, and you might dream about eating something rather than making a touchdown." Alaric shrugs. "Never really learned too much about it. Doesn't make sense to me, and I can't imagine having a Talent where you have to figure out your subconscious just to make it make sense."

"It doesn't work that way for you? The beast is such a part of you, I'd think it'd help to know your own psychology," Chris points out.

Alaric snorts, and there's a small puff of smoke. His gaze narrows. "Maybe. Not something I want to think about right now. So we lost it after Dax went out?"

"We were tied up before that." Chris switches subjects again easily. "Three and a half periods, and we'd each managed to get a field goal, and that's it. But once Dax was out, they took possession and somehow ran it down the field like we weren't even there. Easy touchdown, easy conversion. We made it to their 40-yard line before the buzzer, but we couldn't get close enough to do anything with it." A rustling, like he's shrugged. "Next game will go better."

"Next game I'll be there. It's a double next weekend." Alaric slides down the wall, ends up on his back staring up at the ceiling. He's relaxing finally, loose after the bath, calmed by talking about something that feels so normal. Something that has nothing to do with home. "I want to review tape with you and Dawson this week. Figure out how we can make it work better, get some ideas about the other teams. Figure out a plan."

"Sounds good to me. I'll arrange it with the coaches," Chris says. "Dax had an idea about how we might be able to leverage Dawson's passing game better, avoid him getting picked off before the receiver can get to it."

Alaric grunts agreement. "Tell me about it."

He closes his eyes and breathes easy as Chris speaks. It would be so easy to walk away from home, to go back to PHU and let this be his life. It would feel so good if this could be his normal. If he didn't have to worry about what comes after.

40

ALARIC DREAMS OF flying, waking when he hits the floor with a heavy *thud*. He lies there next to the bed—his skin is hot, burning—and lets the shift come over him. He flaps his wings, hops up to stand on the windowsill, eagle's wings spread in the cool night air, but it doesn't help. The thought of taking flight doesn't feel right, and Alaric lets his humanity return as he falls again to the floor.

He picks up his phone—two o'clock in the morning. It's possible someone will still be awake, but not likely. Chris might have finally managed to get Cass out of his room so he can sleep. Rory's probably either rehearsing or asleep. Alaric could walk down the hall to Drea's room, and he's halfway to the door before he stops. He doesn't want to wake his sister up, and it feels wrong to crawl into bed with them when he feels like this. When it feels like he wants to shift, to run, to fly, to do *something* other than simply burrow down into a pile of people and sleep…

There's one other option.

If you're rehearsing, don't answer this.

He hesitates for a moment before pressing "Send" on the text. A moment later he has an incoming Skype call. Alaric presses his lips together, cradles the phone in his hands as he answers. He frowns, looks at the background behind Thorne. "That's not your apartment."

"I'm not home," Thorne says quietly. "You said not to answer if I was rehearsing. I am not rehearsing. And my current company is asleep, and I happened to be putting on my shoes to head out, so… You okay, Ric?"

"Can't sleep."

Thorne snorts, bends out of range of the phone's camera. His voice echoes slightly. "You do realize that magic isn't going to let me get to your place, or you here, just because you think you want sex."

Alaric feels the heat under his skin get even warmer. "I know," he mutters. " 's not like I can really talk to anyone else about that."

"Don't you have a best friend there? A sister?"

Alaric's mouth drops open. "I am not talking to Drea about my sex life. You might feel comfortable saying anything on your mind, but I don't. And I'm pretty sure you already tell Rory more than he needs to hear."

"Probably," Thorne admits. He picks up the phone and walks out of wherever he is, talks as he heads down the street. "Besides, I don't think sex is what you need."

Alaric's brow furrows. "What makes you think you know what I think I need?"

Thorne motions between himself and the phone. "We've been doing this friends-with-benefits thing for a few weeks now, Ric. I know when you're calling because you want to get rid of energy, and that's fine. You know I have no problems with that. Except right now you've just had a day from hell, and you're surrounded by family, and instead of doing the Clan thing and being buried under a pile of different animals, you're on the phone with me. Why aren't you buried in a puppy pile somewhere, being a literal puppy?"

"Hound." Alaric moves slowly back to the bed, sinks onto the edge of it. "I don't feel right. I don't want to make things worse for Corbin and Drea."

"Was it just you and Drea and Orson?" Thorne asks.

"There are cousins," Alaric says, shrugging one shoulder. "We've done the big family thing. But right now, I don't want them."

"Do you actually want to be with Corbin and Drea?" Thorne asks quietly. "Not feeling right aside—whatever that means—do you want to be with your sister and your best friend?"

Alaric wants to feel the heavy weight of someone over him, sleeping on top of him. He wants to smell familiar scents, the burrow against skin. He wants to feel trapped by someone that feels like family. "Yeah," he admits. "Wouldn't mind Rory, either. Or you." Maybe Chris; a hint of his scent lingers in Alaric's sheets even after a week, just enough to feel familiar and make Alaric want more.

"If you're invoking me and Rory in the same breath, then you're not looking for sex." Thorne stops under a streetlight, raises the phone so he's looking straight into the camera. "Maybe you should give yourself what you want. Do what's going to settle the beast and go be with Clan. You're not going to hurt them, Ric."

Alaric grunts. His skin still feels like it's burning, and he hasn't had much control lately.

"Alaric," Thorne says firmly. "Listen to me. Even when you're out of control, you aren't going to hurt the people you love. And they won't let you hurt them. They need you as much as you need them. So go. You probably need skin-to-skin contact more than anything right now, but you're not going to get that calling me. Go take what you need. I can't give you that. I don't think I'd even be enough if you were here."

Alaric licks his lips, casts his eyes down, past the phone.

"Alaric." Thorne's voice is gentler now. "Talk to me?"

"I almost hurt someone at taekwondo the other night," Alaric mutters. "There's this smoke sometimes. My skin is hot, feels like I'm burning inside and I might explode. And I'm just *angry*. All the fucking time."

"Your brother died; you're allowed to be angry."

Alaric growls, because no matter how true it is, it feels wrong. "I want—" He doesn't have any words for it. "I'm pretty sure sex wouldn't be a *bad* thing."

Thorne laughs softly. "Yeah, well, unless you're going solo, ain't happening. So go for the next best thing. See if you can get that puppy pile, okay?"

This isn't going anywhere, isn't going to get him where he needs to be. Alaric growls in his frustration.

"I'll see you tomorrow when you get back," Thorne says, and it sounds like a promise that Alaric intends to make him keep.

Alaric nods, touches the screen to end the call. He tosses the phone on his bed, leaves it there as he pads into the hallway, lets the hound take over. Drea's door is slightly open, and he noses into her room, whines softly.

"C'mere." Corbin's voice is hoarse; Alaric's not even sure he's awake.

Still, Alaric takes the invitation, leaps onto the bed, and stretches across their feet, his head pillowed on Corbin's hip.

It isn't what he needs, not exactly. It's too soft, too easy. But when Corbin reaches down, lets his fingers curl and grab at the fur behind Alaric's ears, it helps. He tugs a little, until Alaric whines. He's finally able to let go and sleep, anchored by the heat and weight of family and Clan.

Excerpt from *When Magic Entered the World: Interviews With Lineage Talent*, by Pawel Szczek, © 2009

I'm not a historian, not exactly. I am a scholar, however, and I believe in preserving knowledge, whatever it may be. Sometimes that means separating truth from legend, even in our own histories.

The simple truth is that among the Lineage Talents, there are five primary types. Everyone you meet will be one of these. There are Mages, like our community. They may be general Mages with a specialty such as fire. They may not use ritual, but they excel in one area, such as Weather Witches.

There are Clan, our shapeshifters, born as much beast as human. There are Healers, and also those who give pain. There are the Dreamwalkers—I see by your expression that this interests you; unfortunately I don't know of any for you to speak with. And there are the Empaths and Telepaths, those who deal in matters of the mind.

Even the Emergent fall into these categories, in some manner or another. Most have magic, and thus are Mages, whether their Talent is teleportation, or flight, or pausing time. They are people who have specialized as much as the Weather Witches have, able to do that one thing without ritual, but everything else might be lost to them.

And of course, there are the legends.

You want to know about the legends. Remember this: they are only legends, and if they are not, no one has seen anyone of these Talents in decades, if not centuries.

You asked about ghosts. There are no such thing as ghosts. When people die, they pass on. Their souls pass, their bodies decompose. It's that simple.

Yes, we do have souls. There is body and there is mind—there is what makes us human. And there are legends about Talents that can destroy the soul. They are the Shadowwalkers and the Soulstealers. They are the ones who can exist in the darkness around us, emerging anywhere. They are the ones who can touch a body and draw out everything that makes it the person that it is, destroying them from the inside out. They are an embodiment of every Talent, in some ways.

And they do not exist.

Or, if they have ever existed, they are gone now. Destroyed before they could destroy not only the Talented, but the mundane as well. The legends say that they do not care who they kill, only that they feed on terror.

They are the stuff of movies now, the legend behind Bloody Mary and every other bogeyman you'll find in a tale of horror. They are not real.

The thing to remember is that those with Talent are still people. We are all still human, and legends grow out of things we cannot explain and things we do not wish to see. We don't want to think that our neighbor is a psychopath, so he becomes a stealer of souls rather than a giver of pain who delights in tormenting those around him.

We create these stories to save our sanity, when the truth is, we are as dark and light as any human could be. These legends are a cautionary tale, a reminder that we need to be good and follow a path that does not harm others, for what we do will rebound three times back on us.

REVELATIONS

41

ALARIC IS WARY when Pawel pulls into the driveway of a small farmhouse. They left PHU on Sunday afternoon, right after his second game of the weekend. They traveled the distance to the New York State border quickly, and they've been on the road in Vermont for several hours. The last shopping area Alaric spotted was at least twenty minutes back, and when he'd commented on how remote they were, Rory pointed out that the similarities between hippies and Clan were strong. Conor snickered.

They all climb out of the car, and Pawel stands with his hand on Conor's shoulder while Alaric stands behind them.

"You don't need to be afraid of anyone here," Rory says, and heads straight up the stairs onto the porch, then pauses only long enough to knock once on the door. He pushes it open, calls out, "We're here, Gram!" He motions for the others to follow, then he steps inside.

Alaric lingers as long as he can, only following after Pawel and Conor both go up the stairs. He can smell magic in this place. Not just the ozone-bright scent that filled the car with Pawel and Conor both there, but a more subtle scent like clean, fresh cotton. It's pervasive, and it makes him want to sneeze.

He steps inside cautiously, nostrils flared. He expects to smell wariness and concern; instead he's enveloped by a short woman who hugs as hard as any Clan and smells like bright outdoors and calm.

She presses her cheek to his, then draws back, both hands on his shoulders. "Don't be nervous," she says. "Everyone's welcome here, no matter the Talent. And we've heard about you already. You're as good as family."

Alaric looks to Rory, who holds his hands out and shrugs. "This is Gram," Rory says. "Allison Baker; she's Dad's mom, and when you meet

Nana later, that's Dad's other mom."

"We've never been a traditional family." Gram pats his cheeks, then finally steps away, leaving Alaric awash in that fresh, sweet outdoor scent. "From what I know of your folk, we're probably more like that."

"You don't have one big house at the center," Alaric says slowly.

"No one's above anyone else here," Gram responds. "Although most of us have our specialties. This happens to be the library house—our family's always had a thing for books, and Susan's downright obsessive."

"So are you." Rory bends down to kiss her cheek. "Mind if I take Pawel downstairs? We're only here tonight and tomorrow morning, and I want to get started. Ric, Gram will show you and Conor to rooms—Pawel and Conor are going to have to share, and I figured I'd share with you."

Conor looks up at Alaric, his gaze narrowing, and Alaric looks back. He's not babysitting. He didn't plan on babysitting, and he doesn't know this kid particularly well. Conor's head tilts, expression sharpening before he smirks slightly.

Gram shows them to the rooms, then Conor helps Alaric haul their overnight bags upstairs. Conor bounces on the bed in his room, says, "You're not planning on just leaving me here, are you?"

"Do you need watching?"

"Not really, but Dad'd say I do. I'm pretty smart. Talented, too. I make sparks, especially with Alan." Conor has a tablet in his hands, and despite the conversation, he's playing some kind of a game at the same time.

"Who's Alan?" Alaric gets the feeling he's being suckered into a conversation with a purpose, and when Conor peeks at him, he's even more positive. He smells of curiosity and a hint of amusement.

"My husband," Conor tells him, chin lifting slightly.

"You're too young to be married," Alaric says firmly.

Conor smiles, his scent bright and happy, like Alaric passed some kind of a test. "I know. But we got married at recess and that's cool, because someday we'll get married for real. He's my best friend. Are you going to marry Rory? You hold hands."

"I'm Clan; we touch a lot." Alaric sinks onto the bed; he's obviously not going anywhere at this point. He might not want to babysit, but this kid's not Clan, and he's probably too young to be left alone. Besides…Alaric doesn't want to piss off Pawel. "And Rory's…you saw Gram."

"She hugs," Conor says sagely. "And she smells like sunshine, which is weird. I wasn't expecting that."

"You can smell her?"

Conor tilts his head, puts his tablet aside. "Not exactly. I smell magic sometimes. Like Alan smells like lightning and smoke but only when I'm around. And Dad smells like the edge of a candle flame, which does have a smell, kind of waxy and hot and it tickles my nose. Rory smells like nothing, which is really weird."

"Do I smell?" It's a strange conversation to have; Alaric's never thought about this from the other side. "You smell like lightning, like a storm's about to strike."

"That's because I have too much magic." Conor shrugs. "You smell like old smoke, like something burned a long time ago but never got washed out. It gave me a headache in the car. That's why I kept trying to open the window even though Dad yelled at me."

Alaric had thought Conor was playing with the window as it slid up and down until Pawel locked it closed. Huh. "Never met a Mage who smelled magic," Alaric says.

"You've never met a Mage like me." Conor hops off the bed. "And I'm bored. Did she say we could explore? Because I want to go do something, and Dad'll be reading all night. He really likes books."

"Hang on." Alaric pulls his phone out, taps out a text to Rory. *Should I be helping? Conor's bored. I could take him outside or something.*

That'd be a big help. Pawel said he's got ADHD and he gets bored easily. Keep him entertained. There are other kids around too. He might like them.

More kids. Perfect.

It's not that Alaric doesn't like kids. There are plenty of them at home, some of them related, some not. Half of them aren't human when he sees them, and that's fine. It's so much easier when they're the same ones who've been around since he was small. And Clan kids are independent from a young age.

Whereas these are kids who might never have seen someone who's Clan.

277

Alaric is wary.

"Now you smell like dog," Conor grumbles. "Wet dog. It's pretty gross."

"Rory says there are plenty of other kids around. Let's go find them." And if Alaric smells like a dog, then fine, he'll be a dog. He lets the hound take his place and pads on four feet out of the room and down the stairs, whuffing when Conor doesn't follow.

Heavy *thuds* behind him and a *thunk* at the bottom herald Conor's arrival as he runs down the stairs and leaps off the bottom few steps. "Okay, that? Is awesome. I can't do that. I mean, I can make sparks and lightning and I may have broken every light bulb in the room once—don't tell my dad, okay?—but I can't do anything like being an actual dog. Can you smell me? Can you track me? Do you think I could track you? Do you smell different now?" Conor gets down on his hands and knees and throws his arms around Alaric's neck, pressing his face against his ear. "Now you really smell like dog. All over dog, nothing but dog. I mean, if I didn't know better, I'd think that you were just totally a dog."

Alaric puts his paws up against the door and pushes, looks back at Conor.

"Oh, right, door. You can't really do that with paws, can you?" Conor yanks the door open, and Alaric lopes through and down the stairs. He can smell curiosity in the air, a rising scent, and a moment later there's a shout. Several shouts.

Rory wasn't kidding about the kids. There are a half dozen of them in a group, an older teen trailing behind them, and from the way they look around, Alaric's pretty sure this is the tip of the iceberg. The youngest girl is maybe four, her thumb in her mouth and dark hair curling across her face as she peers out through the tangles. The eldest of the children is still a tween, with the mutinous expression and crossed arms that herald the onset of teenage years. He stands with his feet set and brows furrowed. Standing behind the children, the older teen is maybe a year or two younger than Alaric. He has a phone in one hand, typing with one thumb, while his other hand reaches out, fingers splayed.

One of them—a five- or six-year-old boy—rushes forward and runs headlong into some kind of a barrier. The child whines, and Alaric whuffs.

"Ask before you pet the dog," the teenager drawls, not looking at them.

"I mean it, Caleb. You know better. Never touch a strange dog."

The smallest girl takes her thumb from her mouth, lisps, "Annette got bit."

"Exactly. See, listen to Miranda. She knows what's going on." The teenager finally looks over at them, tilts his head. "I'm Shawn. You're the guests Gram said was coming?"

"Is she your Gram too, or do you just call her that?" Conor asks. "Does everyone call her that? She's Rory's Gram, but that's how he introduced her to us. I'm Conor, and we're just visiting. This is Alaric." He puts his hand on Alaric's ruff, pulling it away when Alaric bares his teeth. "I'm not afraid of you," Conor says quietly. "I know you won't bite me."

Pawel would probably fail Alaric if he bit Conor, so yeah, Alaric won't bite him. If he keeps poking, though, he might be tempted.

Shawn points to each of the children in turn, reeling off names. "Miranda, Camden, Caleb, Barbie, Jeff, and Simon." He keeps his hand out; Alaric can smell the ozone in front of him, can almost see the barrier that Caleb keeps pressing against. "Is that a shapeshifter?"

Conor's eyebrows go wide. "*He* is Clan and yes, he's Alaric." He nudges Alaric with his foot. "Maybe you should be a boy for this."

Alaric shakes his head, whuffs as strong a negative as he can. If he's about to be overrun by kids, he is not going to be human for the experience. Instead, he lies down, puts his head on the ground, then carefully rolls over and bares his belly.

It's humiliating to go belly-up for this pack of young Mages, but he doesn't have any other way to say he won't bite.

Shawn lowers his hand, and Caleb barrels forward, skidding to a stop on his knees next to Alaric. He bends down, presses his face to Alaric's ruff. "Good doggie."

There's a tug on his ear, and Alaric rolls his head to see Miranda there, petting him. "Soft," she lisps, and he snorts.

"Shawn." At the sound of Gram's voice, the children roll away from Alaric, and Shawn pauses mid-crouch, straightening up.

"Yeah?"

"Take Conor with you and make sure he gets fed. I suspect his father will be occupied straight through dinner. Conor"—she turns her attention to him—"Shawn will give you the rules, but this place is a magic safe-zone, as long as the magic you do is safe. Please do not do magic without someone else there, and no rituals. Only your own intrinsic magic during playtime. Do no harm."

Conor's eyes are wide, and he raises his hands, fingertips spread. Sparks dance along the tips, and he shows them to her; the air is awash in the scent of ozone. "This is okay." It's not a question, more a bewildered statement.

Gram nods, smiling gently. "It's okay, Conor. We're all Mages here, or families of Mages. Magic is fine. Ask questions. You may think you know a lot, but if there is anything you want to learn, take advantage of being with children like yourself."

"Sorry, Alaric, they're more interesting." Conor slips away from Alaric's side and steps into the group of children. Miranda grabs his hands, pulls them down, and shoves one finger into her mouth, making a face as the sparks continue. Conor snickers.

Alaric rolls back to his feet, hunches his back, and pushes himself into humanity. Caleb watches him, wide-eyed, as he stands, then runs to join Shawn when he calls.

Gram's hand falls on Alaric's shoulder as the children rush off. "I didn't think you'd want to babysit," she says quietly. "Shawn's more than capable, and he's only one of the teens here. He can call in plenty of reinforcements if he feels he needs to. They'll be fine." She tugs slightly, motions for him to follow her around the back of the house. "On the other hand, Conor is right. His father and my grandson will likely be busy for hours. Is there anything you need while you're here?"

"You're not afraid of me?" The side of the house is lined with a garden of late-blooming flowers. The scent is bright and fresh, mixing with the sunshine that Gram seems to exude. Alaric rubs at his nose, tries to tamp down his sensitivity to smell.

"Did you think we would be?" Gram leads him to the back where camp chairs ring a fire pit. She gestures, and the pit lights with a blazing bonfire. As she sinks slowly into one of the chairs, she looks back at where he stands warily, arms crossed. "You did," she answers her own question.

"Clan and Mage," Alaric says. He takes one of the other chairs, leaving space between them.

"Clan and Mage," she echoes. "It's a poisonous thing to perpetuate, don't you think?" She sits back, her hands clasped. "On the other hand, separatism is dangerous, and here we are, more like Clan than other Mages, I know. We like our space. We like having the ability to be ourselves. We don't feel the need to engage in everything that modern society offers, but we also don't want to divorce ourselves entirely."

"Rory says you're hippies."

She laughs softly. "He's not wrong. This commune was started when I was seventeen and first in love with my wife. It wasn't entirely new. We were typical Mages, with our own neighborhoods within towns nearby. Ten of us banded together—my parents, myself and Susan, and six of our friends—to buy this land and create our own space. We've grown since then. There are easily a few hundred of us living here, and we believe in communal family. It takes a village to raise a child. Don't raise your eyebrows at me—Clan aren't the only ones who believe in free-range children."

"It's not what I expected," Alaric admits.

Gram leans forward, tucks her hair behind her ear. "You're not what I expected either," she says softly. "I've met Clan who are more beast than not. I've met Clan who can't handle the smell of magic. But you're settled here, and you have a tangible connection to my grandson." She gets a hand up before Alaric can say anything. "I'm not saying you're romantically involved, and I'm not asking."

"He's like a brother," Alaric says, and that makes Gram snort.

"That only defines the connection in your mind," Gram says. "My point is, you're not locked in the ways of your Clan. You're not our enemy, and we aren't yours. And if there is anything we can do to support you, we will. If you're Rory's family, then you're ours as well."

Alaric licks his lips, inhales the warmth of her scent. "I appreciate the offer," he says slowly. "Thank you. We buried Orson last Saturday, and right now, the thing I need most is a chance to be quiet. To just be."

Gram gestures at the fire. "All I have planned for the evening—aside from dinner—is sitting by the fire with a book or knitting. You're welcome to keep me company."

"Do you keep your own sheep?" Alaric asks, and Gram lifts an eyebrow. "If you do, I'd like to see them. See your process, if you card and spin. I dye. And knit. And weave." The words spill out, his hands clenched as he says them, expecting derision.

Gram pushes to her feet, motions for him to follow. "You seem like you won't mind a walk, but I'm going to take the golf cart," she says, heading for a building. "If you're interested in textiles, then we have quite a lot to talk about. And I've got someone for you to meet." She glances over her shoulder, raises an eyebrow. "Maybe we can talk about doing some trading eventually. It's always good to meet another community that does its own fiber arts."

Alaric's fingers itch with the need to do something, and this is so familiar in such a different place. It's strangely perfect, so he hurries after her. This is something he can offer, something he has experience with. And it's comfortable. Comforting. Just what he needs.

42

IT'S A LONG WEEKEND, but it's not entirely bad. Alaric crashes early on Sunday night, wakes into the sunlit room to find Rory had crawled into bed sometime during the night. When Alaric shifts, Rory mutters in his sleep, and Alaric decides that he doesn't really need to get up. He burrows back under the covers, drags Rory over him like a blanket, and slides down into slumber.

He wakes alone again, his phone blinking from several text messages. Rory, letting him know that he ate and is back in the library. Chris, asking how the research is going. Drea, talking about some party she went to at VIT the night before, sent long after Alaric went to sleep. He sends a quick note to Rory to let him know he's up, and another to Chris to say that he has no idea, then tosses the phone on the nightstand. He leaves it there when he packs up his things, a conscious decision to disconnect and follow Gram to someone else's home to spend the day.

He ends up in David's house, in a bright, airy room at the back, with spun yarn laid out on tables. Alaric shows David the process he uses for his dyes, and together they work through several hanks of a mid-weight yarn, perfect for sweaters. The dye reeks, like it always does, and the scent reminds Alaric of home and comfort. It's easy to let go of his stress as they trade techniques. Somewhere in the middle of the day, Alaric finds Miranda pressed up against his leg, trying to watch. He lifts her up and anchors her on one hip while he works, explaining each step to the small girl.

When he explains that it's best to warm the yarn to fix the dye, he grabs a plastic bag to put it in, intending to let it bake in the sun. But Miranda wiggles her fingers and takes the bag from him. Her small fingers squish it tightly, and her expression furrows deeply, lips pressed together. Alaric can feel the warmth coming from her small body, sees steam rise from her fingers.

"Don't burn it. If it gets too hot, it'll felt," he murmurs, and she leans in against him and holds on. "Don't move your hands, either. Just hold on, keep it still. It needs to be a gentle warmth."

She offers the package back to him, and it's still warm. He sets the bag back down on the bench, and slowly lowers her to the ground. "Let it cool now," he says. "When it's done, you'll have David help you wash it in cold water—very gently, so it doesn't felt. Once the water runs clear, you'll be done."

"I want a sweater," Miranda says firmly.

"I'm sure David will make you one." Alaric smells amusement, glances over at the door to see Rory there, his fingers tapping on the screen of his phone. Pawel is behind him, Conor nowhere to be seen.

Miranda tugs at his jeans. "I want you to make me one."

There's a snort of laughter, and when Alaric glares, Pawel shakes his head.

"I'm not laughing at the idea of you knitting," Pawel says. "I'm laughing at the fact that Rory's cousin seems to have imprinted on you."

Alaric can't deny that Miranda is currently clinging to his leg like a limpet, as if she's afraid that he's going to disappear into thin air. For all he knows, she might know people who do exactly that. He crouches down, and she shoves her thumb back in her mouth, tilts her head, and looks at him.

What the fuck is he supposed to do? He can't make the kid cry.

"I can't take this yarn with me," he tells her quietly. "It's not done yet. But I have stuff of my own. Stuff I made at my home, Clan yarn. I'll make you something, and Rory'll get it to you."

"Promise?" She holds out her hand, sticky with saliva.

Alaric clasps it solemnly. "Promise."

Rory unfolds himself from the doorjamb, passes his phone to Alaric when he joins them. He's got pictures. Several pictures, of Alaric and Miranda with their heads bent close together, working on the yarn. Alaric's cheeks go hot.

Rory takes the phone back and does something. "Sent them to you,"

Rory says. "So you can do what you want. Are you ready to go?"

"We've read everything we could read, and we've got things to talk about, but we can do that in the car," Pawel says. "I'd like to get back before dinner so I can get Conor to wind down in time to sleep tonight. He has to go back to school tomorrow. He's pretty wound up after a weekend of no magic restrictions."

"You can visit any time you like," Rory points out. "Gram invited you back. Especially since Conor probably could use a community, and so could you. We're not really meant to be solitary."

"I might do that." Pawel gives a lingering look to Gram's house as he heads to the car. "I should have thought of this before."

"You do have a lot of interviews talking about Lineage community," Alaric says dryly. One of the most common themes of Pawel's book is magical community. He can't think Pawel missed this.

"I also have a life at Pine Hills, and my son has a life in the town there," Pawel says. "The two are at odds with each other until a magical community happens to move into the space where I live."

Alaric grunts and slides into the back seat. Rory's already thrown their bags into the trunk, and Alaric's phone sits on the seat, waiting for him to reconnect to the world. Conor takes the front seat and buckles in, pulling the seat up to give Rory more leg room. As soon as they're settled and the car is moving, Rory brings out a sheaf of papers and starts shuffling through them.

Alaric sends a quick text off to Drea and Corbin: *On our way home. Be there in a few hours.*

"So we found something," Rory says quietly. "But the problem is, it's not real."

"It's real," Alaric mutters. "My brother is dead, remember?"

"The symbol is real," Pawel tells him. "We found multiple references to it. But it's not magical in nature. It's not meant for a ritual done by Mages."

"I don't get it." Alaric tries to puzzle through Pawel's statement. It's a symbol. A rune, maybe, but it's something for a purpose. It was part of a ritual, and Orson's dead. Of course it's made by Mages.

"It's a word," Rory tells him. He has a drawing of the symbol, clear and precise. "We found two different meanings for it: retribution or recompense."

"So it's a different language?" Alaric asks slowly. "Whose language is it?"

Rory shuffles through the paperwork, but it's not fast enough for Pawel.

"That's the best part of this," Pawel says. He stops at Alaric's growl, his hands tight on the steering wheel. "Of the research, Alaric, not the situation. There is no *best part* to your brother dying."

"Damn right," Alaric growls.

"I'm sorry." Pawel lets the apology sit there while Rory continues going through papers until he finds the one he wants.

The page shows a copy of an old piece of art, the lines thick and rough. The shadows around the edges of the room are dark, while a woman sits in the light, an infant cradled on her lap while she spins. When Alaric looks closer, he sees the shape within the shadow, the tiny white spots of eyes. "What is this?"

"There was an interview in my book," Pawel says, his voice even. "I spoke to a woman who claimed to be more than a century and a half old. Her family said it had to be true—she'd been alive longer than any of them, already old when they were born. And she claimed to have seen Talent that is supposedly a legend. Deathstalkers. I also spoke to a historian of the Talented lines, who talked about Shadowwalkers and Soulstealers. They're also legends. They don't exist. It's possible that some of them are at the root of other myths—Soulstealers may have existed once and still live as the vampire myth. But they aren't real, not any longer."

"The thing he's so excited about is that this is a symbol used by the Deathstalkers. Or Shadowwalkers. Or Soulstealers." Rory pauses, looks at the image. "The problem with legends is that everything's a mess, and it's all hearsay. It's what people remember and stories that have been passed down. But that symbol is part of those stories."

"So it's a copycat," Alaric says flatly. "So what?"

"What if it's not?" Pawel asks, and Alaric smells that flare of interest and curiosity. He bites back the growl because he understands. Pawel is an academic. He wants to learn.

But this is Alaric's *life*.

"What if a Deathstalker came for Orson and his roommates?" Rory asks. "What if this is because they aren't legends, and they're here?"

"Why the fuck would they kill my brother?" Alaric bites out. "What the fuck did he do to them?"

"Language," Conor sing-songs, and it's the first that Alaric remembers that he's even in the car.

"Put in your headphones," Pawel instructs. "Play a game. Watch a video. This isn't a conversation for you."

"You're only angry because Alaric swore," Conor grumbles, but he shoves the earbuds into his ears anyway. Alaric can hear the sound as he turns up the volume on his tablet and sinks into the game.

"No, I really don't want to talk about this in front of you," Pawel says quietly. He glances up, meets Alaric's gaze in the rearview mirror. "I don't know why a legend would come back and kill your brother, Alaric. But if it isn't that, then someone wants us to think it is. Either way, it's the first clue we've got. And more importantly, it means it wasn't a magical ritual. If you want to try to explain that to your father—stave off whatever he means to do—that might help. Orson's roommate was as much of a victim as Orson, probably."

"But we still don't know who or why." Alaric glances at his phone when it chimes.

Call me.

Alaric huffs. "Corbin wants me to call him. Hang on." He presses to dial, lifts the phone to his ear.

"Drea's still here," Corbin says as soon as he picks up. "I'm putting her on a bus back to Unity soon, but right now we're looking into something."

"What?"

"I'm sending you a link to a news article from last night."

Alaric puts the call on speaker, switches to messaging, and clicks on the link Corbin sends. It opens to a local news site, and an article timestamped with the wee hours of the morning. Alaric motions, and Rory slides closer to look at it with him.

"One dead, one in a coma, after ritual gone awry," Alaric reads.

"I know what it says, and am I on speaker?" Corbin asks.

"Yeah. Shut up, I'm reading it so Pawel can hear. He's driving." Alaric frowns, skimming through the article. "Noah Steinberg was found dead in his apartment early this morning after neighbors reported shouts and screaming. A woman, Lorraine Barr, was found unconscious and remains in a coma at the hospital. Noah's boyfriend, Darrik Malone, is missing and is sought for questioning. It appears to be the aftermath of a ritual. There were candles and blood, and there are marks on the body of the unconscious woman implying she may have been the target or a sacrifice." He glances at Rory. "You don't actually sacrifice people."

"We use blood sometimes, yes, but no sacrifices," Rory says firmly. "Corbin, are you calling because of the marks?"

"A friend of a friend has a friend in the police department, and they were able to find out that the mark is on the inside of her left wrist," Corbin says. "It looks like it was both cut and burned into her skin, and it's the same mark. The same exact symbol."

There's a chill down Alaric's spine. His eyes close as a growl rumbles up, and he pulls away when Rory touches him. "What do they know?" he rumbles.

"The girl's still in a coma, and the boyfriend's at large," Corbin says. "Drea and I are going to see what we can do. I mean, if you can sweet-talk case information out of an officer, I should be able to charm one easily." There's a squeak, high-pitched enough to hurt Alaric's ears. "Your sister pinches hard. But she's right, we're going to try tracking Darrik first. We've got advantages the police force doesn't have." Another squeak, and he adds, "And she has a lot of good points. We're also going to talk to people around them. Because I'm sure the police are already doing that, but we're unassuming and just other college students, and I'm pretty sure that they went here."

Alaric feels vaguely sick to his stomach. "Did you know them?"

"No, but they lived on a street that's mostly VIT student apartments, and they seem like they're about the right age," Corbin says.

"They think the boyfriend did it?" Pawel asks, and Alaric repeats the question in case Corbin didn't hear.

"Seems to be what the article's saying, that's why I want to know more about them. What? Oh. Drea's got the school directory up and Alaric, why does your sister know the password on my laptop? Because I am not that predictable. You know it wasn't easy to guess." A shuffling noise. "Noah was a junior, and a comp sci major. Lorraine's also a junior, in math, physics, and apparently a minor in philosophy. The boyfriend is a teacher at the local high school. So he's older."

Alaric huffs; he can't see how any of this intersects with Orson. "Maybe they met while Orson was at VIT?" he thinks out loud. "Fuck. No. This doesn't make sense. Why would some local high-school teacher kill my brother, then kill his own boyfriend?"

"Maybe it wasn't him. He's only under suspicion, Ric."

When Rory touches Alaric's arm, he doesn't pull away this time, just lets the beast and anger bleed away. "See what you can find, Corbin, and send it to me. Drea has my number," Rory says.

"And be careful." Pawel's voice is firm. Flat. "If it is the boyfriend, it's possible that he's a kind of Talent that hasn't been seen in a long time."

"Deathstalker," Rory supplies.

A short, sharp bark of laughter. "Oh God, do you remember the story of the Deathstalker and the lemon, Ric?" Corbin asks, still laughing. "Those things aren't real. They're fairy tales. Told to Clan kids to keep them in line, because how else do you handle a bunch of kids who can shapeshift? You scare the piss out of them."

Alaric had forgotten that story, left it behind in the recesses of his mind long ago. He remembered far scarier childhood stories, like the one about the Clan child who lost his beast. He can feel the weight of Rory's gaze on him, and he shrugs one shoulder. "There are storybooks. I can get them for you."

"They'd be interesting from the purely anthropological and sociological viewpoint," Pawel muses. "Still, my point stands. The symbol isn't magical—it's a Deathstalker word, for lack of a better term. So be careful."

"Always," Corbin says cheerfully, and the call cuts out.

"He's never careful," Alaric mutters. "Never. But Drea is, and she's with him." And she's potentially in danger, too, which *fuck*... "They'll be fine."

"I hate to say it, but this is good news for your investigation," Pawel says quietly. "More evidence. More information. More of a chance to find out what's going on. With a symbol like that, the deaths are most likely linked. The question is what those kids had in common with your brother. And how a legend's come back to life."

Alaric's not sure if he believes in the legend, but he knows something is going on. And it's apparently getting worse. He taps out a message to Drea.

Keep an eye on Corbin; don't let him do anything stupid. And find out if any of them are Mages or Clan. I want to know if someone's trying to start a war.

43

"So, we're pretty sure Darrik didn't do it, but the police are still looking into it officially." Corbin drags the rake across the grounds, moving leaves but not bothering to actually gather them up. Alaric wants to point out that if he's not going to help, he should head back to VIT, but it's kind of nice having Corbin here at PHU for the afternoon.

Terrifying, but nice.

"You're shit at this."

Corbin jumps when Mac whispers in his ear, turns with the rake out. She blocks it easily, knocking it to the side, and raises her hands in a shrug.

Corbin exhales roughly. "How did you—?"

"Ex-military," she says. "I'm good at sneaking up on people. Besides, I knew Ric wouldn't tell you if he saw me."

Alaric hadn't seen her, but that's not a surprise. Mac is disturbingly good at sneaking up on people, especially in a crowd like this. Fifteen sisters from SigPsiEp and twenty OPT brothers, plus Corbin and some random folks from Alaric's floor and elsewhere, are all working on raking leaves on the quad as a service to the school.

"Introduce me," Mac says.

It feels like the hundredth time tonight that he's done this, even though Alaric knows it couldn't have been that many times. "This is Corbin. Grew up with him back home, and he's at VIT now. Decided to get his ass over here to visit today, so I dragged him out to work with us." He pauses, admits, "Drea convinced him."

"Drea's good people." Mac tilts her head, considering. "I've heard of you. The best-friend-slash-brother, right? Be good to Alaric, and be good to Drea. Because I can kick your ass if you're not, and just so you know, I actually will." She points to the rake in Alaric's hand. "Don't overdo it. We've still got practice tomorrow and Saturday, and I need you to help get people ready to compete. You're going with us to Boston, right?"

"Am I supposed to?" Alaric isn't sure about how it works for the Talent on the team.

"This is your kicking thing, right? With the trees?" Corbin asks.

"Trees aren't normal, but Alaric can handle it," Mac says. "And yes, any-one who wants to come cheer the team on can be there. I'll be coaching competitors on the floor along with Pawel—thankfully coaches can be Talent even if we can't compete ourselves. I know Jackson wants you to be there, and Mason's liked working with you."

"Can't disappoint Jackson," Corbin says, smirking.

There are times when Alaric regrets telling Corbin anything, although he can see a small smile from Mac at the words too. Fine. "I'll go."

Mac claps him on the shoulder, then reels him in for a hug. "Good, thanks. We're also taking a few people from outside the team. Pawel's bringing Conor, of course, partly because it's easier than getting child care, and partly so Conor can watch the 'big kids' compete. Chris is coming, because he owes me about a hundred favors, and he can pay off a few by making sure my team doesn't pass out from dehydration. He can also hold paddles for warmups, now that he's in the brace."

"Don't work him too hard; we need him in shape for football," Alaric points out. "Don't undo everything PT is doing for him."

"Do you really think I'd do that?" Mac sidesteps as a pile of leaves show-ers down near them. "I see you, Trish!" she yells out. "Are you trying to start a fight?"

"Wasn't me!" Trish yells back.

Mac squeezes Alaric's shoulder. "We'll talk more about the trip later. I have to go make a leaf pile big enough to jump in."

Corbin leans on his rake, watches her walk away. "Your friends are—"

"If you say hot, I'm going to hurt you," Alaric mutters, and Corbin laughs.

"I was going to say they aren't what I expected." Corbin knocks into him lightly. "It's weird seeing you here. Drea's been telling me more about it than you do, but still, this is all…" He motions with his hand. "It's more social than I expected. So that's Mac, right?"

Alaric nods and points out others that are there as well, even the ones he's already introduced Corbin to. Sera's with Trish; Trish has one hand out and Sera drops leaves over it, looking at something. Dax and Cass are working with Mac to build a huge pile of leaves, and Carolyn is dragging more leaves over. Alaric doesn't recognize the boy with Carolyn, but from the resemblance, he guesses that he must be the twin she mentioned.

He points out Heather to Corbin but avoids actually talking to her, and is pleased that she seems to be avoiding him in return. He's already told Corbin about the incident in the locker room, and Corbin's gaze narrows sharply when he spots her.

It's tempting to let Corbin do whatever he's thinking, but he leans in and whispers "No" before the idea can fully set.

"Hey." Chris walks with a swinging gait, the brace on his knee allowing him to bend it but still giving him support. "You don't seem to be doing much raking."

Alaric grins, makes as if to hand over the rake. "You could help out, but no, you're just here to observe, right?"

"Time off for injury." Chris spreads his hands. "We've got enough workers here, and I'd ask why there are so many people from your floor, but I think I already know the answer."

"First, Sera doesn't actually live on my floor, she just spends a lot of time with Pat. And it's weird seeing Sera without Pat," Alaric admits, "so I figure that he'll show up here eventually, and if Pat's here, Jackson will be here, which means TJ and probably Nik, and…" His voice trails off, staring across the quad, past where they're working, to where a small, dark-haired girl is having an earnest conversation with…nothing. "And I don't know why Pels is here," he says slowly, "but I'm pretty sure it has nothing to do with us."

Corbin's eyebrows go up, and he shoves his rake at Chris, who barely manages to grab it before Corbin disappears in a flurry of wings, flying high.

"Curiosity," Alaric says. "Fatal flaw in birds." He has no idea what Pels's

Talent is, but he's sure she's got one. He's also damned sure she won't want Corbin eavesdropping on whatever she's doing. He glances over at Chris. "How's the PT going?"

Chris makes a face. "It's going. Hurts like fucking hell, but it's worth it. My range of motion is good, the kneecap is tracking well, so they don't think I'm at risk to blow it out when I come back. I just need to keep up the training and the massage therapy, and I get my next official evaluation on the 25th. If I'm cleared, I'll at least get to play in the end-of-season games. I don't want to miss the one against VIT." He nods at where Corbin sits in the tree, tail feathers flicking as he looks down at Pels. "I didn't know Corbin was visiting."

"Neither did I until he texted that he had a ride over because someone he knows had to come here," Alaric says. "We're getting something to eat after—him and me and Drea. I think he's worried about us."

"You just buried your brother, and it looks like there's someone out there targeting Talent. I'm not surprised he's worried," Chris says. He's standing close enough that his shoulder brushes Alaric's, and Alaric leans into his body heat instinctively.

Across the quad, the raven flies out of the tree with a squawk, shooting straight across the grass before flapping its wings hard and flying up. Corbin shrieks, and Pels yells, "It's your own damned fault, bird!"

She turns on her heel and stalks off, avoiding the large crowd raking.

Corbin lands next to them and resolves into human in one smooth motion, brushing leaves from his clothes. "That was unique." He looks at Alaric, eyebrows arched. "She's a telekinetic, and she has conversations with people who either aren't actually here or don't exist. I'd avoid her."

"Nik likes her better than Jennifer." It's not saying that Pels isn't trouble, but she's less trouble for Nikita. "I don't see her much. She's kind of a loner."

"So were you," Corbin says quietly, and Alaric can't deny it.

They get started working again, helping Mac and Dax build a giant pile of leaves. As soon as it's done, Cass calls out from across the quad, takes a running start, and does a series of tumbling jumps before she faces the pile and leaps into it. She comes up sputtering, leaves in her hair, and Dax helps her get out.

They barely clear the space when Mac does a spinning kick in the air, then another one where she twists around, her feet going over her head, hands not touching the ground, then she flips forward and lands in the leaves with a shout.

It seems to be a signal to the girls of SigPsiEp, who all crowd into the leaves and start throwing them at each other. Sera's in the middle, despite not being a sister, and Cass stays off to one side, Dax gently picking leaves from her hair.

"I'm going to be sexiled again," Chris mutters, and Corbin snorts.

Alaric catches the whiff of wariness combined with Rory's scent moments before he hears Thorne call out. "Ric!"

Interest. Unease. Jealousy. Anger. A wash of heated scent as Corbin steps in front of Alaric, and Alaric lets him do it. Nothing will stop Corbin now, not when he's this ramped up, ready for some kind of a fight.

"Thorne Baker," Corbin says easily, planted between Alaric and Thorne like a slightly smaller, rangy wall. He holds out his hand. "And Rory Everett. I've been looking forward to meeting you both."

Thorne takes Corbin's hand, hauls him in for a hard hug and a kiss on the cheek. "And you're Corbin. Ric's got a picture of you on his laptop. Maybe more—I haven't asked if the one of the bird and dog is the two of you, but I've always figured it is. I don't think I'd recognize you as a bird, though."

Corbin's gaze narrows, and his scent flashes with something Alaric can't identify. Alaric gets a hand on Corbin's shoulder, squeezes in warning, and Corbin drops his hand.

"Hey," Rory says, shoving both his hands in his pockets.

Corbin nods. "Are you guys coming out with us to dinner tonight?" His glance includes Chris, his head tilting in challenge.

Rory looks to Alaric before he responds, and when Alaric shrugs, Rory shrugs right back. "Didn't know there was a dinner to go to," Rory replies. "Sure. I'm in. I don't have any plans."

"If you stick around here long enough, someone will make sure you help with the raking," Chris warns. "You'll end up with plans that take all afternoon and hurt your shoulders."

"I don't mind." Thorne's gaze shifts to the pile that's been scattered and is being raked up again. He waves to Dax, then wades in, taking Dax's rake so that Dax and Cass can escape.

Chris mutters under his breath; Alaric doesn't need to hear it to know what he's saying.

"Yes, pet human, you're invited, too," Corbin says.

"Don't," Alaric warns.

"I'm being fond. It's obvious you're keeping him for some reason, along with your Mages." Corbin turns, pats Alaric on the cheek. "Dinner out will give me a chance to get to know them. And for them to get to know me. I don't have to be able to smell scent to know that Rory doesn't like me at all."

"He's not wrong," Rory says dryly. "I'm right here, you know. I don't belong to Alaric. I'm not *his* Mage. And you haven't given me much of a reason to like you, yet."

Alaric's impressed that Rory says "yet," like he's willing to give Corbin a chance.

The small smirk that Corbin wears falls away, expression twisting serious. "He's my brother," Corbin says quietly, "and you share his bed like Clan does. I'm trying to figure out how to deal with my brother having a new family, one I don't know, and one that goes against everything we've been taught is safe. I am *trying*, and if it means throwing all the mattresses on the floor and crashing together in a giant pile of fur, feathers, and humanity until I get it right, then I'll do that. But he's been my brother since we were born, and that's not changing." Corbin swallows, the muscle in his jaw flexing tightly. "I worry about him. Just like I figure you do. The only difference is, you've only been doing it a couple of months."

Rory's shoulders hunch. His gaze flicks from Alaric to where Thorne is carrying Carolyn toward the newly growing pile of leaves. He turns slowly to face Corbin, his chin lifting. "Dinner's fine," Rory says. "I'm going back to the dorm to get my homework done because I have a Skype date with Stormy later, so I won't have time then. Let me know when it's time for dinner, and I'll meet you there."

"I'm thinking Doherty's," Alaric says.

Rory nods. "Just let me know when."

"Is Stormy a significant other?" Corbin asks curiously as Rory walks away, hands shoved deep in his pockets, spine slightly bent, and hair hanging forward.

"Bandmate," Alaric replies. Rory's body language is tight and closed off; Alaric wants to follow but knows he wouldn't be wanted right now. He can feel where Chris is still standing behind him, posture as tight as Rory's. It's supposed to be a fun afternoon, and it's not working. Corbin doesn't mesh with his new life, and that aches more than he expected. "If you keep being an ass, I'm going to let Drea do whatever she feels like in retribution," he mutters. "Because I can't deal with it. You want to keep me from getting hurt? Fine, Corbin, then stop being the one to do it."

It feels like shit, but Alaric needs to get away. He leaves Corbin standing with Chris and makes his way across the quad to where Mac is working with Drea and Trish. Sera sits on the lowest branch of a tree, her feet swinging, her gaze fixed somewhere in the distance. Alaric swears he hears faint music from somewhere, but it isn't enough to drown out the sound of Corbin's voice.

"What'd I do?"

Alaric tilts his head, hates the fact that he listens in and that he needs to know the answer.

Chris lets the silence stretch long enough that there's a hitch in Corbin's breath as if he's about to speak again, and Chris interrupts him. "If you have to ask," Chris says, "then I don't think you know Alaric as well as you think you do."

44

FRIDAY'S A LONG day. Alaric goes from classes to dinner at OPT, and from there to taekwondo. He kicks with everyone else, helps Jackson and Mason focus on their sparring drills, all the while aware that there's a crowd playing cards in the hall and waiting for them to finish.

After the workout, they stop back at the dorm long enough for Jackson and Alaric to get rid of their gear, then the group heads off to the movie on campus. They take over an entire row, and Alaric is thankful PHU has a dedicated movie theater in the campus center, unlike VIT—Corbin has told him their movie nights take place in a lecture hall. Alaric doesn't want to think about sitting in the uncomfortable plastic seats of the hall where he takes magical studies.

Chris knocks his knee into Alaric's; Alaric inhales and lets himself relax. He's surrounded by familiar scent, with Dax and Cass next to him, and Trish, Sera, Patrick, and Jackson on Chris's other side.

It's the kind of movie Alaric normally hates, with complicated relationships and a woman trying to choose between her childhood friend, who's human like her, and the Healer who stole her heart at work. He sits upright when she takes her friend to task over his prejudice, and leans forward when she decides that she doesn't need anyone.

His brow furrows, and he falls back against the seat, his arms crossed through the last fifteen minutes, as she rejects both suitors repeatedly and ends the movie happy and alone.

"I wasn't expecting that," Alaric says as the lights come up.

"It's on the short-list for awards season, I've heard." Trish says.

"High ratings on every site I've checked, and even Terrence Fisher gives it high marks for the realism and the unusual message," Sera adds. She climbs over the back of her seat to get into the empty row behind them. "I have to pee. Teas Please after?"

"Y'know, drinking to excess is the typical college experience," Pat calls out as Sera works her way into the crowd climbing the stairs to escape the hall.

"Sugar first. We can drink on a full stomach!" Sera calls back. "Meet you outside the main doors!"

Alaric is still thinking about the movie. He pulls his phone out, searches for *A Taste of Orange*, and looks at the reviews. He starts with the review and comments on *Fish or Fly*, and he's surprised when they're all positive.

It's great to see a story where the woman doesn't have to give herself up for a man.

It's so rare to find a story where Talent isn't demonized, but also doesn't win.

So true to life. Sometimes we all strike out, and it's okay. No one has to get pissed off.

His fingers hover over the virtual keyboard, and he types quickly to leave one more anonymous comment on the review.

Nice to see someone who might be like me.

He presses "Submit" before he can think twice about it, then shoves his phone back in his pocket as Chris knocks into him.

"You up for Teas Please on a Friday night?"

"Can't be that bad," Alaric says, knowing he's probably lying. "Anyone mind if I let Drea and Rory know where we're going?"

"Already done." Jackson holds up his phone. "And TJ and Nik."

"We won't all fit at one table." It's going to be a large group if everyone suddenly shows up, and eight is already tight.

"That's a problem for later," Pat says easily. "I'm heading out to meet Sera. Trish, Jackson, you coming?"

Cass holds up a hand, wiggles her fingers. "Go."

"You guys coming with us?" Chris leans past Alaric to touch Dax's shoulder.

"I'm thinking—"

"Oh, let's go." Cass's cheerful voice doesn't match her sour scent. "You wanted to do social things. This is social. Even if I'm pretty sure I'm the only—"

"Don't, Cass. Not tonight." Dax stands, offers her his hand. "Come on. You like Trish and Sera."

"I like all of them," Cass snaps. "Maybe I just wanted to spend time with you. Since tomorrow you're off for a game, and Sunday you'll be tired and want to catch up on your work."

"Cass." Dax kisses her lightly. "Come on. Social time, then us time. Compromise."

She sighs. "Compromise. Fine."

Chris holds back, waiting until they walk out of the hall, hand in hand. "And…sexiled again later. They've both got rough schedules this semester, and it seems like every time they do get together, they end up in bed."

"They don't smell like it tonight." All Alaric smells is frustration and the sour scents of jealousy and irritation.

"Give them time. They'll make up." Chris nudges Alaric, hand on his back. "Come on. Let's catch up."

It's slow going, but Chris moves better with the brace than he did on crutches. By the time they reach Teas Please, Sera is riding on Jackson's back, and Pat is trying to carry Trish. Dax and Cass hold hands and are the first into the booth, settling in close together at the far end. The sour smell is gone, although Alaric is thankful that neither of them smells like musk yet.

"I want to know which one of you has the Talent that guarantees this table will be open for you," Nate asks as he drops menus on the table. "Is it you, tall, dark, and handsome?" When Jackson raises his hands and shakes his head, Nate pulls back. "Wait a minute; even numbers. Is this some kind of a date night?"

Alaric slides onto the bench, Chris fitting in next to him. Jackson and Pat are next to Dax, and Sera and Trish squeeze in after Chris. Alaric frowns, looks at each person, pausing when Dax kisses Cass slowly.

"Not dates," he says firmly.

"Well, then, doesn't-like-nuts," Nate grins. "What're you having tonight?"

Mac drops in before Nate finishes taking orders and adds hers to the end of the list. She calls out to Alaric that Drea will be over soon, and she squishes onto the end of the bench. Rory and Thorne walk in when Drea does, and there are too many bodies for one bench. Cass slides onto Dax's lap, and Alaric is wedged between Dax and Chris. Sera leans across the table to make a point, gesturing at Pat, who swats her hand away while Trish tries to haul her back into her seat.

Thorne settles on Mac's lap, while Rory pulls up a chair for the end of the table, and Drea squeezes in next to Jackson, who drops an arm around her shoulders.

Chris shifts, drops his arm across the back of the bench; it gives Alaric room to move closer to him and give Dax and Cass some space. It should be uncomfortable, but the scents are familiar now, the beat of known hearts a soothing sound. Alaric relaxes slowly, lets his body go loose.

"Any room on the bus for a spectator?" Trish asks.

"Tomorrow?" Chris shrugs one shoulder. "Probably, if it's just you."

"You are not dragging me to a football game," Sera says. "Football is not my thing. Not even for a friend."

"Jackson? Pat? Thorne?" Trish looks around. "Aw, c'mon, keep a girl company. Don't any of y'all like football?"

"I'll go," Drea offers. "I mean, my brother's on the team. I might as well show a little support even if I actually hate the game. You can cheer enough for both of us. Or at least tell me when to cheer."

"At least I know where I stand with you," Alaric says dryly. "Not even an ounce of pretending."

Drea blows him a kiss.

"I think it's going to be a hell of a game," Chris says. He reaches behind Alaric to flick Dax's shoulder. "Hey. Tomorrow's game."

"Solid defense against a running game," Dax murmurs, still forehead to forehead with Cass. "Low on interceptions, which is good, especially if we put Dawson in. They have one running back who moves like a jackrabbit—watch out for him. And their kicker's one of the best in the league. She came up from some tiny school in Florida. Totally human."

"I love how all you have to do is poke Dax and he spews stats," Thorne muses. "It's like having a football stat vending machine."

Dax raises a hand, middle finger extended.

"I was being serious. It's an impressive skill. What are they going to do when you graduate?"

"Get a statistician," Chris says. "You should be on the lookout, Alaric. Find someone you trust who can keep stats. Not just someone who can run numbers, but someone who can watch tape and interpret it and work with the team. We're lucky with Dax, but they don't have to be a player."

"That is not a job for me," Rory says, raising his hands in protest.

Alaric snorts. "Didn't think it was. You can write a better fight song instead."

"You don't like *Ode to the Hills*?" Jackson asks. "I've heard worse. There's this one school locally that has a song that sounds like a dirge."

"Did you hear Mac threatening to have us sing it at this weekend's tournament ?"

"That wasn't a threat," Mac says idly. "School spirit. Show unity. Scare the crap out of all the other teams with how off-key we are. I think it's a brilliant idea."

"No," Jackson and Alaric chorus.

"Just no," Jackson adds. "It's a bad idea."

"I'm the coach." Mac smirks. "Brush up on the words. We'll practice on the bus."

"She isn't serious," Alaric mutters. Because she can't be serious. That'd be ridiculous.

"You've met Mac." Chris leans close to whisper in his ear. "I wouldn't put it past her."

"You do know you're going with us, right?" Mac reminds him. "Your voice isn't terrible. Be ready to sing."

Chris groans, letting his head fall against Alaric. "She hates us all."

"Hey." Something hits Alaric in the middle of the forehead; a crumpled-up napkin falls to the table, and Drea smiles innocently at him.

Alaric lifts his eyebrows at his twin.

"Is this going to be the kind of game where you run over the opposition completely, or will it actually be exciting?" Drea asks.

"Lots of passing, and I hear the receiver for our team is better than the

QB," Dax deadpans. "So keep an eye on him while he saves the day. I don't think they'll be a pushover team, but we should win as long as we're consistent. Ric and I have been working on placement, and we've got some good fakes. Haven't missed our first string QB at all lately."

"Hah," Chris says dryly, and Alaric nudges him, pressing his knee against Chris's in solidarity against Dax being an ass.

Dax grins. "You'll be back just in time for the game against VIT. When they have to deal with both of you? They won't know what hit them."

The conversation is interrupted by the arrival of food. Alaric reaches for his tea, inhales the sharp ginger scent as he pours a cup for himself and one for Chris. They have two pots, but there's no point in keeping them separate since they're both drinking the same thing.

Drea asks Rory something about music—some band that Alaric's never heard of—and Alaric lets himself tune out as the conversation shifts around him. The scent of musk is slowly rising to his right, but everyone else smells like contentment and pleasure. Alaric holds the scent in his lungs, lets it suffuse him. It settles his beast to be here.

There's a hint of curiosity in the air; Alaric glances over to see Thorne watching him. Thorne tilts his head, and Alaric frowns, no idea what he's silently asking. Thorne jumps, and Mac smirks; Alaric winces at the spike of arousal in the air, familiar and strong from Thorne. It doesn't fade even when Mac shoves Thorne off her lap, forcing him to get his own chair to pull up next to Rory at the end of the table. Mac's attention shifts away from Thorne—whatever Thorne's interest is, it smells one-sided—but Thorne's focus returns to Alaric. Thorne raises an eyebrow, lifts his cup of tea, and sips it.

Alaric shrugs; he still has no idea how to respond. He's fine. For once his skin doesn't itch. He's perfectly comfortable.

When Cass turns on Dax's lap, bumping into Alaric as she does, Alaric slides a tiny bit closer to Chris. Small movement as Chris turns to look at him; Alaric offers a wry smile and leans in so he can speak quietly. "If Rory's okay with it, you can crash in our room. Looks like yours is definitely going to be occupied."

"There's a couch at OPT, too," Chris says easily. "We can play it by ear.

I don't want to annoy Rory."

Alaric glances over at Rory, but he's involved in a close conversation with Drea. Doesn't really matter; they can sort it out later. Alaric doesn't need to move right now.

45

WATCHING TAEKWONDO MAKES Alaric's skin itch.

It's not bad during the forms competition. He doesn't know the forms other than white belt, so it's interesting to see the different patterns of movement. For a single color of belt, every form is exactly the same, but each competitor does it slightly differently. He tries to judge each group mentally, but he only agrees with the judges on occasion; he's still not sure exactly what they're looking for.

The PHU team has claimed a space to sit and spread out their gear near the bottom of the stands, so Chris won't have to climb up and down constantly. Mac gave them all assignments as soon as they arrived: Chris is in charge of making sure no one misses an announcement for staging, while Alaric is on the move, carrying water bottles, sports drinks, and small snacks to his teammates who are competing.

He feels like he's wearing a uniform even though it's just his PHU taekwondo T-shirt and a jacket that Mac handed him when he got on the bus. Every competitor wears the same jacket, and even Chris has one that he says was left at the house long ago when someone moved out. Alaric is wearing purple and gold, the kicker emblazoned on his back, and it feels good to be part of this particular team.

Neither Mac nor Pawel has stopped moving since they arrived, bustling around and talking to the competition organizers and the judges. With only two coaches for the PHU team, Mac wants to make sure that they don't have more than two people competing at any time; no one should compete without a coach at their ring. Pawel smells supercharged, and the stink of lightning makes Alaric's nose itch. He almost wishes Rory were there to touch Pawel, bleed some of the power off, but he's not sure it'd work like that with him. He suspects that shutting down Pawel's Talent would result in an explosion when it flooded back into him.

"Ric." Mac's right there by his elbow; Alaric flinches away, turns to face her. When she holds out her hand, he gives her two water bottles and a granola bar. "Thanks," she says, and she turns on her heel.

"Who do you want me to warm up?" Alaric asks, and Mac pauses.

"I've got Chris working with the black belts already," Mac says, her gaze drifting to the spot Chris has claimed with their team. "Black belts compete first, which means the color belts are going to get bored. Especially the newer ones. Round them up and get them stationed at ringside for our team as soon as we know who's competing where. Keep them interested in the bouts. Keep them fired up for the team."

Alaric nods. He can't understand how anyone would get bored here. There's always something happening, someone moving. And it's all things he understands. It's different than football. More visceral. Personal.

He gathers up a group just as the first ring assignments are announced. He leaves half of them at a ring for Mason and hands off a water bottle to Pawel. Then he takes the rest of the color belts to Jackson's ring. He hands yet another bottle to Mac, then finds a space to sit where he can watch.

There are two matches before Jackson's, and even those dig deep under Alaric's skin. The men are fairly evenly matched, so he focuses on technique, brow furrowing as he tries to work out how the footwork affects the kicks. Manny leans toward him and offers commentary on each move, pointing out how, despite being even in height, one of the competitors has longer legs than the other.

By the time the fight ends, Alaric is standing again, fists tightly clenched, itching to be out there fighting too. Manny is on her feet cheering when Jackson steps into the ring. Jackson puts his arms out, lets the referee check his gear before he puts his helmet on. When he drops into ready position, Jackson's kihap makes Alaric want to roar in response and fight with him.

This is not the Jackson that Alaric spars on a regular basis. He can see now that Jackson has been holding back, both in speed and style. Jackson dances on light feet, sliding sideways out of the way when his opponent kicks, retaliating by lifting his foot and bouncing it off of the other man's headgear. Alaric watches the scoreboard change—up by four for Jackson, then sliding back to even, then up by two for his opponent. A flurried exchange of kicks, including two quick spinning head kicks from Jackson, leaves Jackson up by six when the timer ends the round.

Jackson sits, breathing hard, and sips at the water. Mac crouches in front of him, and Alaric focuses to hear her soft words.

"He's angry," Mac whispers. "You nailed him four times in the head, and he's pissed off about it. You know his coach is telling him to change things up, avoid letting you get those same kicks on him. That means he's going to change his distance. I want you to take it in close. You need some time to breathe, too. Get in the clinch and use tight kicks, both to his back and to his head. When he realizes that the clinch isn't doing him any good, let him give you the space you need again and finish it off. You're already up by six. If you do this right, you can gap him before the round ends."

A gap means a twelve-point lead. Two more head kicks would get him there.

Jackson nods, takes one last gulp of water, and hands the bottle to Mac. He's already pulling his helmet back on when the referee calls him out on the mat. He drops into ready position and meets the gaze of his opponent.

Mac was right about the anger. It flows off of Jackson's opponents in waves, mixing with the rank, salty scent of sweat. Jackson sits back and lets him come in close; they lean on each other, chest to chest, then Jackson rocks back on his foot and lifts his other leg to somehow tap the guy in the back of the head.

The points don't go up, and Mac raises her hand, calling for a review. The sharp scent of anger increases when the points hit the scoreboard after the judges confer.

Jackson's expression is solemn as he returns to the fight. They dance around each other, are told to *fight* by the referee in the ring. The opponent tests, then explodes into motion. Jackson circles, throws a spin back kick, then follows it with a crescent kick that strikes the side of his head, knocking his opponent back.

The points go up, and a buzzer sounds. The match is over with a minute left; Jackson made the twelve-point gap.

Manny's screaming loud enough to hurt Alaric's ears. Something touches his hand, and he turns, twisting as a hand falls to his lower back. Chris smells like he aches, sour pain and elation in his scent.

"You okay?" Chris asks, and Alaric nods.

"Wish I could fight," he admits, which is no surprise. "Come on. Let's get Jackson some food. Mason's probably done now, too."

It's a long day, overall. Alaric hadn't thought about how many hours it would take for everyone to fight, then for the medal ceremonies, then for the team to gather up equipment once they're done. They load everything onto the bus and climb in after the tournament is finally over, and Alaric's thankful he's not the one driving.

He slides into a seat next to Chris while Mac sits in front of them. "We've got three hours on the road," she says. "Get some sleep."

Chris makes a noise, rearranges himself so that he's leaning on Alaric's shoulder. He's asleep before Alaric can say anything, still smelling of pain.

"I think we broke Chris," Alaric says quietly. "Better not have done anything bad to his knee."

"I think he'll be okay once he's rested. He's got PT this week, right?" Mac asks. She holds out a hand as Mason walks by, and Mason puts a chocolate-chip cookie in it. Alaric has no idea where the cookies came from or how Mac knew to ask for them, but he silently requests one as well. Mason hands him two and moves on to offer his plastic bin of cookies to the next person.

Alaric nods. "He does. But we're hoping he's cleared next week so he can be back before the end of the season."

"At least he's not a senior."

Alaric glances at where Chris is sleeping. "Mm." It's strange to think that everything here has a time limit. Not only does he have a mere four years himself, but Mac and Chris will be leaving two years before he does. He grumbles, and Mac reaches out to ruffle his hair.

"Everything's going to be okay. Take a nap. I'm going to, after I eat the cookie," she says. She turns around, slumps down in her seat.

The cookies are homemade, soft and chewy and full of chocolate chips. They fill the sugar craving Alaric didn't know he had, and he drinks an entire bottle of water after, dehydrated from how dry the arena was.

He digs out his phone, checks for messages, and isn't surprised that there aren't many. He lets Drea know that everything went fine and he's on his way back to PHU, then lets Rory know how late they'll be getting in.

How are you feeling? Rory texts back.

It's complicated. Alaric's at ease, loose-limbed and comfortable in the bus, but there's still an itch under his skin from not being able to compete. *I'm okay*, he texts back. *Probably going to be restless.*

Fine, Rory replies. *Just don't sleep on me. You're heavy. You know where I'll be.*

Alaric smiles slightly, touches the screen of the phone, thankful that Rory understands the need for being Clan sometimes. *I might be really late. Don't know if we're stopping.*

It's only a small lie; Alaric isn't going to explain everything to Rory.

I'll be asleep. I won't care as long as you don't sleep actually on top of me.

Alaric smiles more widely, types back, *Okay.*

He switches over to a different conversation, one not nearly as long and definitely not as varied or constant. He starts typing several times, finally decides on something and sends it.

Bus should be pulling in from the tournament between 11 and midnight tonight. Will you still be up?

It's a badly phrased question. Even though it's a Sunday and there are classes tomorrow, Alaric's pretty damned sure Thorne will be awake. That's not the question Alaric's really asking.

The three dots taunt him, appearing and disappearing several times.

I don't think so. Not tonight. Sorry, Ric.

He's probably got other plans. It's not like Thorne's going to drop everything just to soothe the itch under Alaric's skin. He types back quickly: *Okay, fine.* Then he sets his phone to silent and shoves it in his pocket. He crosses his arms, sinks down a little in the seat. Chris shifts closer in his sleep, and Alaric's arm is wedged uncomfortably, so he lifts it, ending with his arm across Chris's shoulders as they lean together.

Fine. He'll try to rest here. At least he won't be getting in so late that he'll piss off Rory.

46

THERE'S NO CHANGE. No new information, no movement. Orson's still dead, there's no new information on the mark, and the girl is still in a coma. The boyfriend of the guy from VIT is finally cleared, and Alaric finds his investigation—such as it is—back at square one.

It's frustrating.

When the topic of legendary Talent comes up during magical studies, Alaric sinks down in his seat, arms crossed, and refuses to participate. It seems like every Lineage has children's stories, often surreal cautionary tales that make Alaric wonder how real it is. Or maybe there are clues in the stories, clues to reality that make more sense than a grove of lemon trees keeping Deathstalkers from attacking.

Alaric remembers asking once, when he was very young, why human children liked their lemonade so sweet. And his grandmother twisted a lemon, squeezed the juice over ice cubes, and added water and a hint of sugar before handing him the glass. "Because they don't know that the lemon keeps the Deathstalkers at bay," she said solemnly, and Alaric drank the glass down in one long gulp.

He makes an idle note to look into where lemonade came from, and who else uses lemons at full strength, then scratches it out because it's a ridiculous thought.

It's a story to keep children in line somehow, nothing more.

By the time he gets to taekwondo on Wednesday night, Alaric feels as if he's spinning in place. He's attended classes, taken exams, handed in homework, and none of it feels quite real. He's more than ready to get back out on the floor and fight.

After a solid hour of drills, he's sweating and aching when they finally gear up for a short round of sparring. Alaric crooks his fingers at Jackson. "Don't hold back. I saw you spar on Sunday. Don't hold back on me."

Both of Jackson's eyebrows rise. "I like you, Alaric. I'd like to stay friends, and I'm pretty sure you're not ready for me to go all-out."

Alaric gestures, negating the thought. " 's fine," he says curtly. "I want to push myself tonight. If you hit me, you hit me. 's all good."

Jackson shrugs and waves for Mac to join them and judge their ring. As Pawel calls out to start, Alaric readies himself.

Jackson starts as soon as Pawel says, skipping forward with a quick strike to the body and one to the head. Alaric manages to get his hand up and shoves Jackson's foot out of the way before he connects with his helmet. Alaric growls low in his throat, circles out of the way. He exhales, and there's a soft puff of smoke.

"Ric," Mac says, and Alaric tries to rein it in.

He loses badly to Jackson. He manages to land shots, including one spin back to the gut that leaves Jackson groaning, but Jackson outpoints him with quick shots to the head. As they bow and shake hands, Alaric yanks Jackson forward, claps him on the back. "Thanks," he says, because it feels good to let go and not worry about someone getting hurt.

Mac slips her head gear on. "Don't go away, Jackson. You ref. I'm fighting."

Well, fuck. This ought to be interesting.

She seats her mouthguard and grins around it at Ric. They both bow and shake hands, and then kihap, ready for the fight.

Mac is fast. She's faster than Jackson, faster than anyone Ric's fought. She sidesteps so quickly that she seems to disappear from view, and then she's kicking up, jumping high enough to strike his head before she bounces away. He feels like a lumbering ox as he fights her, and the itch under his skin grow hot. He huffs out smoke, and she slides in close, gets in his face.

"Don't lose control," she whispers, then she's gone again.

He strikes out at her, catches her in the side with a roundhouse that makes her grunt, then she skips sideways and throws a spin hook that catches him in the back of the head. By the time the bout ends, his ears are ringing and his head is spinning, dizzy from trying to keep up.

Pawel calls for gear off. Jackson loosens his chest protector as he asks, "Teas Please?"

"I'm stealing Ric tonight," Mac says. She looks at Alaric while she speaks. "There's something I want to talk to him about."

"We'll all do that movie thing on Friday again," Alaric says when Jackson hesitates. As Jackson walks away, Alaric quickly strips off his gear to stow it. "Corbin's right. My life is weirdly social."

"You don't have to go every time," Mac points out. "They'll understand if you want time on your own."

"It's fine. It's been okay." That's the strangest part of it. Alaric never expected to be this comfortable with all these people who aren't Clan.

"Cool." Mac balls up her bandana and tosses it into her bag. "I'm going to walk back to the house and drop off my stuff. Walk with me, and we'll drop off yours, then go get something to eat?" When he hesitates, she grins. "Not a date, Ric. There really is something we need to talk about."

She doesn't say anything as they head first to SigPsiEp then to Douglass. It's starting to get cool as October fades into November; Mac walks with hunched shoulders, pulled in on herself with her jacket, hands shoved into her pockets. Alaric's too warm from the inside out, so he leaves his jacket at the dorm and hopes he doesn't cool off enough to regret the decision.

Mac drifts closer to him as they walk, her shoulder bumping him as they cross off campus. "I'm thinking Minnisale's," she says idly, and Alaric nods his agreement. He's not sure he's hungry enough for one of their huge plates, but he can always eat leftovers tomorrow.

She's close enough that she keeps bumping him. Alaric looks down at her. "What?"

"You're warm," she says. "Warm enough that you're walking around in short sleeves and when I get close to you, I can feel it."

He can't deny it. "So?"

"You puffed smoke again today. The more frustrated you got, the more smoke came out." Mac's gaze shifts sideways. "Do you think they're related? Or do you normally run this hot?"

"Only since things started getting bad," Alaric admits. "What are you thinking?"

"I'm thinking something's happening to you." Mac stops, tilts her head to look at him. "Probably something to do with being Clan. Maybe something's changing."

Alaric snorts. "Clan doesn't change."

"You're not typical Clan."

No, he's not. He's nothing like typical Clan. He's not right. "Thanks for reminding me."

There's a flash, and the streetlight above their head goes out, leaving them in darkness. Alaric blinks, catches Mac's shoulder. Seems like it was the last light working on the street; there's nothing left but shadow.

"Don't like this," Alaric mutters, and Mac nods. Her body is stiff, scent wary.

"Yeah, if I were overseas, I'd say we're being set up for an ambush," she whispers, barely vocalizing. "This might be the first time I've ever missed carrying a gun. Not because I like guns, but because it feels like I should have one in my hand. And be in uniform. Fuck. I don't like this, Ric."

She's shivering, and Alaric squeezes her shoulder, pulls her closer as if he can shelter her completely. A rasp in the alley nearby, and Alaric turns, tries to see into the darkness.

"We're not alone," Mac says quietly.

The shadows come to life.

They swell up, darkness on top of darkness, surging toward them. Mac grabs Alaric, and suddenly they're up against the wall and Mac's letting go. "I can't move both of us far enough," she says sharply. "We have to fight or run."

Alaric wants to say run. He wants to tell her to flee however she can. But there are no words in his mouth, only teeth and a roar that drowns out every other thought. Heat spreads under his skin, bursting through as he flaps wings in a rush of wind that seems to blow the Shadows back.

The sound they make is inhuman, a high-pitched howling that reaches into his soul and twists darkly.

Alaric pounces, and the world slips away as his claws rip through the darkness.

He comes to lying on the ground, Mac crouched over him, her hand on his chest. As soon as his eyes flicker open, she sits back on her heels. "Well, that was interesting," she says.

There's dirt on her face and blood under her fingernails. Alaric smells soot, salt, and iron in the air, mixed with a dusty smell of old books and ancient cloth. He sneezes, and Mac smiles.

"What happened?" Alaric pushes himself up on one elbow. "I passed out. I left you to the—" He doesn't know how to finish the sentence.

"Shadows," Mac suggests. "Two of them, and no, you didn't. We fought together. I distracted them, and every time they turned away from you to get me, you ripped at them. I'm sure they're injured, but they left, just melted back into the darkness."

Alaric rubs at his head, an ache building behind the eyes. A breeze blows through, and he shivers, finally cold. "I don't remember."

"You changed," Mac says slowly. "I was a little too busy, or I would've recorded it for you, but I'm pretty damned sure I know where the smoke is from now. You have another form."

Alaric blinks.

Mac sits cross-legged with her elbows on her knees. "You were seven feet tall, and you had scales. Your wing span was easily ten feet across. You had claws on every foot, and more teeth than I care to think about. I'm suspect you could breathe fire, even though you didn't."

"Dragons aren't real."

"Neither are Shadowwalkers, and I'm pretty sure we just ran into two of them," Mac says dryly. "It might be time to re-evaluate what's a legend and what's merely so unusual that no one has ever seen it before. And let me tell you, I am the queen of being unique at the wrong place and time."

Sorrow and regret, thick and dark in her scent. She's looking at him like she's waiting for something, wary and on edge. Alaric tries his best to remember, and all he gets is that feeling of suddenly being somewhere else. Only a few feet away, but out of reach of the darkness that reached out for them.

Wait.

"You teleport. That's your Talent."

Mac nods slowly. "Keep going, Ric. You're almost there."

The penny drops, and it's like someone punches him in the gut. "Mac is short for Mackenzie."

Mac's mouth twists ruefully. "Yes. Yes it is. And in the interest of forgoing some of the next questions, my stepfather is Senator Palmer, which is how my last name changed—he adopted both me and my brother. I didn't want to be Kenzie Davis anymore. Can you blame me?"

"Not really, no." Alaric wonders how he didn't see it before. Now that he looks, he can see it in the shape of her face, in her height and her build. It's her eyes that are different. Kenzie Davis was all bright eyes and hope when she went into that competition. Mac looks like the world already chewed her up and spit her out. "Who knows?"

"Out of people you know? Not many. Chris. Pawel. Some of my sisters," Mac says. "I don't deny it if someone asks, but I don't want to talk about it, either. I'm pretty sure Cass suspects; she's said some things. But unless she's willing to be blunt, I'm not going to offer."

Mac pushes to her feet, offers Alaric a hand. He's cold now, shaking in the aftermath, and he accepts the hug she offers, holds on for longer than is strictly necessary.

"So, after that, I think a few more people deserve to know," Mac says quietly. "And I think some people might need to know that you're a legendary shapeshifter. Because I'm guessing that the Shadows that attacked us were legendary as well. And maybe they attacked us for a reason, because of who we are. And maybe that'll help us figure out why they went after your brother, and the kids from VIT, and more importantly, how to get back at them."

Alaric looks at the darkness around them. "You think those were Deathstalkers."

"Shadowwalkers. Soulstealers. Deathstalkers. Whatever you want to call them, yeah, I think those were them," Mac says evenly. "And when you look at the fact that you're able to turn into a fucking *dragon*, and I'm the girl who everyone says started the Emergence, we might be on track to figuring something out that makes sense."

47

IT SEEMS LIKE that one breakthrough should send them tumbling down a path to resolution, but it doesn't. Over the next few days, Alaric meets with Pawel and Rory. He has a conference call with Rory's Gram and Nana. He absolutely refuses to discuss anything with his father. Until he knows more about this new shape, he doesn't want to try to explain to his father that he's broken again.

Each new conversation breeds new questions. He smells exhaustion coming off of Mac as she explains her identity to Rory and Thorne, to Drea and Corbin. Rory claps a hand over Thorne's mouth, forestalling any questions, but Alaric can't be sure Thorne won't try again later.

They all try to convince Alaric to shift again into the dragon form, but Alaric can't seem to call it forth. He wonders if it might be for emergencies only, and he doesn't want to get into that level of emergency again just so he can test the theory.

By the time Friday evening rolls around, he's frustrated enough that the walls at OPT feel like they're closing in on him. After dinner, he leaves without a word and walks around campus until he cools off. When he's back in his room, he stares at the walls, tries to think of something to do while his friends are at the campus movie.

He grabs his phone, texts, *What about tonight?*, then sets it down on the desk.

It buzzes. *Where are you?*

My room. I can be at your place in ten, Alaric texts back.

NO.

It pauses after that, and Alaric's breath catches, his heart ratcheting faster until the phone buzzes again.

Stay put. I'm coming to you.

Alaric relaxes. He doesn't know why the caps—why Thorne would yell like that—but he's coming here. Alaric didn't fuck everything up. He closes his eyes, breathes in slowly, breathes out. When the door creaks open and Thorne is standing there in the doorway, hair disheveled, chest rising and falling as if he's run the whole way, Alaric suddenly realizes where they actually are.

"Wait." He jumps up, looks at Rory's bed, then at Thorne. "Not here. Not in this room."

Thorne pushes a hand through his hair, which does nothing to tame it. He gently closes the door behind him. "Sit down, Alaric. We're not doing anything Rory wouldn't approve of." He pauses, makes a face. "Strike that. We're not having sex in this room. We're going to talk."

They end up sitting on the floor, cross-legged and facing each other, knees almost touching. Thorne's scent has a sour edge, sorrowed.

"I don't get it," Alaric says.

"I know." Thorne pushes at his hair again, gives up and digs a band out of his pocket. He wraps it around to pull the thick mess back into a rough ponytail. "And that's why we're going to talk. I don't think we should keep having sex, Ric."

"Why not?" Alaric still doesn't get it. It's been good. It's really good to get off with someone else, and he trusts Thorne. He trusts him with all the little details that he's afraid to tell anyone else about what he wants. What he needs sometimes. "Is this about the dragon?"

Thorne flips one hand palm up, cradles a tiny ball of flame. "I am not afraid of a fire-breathing dragon," Thorne says with a small smile. "In fact, that makes me appreciate you even more as a friend. Seriously. Have you thought about whether you could carry someone on your back? If there's ever actually a war, I could ride you into battle and we could rain flames down on all the evil."

"You've really thought about this." Alaric shakes his head, tries to clear the image away. "You do realize that if there's a war, our families will be on different sides."

"That depends on if we take sides and play along like traditional Clan and Mage." Thorne waves his hand like he's erasing the conversation. "We're getting sidetracked, and I need you to understand this. It's not about the dragon. It isn't even about you, Ric. I like you. I'm glad we became friends this year, and frankly, the sex is good," Thorne admits.

"Then why?" Because Alaric still doesn't understand. "We're friends. The sex is good. What's wrong with that?"

"Are you having sex with anyone else?" Thorne asks quietly.

Alaric's brow furrows. "No. Why?"

Thorne's breath huffs out. "Because the first thing you told me is that you didn't want a relationship. And you and me?" Thorne points to the space between them. "You're starting to treat this like a relationship. It's like a crutch. You know you want sex, so you text me. We fuck, that's it, we go on. But then it happens again, and in its own way, that's a relationship, Ric."

"We don't date."

Thorne laughs softly. "Relationships aren't always about dating. There are so many kinds of relationships. And you keep glaring at me when I flirt with someone else."

"Mac's not interested in anyone." That's the last person Alaric can remember Thorne flirting with.

"I'm not going to sleep with Mac," Thorne replies. "I know she's not interested. On the other hand, if Nate's interested? I'm willing to get in bed with him. The girl who was at my place on Sunday when you were coming back from the tournament in Boston? Pretty sure we'll hook up again, and she said something about bringing a friend."

Alaric growls softly. "So you'll sleep with them, not me."

"Would you be angry if you texted me and I was in bed with Nate?" Thorne asks

Alaric turns his head, clamps down until his jaw is tight as he stares at the floor. Because yes. Because he's used to this, accustomed to the idea that Thorne's there when he wants him. That they have this thing.

"You don't love me," Thorne says plainly, and it's not a question.

Alaric shakes his head.

"But you want to keep me for yourself."

Alaric licks his lips. "Sounds about right," he admits.

"I'm not sure what we're doing is healthy for you anymore," Thorne says softly. "It helped in the beginning, but you're hiding from things now."

"What the fuck am I hiding from?" Alaric bursts out, because…what the fuck?

"That's the point. You don't know because you're hiding," Thorne tells him. "I think that maybe you need to give yourself a chance. Look more closely at what you think you're looking for. Think about it. Figure it out. That might mean trying something with someone else, I don't know. And you can always talk to me about anything. You want to figure out how to tell someone what you like? I can help with that. You want to rant about something? Fine. I'll listen. Given what we've already done, I'm pretty sure there's not much left to be embarrassed about."

There's heat in Alaric's cheeks. He's flushed red. It's different than when the dragon slips under his skin. He can smell his own embarrassment, his own frustration. "I don't know what I want. This was—it was…"

"Convenient?" Thorne says, and huffs a laugh when Alaric nods. "It was good, too. I don't regret it, and I hope you don't. I just think—I think you're ready to take off the training wheels. Figure out where you want to go, and go there. Give yourself a chance."

"But I don't—" Alaric stops, frustrated by the lack of words to express what he's trying to say.

"You don't understand love?" Thorne says, and Alaric nods. "And you don't fully understand the concept of romantic relationships?" And Alaric nods again.

Thorne leans forward, gets a hand at the nape of Alaric's neck, holds him there while he kisses him gently. "Just remember that you can find someone who understands you. Who won't push for more than you can give, but who can give you what you do want. Like regular sex, just with you. And being there as your friend. I'm sure he's out there."

Alaric nods again. He's out of words, out of any way to make sense of this. He feels like he's losing something, but when he reaches inside his mind to touch the concept, he's not upset. He's certainly not heartbroken. As Thorne pushes to his feet, Alaric watches him get farther away.

"Thanks," Alaric mutters.

Thorne grins. "The pleasure was all mine. You okay?"

"Yeah." He feels like he shouldn't be, but he really is fine.

Thorne leaves, and Alaric sits there, cross-legged on the floor, still trying to process.

Something where he's with someone. One person. Just them. Friends. Sex. It's what he wanted with Corbin. It's what he had, in a way, with Thorne. And when he thinks about it, it's as close as he can get to explaining that he does want *something*, but he doesn't want traditional hearts and romance.

He's still sitting when Rory pushes through the door, drops his bag on the floor, and throws his notebook up on the bed, then stops dead. "What are you doing here?"

Alaric blinks up at him. "Thinking."

Rory folds abruptly, kneeling in front of Alaric. "What did he do? Because Thorne ran out on a session after getting a text, and he only does that when it's you. But you're here, and you look a little like you've been run over by a bus."

"We didn't have sex in the room," Alaric assures him. "He just broke up with me."

"Shit." Rory sits back on his heels, mouth twisted into a frown. "I'm going to kill him for hurting you."

"Don't. It's okay." Alaric pushes to his feet, unfolding himself slowly. He rubs the back of his neck, seeks words that aren't anywhere to be found. "I mean it. It's really okay. I wasn't in love with him. He didn't hurt me. He just…he gave me something to think about."

"Something to think about." Rory's expression is dubious as he comes to his feet. He holds his arms out to the side, and Alaric slides closer without thinking, accepts the hug that's offered. They stand there, Rory rubbing Alaric's back in small circles, and Alaric can't stop thinking.

"I don't know what I want," Alaric admits. "I know what I don't want, but it's harder to figure out what I do want."

"Do you want a sounding board to figure it out?" Rory offers.

"No." Alaric steps back, looks at the bed. "Not yet. I think I just want to sleep. And maybe—" Yeah, no, he's not going to say that part out loud. He doesn't want to get into this conversation with Rory.

"You know what? I came up with a potential start to that piece for TJ." Rory reaches for his notebook. "Thorne had this idea about opening with a piano—like an old-fashioned music box—then twisting the sound into something more modern. So I'm going to go see if TJ's around to talk to him about it. I'll be gone a while."

Alaric relaxes, smiles slightly. "I'll probably be asleep before you get back."

"Better that than traumatizing either of us," Rory quips. "Yell if you need anything. I'll be right down the hall."

The only thing Alaric needs is answers, and he's not ready for help with that yet. He waits until Rory's gone before he climbs into his loft, closes his eyes, and tries to find a way to finally relax.

48

ALARIC STARES DOWN at his phone as his late calculus recitation ends. His stomach is already growling, but he stays in his seat while everyone else quickly leaves and types out a response to Corbin's last text. *No game this weekend*, Alaric sends. *Why?*

Someone I know is going to a party at PHU, and I thought maybe I'd come over, Corbin responds.

Alaric tries to imagine Corbin actually in the house with the rest of his OPT brothers. It's easy to think of Corbin at a party; he takes to social events easily. But in terms of assimilating with Alaric's fraternity, it was traumatic enough just having him visit for the day.

Still.

Corbin's his brother. And he misses him.

We're having a Halloween party at OPT on Saturday, Alaric sends. *I can see if Rory would mind if you crash in our room. I think SigPsiEp is having a party too.* He hesitates, then smiles slightly as he adds, *OPT is costumes required.*

It's not entirely the truth; costumes are optional but heavily recommended. Corbin, on the other hand, will love the idea that he has to dress up.

Let me know about Rory. Remember the part where we don't seem to like each other much.

Alaric pinches the bridge of his nose, finishes packing his bag before he's ready to respond. *One: you said you'd puppy pile if you have to in order to get to know my friends. This is a chance. And two: you two are stuck with each other. Deal with it.*

He shoves his phone in his pocket, ignores when it chimes with a response. He grabs his bag, throws it over his shoulder, and turns toward the door. "Oh." He stops; Chris is standing in the doorway. "Hey."

Chris spreads his hands. "No crutches. No more brace. Range of movement is in acceptable parameters, and the kneecap is tracking fine, so I'm not at any elevated risk for it dislocating. Well, any more than anyone else getting tackled on a regular basis is. I'm done with PT, and while they think I should keep it light in the next game, the fact that it's more than a week away means I get to play."

" 's good." Alaric grins, pulls Chris into a one-armed hug, slapping his back. "There're only two games left, but you get to play against VIT. You shouldn't miss that one."

"Neither should you. We'll both get time on the field," Chris says. He lets Alaric leave the classroom first, following close behind and nudging him with his shoulder. "I want to celebrate."

"Teas Please?" It's become the default place to go whenever they're out.

Chris shakes his head. "Minnisale's? Or maybe Doherty's, if you're more interested in pub food?"

"Never made it to Minnisale's last week with Mac, so let's do that." Alaric's in the mood for pasta. Lots of pasta, and Minnisale's is the best Italian near campus. It's dirt cheap and has large portions, made for the college budget.

Alaric's nostrils flare as they walk; there's still a hint of pain in Chris's scent, but he seems at ease. Happy. A little excited. Despite the lingering pain and a slight limp, he's in a good mood.

Alaric can't help but slow when they get near the alley where he and Mac were attacked. He glances up at the streetlight; it's on now, shining brightly, along with one a block behind them and another a block ahead. "Feels like everything should've changed, and nothing did," he mutters, squaring his shoulders as they walk by.

"Are you angry that I knew and didn't tell you?"

Alaric's brows furrow. "Wasn't yours to tell, so no. She shouldn't have to deal with all the shit that comes with what happened. Wrong place, wrong time, and everyone gave her shit for it. I'm fine with her being quiet about it. And you keeping her secret."

Chris snorts softly. "Most people would be mad."

"Most people don't get why secrets are necessary," Alaric grumbles. "I get it. And fuck, now that I know, I can think of a dozen times she did it, and I didn't realize."

Chris knocks into his arm, bumping him gently. "She does that. Sometimes just to see if she gets a reaction. And no one ever notices." He pulls the door open for Minnisale's, motions for Alaric to head inside first.

The hostess grabs two menus, shows them to a small table off to one side. It's a little dark, but it's better than one of the tiny booths where their legs would be knocking under the table. She brings water and silverware once they're settled, then leaves them with the menus.

Compared to the chaos that strikes every time they go into Teas Please, particularly with Nate waiting on them, it's strangely quiet. Alaric picks up the menu, glances at the specials on the front, then sets it down with a small smile as he pushes it aside.

"Figured it out that fast?" Chris asks, the menu open in front of him.

"Meant to get pasta, but the special is braised lamb shank. Can't resist," Alaric admits. "Too used to lamb only being a spring food." He makes a face at the table. "Not going to tell Rory, though. He might be horrified."

"Vegetarians tend to like lamb or veal even less than everything else," Chris agrees. He closes his own menu, sets it on top of Alaric's. "Lasagna. It was between that and the hand-stuffed shells. They have ones stuffed with ricotta, spinach, and mushrooms that are fantastic."

Alaric makes a mental note to get that next time, because it sounds good. As soon as they've got their order in, the menus are whisked away and a basket of fresh bread is dropped on the table. It's hot, with a chewy crust, and even though it's not fresh butter, it's good.

"So, you've been working with Dawson." Chris gestures with the piece of bread in his hand. "Do we bench him until we need him? Do we keep him in the rotation? What strengths and weaknesses are you seeing?"

"His passing game's not as bad as Dax says." Alaric's been paying close attention. "Dawson can't pass to Dax. Can't say why, and that doesn't help since he's our best receiver. But if we put him out there with Jameson? Ball falls right in his hands."

"Jameson's second string; they're not going to be in the game together often," Chris points out.

"Exactly. Not unless you pitch it to Coach." Alaric moves the bread basket to the side, grabs the little ceramic container of sugar packets. He has them all lined up neatly, moving them one by one as he and Chris go over plays and ideas, when the waitress stops by their table. She has a tray held high, and both eyes are wide as she looks at the table.

"Moved on to dessert?" she asks, and Chris laughs.

"Football," Alaric says, a flush staining his cheeks. He gathers the sugar packets together again, shoves them back into the container to make space. "Sorry."

"Not a problem, boys." She sets a bowl in front of him with a huge shank of lamb settled atop a fragrant layer of greens and polenta. Alaric leans in, inhales. Every herb smells fresh, and it makes him think of home.

The waitress puts Chris's lasagna in front of him, and Alaric swears it's a quarter pan on one plate. The waitress grins at them both, winks. "I'll leave you two alone. My name's Jenny if you need anything, so just give a yell; otherwise I won't be back until either these plates are clean or you're looking for boxes."

"I bet I'm the only one who'll need a box."

"I'm not that hungry. Haven't been working out, haven't shifted." Alaric digs in by slicing off a thick hunk of meat, dredging it through the greens and polenta. It's a big bite, but flavors explode across his tongue, and it's worth it. He makes a small, pleased sound. "Fuck. Almost like home."

"Your parents aren't Italian," Chris says, his attention entirely on trying to slice off one side of his lasagna.

"No, we do things differently, but this is all fresh." Alaric gestures at the plate. " 's all ingredients we use. Lamb in the spring, and greens are the first things that grow for vegetables. We dry corn from the fall and grind it, and the roughest milled corn makes porridge. Great for a hot meal in the morning with syrup, but also good with herbs and garlic like this. Or cheese and eggs."

"It's strange to think your family's so self-sufficient." Chris leans his free elbow on the table, leaves his fork on the plate as he leans forward. "You're your own world."

"Exactly. Rory's family's like that, up in Burlington. Sheep for wool. Hemp, too. I've never spun with hemp, but I'd like to try it sometime," Alaric admits. "David said they were thinking of trying bamboo, but it's a long process to work with it, even though it grows fast. No livestock for food, but they've got cows and goats for milk. All kinds of cheese. Good food."

"Is that what you'll do eventually?" Chris picks up his fork, stabs a bite of lasagna. "Go home and herd sheep?"

Alaric grumbles, halfway to a growl. There's a hint of smoke from his nose, and he puts his fork down, breathes slowly in and out. "Was that supposed to be derogatory?"

"No." Chris sets his own fork down again. He leans back, crosses his arms. "I know you have different ideas, but I also know they want you to go home. And you hate engineering, but you'll have to do something if you go back there. Honestly, out of everything you showed me there, the things you seemed to like best were flying and weaving."

He has a point. And Alaric felt at home with Rory's relatives when he was talking about dyeing and discussing technique. He grunts. "You're right. I like working with it. But it's not something that's going to lead the Clan or change our world. It'll be a hobby for me. I'll need to do something more." His appetite is waning. "If I go back."

Chris's head tilts. "If?"

Alaric shrugs one shoulder. "What if pro teams are taking Talented players by the time I graduate? Before Orson died, I thought that if that happened, I could try for it. Play football. Do something I love for as long as I could. But I've only got four years now. Five if I switch majors to something that keeps me here longer."

"Things could change," Chris says quietly.

"They could. My father could start a war." Alaric picks up his fork again. The polenta and greens are still good, and his stomach rumbles as soon as he takes a bit. He might not feel like eating, but his body has other plans. He digs in, lets the silence stretch while he eats.

"Think that beer you bottled is ready to taste?" Chris asks as he winds down finally, pushing half of his lasagna to the side and taking another hunk of bread. "We could try it tonight."

Alaric makes a face. "The coffee beer isn't ready yet; it hasn't even been in the bottles a week. Drea's lager is probably fine, if you want to crack a bottle open."

"You have to be there for the first bottle," Chris points out. "No one's touching that beer without you there."

They've already brewed three batches. The coffee beer took two weeks in a secondary, so it's just barely been in bottles. The lager was a quick kit that Drea picked out. And there's cider fermenting now, ready to go into a keg when it's done, probably sometime after the party on Saturday.

In a way, cracking open a bottle will be a good memorial.

"Sure. Yeah. We'll do that," Alaric agrees. He's made headway, finally, on his dinner, and there's plenty left to eat another time.

Chris waves for the waitress, and when she comes over, he hands her a card. When Alaric gets his wallet out, Chris shakes his head. "You can get it the next time. It's a pain to split the bill; if it's just us, this is simpler."

Alaric can't argue, and he figures he'll get the chance to pay him back soon enough. The waitress brings over boxes, and they pack up the leftovers and put them in one bag for the hike back on campus to OPT.

The walk back is quiet, the fall air crisp and cold. Weather report says there's a storm coming in the morning, and Alaric can taste it on the air. It's not the same as summer, when the storms taste like ozone and electricity, or like the wet scent of mud. This is cold and harsh, crisp and clear, like ice hangs waiting nearby to turn into the first snowfall of the coming winter. Chris hunches his shoulders against the cold, and Alaric drifts closer, bumping into him as if he can share his body heat.

As soon as they reach OPT, Chris ducks inside, taking the bag and shoving the leftovers into the fridge. They end up in their usual spots on the couch in the living room, a red cup and one bottle of beer sitting on the coffee table waiting to be opened. Lewis spots them in the kitchen and follows them to sit in the chair opposite, leaning forward.

"Go on," Lewis says. "Open it."

"You don't even like beer," Chris points out, and Lewis shrugs.

"Doesn't stop me from appreciating a concoction someone else will like.

Besides, how am I going to know how to mix with it if I don't try it?" Lewis says.

Alaric can't stop the expression of horror from welling up. "This isn't some fucking light beer, Lewis. It's homebrew. It's *good*. You won't be mixing anything with it." He grabs the bottle opener and carefully pops the top, giving it a moment to make sure he hasn't over-carbonated it and that it isn't going to foam up. When he's sure it's safe, he takes the top off and grabs the cup.

"Why not go straight from the bottle?"

Alaric gives Lewis a look. "Sediment," he tells him. "Homebrew has sediment at the bottom, can't help it, so you always pour it into a glass and leave the dregs in the bottle. Need to rinse 'em out soon, before it sets into something we can't clean."

"Noted." Chris nudges him with his knee. "Go on, pour already."

It foams up as Alaric pours, but it's not too bad. He thinks he got close, especially for a first try. Of course, this one's a kit, so it's easy. Dump everything in, cook it together, ferment, and bottle. He notes the color—a little reddish, darker than a typical mass-produced beer—then lifts it to inhale the scent of hops. He takes a sip at first, then nods approvingly and takes a long swallow.

"Not bad," he says, handing the cup to Chris.

Chris inhales as well, raises an eyebrow, and starts with a long gulp. "I could definitely drink this," he says. "Is it any stronger than what we buy?"

"Same alcohol content, just better taste," Alaric says. "We don't brew to get drunk. We brew because we don't get drunk easily and we want it to taste good." He takes the cup when Chris passes it back, holds it out to Lewis.

Lewis raises a hand, shakes his head. "I can smell the beer-flavored beer from here, so no thanks. I'll stick to my fruity concoctions. And I won't touch your homebrew for anything mixed, promise."

"If I do the fall spice one you can drop a fireball shot in it," Alaric decides. "They'd go well. Might work with the cider, too."

"That's one I'm looking forward to." Lewis pushes himself to standing. "I'm heading up. I've still got a solid few hours of orgo work to do before lab tomorrow. Glad the beer worked, Alaric."

"Movie?" Chris has the remote in his hand, gets the TV going, and starts flipping through a list of really bad movies to stream. Alaric takes another drink from the cup, reaches out to stop Chris from changing movies, and hits play, then hands him the cup.

It's quiet and easy, a decent way to spend the night.

The movie's half done when the front door slams open, and Dax comes in, dropping onto the other end of the sofa and pushing Chris closer to Alaric. The beer's gone, and they've shared a second one as well, the cup sitting empty on the table. Alaric feels warm in a pleasant way, loose and easy.

"Movie Friday night?" Dax asks. "Showing after taekwondo, of course."

Chris glances over at Alaric, who shrugs in response. He has no idea what's showing on campus, but fine, he's happy to go. "Why not?" Alaric decides.

"I'll bring takeout to the movie for you," Chris offers. "You're always hungry after your class. Chinese or Indian?"

"Chinese." Alaric twists slightly to make room when Chris leans into him. It's easier to slip his arm behind Chris's shoulders and give him space, and it slots them together neatly enough that Alaric can offer his body heat to Chris. There's a low sound; Dax nods.

"Settled then. See you there." Dax gets up, stops after two steps and turns back, spreading his hands. "No Cass tonight, Chris. So no need to sleep on the couch."

"I'll be up when the movie's done, probably." Chris presses play, and the stream restarts.

Excerpt from *When Magic Entered the World: Interviews With Lineage Talent*, by Pawel Szczek, © 2009

Why would you think we're all atheists?

Tell me how you were raised. Catholic? Now tell me why you don't believe that God and Talent can intersect. No, wait, don't tell me. I'll tell you about how I was raised, and maybe that will help you understand.

I was raised Catholic. Now I attend the Episcopalian church in Springfield—the one down on Main Street—but that has nothing to do with Talent. I still feel Catholic. No matter how much I may disagree with certain points of the Catholic church and teachings, in my heart, those are my roots.

I learned from an early age that there are miracles. That there are those who brought God into our lives, and those who channel him. I believed, from my earliest moments working with the Earth, that the Talent that flows in my hands was given to me by God.

He created everything around us. Why wouldn't He have created me? Why would He be angry that I can plunge my hands into the dirt and warm it, bring life to it? I believe He created me for a reason, to help feed the people who need food, to help bring green back to a world which seems determined to push it away.

I think Talent is religion. No, we aren't gods. We aren't Him, walking the Earth. But we have been touched by Him. Everyone has been, in different ways. Some have talents like music or gifts with math and science. Some have Talent that allows them to grow plants in barren ground or to bring light and fire where there is none.

I believe in all of it. There are angels watching over us and demons tempting us. There are those who walk in the light and those who remain in the shadows. There is good and there is evil, and it is up to us to know which is which and where to look. Sometimes good is ugly, sometimes evil is beautiful. Sometimes it's the other way around.

If you sit quietly outside, you might hear the whispers of angels on the breeze. I knew a girl once who said she could talk to them, that they spoke to her. Encouraged her. Protected her.

I believe her.

I talk to God because I believe He listens, not because I think He is there to change my life. He has already given me everything I need. I am blessed from birth; it is up to me to do good with what I've been given.

It's okay if your own Emergence has led you down a different path. I'm not telling you this to try to change you. All I ask is please don't believe that having Talent means we can't have faith as well.

GHOSTS

49

HALLOWEEN COMES AND goes, and November slips in with cooling weather and the brisk scent of fall. The afternoon of the final football game of the season is chilly enough for Alaric to see his breath as he warms up on the sidelines before the game begins.

His gaze slips to Chris, who had played his first game back the week before. The coaches had still let most of the game rest on Alaric's shoulders, giving Chris more time on the field when he played with confidence and strength.

Chris is starting for this last game, and Alaric's okay with that. It's strange to think that they're already here, about to play the annual final game against VIT. It's a long-standing rivalry, and the crowd shows how popular it is.

The stands are roughly split with PHU on one side and VIT on the other, but signs for both schools are interspersed. The signs from SigPsiEp are obvious as Drea and Mac both wave, and only a few people away, Alaric spots a sign naming the quarterback for VIT. He suspects that Corbin has convinced his friends to sit among the PHU fans.

Chris knocks into him. "You ready for this?"

It should be sad. It's the end of his first season, the end of his sports for the year. It's time to step away from football and cross-train so he won't lose conditioning. He won't have this again until summer training returns.

And yet.

Alaric grins. "Ready," he agrees. "We're going to crush them."

Chris waves a hand in front of Alaric's mouth as he huffs out a breath.

"I'm not going to start breathing fire," Alaric grumbles, rolling his eyes. "It's just really fucking cold."

"It's only going to get worse, but we won't be out in it as much after the season's done. Unless we go sledding—there's a great hill on the back side of campus, heading down from the field." Chris points, and Alaric's gaze follows. He knows the stretch of grass Chris means, and he can imagine sledding down it.

Or going down on his belly as the hound. It sounds like fun, if they get the snow.

They head over to the bench as Coach calls them in, stand at attention for the national anthem. When VIT wins the coin toss, they elect to receive, so Chris and Alaric take their seats on the bench. Dax joins them, and Alaric slides closer to Chris as they all lean together and talk strategy.

The PHU defense holds VIT back, keeps them out of field goal range. Alaric claps Chris on the shoulder as he and Dax get up to go in when PHU takes possession.

It's an intense game. Chris comes out after the first drive results in a field goal, and Coach Young brings ice as Alaric helps Chris position his knee over a rolled towel on the bench. When Coach Campbell calls, Alaric heads over, raises his hand to cover his mouth as he discusses plays.

They're in the middle of debating running versus passing when VIT scores at the very end of the first quarter, and they're down seven to three.

Alaric takes the field, fastening his helmet and tuning everything out but the game. He's got only one goal in mind—get the ball down the field and over the line. Nothing else matters.

He starts with a short throw, picking up thirteen yards for a first down. It's not pretty, falling into Jensen's hands just in time for Jensen to be taken down by the opposing team, but Alaric will take it. He doesn't need pretty. He needs efficient.

The next two passes are thrown directly to Dax, but neither makes it. He's covered too well, the VIT team all over him, and the second one is almost picked off as an interception.

New plan, because that one's not going to get him to a first down.

Alaric takes the snap and falls back, looking for his spot. He twists like he's going to throw a short pop to Jensen, then shifts back to see that Dax has broken through and is running down the field. Alaric barely manages to loose the ball for a long bomb when the impact hits him from the side, rolling through him and taking him down under a pile of bodies.

When he gets back up, they're moving down the field. Dax made the catch.

Alaric's side aches; he can feel the imprint of the shoulder that went into his ribs. He'll be fine, but it's rough now with adrenalin surging through him. He growls softly, shows his teeth to the VIT defenders that are trying to stare him down. He won't give ground.

He's sacked when VIT pushes through his offensive line, but he doesn't let the ball go wild. Second attempt leaves him no choice but to throw a lateral pass to Damon and hope he can run through.

It feels like every play they make, VIT knows about it before they can even get started.

They move down the field by inches, making the first down at the last moment every time until they stall on the 35-yard line. It's fourth down and too long for a field goal but too close for a punt. They have to make the attempt to get the first down.

The clock is ticking, time running out on the half, and Alaric keeps his head down. He doesn't look at any of his team, tries not to telegraph what he's thinking. As soon as the snap occurs, Dax is off, racing down the field. Alaric drops back, arm up. VIT breaks through the line.

Throw. Or run.

Alaric tucks the ball and darts to the side with all the speed he can manage. He tucks his shoulder down, pushes through the defensive player who comes after him and ends up running too close to the sideline. Another player dives at him, and Alaric slides, foot slipping out of bounds as he goes down and rolls hard on his shoulder.

He comes up and tosses the ball to the official, getting himself back in position. They're twenty-two yards out, and Alaric's done with this. The half's almost over. He needs to finish this now.

Dax is perfect, sliding away from the defensive line and into an empty space as he heads for the goal. Alaric places the ball just past him, watches as Dax reaches for it and keeps going, diving across the goal line and popping back up, ball in hand.

Alaric can rest.

The extra point is easy, and VIT only manages two plays before the buzzer sounds and the half is over. PHU is up by three.

Back in the locker room for halftime, Coach Campbell goes over plays with the offensive line while Alaric presses ice to his ribs and Chris swings his leg, stretching and trying to warm up all over again.

"We can't lose the advantage," Chris says tightly. "We're going to win this game."

"We're a better team." Dax claps him on the back. "Don't worry, we've got this. My little sister is in the stands. We can't lose when she's here."

"No pressure, Dax. Thanks," Chris mutters.

"How's the knee?" Alaric straddles the bench and pats the space across from him, and Chris takes it.

"Stiff," Chris admits. "You looked good out there."

Alaric huffs. "I got sacked. Their defense is good. I'm glad their offense sucks."

They head back, Coach Campbell checking in on Chris before sending him out as soon as special teams is done with the kickoff return. They're starting on the VIT 40-yard line, which is a good position.

Coach Campbell sinks onto the bench next to Alaric. "Ribs?"

Alaric still has the ice pressed to his side, and he drops it now. " 's okay, I'll live. It just aches. Better me than anyone else. They kept hitting the same damned spot. How's Chris holding up?"

"Looks better now than he did in the first half." Campbell nods at the field. "He's determined to end the season on top."

"One of the best QBs in the Blended league," Alaric says. "He should finish the game, if he can." When Campbell looks at him, Alaric shrugs one shoulder. "I've got three years left. He doesn't. And he's the starter. Let him finish it out."

"I'm pulling him if it looks like he'll risk permanent damage," Campbell says.

Alaric's pretty damned sure that Chris is in the game to stay.

Chris takes the team down the field to add another seven to their score. He only gets to sit for four plays before PHU manages an interception on one of VIT's passes. The tide is turning. Alaric can smell it in the air, a rising scent of excitement. And Chris marches his team down the field again to bring their lead to seventeen points.

Alaric can't sit still through the final quarter. He's on the sidelines, yelling as loud as anyone else, cheering on his team. The game ends on a pass by VIT, a desperate long bomb that falls short of the endzone. They'd managed to pull the score up, but in the end, it's 27 to 10, and PHU wins.

Chris yanks Alaric in, clapping his hands against his back as he shouts. Dax jumps both of them as the entire team rushes the sidelines, gathering together in a clump of yelling and hugs. Alaric sees the fans spilling out of the stands onto the field as the team moves back out, meeting them there. It's a chaotic mess that smells crisp, like rising energy and excitement. It shivers under Alaric's skin, and he loses sight of Chris and Dax as he turns from person to person, slapping backs and offering congratulations.

He growls and spins when someone jumps onto his back, but he recognizes the scent quickly and catches Corbin's legs before he can slip down. There's a wet smack against his neck, and Corbin coughs. "Gross. You're covered in sweat."

"What did you expect?" Alaric asks. It may be cold, but he's been buried under his heavy equipment and played a hard game when he was on the field. "Shouldn't you be consoling your friends over a devastating loss?"

"Eh, I'm not friends with anyone on the team." Corbin's shrug is a solid thing against Alaric's back. He scrambles upward, and Alaric hitches him, ending up with Corbin on his shoulders. It's awkward as fuck and gains him an odd look or two, but it's Corbin. This is normal, as far as Alaric's concerned.

"I'd rather celebrate with you." Corbin pats the top of Alaric's head. "Sweat and all. I've told the guys I came with to go back without me. I'll catch a bus or something later. So where are we going?"

"Good question." Mac is there, hand on Alaric's shoulder, leaning up to kiss his cheek. "Good game. Where the hell is Chris in this mess?" She twists away, keeping her hand on Alaric as if she's afraid she'll lose him.

Corbin points. "Chris is there." His hand shifts to the left. "Drea's over there with a whole crowd of people, including your Mages, Ric."

"Not *my* Mages."

Corbin pats his head. "It's fun how pissed off you get when I say it, though." His amusement is a tangible thing, a shift from the anger that used to accompany the words. "Besides, yes, I paid attention." The touch to the side of his face is softer now, sympathy in his scent.

"Don't," Alaric warns. "Because remember the part where I didn't actually give a shit?"

"Yeah, well."

It's obvious that Corbin doesn't get that Alaric was never romantically attached, worry still in his scent. Mac's brow furrows in confusion, and Alaric shakes his head. He squeezes Corbin's shins. "Wave. Get their attention."

An ear-splitting whistle, and Alaric winces as Corbin rocks on his shoulders, obviously waving. A few minutes later, Drea pushes through the crowd with what seems like half of his floor in her wake, plus a few extras. It amazes Alaric how the random group of people he hangs out with seems to constantly shift and change.

"That way." Corbin taps Alaric's head. "Let's go get Chris."

Mac's lost in the crowd, and Alaric wishes he could do the same, simply pop from place to place rather than having to wedge his way through people who seem determined to get closer to him. There are slaps against his back, laughs at Corbin's perch. But the group somehow manages to get through, pushing to the sideline where they can meet up with Chris, Mac, Dax, and Cass.

Corbin finally slides down Alaric's back to the ground. "So. Again. Where are we going to celebrate?"

"Teas Please?" Cass asks dryly. "Isn't it always Teas Please?"

"I'm not on-shift, so there's no point in stopping in to bother me," Nate points out. "Besides, what's the point of going when I'm not there?"

"We could give our hard-earned cash for tips to someone else," Jackson points out. "Every once in a while I've sat in someone else's section."

"And I have resented you for it every single time," Nate says cheerfully, throwing an arm around Jackson's shoulders and squeezing quickly before he lets go. "C'mon, I know you guys only go there for me."

"And the tea," Trish says.

"And the chocolate," Sera adds. "Don't forget the chocolate."

"Personally, I like the scones," TJ says, hands spread. "Best scones that I've found up here, and I'm picky."

"So we're going to Teas Please again." Cass smells like resignation and prickly, sour irritation. "Of course we are."

Dax doesn't say a word, but he draws Cass closer, presses a kiss to her forehead that she doesn't acknowledge. She keeps her arms tightly crossed over her chest, her jaw tight.

"Ice cream," Pat suggests. "I mean, I know it's cold, but I'm a New Englander. We eat ice cream during nor'easters. This is still balmy as far as I'm concerned. Besides, doesn't the place on West Hanover have indoor seating? It's a few blocks away, so it probably won't get overrun immediately after the game."

"And they have that thirty-scoop bowl we could share," Sera says.

"I'm not sharing my ice cream," Nate comments, eyebrows raised. He glances at Dax and Cass, then at the various groupings. "You guys can share. I don't currently have anyone I'm interested in sharing with."

"I was thinking solo ice cream." Pat gestures for the group to follow. "Come on, I know a shortcut out the west side of campus."

"Not changed yet," Alaric points out, as if they've somehow forgotten that the game just ended and he, Chris, and Dax are still in full gear.

Pat stops, glances back, head tilted. "You've got a point."

"We're going to find a place to hang out, and we'll text you where we're waiting so you can catch up," Mac decides. "What? Someone has to be organized here. If I can herd an entire taekwondo team, I can deal with all of you. Thorne, help me out here. Keep them in line."

"Are there any restrictions on how?" Thorne asks, lips pursed in a blooming smirk, eyebrows raised.

"Just no," Rory comments, and Thorne laughs.

Chris claps Alaric on the shoulder. "C'mon. Let's go get our gear off and wash up."

Dax is still with Cass when they walk away, talking quietly enough that Alaric would have to try to overhear. He figures Dax'll be along eventually. Or he won't. It's not Alaric's problem.

50

"I FEEL LIKE I'm cheating on Teas Please," Nate complains. "The gods of desserts are going to smite me."

"There are no gods of desserts," Sera tells him.

"Besides, Teas Please is lacking in ice cream," Trish adds. "It's okay. You're on a journey to get something new. Entering places unknown for treats untasted."

"Poetic," Nate says.

"Please tell me you're not writing a song about going for ice cream."

Trish glances at Thorne. "Why not? I wrote a song about iced tea once. And it was popular. I bet if you and I teamed up, we could write something about ice cream that the whole world would decide was actually about sex, and it'd get great airplay."

Thorne tilts his head, tucks his hair back behind his ear. "I might take that challenge, but not tonight."

It's an even larger group than usual walking together, and Alaric can see the ways different groups overlap. Corbin sticks close to him on one side, Chris bumping Alaric slightly as he tries to stay on the sidewalk on his other side. They trail behind Drea, Cass, and Dax. Sera, TJ, Pat, Nik, and Jackson are a clump moving faster than the rest, while Rory, Trish, Mac, and Thorne take up the middle space.

Rory glances back at Alaric, raises an eyebrow, and Alaric tries to make a face to show that he's fine.

It all seems okay right now, anyway.

Dax slows, Cass and Drea slowing with him. Alaric stops walking before he bumps into them, following when Dax takes a step toward a wrought iron fence alongside the road.

"Fuck," Dax mutters, and Rory turns back again, brow furrowing.

"Hey, guys," Thorne calls out, and the entire group slows, looking back where Dax stands, visibly holding himself still.

"Go on," Dax says quietly. "I'll be there in a few minutes."

"I'm not leaving," Cass says flatly, her arms crossed. "Do you want to tell us what's going on here?"

"Cass…" Drea's voice trails off.

Trish touches Cass's shoulder. "Come on. We'll go get seats. Dax'll be there soon enough."

Cass shakes off Trish's hand. "I'll wait here," she says. "You go. We'll be fine."

Alaric isn't sure he wants to walk away, either. Dax looks pained, hands clenched by his side. There's a faint smell of citrus in the air, and Alaric meets Drea's gaze. He shakes his head, and Drea nods.

They're staying.

Dax starts walking toward the fence, hitching himself up to climb up and over, jumping down to the other side. Alaric spots a gate and heads toward that, Drea and Nate close behind him. He can hear the soft rush of conversation behind them, but he doesn't worry about it, putting on a burst of speed and knowing Drea will be able to keep up. He's only a little surprised when Nate lopes along next to him, meeting stride and speed with ease.

They enter the graveyard through the gate, then follow the path, veering off when they spot Dax standing in front of a freshly dug grave. Dax slowly sinks to his knees, presses one hand in the dirt for a moment. Dax's shoulders rise and fall with a heavy breath, and the scent of citrus floods the space, stopping him in his tracks.

Empath.

"What would you have of me?" Dax asks, voice ringing clearly. He sits back on his heels, then comes to his feet, standing with his arms crossed over his chest.

Heavy breath and footsteps behind them. Alaric's nostrils flare; Chris, Mac, Rory, Thorne, and Cass. He suspects Corbin's in a tree somewhere. Drea's fingers brush Alaric's, and he takes her hand, squeezing lightly.

"It's okay, take your time," Dax says. "I know it's not easy." Slow inhalation, exhalation, then the same words all over again. Quietly. Softly. Formally spoken, as if Dax has said them a hundred times before. "What would you have of me?"

Nate takes a step forward, feet sliding in the grass, leaves crunching under his toes. Dax doesn't even twitch.

"Let him be," Cass hisses, her fingers wrapping tightly around Nate's wrist. "Let him do whatever he's going to do." Her body tilts toward Dax, her attention avid.

There's pain in the air, and Nate shakes her off. "Does he look bewitched to you?" Nate whispers back. "What's going on?"

"Empathic Talent." Alaric can't help the way he twitches when he says it. His beast is calm; nothing's directed at him, but it still pricks under his skin. "I can smell it."

"Ritual," Rory says, glancing at Thorne, who nods his agreement.

Dax steps forward, puts both hands on the gravestone and bows his head. There's a twist of pain threading through the citrus hanging in the air. His fingers curl over the stone, and Alaric catches a faint scent of blood. "What would you have of me?" Dax repeats for the third time, breath hissing out in a sigh when he finishes.

Dax steps back abruptly, like he's been punched in the gut, his hands dropping to his stomach. Alarm flares in the air, then recedes quickly. "It's okay. I'm not going to hurt you. Can't, really. I just need you to tell me what you need," Dax says.

"We're not supposed to be hearing the other side of this conversation, are we?" Nate asks quietly.

"Pretty sure no." Mac knocks her hand into his shoulder. "Hush. Let him be."

Dax closes his eyes, shoulders slumping. "Are you sure you want me to call? I can go there—" He cuts off, takes a step back. "Slow down."

Dax raises his hands, holds them out as if placating someone. "Slow down, slow down. I can't understand a word of—*yes*, I can call. I promise. I'll call. But if you'd rather I go—" Dax sidesteps, swings one hand out as if he's blocking a blow. "Hey! I'm trying to help here. You reached out to me."

Dax spins in place, and the scent of dead earth rises in the air. Alaric pushes at his nose, wishing he could get rid of the odor. It almost looks as if Dax is fighting, every line of his body reluctant until he manages to hold his hands out, fingers curled around something that isn't there. Dax stands steady, his arms shaking slightly with the effort.

"You need to give me the number," Dax says softly. Gently. He cocks his head, listens, and speaks numbers as if repeating them back to someone. Nate tugs his phone out of his pocket and when Dax repeats them for the second time, Nate notes them down on his phone.

Dax sags after the numbers are spoken, his voice tired when he asks, "Just a phone call, then? That's all you need?"

He listens intently, murmurs, "Third brick from the left, fourth row down, seriously?" Nate taps every word Dax says. Dax straightens up, pushes his fingers through his short hair until the curls stick up. "I hear your words," Dax says solemnly. "I accept your charge. It will be done."

The scents of earth and citrus fade into the breeze.

"Well, that was unique," Corbin murmurs, and Mac jerks back.

"Where the hell did you come from?"

"You're not the only one good at sneaking." Corbin grins. "Just flew in from a bird's eye view."

Dax turns slowly, sees the group standing there. "So. You saw that."

"You might need this." Nate holds out his phone. "I mean, I'm guessing your memory is good and that wasn't the first time something like that happened, but you also looked like you were half in a trance. So, notes."

Dax's laugh is dry. "Yeah, definitely not the first time. You guys should've gone on to the ice cream place."

"Of course I waited for you." Cass's tone is light, concerned, but there's anger in her scent, mixed with a hint of fear. "I wasn't going to leave you standing in a graveyard, talking to…" She waves at the grave.

"Newly dead person," Dax says. "Her name's Tiffany, and she's still unsettled by the entire experience, and she's worried about her kid, and this…" He rubs at his forehead. "Okay, yeah, Nate, mind if I borrow that for a second?" He takes the phone in one hand, uses his other thumb to tap numbers into his own phone. He hands Nate's phone back to him, holds up a hand to Cass when she takes a step toward him. "I'm not done yet. Let me do this, then we can go get ice cream. Okay?"

Dax walks away, far enough that he's out of Alaric's hearing. When Corbin twitches, Drea reaches for him, holds him in place. "Let him be," Drea murmurs.

"I don't know about you guys, but I am not thinking *ice cream* after that," Thorne says quietly. "I've never seen a Talent like that. Didn't Dax say he's Lineage?"

"Yeah, but he never talks about it," Chris says. "We've known each other since football started before his freshman year, and he's never said a word." He glances over at Cass, who shakes her head, lips pursed.

"Don't look at me. Obviously he didn't confide in me." Anger and hurt in her scent, her arms crossed tightly like a shield. "I've never seen him do anything like this."

"It might be private," Nate points out.

"We've been together almost two years," Cass snaps back. "You'd think we'd know intimate details."

Rory twitches, and Alaric would lean into him, but he's not close enough. He looks over, and Rory's attention is entirely on where Dax stands curled around the phone, his words muffled.

"Give it a rest, Cass." Thorne manages to slip between her and Nate, getting an arm around Cass's shoulders. "Some of us are open about our Talent, some have no choice, and others like keeping it private. Unless you've had the *I'll show you mine and you show me yours* conversation and he lied, leave it."

"That's not the point," Cass hisses. "And yes, I knew he's Talented. But Empathic? Talking to ghosts? Whatever"—she waves a hand at the gravesite—"that was?"

"Maybe it's personal." Rory's words are soft and slow, echoing Nate's sentiment. Nate gestures at Rory as if he's agreeing, while Rory continues, "Not everyone likes to have their Talent public."

"You're a Mage. Everyone knows you're a Mage."

Rory's expression is even as he looks down at her. "I wasn't talking about me. Give him a break. And maybe try listening to his explanation before you go off on him. If you've been together two years, why blow it up over this?"

This is exactly why love isn't worth it. This is a mess. Alaric takes a step back as if he can separate himself from the intensity of the emotions and charged scents thick in the air around him. Cass's anger chokes him, and he raises a hand to his throat as if he can clear it somehow.

There are shoulders on either side of him, familiar scents to cloud the air around him. Corbin on one side, Chris on the other.

And footsteps through the leaves as Dax returns.

"You're an Empath."

Dax stops at Alaric's blunt words, his phone held loosely in his hand. He lowers it slowly, tucks it into a pocket. "Sort of," he says. "But only for dead people, and only if they're lingering around, needing to get something done. And when it happens, I don't exactly have a choice about it, either. It's not the kind of thing that comes up all the time." He spreads his hands, "Unless I pass a graveyard at the wrong time, like tonight."

"So what happened?" Thorne sounds as curious as he ever is. "You literally hopped the fence to get in here."

"It's urgent when I hear someone calling. I can't ignore it," Dax says. "I felt her, and I had to come in and that was the quickest way. I just wanted to get it done, and I figured you'd all go on to get ice cream and I'd catch up."

Cass makes a soft sound of disbelief, her lips pressed tightly, scent sour.

"We weren't going to abandon you," Nate says.

"Well, now that we've all taken a detour so I could phone someone's mother to let her know where her daughter hid the cash she'd been paid under the table while working so she can take care of her granddaughter, can we go on?" Dax pauses as he walks past Alaric, puts a hand on his shoulders. "I can't do anything to you," he says quietly. "I can't even do anything to them. All I can do is listen and promise to help, and it's more like they control me than the other way around. But I won't get in your head."

"I know." Alaric's beast can tell the difference. He claps Dax's shoulder, nudges him to keep walking. "I'm okay with it. I'm not going to let the dragon out just because you reek like an Empath."

Dax slides an arm around Cass's shoulders, tugs her close, and kisses her forehead.

"We'll talk later," he murmurs, and she makes a displeased noise.

Alaric glances at Chris as the group begins to move again, heading out of the graveyard. He doesn't smell surprised, but he doesn't smell settled either. Concern, confusion. When his gaze shifts, Alaric realizes that Drea's looking right at him. She tilts her head, asking a question, and it takes him a moment to follow what she's thinking.

When her gaze flicks to Dax, he catches on.

Oh.

He's going to need to think about that.

51

Sweet Scoops is busier than they expected, and they aren't able to fit the entirety of their large group inside. They split up, with Pat and Sera insisting on staying inside because they're always cold. Trish, Jackson, Pat, and TJ pull up chairs and sit on the windowsill to stay nearby. Alaric tries not to notice how Thorne is also perched on the windowsill, leaning in close to talk to Nate.

"You upset?" Corbin asks, and Alaric shakes his head.

"Not really, but the sex was good," he admits.

"Does that mean you and Thorne...?" Chris lets the question trail off. Alaric shrugs, motions at the door where he saw Dax and Cass disappear not long ago.

"Let's go outside. I want to talk to Dax." Alaric is aware that he hasn't answered Chris and that Chris still smells like curiosity and concern. He huffs a sigh as he pushes through the door into the cool night air, the outdoors at least slightly warmer than the taste of the ice cream on his tongue. "You know I wasn't in love with him," he responds to Chris's question.

"But he's been cut off from booty calls," Corbin points out.

"Sorry to hear that."

Alaric is relieved that Chris doesn't say *I told you so*, which he half expected after the way Chris warned him about Thorne. He's just frustrated now with no outlet.

The door jingles as it opens, and Drea, Rory, and Mac join them. Alaric lifts his head, taking in the scent of the air; Dax and Cass are down the block. He catches Drea's eye and points in the correct direction just as Dax walks back toward them alone.

Alaric's gaze narrows, taking in the scent of irritation and frustration in the air. "Dax isn't okay," he mutters.

"Do you think Cass broke up with him? She seemed pretty pissed off about not knowing what happened back there." Corbin's tone is more serious, not teasing like he would if it were Alaric.

Alaric shakes his head, exchanges a glance with Drea. "Doesn't smell like it. You want to talk to him about this, or should I?"

"What—oh." Corbin goes silent, gaze flicking between the two of them. "Are you thinking—?"

Dax's steps slow as he spots them all standing outside. He has a bowl of ice cream in one hand, the spoon sitting in it while it slowly melts. It looks like it hasn't been touched. Dax sets it down on one of the nearby picnic tables, sinks onto the bench. "Go ahead and ask questions, but I don't know if I can answer them," Dax says. "I don't know a lot about how this works other than what I already said." He sounds tired, like he's already been grilled.

"You're Lineage," Mac says, sitting down on the bench opposite him. "Doesn't that mean your entire family has this Talent?"

Dax shakes his head. "Not exactly. We're an odd branch. Pretty sure we were purely Empathic somewhere back in the line, but there was a point in Greece where someone got tangled up with a Seer, someone else married a Mage, and somehow the lines crossed and merged. Now we're all Empathic, but with different specialties. Not just something like being a Mage with a tendency toward fire." Dax looks around as if he's going to point at Thorne and is surprised to find only Rory there. "These are distinct abilities. I'm not the first who speaks to the dead, but that's not what my mother or my sister do. It's not even what my grandparents did, or any of my other living relatives. So I've been pretty much on my own figuring it out."

"There's an element of ritual to it." Rory sits next to Mac, hunched over with his elbows on the table as he leans forward, intrigued. "You've crosswired the Talent. Professor Szczek would be fascinated."

"He is." Dax shrugs one shoulder. "I talked to him last year when I took the intro class. He knows a guy who's looking into the genetics of Talent, and he thinks I could intern with him over the summer, if that's the direction I want to go with my degree. It isn't, so I said no thanks. I'm more interested in the psychology of Talent." He laughs dryly. "Because all Empaths want to be in psych, right? Except I can't read people unless they're dead."

"I wanted to ask you about that." Alaric's the only one left standing. Drea's taken up the space next to Dax, straddling the bench, with Corbin fit in close behind her. Chris sits on the edge of the bench next to Rory. But Alaric doesn't want to squeeze in, can't even think about sitting still. He has his legs spread for balance, his arms crossed tightly, his ice cream cone held at an awkward tilt. "I want to know if they have to have just died."

Dax's expression goes blank. "How long dead are you thinking? The oldest one I've ever talked to was three centuries gone, when a cousin was buying a farmhouse in the middle of nowhere. She refused to leave—the ghost, that is—because she was protecting the well. I don't know from what because she wouldn't say. All I know is she died there, and my cousin had to dig a new well because the old one had a habit of going bone dry at random times. It's a good farm. He's happy out there."

Drea coughs. "We're thinking maybe a little more than a month."

"Our brother," Alaric says quietly. "He's Clan, and they're saying he was in the middle of a Mage ritual when he died. We haven't been able to find much, only things that talk about Talent that doesn't exist. But if he's still around, if he's restless because he was killed, maybe you can talk to him."

There's a knot in Dax's jaw, a sour tension to his scent, but he nods slowly. "Sure. I can try, anyway. Where's he buried, and when are you thinking?"

"Haverhill," Alaric says. He keeps his tone as even as Dax's. "And I'm thinking that if you can borrow your mom's van, we can go out tonight."

Drea makes a face. "Dad—"

"—doesn't need to know we're coming." Alaric doesn't want to give Theobald the chance to say no. "We show up. We get some rest tonight, and we go talk to Orson first thing in the morning. Then we leave. We won't be in his hair for long."

"How close is your house to the gravesite?" Dax asks. "If it's close, I might not have a choice about timing. And you're assuming he'll be at the grave. He might be where he died."

Alaric winces; he hadn't thought of that. "We'll have to take that chance.

And not close. From here to campus," he estimates. It seems about right. Maybe farther. "You didn't feel that girl from campus, so it should be all right."

Dax picks up his phone, taps out a text and sends it. "Should be, yeah. Who are you thinking of as '*we*'?"

"You, me, Drea, Corbin," Alaric says firmly.

"I'll go," Rory offers. "For moral support. And in case..." He gestures, and Alaric nods, knowing what kind of support he means. He really hopes it doesn't come to that.

"I'll go," Chris says.

"Me too," Mac offers, expression serious. "This isn't going to be easy for any of you."

"Mac can't." Alaric's mouth thins, lips pressed together. "I didn't recognize you, but my father might. He's not interested in gymnastics, but he'd definitely remember the girl who changed everything."

Mac's expression twists. "Can't argue that point."

"Rory, are you sure?" Drea says, and Rory just looks at her.

"If Dax is there, your father will already be pissed off about you bringing an Empath. He's not going to get more pissed about a Mage. Besides"—he tilts his hand—"I might be able to help. And Alaric'll text me half the time anyway. It's not like I'm going to get song writing done wondering what's going on."

"Let him come." Corbin says. "Maybe Theobald will have a heart attack and leave Alaric in charge, and it won't matter anymore."

"Don't talk like that." Drea swats at him. "He's still our father."

"Until he disowns you," Corbin murmurs, leaning his chin on her shoulder. "This isn't going to make him happy. I'm actually more worried about him trying to kill Alaric when he realizes there are Mages in his house. Maybe we should bring Thorne, too, because anyone with eyes can see that Rory's offer isn't a suggestion—pretty sure he's going with Alaric whether we want him to or not."

"We can't take Thorne; I need the seat for Cass," Dax says, his fingers tapping at the keyboard on his phone. "Chris, would you be willing to loan your car to my mom until we're back? We can drive out after we get back to campus, pick up the van, then come back and get everyone else."

Chris's hand is curled tight. He glances at Alaric, and his expression eases, his hand uncurling to lie flat against his thigh. "Yeah. We can do that."

"Bringing Cass means bringing two humans," Alaric points out. "I'm not sure that's a good idea."

Dax finishes what he's typing, then sets the phone down on the picnic table. "It'll be you, Corbin, Drea, Chris, Rory, me, and Cass. That's an Empath and a Mage, and we're planning on talking to your father's dead son. I'm guessing that one more human isn't going to make things much worse."

"Where is Cass, anyway?" Mac looks down the street in the same direction where Dax came from not long ago.

Dax's jaw goes tight at the corner, his smile thin. "Taking a moment to cool down. But if I take off without her, it's going to make things worse. I know she'll want to go—she's got this thing in her head about secrets right now, and it'll be easier if she's there. So please, if you think your house can handle it, let's bring Cass instead of Thorne. I'm pretty sure she's less likely to say or do anything to poke at your father, at least."

Alaric can't argue that. Bringing Mac might cause an explosion if his father recognizes her, and he's certain Thorne won't stay quiet where Theobald's concerned. His nostrils flare, seeking some scent from Cass, but she's too far away to smell or hear. He nods slowly. "Fine. We can bring Cass. But don't plan on makeup sex. No one's getting sexiled, and you'll probably be staying in my room or Drea's room."

"There are guest rooms," Corbin points out.

"Do you think we should leave any of them on their own?" Alaric counters. "They'll be safer with us."

"If we're going to do this, we should finish up the ice cream and get back so we can get the van," Chris says, taking a bite out of his cone. He holds it up, gestures to Alaric. "Eat."

The ice cream is good—sweet and creamy and full of flavor, obviously handmade in small batches. It's supposed to be a celebration of their victory earlier that afternoon, but it doesn't taste like that to Alaric. It's just something to get through so they can move on to the next thing. So they can find out more about Orson.

52

ALARIC TAGS ALONG when Dax and Chris go to pick up the van, in case Dax's mother has questions. "All I told her was that I needed the car for the night," Dax says quietly. "I didn't mention that we're going to your place. Pretty sure she thinks I'm heading to another concert."

Alaric sits awkwardly in the back of Chris's car, his knees bent too tightly, legs cramped. "Might be for the best. How does your family feel about Clan?"

"Don't really care, I think," Dax says. "My dad's not Talented. We've got enough variety that we're used to things being a little different. We've got our own little corner of Valiant, and our house that's been there for centuries. Turn here." He points to the right as Chris pulls up to a light and puts his blinker on. Alaric can see VIT on the hill ahead of them, the brick buildings stretching up toward the sky. The route Dax points out takes them around the lower edge of campus, then pushes out farther to the east.

"How much driving does your mom need to do?" Chris asks tightly, and Dax chuckles.

"You are so possessive about your car." Dax taps his shoulder. "Right here, then second left, then it's the third driveway on the right. Pull in on the right hand side; that's where dad usually parks. So we can get the van out of the garage."

"That's not an answer."

Dax snorts softly. "Nothing guaranteed, but Dad's on shift at the hospital tonight, so Mom doesn't want to be left without a car in case of an emergency. Not that there will be an emergency, but you never know. When he gets home tomorrow morning, she'll use his car to get Alex to her dance class. So your car will be ignored and fine, don't worry."

It's somehow good to know that Chris is worried about his car all the time, not only when Alaric is driving it. Alaric leans forward, gets a hand on Chris's shoulder. "Thanks for doing this," he says quietly.

Chris huffs. "Yeah, well." He reaches up, touches Alaric's hand, then drops his grip back to the steering wheel. He maneuvers into the driveway as the garage door opens; a lanky girl stands there in the opening in front of a familiar-looking minivan.

Alaric can see the shape of Dax's face in her features, a similar curl to her hair where it falls around her face. She has his broad shoulders and long torso, but her legs and arms are also long; Alaric suspects she might end up as tall as her brother when she's done growing. She's already close.

She smiles with a mouth full of braces, starts talking as soon as they open the doors to the car. "Dimitri Maximilian Katsoulis, where do you think you're going?" she asks sharply. "Not telling Mom that you're taking a road trip is rude."

"Hey, Alex." Dax reaches out, tugs her for a hug and ruffles the hair atop her head. "Keys?"

She sighs and drops them into his hand. "Were you going to say anything?"

"Should I bother? You always know everything anyway." Dax keeps an arm around her shoulders, gestures at the car. "You've met Chris. This is Alaric."

"The other quarterback." Alex's gaze narrows, thoughtful. "You were good today. You both were. It was an awesome game. Why are you going to his house now?"

Alaric's jaw works and he rocks backward on his heels. "Dax."

"I didn't say a word," Dax says, his tone resigned. "Like I said, I let Mom think we're just going out. Alex, did you tell her?"

"Only just figured it out, and she didn't tell me you're taking the van, so we're even," Alex says. "Is this one of those times I'm supposed to keep things to myself?"

"It'd be appreciated."

Alex reaches up, frames Dax's face with her hands, and stares at him for an uncomfortable moment. She finally lets go, steps back, and huffs a sigh. She crosses her arms again. "Fine. Go inside. Mom's baking, and she's already got the apple fritters out of the oven and there are these strawberry-rhubarb tartlets that she's trying that are almost done. Those must be for Alaric. You two help her package things up so you can take them. I want to talk to Alaric."

"I…"

"She's harmless, I promise," Dax says, clapping a hand on Alaric's shoulder. "Whatever she has to say, listen."

Dax and Chris head inside, and for a moment the scent of warm fruit and pastry wafts out. Alex takes Alaric's hand, and she tugs, leading him around the outside of the house toward the back.

"If you were Clan, you'd be a colt," Alaric mutters, and Alex nods as if that weren't strange to say.

"I dream about running sometimes," she says. "The fields are full of these purple flowers, and I know they taste sweet if I want to stop to eat. But I never want to stop running long enough to do that."

Alaric is off-balance. Her small hand is still tucked in his, her scent as trusting as if she's known him for years. She comes up past his shoulder, and when he turns to glance at her, she's looking at him rather than toward where they're going.

"I'm unnerving, I know," she says easily. "It's okay. I'm weird. You can think that." She lets go of his hand as they reach the swing set behind the house and sinks down onto one of the two swings. She motions, and Alaric carefully sits on the other. It bends under his weight, but it holds. He's wary of letting it move, afraid the entire structure will tip over.

Alex has no compunctions, leaning back and pumping her legs as she starts to swing.

"What?" Alaric asks, still waiting for the other shoe to drop.

"Aren't you going to ask other questions?" Alex counters. "How did I know you were coming?"

"Dax texted your mom."

Alex makes a buzzing noise. "Wrong. Mom didn't tell me anything, just started baking. And yes, apple fritters are a good tell that Dax is coming home, but the new recipe meant he was bringing someone else. I didn't know who, and I didn't know why. But I knew he needed the keys. The rest snapped into place as soon as I saw you, and it made sense of some other things, too."

Alaric swallows hard, closes his eyes, and focuses on the scents around him. There's no citrus in the air, only curiosity and a fresh vanilla-and-strawberry that complements the faint scent of baking that wafts from the house. Probably shampoo, or soap. "You're an Empath," he says, because Dax is one, and she should smell like it too.

"Sort of. There's a bit of Seer in me. So sometimes I know things. But I don't always know who they're for or why until I see the person." She lets her feet drag in the sand under the swing, slowing abruptly. "I'm glad you came with Dax to pick up the car, or I wouldn't have figured it out, and I wouldn't have been able to warn you. You need to watch out for the darkness, Alaric."

He snorts because that's obvious. "Thanks, but I've already run into that."

Her brow furrows, and she leans across the space between them, wrapping her fingers around his wrist. Her tongue pokes out between her lips, and she shakes her head. "Okay, so yes, I can feel that, but that's not all of it. It's going to touch you again, and I don't think it's the same, and it's bigger than you think. And when it comes after you, don't fall into the split."

That makes no sense. "What do you know about Shadowwalkers?" Alaric asks.

"Legends," Alex answers promptly, finally letting him go. She starts to swing again as if the intense moment never happened. "There's a story about a dead soul trying to cross into the afterlife, and a Soulstealer who nearly steals their essence, but an Empath protects the soul. My grandmother used to tell me that when I was young. Also a story about Seers losing their sight after walking into shadows."

Alaric's jaw works, and he tries to put his words into a sentence that will make sense. Alex's eyes are wide, waiting, her body at ease. She pumps her feet, swinging high, then leaps off and lands with coltish grace. "Come on," she says. "You want one of the tartlets while they're still warm. You don't have to share them, if you don't want. She only made half a recipe because she didn't know how it would work. If you were staying longer, she'd probably cook more."

"I don't understand."

Alex stops at the back door of the house. "Mom knows what people need, and she usually ends up feeding them, although that's not always it. So right now you're getting a minivan and strawberry-rhubarb tartlets. Just accept it and move on; it's easier that way."

She pushes open the door, and Alaric trails after her, still uncertain about the entire conversation. Alex pauses as they get inside the mudroom, stomps dirt from her shoes, and hangs up her jacket. "Remember what I said about the split," she says, and walks away.

Chris is waiting as Alaric follows her into the kitchen; he budges up shoulder to shoulder with Alaric. "What was that about?" Chris murmurs, and Alaric watches as Alex bustles around the kitchen. She gets out plates and forks, puts pastries onto plates and hands them out, pointing to where they should sit and eat before they go.

Dax's expression is apologetic. "We should eat before we go," he echoes.

"Your family is…unique." Alaric flounders picking the right word because it would rude to say *odd*, but that's the best impression that he's got.

"There's a reason I don't talk about my Lineage," Dax says, pushing his fork through the apple fritter on his plate. "We're not easy to explain."

They join Alex and Dax's mom in the living room, sitting politely while they eat. Alex chatters about the game that day, asking questions and pointing out what she could see from the stands, then she reciprocates with plans for her upcoming dance recital. She presses Dax to promise to attend, and it's all very normal. Very family, and almost human.

And despite all the normalcy, and the fantastic taste of the strawberry-rhubarb tartlet, Alaric can't forget what Alex said. He has no idea what it means.

53

"I THOUGHT PREDICTIVE Talent always had a focus," Chris says. The thrum of the engine is the loudest sound in the minivan; the stereo is off so that everyone can hear. "Weren't we just talking about that?" He nudges Alaric.

Rory reaches forward from the third seat, taps Alaric on the shoulder before he can answer. "It depends on the type of predictive Talent," Rory says. "Sometimes it's a specialty for a Mage, like my mom, who can sense Talent. It's not the same as reading cards or having prophetic nightmares, but it's predictive in its own way."

"Alex isn't like any of that." Alaric is at a loss trying to find the words to explain it. He meets Dax's gaze in the rearview mirror. He'd lean forward, but Cass is in the front passenger seat and she has it reclined while she curls to one side, her eyes closed, breath soft and even with sleep. Alaric frowns, tries to tease out from the scents whether Cass and Dax are still fighting and how badly that will go when they get to his home.

"Alex is— We're a different kind of family," Dax says. "The predictive Talent in our bloodline is from a Seer. Think the Oracle of Delphi, and yes, it probably goes back that far into our Greek roots. I don't think there are any pure Seers left anymore, but it seems to infuse our bloodline. So we're each unique. Alex has no control over it—she'd be useless in something like a football game. She'd never be able to predict what was going to happen next. She gets random flashes, and she doesn't always know how it fits together until she happens to find the right puzzle piece."

Like when Alaric walked in. And he's pretty sure Alex still doesn't know the whole story, and he's damn sure he doesn't understand the parts she told him.

"Did she happen to mention what Theobald's going to do when we pull in the drive?" Corbin asks. He's joking, but only barely; Alaric can hear the thread of sincerity in the question.

Dax turns as the GPS directs, and they head out of downtown Haverhill toward the community. It won't be long now.

"Don't need to be predictive for that," Alaric mutters. He crosses his arms, sinks down in his seat. There's a bump against his knee, and he catches the scent of worry from Chris. "It'll be fine," Alaric adds. "This is my plan, and I am exercising my authority."

"I don't think this is what Theobald's expecting you to do."

Drea snorts softly. "I think in some ways it's exactly what our father's expecting Alaric to do. The problem is that he doesn't know that maybe it's the right thing to do. Dax—" She waits until Dax raises a hand to acknowledge her, then continues, "Turn's coming up on the right. Look for the sign for Herne Way. It'll be about five minutes down that road. Watch out for small animals and children."

"They're probably all children," Corbin points out.

"Got it." Dax navigates slowly down the road, and Alaric spots more than a few forms that he recognizes. When a pair of wolves dart away, cutting through the woods straight for the house and avoiding the road, Alaric knows his cousins will warn his father.

He curls his hand together, presses his nails against his palm. Rory's fingertips are cool against the back of his neck, a light touch with no magic. Chris covers Alaric's hand with his own briefly, and Alaric breathes in, inhales the familiar scents in the car. The only one that feels out of place is Cass, but enough of Dax's scent is mixed with hers that Alaric can accept it.

"Park here." Drea points, and Dax pulls into the spot.

He reaches up, pushes a button, and both back doors slide open in time for them to hear a roar from the house. A lion bursts through the quickly opened door, leaps off the steps, and stands in front of them, roaring again. A blink later, Theobald stands before them, arms crossed, scent furious. "There are Mages in that car."

Rory's hand slips from Alaric's skin, and Chris draws away. Alaric doesn't say he'll go first, but they all stay in place anyway as Alaric climbs out of the back of the car, walks the few short steps to greet his father. He doesn't tilt his head, refuses to bare his throat.

"One Mage," Alaric says. "My roommate, Rory. One other Lineage Talent, and two humans, plus Corbin and Drea. We've come to visit Orson's grave."

Fury rises in the air, hot and tangible, not just to Alaric's nose but to his skin. He feels answering heat under his own skin, and he clenches his fists tight against the beast that wants to burst free. Not in front of his father. Not now, not when he needs control.

His twin's scent washes over him; she stands at his left hand, Corbin to his right. Rory lingers at the door to the van after unfolding himself from the back seat, one hand pressed to the small of his back while he stretches. Chris and Dax speak quietly, while Cass still somehow snoozes in the front seat.

"Go home," Theobald says. Each word is low and separate, ringing with authority. Corbin grips Alaric's elbow; Drea has her hand at his waist. "You will not disturb Orson's rest."

"He's dead, old man," Corbin says, tone light despite the tension in his body. "We can't disturb him because he's not resting."

"You will not disrespect my son!"

Corbin takes a step back, and Alaric goes with him. He's never heard Theobald yell at Corbin before, and he can smell Corbin's rush of surprise and flash of fear. Alia is there a moment later, her hand on Theobald's arm, and Alaric feels Rory and Chris at his back. He hears murmurs near the van as Dax wakes Cass.

"Theobald," Alia says gently; it does nothing to quench the scent of fury in the air.

"Let's do introductions, since we're here for the night no matter what," Drea says firmly. "This is Rory—he's Ric's roommate, and he's a good guy, and he's not going to attack any of us, nor is he part of what happened to Orson. You remember Chris. That's Dax over by the car, and he's the reason we're here—which Ric can explain to you—and that's Dax's girlfriend, Cass."

Cass slides from the seat, stands on wobbly legs, and pushes her hair out of her face. "What's going on?" she asks.

"Later," Dax says.

"You are all welcome in our home," Alia informs them, voice tight. "Andrea, perhaps you should take your friends upstairs and settle them in your rooms while Alaric and your father continue this discussion in private."

"C'mon, let's get our stuff out of the car." Drea kisses Alaric's cheek, then shoves Corbin toward the car in a familiar roughhousing gesture.

Rory hesitates, holds his hand out where only they can see it, and Alaric shakes his head slightly. " 'm fine," Alaric says quietly. "As long as he can see you here, my father's going to be pissed off."

"How did he even know I was in the car? Usually I fly under the radar," Rory responds, and Alaric shrugs. He can't smell Rory. He has no idea how his father knew, but somehow, he did. "Does he get that I'm not here to hurt anyone?" Rory's glance flicks past Alaric, then back to meet his eyes. "You're as good as family to me."

"Yeah," Alaric says gruffly. He yanks Rory in, hugs him hard, rubs his cheek against Rory in a gesture that he knows his parents won't miss. "Stick with Drea and Corbin. You'll be safe."

"What about you?" Chris hasn't moved yet, his jaw tight. "This looks worse than last time."

"Last time might have been right after Orson's passing, but I only brought you," Alaric says quietly. "This time I brought an entire van-load of people into Clan territory. He's not going to trust anyone."

"So we stick together, we do what we came to do, and we leave," Chris says. "We're with you on this, Ric. Like you said to Drea: you made this decision, and he needs to recognize that if he's asking you to lead, you can do it in your own way."

Alaric huffs. "I know. Think I would've let you all get in that van if I didn't?" He nudges Chris. "Go. Get upstairs with the rest. My room or Drea's; stay put until I get this settled. Pretty sure that the only one here you can't trust is him, but you don't need a bunch of curious Clan kids sniffing around, either."

"Should I still be wary if Corbin offers to show us the baths?" Chris asks, and his grin crinkles the corners of his eyes.

Theobald clears his throat, and there's a small sound from Alia.

"Go," Alaric says. "I need to talk to my father."

"You are not leader yet," Theobald says solemnly when Alaric finally gives him his attention.

"No, I'm not," Alaric tells him, "but I'm going to be, and if you want to leave me something to lead, then don't interfere with what I'm doing."

"Inside," Alia says, shushing them. "There are too many curious ears out here. Alaric, join us in your father's study, then the two of you can discuss what is to be done."

"There haven't been Mages on Clan land in a century."

Alaric trails after his father. He can't resist getting a final dig in. "There haven't been Mages on *this* Clan land in a century," he says. "Others haven't remained so separate. What happened to Orson wasn't about magic. We're here to find out what it was about."

54

"YOU WANT ME to lead, but you won't let me do anything!" Alaric yells, his voice echoing off the walls. He feels Alia's flinch, but he can't stand down, not when his father postures, command evident in his stance. They've been yelling long enough that Alaric's lost track of time; they're going around in circles, saying the same things over and over. He's sure that there are cousins and others in the halls, listening in. He's sure that Drea's relaying everything to his friends upstairs.

But he can't stop, and he can't give ground. He can't lose to Theobald.

"This isn't leadership. This is interference in Clan affairs," Theobald growls. "This is putting yourself in the midst of something you do not understand."

Heat ripples under Alaric's skin, thin tendrils of smoke spiraling out from his nostrils. "I can't understand something if you refuse to allow me to," Alaric grinds out between gritted teeth. "You want me to lead, but you shut me out. You refuse to allow me to investigate my own brother's death."

"Murder!"

Alaric can't dispute that. He cuts the word away with a gesture, moves on. He tries to keep his voice low, even, while vibrating with the need to shout. He needs to push this into his father's ears, make him understand by sheer force of will. "I understand more than you think," he growls. "I know that it's not because his roommate was a Mage. I know that there's more to this than the ancient wars that have happened between our kind. I know that we don't need another war, not now, not when the eyes of the entire world are still staring at us, waiting for us to fuck up. Humans think we're violent. Animals. They expect us to start ripping each other apart, and if you go to war over this, you'll prove them right!"

"This is exactly why we shouldn't mix!" Theobald roars. "We are not like humans. We are not like Mages. We are *Clan*, and they know this. They *know* we are something different."

A thick scent is in the air, wrapped around them. Alaric smells fur and fury, knows that Theobald teeters on the edge. He feels claws prick his palms in reaction, his mouth full of teeth, and he snarls, lip curling, to show those teeth to his father. Theobald snarls back, stalking close, staring Alaric in the eye to force him to back down.

Alaric won't back down.

There's a hand on his chest, small and warm, pushing him back. Alaric goes when Theobald does, relenting to his mother's touch when he refuses to give way for his father.

"I won't lose my husband and another child," Alia says quietly. "And certainly not to each other. Be civil, or this community will be left with nothing. You can't argue about leadership when you would both destroy each other and leave us with none."

Breath shudders in his chest, and Alaric takes another step back. He flexes his hands, forces his fingers back to human, swallows the roar that wants to slip free. Smoke swirls around his head, and he smells the sharp scent of curiosity as his mother and father both take notice. "I have control," he says, clearly implying that perhaps it's his father who doesn't.

Theobald growls, mouth still full of teeth, and Alia wraps one arm around his shoulders, her other palm pressed against his chest. The teeth disappear on an inhale, and Theobald seems smaller. Quieter.

Alaric licks his lips. Waits.

"I want the Mages off my property," Theobald says quietly. "Now. Get back in that van and leave."

"Only Rory's a Mage," Alaric says. "He's my roommate, and you can trust him. He doesn't mean any harm. Fuck, you'd actually like his family if you gave them the chance. I'm thinking about setting up some trade with them. Wool and other fibers." His gaze flicks to his mother. "We can talk about it later."

"No, you can't," Theobald insists, but Alia gives a shallow nod where Theobald can't see.

Alaric feels a thread of tension go loose in his shoulders. He curls his fingers, then spreads them, his hands loose at his sides now. "It would be good for us," he says as if Theobald has said nothing.

"I want no interaction with Mages, and I want the ones you brought gone. Tonight," Theobald repeats. "All of them. And when they're gone, you will return. If this is what you *learn*, then perhaps you should be here, instead. Learning how to be Clan. Corbin disrespects authority, but he knows what it means to be a part of this community. Even your sister would lead better than you."

"It's funny how you don't want her to come back," Alaric says. "We're not all that different. We're twins, remember?"

"She's not going to lead, and you are. You need to learn how."

"Maybe I am." Alaric huffs, crosses his arms. "We'll leave tomorrow after we talk to Orson. We need to know what he knows. If his spirit is still here, it's here for a reason, and Dax can talk to him. He can find out why, and we can fix it. Because it's *not Mages*. That symbol—it's happened to someone else after Orson. And we found a reference for it."

Doubt in the air. Disbelief, heavy and thick, layered with disappointment. "What do you think you've found?"

"Legends," Alaric admits. Theobald goes stiff, gaze narrowing. Alia's eyes go wide, her nostrils flaring. Alaric speaks slowly. Carefully. "The symbol is a word in the language of the Shadowwalkers—"

He gets no further as Theobald barks out a sharp, short burst of laughter. "Legends," Theobald snarls. "Stories. Would you protect us with lemon trees, Alaric? Do you want our children to be afraid of the dark?"

"I want to find out the truth!" Alaric steps forward, the anger flickering into rage beneath his skin, warming him from the inside out. His beast is gratified to see Theobald take a step back, leaning into Alia. Alaric's lip curls as he growls, the sound thick and deep, burgeoning into a roar filled with smoke.

Alia moves forward, presses both her hands against his chest, and Alaric huffs, goes quiet.

"I want you to come back after you take them off our land," Theobald says quietly. "You will return and learn what it means to be a leader."

Alaric's breath catches in his chest, twists tight at the idea of never returning to school. Of never seeing Rory again, or Chris, or Mac, or any of his friends. Of never playing football. He shakes his head. "Maybe I should make my own community," he whispers. Theobald's skin goes pale with fury. "Maybe I should make my own space, where Clan thinks for itself and sees the world around it, rather than hiding from it."

"Alaric," Alia says, and Alaric's mouth snaps shut at the hushed tone of his mother's voice. "Theobald. This discussion is done."

"It's far from done," Theobald responds, and Alia turns to him. Alaric can't see her face, but he can feel the shift in the air around them, can see the way Theobald's eyes widen as Alia growls, baring her teeth.

"You will not drive our only son from his family," Alia snarls quietly. "And you." She spins and jabs a finger hard into Alaric's chest. "You will not leave. Alaric and his friends will remain overnight. You will do what you came to do, and then you will go, and that's it. Do not continue down this road, and do not say things that you will regret, either of you. I have already lost one child; I will not lose another."

The conversation is far from over, merely paused. Alaric can see it in Theobald's posture, in the way his jaw tightens against words bursting forth. Alaric nods, giving way first as he turns his back on his parents and stalks to the door. There's movement behind him, and he keeps his back stiff, refusing to turn back at the sound.

He pulls open the door, pauses when Theobald clears his throat.

"I want them gone by lunch tomorrow," Theobald growls softly, and Alaric nods once.

"We'll be gone by then," he says. "I won't see you again until Harvest. And only then if I decide to come home." Alaric's fingers are tight on the door knob, pressing hard against the cool metal. "I'll let you know if I decide to stay at PHU for the long weekend." His tone is careful, even. "It might be for the best."

He tugs open the door and steps through. He pulls it shut with a *thunk*, lets it put the final stop to the argument, closing the space between himself and his parents.

55

DREA SITS ON the floor, working to plug in the pump to an air mattress while Chris and Dax tug out the corners to lay the mattress flat on the floor. Drea starts the pump, and the sound fills the room, buzzing loud enough to hurt Alaric's ears. He pushes at his ears, stopping when Corbin reaches over to scritch him like a puppy.

"Quit it." Alaric swats at Corbin's hands.

"You know, we could probably all fit in your bed," Corbin points out, pulling away as he leans against the wall, legs sprawled, foot knocking into Rory. "It's pretty big. Didn't we have ten of us on it once, for that sleepover?"

"We were seven years old," Alaric says dryly. "I wasn't even five feet tall yet. Pretty sure that now me, Chris, and Rory would take up half the bed on our own. Add Dax and I don't know where the rest of you would sleep."

"On top of you," Corbin tells him. "It's not like we need a lot of room in a puppy pile." He glances at the others. "I know I said I'd puppy pile to get to know your friends, but I didn't think it would actually happen."

"You know, you spend an awful lot of time trying to sound like an ass-hole," Rory says quietly. "Maybe it'd be easier if you just stopped trying to be an ass and accepted that this is how it is."

Corbin glances sideways at Rory, and Alaric smells apprehension in the air. "You try losing your best friend since birth," Corbin snaps.

Rory blinks. "Already went through that." He leans forward, crawls over Chris, his jaw set with determination. He slides into the spot between Corbin and Chris, crosses his arms as his shoulder pushes against Corbin. "My family's more like your Clan than anything else. We're close. We sleep in piles sometimes. We don't have a lot of barriers—which you might have noticed from talking to Thorne for more than five minutes. And when

Thorne left for his first year at PHU, it was like half my life walked away." He elbows Corbin, and Corbin bites his tongue. "So I get it. Ric's my friend, and he's your friend, and we're all here to support him, and it's obvious that things are shit here right now."

"So?"

Alaric recognizes the quaver in Corbin's voice, barely audible, the wariness more in his scent than his prickly posture. Corbin's head tilts, then his chin lowers, gaze narrowed and sharp. Rory meets that gaze, shrugs one shoulder.

"So, if you're his family, and I'm his family, then we're stuck with each other as family," Rory says carefully. "You should know I don't like touching people. There are reasons, and we're not going to go into them. But I'm here, and I'm not pushing you out of bed, so how about you stop trying to push me out of Ric's life. Okay?"

Air from the pump hisses in the background through the long silent moment. Corbin's jaw is tight, a muscle clenching near his ear, then he nods sharply. "Fine." It sounds begrudging, but Alaric sees how Corbin goes quiet, curls closer to Rory, and tentatively checks to see if Rory will take his weight. Rory huffs and lifts an arm as he rolls his eyes.

"We don't all have to sleep in the bed, do we?" Cass's voice is soft, scent thick with discomfort.

"We'll take the air mattress," Dax tells her, kissing the top of her head. "No one has to do anything they're uncomfortable with."

"I'm not—" She breaks off, licks her lips, and looks up at where Alaric sits on the edge of the bed. "Thank you for your hospitality and for not minding that I've tagged along. I'm not trying to be a bitch."

"Not a slur around here," Drea says. "Half the time, I'm a literal bitch."

Cass laughs, the sound bursting out bright and surprised. "I hadn't thought of that," she admits. "I just—I'm pretty traditional. I'm not into this puppy-pile sharing thing. I'd rather have our own space."

"We're not all going to be having sex, if that's what you're worried about," Corbin says.

"Please no one have sex while we're in this room," Rory mutters. "Go find privacy if you're that desperate to get off."

"I'm pretty sure everyone here can wait until we get back to wherever," Dax says.

"There." The air pump turns off, and Drea unplugs it. The air mattress is raised, not quite as high as Alaric's bed. Drea tosses a pile of blankets, sleeping bags, and pillows on top, and Dax and Cass climb up to make sure it doesn't sink under their weight.

Drea flops onto Alaric's bed, her hip wedged in against Corbin's, her head falling back against Rory's chest. Rory's eyes open for a moment, then he lets his hand fall against Drea's head, fingers combing through her hair. She sighs softly and closes her eyes, letting out a noise that sounds suspiciously like a purr.

"Come on." Chris slides over, pats the space he makes between himself and Rory.

Alaric crawls across the bed and fits himself into the spot that's left. He ends up with one arm across Rory's shoulder, while Chris lies half on Alaric with Alaric's hand on his chest. He can feel the steady beat of Chris's heart, and it echoes in his own chest, calming him.

"There's room for more if you change your mind," Corbin says, and Cass snorts. She's lying on her side on the air mattress, Dax's arm around her as he spoons behind her. She pats Dax's hand where it lies against her belly.

"I think we're good," Cass says, then threads her fingers together with Dax's.

"Someone should get the light," Corbin says, grunting as Drea shoves him to the edge of the bed. "I said *someone*. Not me."

"You're closest," she points out. "So go. Kill the light, then maybe we can all get some sleep."

Corbin grumbles, rolls off the side of the bed, and disappears in a flurry of wings. The raven stops just before hitting the wall, manages to flick the switch, and resolves back into Corbin at the edge of the bed. "Fine," Corbin grumbles. "Light's off. Shove over and give me back my space."

They rearrange again, and Alaric ends up with Rory sprawled over him stomach to stomach. Chris is still tight against his other side, Alaric's arm over his shoulder. "This okay?" Chris asks, and Alaric nods.

"Yeah. Yeah, this is good." Alaric huffs as Rory pats his shoulder. He's trapped between the warmth of his friends, surrounded by their scent. It feels odd to have them all here, but it's everything that his beast wants and needs. Something pokes at his foot, and he realizes that it's Drea, her leg draped across Rory to get to Alaric. He reaches out in return, past Rory, to skim his fingers over Drea's head, then touches Corbin's shoulder.

This is exactly what he needs.

"You're thinking too loudly," Rory mutters. "Isn't this supposed to be the part where we sleep?"

"Yep," Corbin says, voice already low and loose. "Quit it, Alaric."

"What if I left?" Alaric whispers. He doesn't mean to let the words loose, but they come out anyway, soft and slow. Once they're in the air, there's nothing to do but finish the thought. "If I left, would you come with me, Drea?"

"Always," Drea says.

"In a heartbeat," Corbin adds. "But you know that."

Alaric isn't sure that he did. "I do now," he says quietly. "Even after—?" He stops, not sure how to end that question.

"Even if it means living with Mages and humans?" Corbin murmurs. He rolls over, presses his face against Drea's hair, words muffled. "Yes, Ric, I'm with you. You and all your terrible taste." The tone is dry, teasing. "I am literally in bed with your friends right now. I'm pretty sure that's Rory's cold toe on my ankle. We're all good. You leave, I follow. That's how it is."

"Me too." Rory's breath puffs out against Alaric's chest. "Which means you're stuck with Thorne, too, but honestly, if you haven't figured out yet that we've adopted you, then you haven't been paying attention. I mean, I followed you home."

"I've followed you home twice," Chris points out. "Despite being threatened with drowning."

"I wouldn't have actually drowned you in the baths," Corbin says idly. "It would've pissed off and hurt Alaric. Which I don't want to do."

Truth. Alaric can smell the honesty in his scent, the wariness that still lingers as Corbin is surrounded by Alaric's friends. "I know," Alaric says, and Corbin eases. Alaric closes his eyes, breathes deep as Chris twists next to him, throws one arm and a leg across Alaric's body.

"Are we good now?" Rory asks. He pats Alaric's face, snorting when he feels his nose. "Sorry, meant to pat your head."

Alaric rumbles, the sound deep in his chest. Chris exhales, relaxing, and Drea murmurs something Alaric doesn't catch. On the air mattress, Cass and Dax have already managed to slip away into sleep, their breath in sync.

Rory raises up a little; Alaric can see him clearly despite the dark. Alaric nods once. "Yeah. We're all good."

Despite what he said to his father, Alaric isn't planning on walking away from his family. Not yet. But for the first time, he's halfway to believing that if he needed to, he could.

56

"I WAS GOING to ask if we really had to walk the whole way, but I can see we do," Cass mutters, picking her way along the path. Alaric doesn't dignify her grumblings with a response; the graveyard is a far easier flight than walk, and a better walk than a drive.

It's possible they could've borrowed a golf cart, or a four-wheeler, or a horse, but in the end, feet are the simplest method.

Corbin flies overhead, flitting from treetop to treetop, while Drea chases him as a squirrel. She runs out to the ends of branches and launches herself through the air, chittering before she grabs hold of the next branch and races along.

It's a light moment in an otherwise somber task, and Alaric's heart feels better for it.

"We didn't create our land for humans," Alaric says. He's tempted to drop to four legs, lope along as the hound, but he stays human in deference to the others. "Most of us can run or fly; very few of us walk on two legs. And those who can't get around easily have family or friends who can. It's not odd to see a mouse carried safely in the beak of an owl or to spot a cat riding on the back of a horse." Everyone has their own favorite forms, some more mobile than others.

"You'd rather be flying." Chris bumps Alaric's arm; Alaric ducks his head.

"Or running," he admits with a shrug of one shoulder.

Rory has his hands shoved in his pockets, back hunched slightly as he walks. His gaze slips around, shifting from the path to the tree line, then following where Corbin and Drea chase each other through the branches. "It's not so bad. The hard part will be walking back."

"We're well-fueled," Dax says. "You guys know how to set a table."

It was less of a table and more of a series of trays in Alaric's room. And Alaric doesn't want to explain how little food that was compared to a traditional Clan meal. "Clan have big appetites," Alaric says. "It takes a lot of energy to change, and most of us do it without thinking." He glances at Rory. "Sorry about all the bacon. It's a tradition here."

"As long as I don't have to eat it, it's fine." Rory makes a face. "Sorry, vegetarian since birth. If your family thinks I'm rude, I apologize, but there is nothing in this world that's going to convince me to eat meat."

"I don't care what my family thinks." Alaric suspects that Rory's eating habits would be one more strike against him, but it hardly measures up to his Talent. "There are late greens in the greenhouse, and some good cheeses. I'll make up lunch before we go. Dax—how hard is this going to be on you?"

Dax steps awkwardly, pauses, and turns to face Alaric. "Haven't really thought about it that way. You mean, am I going to be starving? Not usually. If anything, I lose my appetite, and I'll be hungry later. I don't think the impact is as physical as changing your shape is for you. It's a mental and emotional Talent. I'm just hoping he's not upset. Sometimes they fight when they don't understand what's going on."

Dax goes silent. As they start walking, he waits for Alaric to fall into step next to him. "I'm sorry I can't let you talk to him. He might hear you, he might not. But you won't be able to see or hear him."

"Can you see him, too? Not just hear him?" Alaric keeps his voice low, his attention on how far ahead Corbin and Drea are.

"See him, sense him even if I'm not looking, talk to him, and possibly touch—that one's not all the time, usually only when they're pissed off." Dax's expression twists wry. "Like the one you were there for. She was angry that I wasn't acting quickly enough and started throwing punches. It's ridiculous, like trying to wrestle solid air. If I could let you see him too, I would, Ric. But that's not how it works."

There's a piece of Alaric that regrets it, that wishes that it could work in a different way. He shoves his hands into his jacket pockets and shrugs. " 't's okay, I've already talked to him. And if he's there when you talk to him, then he was there when I did. And that means he probably heard me. Pretty much said all I needed to say then." A small, soft snort. "He heard some of Rory's music then, too."

"Over the phone," Rory says, smiling slightly.

There's a rustle of leaves up ahead, and Corbin flies down from the tree, shifting from bird to man as he lands. "Drea's gone on ahead."

It's code for "slow down, let her have her moment," and Alaric's willing to listen. As his steps slow, Rory and Chris bracket him, their warmth solid against his sides. He doesn't need to be carried forward, but he appreciates that they're willing to try.

Drea pushes to her feet when they enter the graveyard. She gives a shallow nod, moves away from the headstone.

Dax has one hand clenched into a fist, tension thick in the air around him. "Didn't really think this through," he mutters. "There are a lot of people buried here."

"Most of the dead from our community end up here," Alaric tells him. "Someone else calling to you?"

Dax shakes his head. "Not loudly, no. I can ignore them for now, but I can also feel them. Hundreds."

"Maybe more." It's been a long time since the community was founded, and Alaric has no idea how many people have died here over the years. "Sorry."

"It's fine." Dax veers off, heads directly to the tender, fresh grass that covers Orson's grave. He stops in front of it, expression set. "What would you have of me?"

"Guess that answers the question of whether Orson's hanging around," Rory murmurs.

Chris's fingers brush against Alaric's arm, slide up until his hand is on Alaric's back. "You okay?"

"No." Alaric feels like there's a grip at his throat pressing the breath from his body. Drea is on the other side of the grave, curled close to Corbin while Corbin strokes idle circles on her back. Alaric takes a low, shuddering breath, shifts closer to the warmth that Chris offers, and is grateful when Rory presses close on his other side. Only Cass stands alone, her feet planted in a steady stance, arms crossed over her chest. She smells sourly wary yet attentive, brow furrowed as she watches Dax.

"There's not going to be a war," Dax says, voice low. He has both hands out, palms down. "Slow down. I've got it. Don't worry. We'll make sure that your family's safe, and there won't be a war." His gaze shifts toward Alaric for a moment, then he stares straight ahead again, as if someone else stands on the grave with him. "I'll let him know."

"Let me know what?" Alaric asks.

Dax licks his lips. "That he heard you." He goes silent, expression intent. He nods twice, then takes a step back. "I'm Dax, and obviously my Talent is talking to ghosts. That's my girlfriend Cass, and Alaric's squished between Rory and Chris. And they're waiting for me to ask you some questions. About what happened."

Dax winces, takes a quick step forward, both hands out where Alaric could imagine Orson's shoulders being. "No, no, I get it. No one really wants to relive their death. That's not what we're asking. The news said it looked like you were doing a ritual."

Corbin's head comes up, and he swivels to look at the empty space in front of Dax. "Orson wouldn't do—"

Dax's hand comes up. "Quiet." He lowers himself to sit cross-legged on the ground, hands on his knees. Silence lengthens as Dax listens, nodding intermittently. "Shadows?" Dax asks, and nods at whatever answer he hears.

Dax leans back, raises one hand, and stops there, hand hanging in mid-air. "Are you sure you don't want me to relay something more specific? A message for Ric and Drea, or something for your parents?" He huffs a sigh, lowers his hand. "Protect them, stop the war. Yeah. Got it."

He pushes to his feet, his tone formal as he says quietly, "I hear your words. I accept your charge. It will be done."

There's a rush of scent in the air, pine and apples, crisp with cinnamon, then it's gone as quick as it came. Alaric shudders, and Drea gulps loudly, sniffling back tears.

"Is he gone now?" Chris asks.

"Not sure." Dax rubs his hands against his jeans. "Normally I'd say yes, but this wasn't... Maybe it's because I've never talked to Clan before. He had more of a sense of himself than they usually do. I don't know if it's how he died, or because he's Clan, or what. The thing is, talking to me is supposed to release them. Give them enough ease that they can cross, because once they've passed along their need to me, I have to do it." He pushes his hand through his hair. "Specific tasks are easiest. I'm not sure exactly what's going to satisfy this one." He scratches at his forearm. "And this is going to suck until it's done."

"Sorry." It's not what Alaric meant to happen. But at the same time, if it helps, it's exactly what Alaric needs. "What did he say?"

"Can we go somewhere else to talk about this?" Dax gestures back the direction they came. "Having a conversation here is like trying to chat while sitting on a hive of a few hundred bees. I can hear them buzzing, and some of them feel like they might be getting ready to sting. I'd like to get far away before they get the chance."

Cass slides in close to Dax, tilts toward him as he drops an arm over her shoulder and pulls her in to kiss her forehead. Her scent eases as she relaxes against him. "I'm ready to go," she says.

Corbin and Drea walk slowly with them, Drea riding on Corbin's back, her arms looped loosely across his chest, her cheek pressed to his. Rory has his hands in his pockets, moves a bit apart, but Chris stays close enough that his fingers brush Alaric's regularly. Alaric flexes his hands, torn between shoving them into his pockets to pull in on himself or reaching out for more contact.

When he feels the brush of fingers again, he reaches for Chris, grabs his hand to stop the movement. A low growl of irritation, then Chris twists his hand, meets Alaric palm to palm, and the irritation slips away. Alaric bites his tongue against the whine that almost slips out. He lets Chris thread their fingers together, the point of contact an anchor that cools the heat rising under Alaric's skin.

Dax's shoulders are tight, tension sliding slowly away the farther they get from the graveyard. There's a low sigh when they're far enough, and Dax halts, inhales deeply, and lets it go. "We can talk now."

"We could also keep walking back to the car and get out of here," Cass points out. "Talking and walking aren't exclusive activities."

"Honestly, I'd rather sit down." Dax looks around, heads off the path enough to find a place where he can sit with his back to a tree. He pulls Cass onto his lap, wraps his arms around her. "Besides, they aren't going to like this, and I'd rather get it said before we're within earshot of the house. Are any of your family or friends around?"

"You mean, did Theobald send someone to follow us and spy on us?" Corbin translates. "I didn't see anyone earlier, but let me check again." He jumps up in a flurry of wings, flying into the trees. Drea follows quickly after him, squirrel scampering up the tree trunk and out onto the branches.

"Some leader," Alaric mutters. "Didn't even think of that."

"I get the feeling that Corbin's more naturally suspicious than you are," Rory says. He's found a tree to lean against, arms crossed as he looks up into the rustling tree branches. "He's a good right-hand for you. You may not be suspicious, but you know how to surround yourself with people whose Talent complements yours, and that's the best thing you can do when you lead, right?" When he realizes everyone's looking at him, he shrugs one shoulder. "I paid attention in high school history. I might not give a shit about politics generally, but I at least know what goes into a good administration."

"He has a point," Chris says. "And you're already ahead of your father because you know that family doesn't need to mean just people from Clan."

Alaric grunts, not wanting to get any more into details.

Corbin drops out of the sky, landing on human feet. He pushes a hand through his hair, calming it. "Pretty sure we're on our own. Theobald probably warned everyone away from the Mages. He wouldn't want his people corrupted." Sarcasm drips in the thick, dry tone of his words. He reaches a hand out; Drea leaps down from the tree, scrambles up his shoulder, and chitters before she slips back into her human skin and her place on his back.

"Okay." Dax breathes roughly, makes a face. "So. Orson was doing a ritual. But that's not what killed him."

Alaric feels the world drop away, and only Chris's grip on his hand keeps him from falling. He tugs himself free, lets his legs fold so he can sit roughly. "What? Orson wouldn't."

"Orson would," Dax says quietly. "Dionne wasn't dating either of them. She was a good friend, and her Talent was out of control. She vibrated so fast she couldn't interact with the world, and Sal came up with a ritual to use his and Orson's blood to ground Dionne so she could slow down."

"Huh." Rory wrinkles his nose, slides down the tree to sit as well, his hands loose on his knees. "I've never heard of something specifically like that, but I'm sure it could be developed. Pretty much any ritual can be made if you need it. It's just a question of figuring it out. That's a lot of what we talk about at Coven, and then there's Pawel's ritual design course."

"Orson said something about going to VIT with Dionne, but Sal went to PHU, so Sal probably did that course if he majored in magical studies," Dax says. "Orson left out a lot of details; he was talking almost too fast to follow. I just had to remember what he said. Anyway, the point is that there wasn't much blood, and it shouldn't have killed any of them. The ritual they planned had nothing to do with the way the darkness in the room came alive and attacked them."

"Shadowwalkers," Chris says softly.

"Deathstalkers," Alaric says at the same time Corbin does. They look at each other, Corbin's gaze unsettlingly serious.

"Same things that attacked me and Mac," Alaric mutters. "And the symbol's their language."

"Retribution," Rory says. "Or recompense. But for what?"

"And why Orson? And Alaric?" Drea asks.

"Or those people from VIT?" Corbin adds. "What do they have to do with any of us?"

"Maybe it was the Emergent ones," Chris says. "Dionne was Emergent. Mac's Emergent. Were any of the ones from VIT also Emergent?"

Alaric doesn't remember. "We'll check when we get back," he grumbles, burying his head in his hands. His elbows dig into his knees, and the pain grounds him, keeps the beast from pricking under his skin. "We'll keep digging, and we'll figure it out."

"I don't know about you, but I think stopping to buy some lemon on the way back might be good," Corbin says, tone lighter than his scent.

It sounds ridiculous, but at the moment, it's the only thing they know about Deathstalkers. It's a story—the lemon tree—but then, Deathstalkers are just legend. Stories might be all they have to fight with.

Excerpt from *When Magic Entered the World: Interviews With Lineage Talent,* by Pawel Szczek, © 2009

So you're talking to Lineage Talent about what Talent means to them. You've just started on this project, haven't you? You'll get a lot of different answers depending on who you talk to, but one thing will come through in every conversation: family.

When you have Talent, it's important to keep track of your genealogy, to know where your Talent intertwines with other lines. It's important to know who becomes a part of your family and where your family travels. Family is much more than who gives birth to whom; it's about who becomes a part of your life.

Yes, Pawel, it is exactly that simple, and that complicated. Remember, Talent is magic, and while it has rules, sometimes those rules may seem obscure, even to those of us who live with them on a daily basis.

Did you know that if someone has the possibility to Emerge, they might also have the possibility for that Talent to remain dormant their entire life? But if they were to become a part of a Lineage family, that Talent might be called forth, even late in life.

Talent can be a strange thing. It is what we need it to be, even if we don't know what it is that we need.

Ours is an intertwined Lineage. We can trace our roots back to the temples of Greece, perhaps to Delphi itself. We also trace our roots to the cradle of civilization; Empaths were one of the first Talents to exist. But we have changed over the years. Lines merge, become something new, something different.

But family—that core around which you grow and shift and change—that becomes your rock. That is your Lineage, not the Talent you display. The ties between family—by blood or bond—can be stronger than life and death itself.

Yes, dear, I was going to tell him about Great Uncle Dimitrios. He was the first of our line to come to this area, settled here on the hill long ago, and he remains here still. Every once in a while, there is a member of the family who can speak with him. We all sense him in some way. We're drawn from Empaths, and he is family after all, but few can converse. He's found a new friend in our young grandson.

Remember as you interview those who respond to your query. Remember as you search through what it means to be Lineage Talent. Remember that Talent is personal, it is inherited, and it is shared. And remember that even as an Emergent, you are not alone in this world, Pawel Szczek. Find your family and make your space.

HARVEST

57

"HERE." DAX TOSSES a pile of sheets at Alaric; they unravel into a fall of fabric by the time they reach him, tangling around his arms. "Clean sheets." Dax turns away, yanking the dirty ones from his bed and tossing them on top of the rest of his laundry in a cloth bin. "The blankets are in the dryer in the basement."

Alaric wrinkles his nose, tries not to inhale. "Thanks," he says dryly.

"You know, you could come over to Thanksgiving at my place," Dax says. "Both of you." He nods at Chris. "Mom's always happy to put another plate or two on the table, and it's not like any of the dining halls are open here on campus."

There's a piece of Alaric that still thinks he should be heading out to Haverhill; choosing to eat with someone else's family feels like a betrayal of his own. He shakes his head. "No thanks. I'll be fine here."

"And I figure it's rude to leave Alaric stuck here on his own," Chris says. There's something in his scent that Alaric can't tease out, and Dax smells amused. "I figure we'll go out and get something to cook, or we'll order in, or something. There's a functional kitchen in the house. We're not going to starve, Dax. Besides. This is one of those rare breaks I get from living with you and Cass." He grins, but the statement is honest.

"Yeah, well, if you change your mind, you know where I live now," Dax points out. "If I see anything strawberry rhubarb appear in the kitchen, I'll assume you're on your way over. You don't need to actually text that you're coming; Mom will know what's needed."

"I don't know if I could get used to that," Alaric mutters. Dax is fine; he doesn't make Alaric's skin itch, even knowing that he's an Empath. And what his mother does—what Alex does, too—doesn't really bother Alaric. But at the same time, that strange level of knowing leaves him uncomfortable, as if he's been stripped bare.

"It's the way my family is," Dax says. "Trust me, you really do get used to it. Besides, they needed to get used to the way I talked to things they couldn't see. I was pretty amusing as a toddler, I've heard. My invisible friends were real and actually invisible. Just dead."

Outside, a car stops; there's a whir of a sliding door, then the slam of the front door. "Your parents are here," Alaric says, and Dax swears.

"And Dad's going to be in a rush because Mom's probably got dinner planned down to the second for when we get home," Dax mutters. He starts shoving clothes into his gray PHU football duffle, then drops it on his bed and grabs a smaller gray bag instead. He heads out of the room. "Gonna grab my stuff from the bathroom. You know they'll just walk in."

The front door opens and closes right on cue, and footsteps run lightly up the stairs as Alex calls out, "I know you're running late, Dax!"

Dax waves to his sister, passes her on his way down the hall. She ends up in the doorway, leaning awkwardly in. "Hi, Chris. Alaric."

Alaric's nostrils flare wide; there's no citrus, but he doesn't know what to expect from Alex. "Hey," he says warily.

"You already know," she says. "I mean, you think you don't, but you do, so it's okay. Just give yourself some time to deal with it."

Alaric blinks, sits down on the edge of Chris's bed. Chris slides closer, his knee warm against Alaric's. "What?" Alaric says.

Alex shrugs. "That's it, sorry. Isn't it handy Dax was running late so I could come in and say hi?" She plops down on Dax's bed, puts one hand on the mattress, and looks at Alaric. "Are those clean sheets? I'll help you make the bed."

They've just managed to get the sheets on when Dax walks back in and shoves the toiletry bag into his duffle. Alex tosses his pillow on top of the laundry bin and picks that up while Dax shoulders the duffle and grabs his backpack full of books. "I texted Cass to let her know we'll be there in five," Dax says. "If you guys change your mind, text me."

"They won't. Dad's waiting." Alex heads out the door and down the stairs. Dax lingers.

"I mean it," Dax says. "Alex might think she's right, but she doesn't actually know everything. We've got a five-day weekend. You don't have to spend it here at the house."

"I'm planning on leaving to go to Teas Please eventually. I'm pretty sure they'll feed us," Chris deadpans. "We can take care of ourselves, Dax. Don't worry."

"They're *fine*," Alex yells from the bottom of the stairs. "Come on!"

Dax hesitates, but when Alaric stands, curls his lips, and growls, Dax quickly ducks out of the room. The front door slams a moment later, and Alaric sinks down to sit on Dax's bed. He inhales, tastes a hint of Dax and Cass in the scent of the room, but it's mostly Chris. His own scent is fleeting, and without thinking, Alaric rubs his hand over the sheets, claiming this space as his own. At least for the weekend.

Chris's phone buzzes, and he glances at it and shakes his head. "That's the fifth time my family's checked to make sure I'm okay." He laughs. "My mom offered to buy my ticket to Atlanta because everyone's going down to see Damon for his freshman year at Georgia Tech, but I can't."

Alaric's gaze narrows. "Why are you staying if they'd buy your ticket? You like your family, don't you?"

"We're close," Chris admits. "I have six brothers, plus Mom and Dad. We never really had a choice about sharing space, or clothes, or anything else. We all play football—three of my brothers already graduated, and Les graduates this year. One more still in high school. But we do everything together. But I have a huge paper due for my independent study, and if I go, I won't get anything done. With everything else that's happened, I could use some time to work on it. We'll all be home for Christmas; Mom and Dad will be happy with that."

"I'm going to distract you," Alaric mutters, and Chris laughs.

"You're going to remind me to take breaks," Chris tells him. "It's fine. If I get some blocks of time to get my notes together, it'll all work out. If I have to drive back to Portal, then get in a van to go to Boston so the whole family can make it to Logan in time to get through security, then fly down to Atlanta..." He shakes his head rather than finish the thought. "We'll be squished in a hotel room because, while two of my brothers are getting their own rooms with their girlfriends, the rest of us will have to share.

There won't be any time to myself, Ric. This way, if I need time, all I have to do is ask. I know you'll give me space."

Something else sits beneath those words, something in Chris's scent that puts Alaric at ease. Alaric nods. He feels as if there's something he's supposed to say, but there aren't any words at the tip of his tongue.

His phone chimes, and when he looks, it's from Drea.

Just got in. Mom's surprised you're not in the car. She said to tell you she misses you. Also, Corbin's family is staying at the house for Harvest. A lot of the community is this year. Dad is angry that you're not here.

Alaric stares down at his phone, holding it loose in his hand. His jaw is tight, and there's a soft puff of smoke swirling around his head as he exhales. The bed sinks as Chris sits next to him, leans in shoulder to shoulder.

"I'm not Rory," Chris says quietly. "I can't bleed it away. But if I can help you center yourself…"

"It helps," Alaric admits. He tilts the phone to show Drea's text. "They made it home, and my parents are pissed off. Doesn't surprise me."

"Sounds more like your mother is sad."

Alaric snorts. "You're probably right. But Theobald's pissed off. If I walked in right now, he'd rip me apart and send me to heal before I show my face in public."

"Do you heal that fast?" Chris looks and smells dubious, and it makes Alaric laugh.

"Faster than humans, but not that fast," he admits. "There's a reason my mother tends to get involved when we're arguing. She can get him to back down." He lifts the phone again, carefully types out a message.

Tell Mom I miss her, too. But I'm not coming home, not unless there's good reason, and him expecting me to act like a perfect successor when he won't listen to me isn't enough of a reason. I'm not ready to see him. And he's not ready to see me.

Alaric tosses the phone aside, letting it fall face down on the sheets. It chimes again, but he doesn't need to continue the conversation. It'll only go in circles, and that's not good for either of them. Drea and Corbin will be fine without him for one Harvest.

"So why is it Harvest?" Chris asks, and Alaric huffs.

"Because Thanksgiving celebrates the beginning of the annihilation of the Native people, and a long time ago our Clan lived peacefully among the Mohawk people. Some of us have Mohawk blood," Alaric says dryly. "Thanksgiving isn't a thing you can get away from—you get days off from school, and everyone talks about family. But we know what it meant to our ancestors. So instead, we celebrate what this time means to Clan. This is our Harvest. Our time to gather before winter comes and separates us from others. A time to eat well, and to enjoy the last bounties before the frost. It's when we slaughter and cure our meat for winter—my cousins have been working for weeks. Autumn is a busy time getting ready for winter, and this is our gathering to celebrate that now it's time to rest and to stay safe through the cold months. It's Harvest."

"Aren't you going to miss them?" Chris asks quietly. "This must be your first year that you're not involved."

His first year without gathering up the green tomatoes before the first frost and bringing them to be preserved. His first year without ensuring that there were enough hats and gloves, that socks were mended and tapestries hung on new walls. His first year without preparing for winter by creating, as well as shopping. Alaric grumbles and shrugs. "Do you think when I move into the house there'll be a place for my loom?" he asks, and Chris knocks his knee into him.

"We'll make space."

Alaric breathes more easily when Chris doesn't point out that the guys might wonder why a loom; he just accepts it. Maybe after winter break, he should bring back his basket so he has yarn and projects and something small to do with his hands. Maybe it'll help with the stress. "Thanks."

There's a shout somewhere in the house, footsteps overhead. "How many people are still here?" Alaric asks.

"Not many. Lewis, because Lewis is pretty much always here. Why?" Chris nudges him. "Is this because you want more people around, or fewer?"

"Fewer." Alaric goes to the window, cracks it open, and inhales the crisp, fresh air. "Is that too cold for you?"

"It's cold, but I'll survive." Chris fits in behind him, hand on the small of

Alaric's back. "Blame Dax for anything in this room that reeks."

"Oh, I do." The window will make it better, and the clean sheets on the bed. But nothing can completely get rid of the idea that Dax has thoroughly claimed this space as his, and that itches under Alaric's skin. "Let's get the blankets from the dryer."

"Let's order pizza first." Chris opens the app for the place just off campus and places the order, not even needing to ask what Alaric wants.

By the time they get the blankets out and on the bed, then head back downstairs to grab a few beers and an opener, the pizza has arrived. Lewis drifts into the kitchen, and at Alaric's growl he raises both hands. "Your pizza, got it," Lewis says and slips away again.

"You're going to be an interesting captain someday," Chris says, and that makes Alaric pause.

"What makes you think I'll be captain?"

"For one, you're the quarterback; you'll be a driving force on the team no matter what," Chris points out. "You won't want to lead here at the house—you'll let someone else be the fraternity president. But people listen to you, and you have good instincts. You and Dax would work well together, but they'll want one offensive team member and one defensive for co-captains. Although for the way you two seem to read each other, they might make an exception." Chris grabs a roll of paper towels and tucks it under his arm, then picks up the pizza boxes.

They head back up to Chris's room and Chris drops the pizza on the floor, opens one box, and takes a slice of supreme meat before nudging the box toward Alaric. The room is chill, and once they get a movie started, Chris drifts closer to Alaric.

Alaric drops an arm behind Chris, letting him get in close enough to share body heat. There's no point in pouring more than one cup of beer and risking getting it on the bed, so they share the one cup, placing it carefully out of the way when neither one is drinking.

Halfway into the movie, Alaric is warm and comfortable. He's at ease, but not quite drowsing, when his phone chimes. He ignores it, but it chimes again, and then again, until Chris huffs a laugh and pushes at Alaric. "Answer it. It's either Drea, Corbin, or Rory, if it's going off that much.

Either way, it's family."

When Alaric picks up his phone and unlocks it, his conversation with Drea from earlier is still on the screen.

You have to deal with him sometime, Ric.

Unless we're leaving. Give us some warning if we're leaving.

His breath goes tight over her words, and he quickly types back *we're not leaving* and sends it, just so he can exhale without choking on the thought.

Not yet, at least. They're not leaving yet.

Chris's hand is warm between his shoulders as Alaric hunches over his phone. Chris doesn't seem to be paying any attention to him, but Alaric can feel his tension in the way Chris's fingers curl and flex against him.

" 'm okay," Alaric mutters, and opens the new text from Rory.

We're home. Thorne says hi and thinks I should tell you to get out of your own head. Is he being a dick when he says that?

A small smile quirks the corner of Alaric's mouth. He sits up, and Chris shifts; when they rearrange, Chris's arm is behind Alaric, and Alaric is leaning back against him, letting Chris take his weight. *He's not being a dick. He's probably right, but I'm not stuck in my head right now. I just don't want to go home.*

I really don't blame you, now that I've met your father. The phone goes quiet for a moment, dots appearing and disappearing a few times before Rory texts again. *I left a menu on your bed. It's a place Mom ate at when she was at school, before she became a vegetarian with Dad and Dad. She said it's still there, and if it wouldn't make her sick, she'd go there herself. She thought you'd like it.*

"What is it?" Chris's breath is close to Alaric's face; when Alaric turns slightly, Chris is still watching the movie. At Alaric's movement, Chris grabs the remote, hits pause. "You okay?"

"Rory's mom told him to tell me about a place to go eat over break, I think," Alaric says. "It has meat."

Chris huffs, amused. "So maybe we'll try it."

Alaric frowns, something pricking at him. He types out a quick note on the phone to thank Rory and wish him a good weekend before he tosses it aside. As he settles back against Chris's warmth, he figures it out. "My turn to pay this time."

"Okay," Chris says easily. "We go out, it's your turn to pay."

Alaric makes a rumbling noise, lets his body go slack as he sinks down. His head tilts to rest against Chris as the movie plays. Having that settled helps, lets him relax. As long as he doesn't think about Harvest and home.

58

"Date night?" Nate asks as he meets Chris and Alaric at the door to Teas Please. "I figured you'd be gone by now; everyone seems to have rushed off to get home in time for the holiday."

Alaric growls, and Chris makes a face. "Sore subject," Chris says, and Nate nods.

"Are you planning on anyone else joining you? We're not packed tonight, so I can put you at a larger table or at one of the smaller ones." Nate heads toward the back corner table, but he veers off and drops the menus on a table for four that has a bench on the wall side and chairs on the other. "If any more of your crew come in, let me know, and we can pull up more tables or get you moved. But it's quiet back here, and I thought Alaric might like that."

There's no one else in this section. There aren't many people there—a few groups on the couches and chairs at the front, and Alaric can see two booths and a few tables on the other side, but no one is in this section. In fact, one table has the chairs atop it, like it's been packed up. It's a little darker than the rest of the place, half the lights not lit, and Alaric gets the feeling it's not supposed to be used.

He gives Nate a grateful smile, says gruffly, "Thanks."

"You're regulars," Nate says. For a moment, Alaric thinks Nate's going to hug him, then Nate steps back and makes space between them. "So, ginger tea. Do you need to look at the menu, or do you want me to surprise you? No nuts, Alaric," he says, biting back a grin.

"Food, not desserts." Chris slides onto one side of the bench, stretches his legs out as he leans back. Nate gathers up the menus and heads into the kitchen.

Alaric could sit on the other side, but it's cramped enough that they'd knock knees even if he sat on the opposite corner. So he sinks onto the other side of the bench, next to Chris. He pushes the chair out with his foot to make room for his long legs, and when he crosses his arms, his shoulder brushes up against Chris's.

"If we'd brought a laptop, we could've streamed another movie," Chris points out, and Alaric rolls his eyes.

"We deserve a chance to do nothing," Alaric grumbles. They spend enough time working out—including Chris dragging him out of bed early this morning to run while the sun was still low. It's been nice to take a day and do nothing productive at all. " 'course, that's not helping your project."

"I'll work on it tonight," Chris promises. "I've got piles of research and notes, I just have to start pulling it together and figuring out how I want to present it in the paper. I'll probably end up spreading it out on the floor; my bed's too small."

"All the beds here are too small." Not that Alaric minds when he shares with someone else and they end up pressed close together. Not that he's shared with anyone but Rory. Still. He likes his bed at home and knowing that everyone fits together neatly there.

Chris's foot nudges Alaric's. "Homesick?"

"No," Alaric lies.

"I could drive you out there tomorrow morning," Chris offers. "You'd get there in time for dinner—I'm assuming you have some kind of big meal, right? We could stay until Friday. You do family things; I'll stay in your room and do my project, so I'll be out of the way enough that I don't piss off your father. We'll come back Friday night. Then you get home for a couple of days, but you don't have to be there as long as Corbin and Drea."

"You can't avoid pissing off my father," Alaric mutters. "All you have to do is enter the grounds, and he'll know, and he'll be angry. You're not Clan, and he doesn't want you in Clan spaces."

"Me? Or humans in general?"

Alaric folds his legs, tucks his feet back as he leans forward, elbows on the table. His head drops, and he shrugs. "Mages. Humans. And you in particular. You've been there twice. He thinks I'm getting attached."

"We're friends." Chris's voice is low and quiet. "I can stay here and never go there again, and that isn't going to change."

"I know that. He seems to think we need to stay isolated, and he's not ready to listen to why I think that's the whole problem." It's been on Alaric's mind for too long, and he doesn't want to spiral down that hole right now. "Change the subject." It's not meant to be an order, and Alaric winces inwardly at the way his voice snaps sharply.

"Okay, housing for next year." Chris waits until Alaric leans back again so he can look over and meet his eyes. "I know you want to live with Drea, and I know you talked to Rory about rooming again, but have you considered moving into OPT?"

"I don't have to make a decision until February," Alaric says. He picks up the napkin from the table, unwraps his silverware, and turns the knife over in his hand.

"You need to plan with OPT now, if you're moving into the house," Chris says quietly. "There's an application to file on campus to remove yourself from the general room selection. Or you can go into the lottery, or you can get an apartment off campus."

"Semester's not even fucking over yet. 'm not ready to make that decision." Alaric taps at the wood with his knife. He stops when a pot of tea lands on the table, pulls back enough to give Nate space to put down the two cups and a small bowl of crackers.

"Homemade herb-and-cheese crackers from the kitchen," Nate says. "I'll bring out another pot when you finish that one. There's no point in letting the second one get cold 'cause you're both drinking the same thing."

Chris pours the tea, slides one cup over. Alaric lets it sit for a moment, his hand still curled around the knife, resting on the table next to the cup.

"Hard to believe the semester's almost over already." Alaric lets his head fall back against the wall, closes his eyes. "Still feel like I just got here."

"Season's over, Thanksgiving's here," Chris says. "It's only a month until Christmas. Depending on your finals schedule, you might be done in three weeks."

Alaric grunts, unable to find the right response to that. So much has changed in his life in the few months since he arrived at PHU, and he doesn't know how to assimilate it. He hasn't talked to Drea about housing, hasn't even thought about how the deadline is approaching. And he suspects she already knows what she's going to do.

The fact that she hasn't talked to him means she's not planning on getting an apartment off campus.

"How do you figure who you're living with at OPT?" He's not sure it's the right decision for him, but he also figures he should know the answer. Alaric needs to know all the options before he makes a choice.

"Either come in with one of the other new guys," Chris tells him. "Or if there's a spot opening up in a room, you can move into that."

Alaric's gaze narrows at the shift in Chris's scent. "What," he says, and it's not a question, just an expectation that there's something not being said.

"Dax has been talking about getting an apartment with Cass," Chris admits. "Out of everyone who might move in, I figured I'd rather room with you than any of them." He pulls the bowl of crackers close, takes one, and bites into it; the air is suffused with a sharp scent of cheddar and thyme.

"Mm." Alaric understands that wariness, that need to control who will be in his space. He takes one of the crackers as well, knocking knuckles with Chris as they reach into the bowl at the same time. "I'll think about it."

It isn't such a bad idea.

"You probably don't really want to share an apartment with Rory, if it means sharing with Thorne, too," Chris points out, and Alaric makes a face, nose wrinkled.

"I don't know how Rory could share an apartment with him. It has to reek of sex," Alaric says flatly. "I could live with Thorne; it wouldn't be a problem. But it would—" He cuts off, not sure how to phrase it. He licks his lip, mouth twisting, sour. "It would make my skin itch. The beast would—I'd want—not with Thorne." He fails to find the right words. "It'd make me need things. And well." Alaric shrugs. "You already know that it's fucking complicated."

"I do." Chris glances up and moves the bowl of crackers, making space for Nate to set down plates. "We barely started on the crackers. They're good."

Alaric is still holding his. He feels Nate's gaze on him and quickly shoves it in his mouth, biting down and tasting the more subtle sage that underlies the thyme. Maybe parmesan. Something smoky. " 's good," he agrees.

"Hope I'm not interrupting anything." Nate slides one plate in front of Alaric, one in front of Chris, and then puts two empty plates on the table. "I told Mallory to just have fun and make two complementary crêpes. One is steak with smoked gouda, caramelized onions, and sautéed mushrooms. The other one is chicken paprika in a crêpe. Take whichever one you want, or share."

"You're not interrupting anything," Alaric mutters.

Chris nudges a chair out with his foot. "It's quiet. Go ahead and take a break and sit if you want."

Nate pauses, and the chair squeaks on the floor as Chris nudges it again. Nate finally sinks into it. "Okay," he says slowly. He takes a cracker, gestures as he asks, "So what are you two doing over the break?"

"Avoiding going home," Alaric says dryly.

"Didn't go so well when you went with Dax?" Nate asks, popping the cracker in his mouth. He makes a pleased sound and grabs a handful to eat one by one.

"Not really, no, but—" Alaric stops when Nate raises a hand.

"One, I saw you all talking through the window that night, and two, all of you disappeared and Thorne said something about Rory and a road trip." Nate shrugs. "It wasn't difficult to put two and two together, considering."

He doesn't mention Orson, but the meaning is clear. "Yeah," Alaric says gruffly. "Considering. My father wasn't thrilled that I brought Mages into Clan spaces. Or humans."

"I'm just working on a project," Chris says. "Figured since I'm there at OPT, Ric could crash in Dax's space because Dax went home for the holiday. What about you?"

"I'm local enough to work over the holiday." Nate brushes it off, elbows on the table as he leans forward. "What happened with Dax was intense."

"All Talent is intense," Chris replies, glancing at Alaric. "I can try to understand it, but it's outside of everything I've done."

"I don't know; is it really?" Nate asks. "I run. It's not a Talent—and I don't have a Talent—but when I run, it's like there's something inside me that I'm letting out. And for that time, I'm exactly who I'm supposed to be and no one else. I wonder sometimes if being able to actually use your Talent is like that."

"You mean changing shape is like playing football?" It makes a strange sort of sense in Alaric's head when put that way, so he nods once. "Yeah. Kind of."

Chris cuts his crêpe in half, nudges Alaric's knee under the table. Alaric does the same, and they trade halves. The scent is warm and woodsy, and Alaric's stomach grumbles.

"See, that's what I mean. It's like letting go. Being free. Dax's Talent didn't look like that; it looked like it wound him up even more." Nate picks up another cracker while talking, and Alaric wonders if he's going to eat the entire bowl.

"You'd have to ask Dax that," Chris tells him. "And Dax tends to be pretty quiet about his Talent. I've known him for a year and a half, and that was the first time I had any idea what his Talent even is."

"Mm." Nate pushes to his feet quickly, chair scraping along the floor. "I need to get back to work, but thanks for letting me sit a while." He flashes a sudden grin, but it doesn't color his scent or reach his eyes. "You guys eat. I'll refill your tea and bring out one dessert and two forks when you're done. Just trust Mallory to make something you'll like. Nothing with an overwhelming scent, right, Ric?"

Alaric's phone chimes, and he fishes it out of his pocket, grunting instead of replying properly to Nate. He thumbs it open, stares down at the text from Drea.

Orson's things have arrived from his apartment. They were all packed up for the investigation. Now that it's been canceled, they've been released to us.

Alaric touches the screen with his finger.

"What's up?" Chris leans into him, weight heavy against his shoulder.

"Orson's things are back. Boxed up. Official police investigation is over." Alaric keeps touching the screen, trying to decide what to write. So many options, and none of them seem to say enough. Do enough.

"Ah." Chris straightens, cuts a piece of his crêpe. "We'll go tomorrow morning. You decide if you want to set an alarm and get there early, or if we'll go when we wake up."

Alaric's next breath comes more easily. "After we wake up," he says as the keyboard lights up from typing.

Chris is bringing me tomorrow. Tell Mom. Not sure when we'll get there. Maybe there's something in the boxes that'll help. Feels like we're just missing a link somewhere.

He sets the phone down on the table between himself and Chris where it lies silent, dots appearing and disappearing while Drea types. Alaric takes the time to finally taste his own crêpe, savoring the flavors. He likes the beef better than the chicken, and when he sees that Chris has finished his chicken, he offers to trade back. He's mostly finished by the time Drea finally texts back.

Told Mom and Dad. We'll see you when you get here. Love you, Ric.

"We can leave again any time you want."

It feels good knowing that Chris will get Alaric out of there if he needs to go. He nods, glancing up to see Nate approaching with something in his hands. "Thanks," he says quietly, and he tries to let it all go and only think about dessert.

59

CHRIS DOESN'T NEED directions to get to Haverhill this time, nor to find the entrance to the community. When they pull up in front of the house, Alaric is surprised that Theobald isn't standing on the steps ready to rage.

"Maybe he expected us to arrive earlier or later," Chris says as he climbs out. He reaches into the back and grabs his backpack and the duffle they'd both thrown clothes into earlier. It didn't make sense to pack separate bags for one night.

"Or he's avoiding me," Alaric says quietly. "That wouldn't be a bad thing. If we don't talk, I can get through this. We won't try to kill each other."

"I really hope you don't mean that literally, but I bet you do," Chris comments. He shrugs the backpack over his shoulders, heads for the front steps as the door opens and Alia steps out.

"Alaric," Alia says softly. "And Chris, yes?"

"Thank you for your hospitality, Mrs. Herne," Chris says, "and for having me here for your Harvest."

"It's never difficult to set another plate for a Gather, here," she tells him, coming down the steps to greet him. Both hands on his shoulders, she leans up to kiss his cheek. It's quick and perfunctory, but it's more polite than recent visits have seen. "We're always sure to cook for more than are here. After all, we never know when we might have unanticipated arrivals." Her gaze drifts to Alaric, and he feels pinned beneath it.

He shifts stance uncomfortably.

"Come in." Alia leads the way back inside, closes the door behind them. "Alaric, if you don't mind, I'd like to speak with you briefly."

Chris raises the bag. "Pretty sure I know the way to your room," he says, heading for the stairs. "I've got plenty of work to keep me busy. I'll do my best to not start watching movies instead."

Alia waves him off, then grips Alaric's hand, gently tugging him with her down the hall, past the kitchens and into one of the private rooms. It's bright inside, the entire back wall made of glass from floor to ceiling. Plants hang, vibrant in green and flowering color. Off to one side sits Alia's spinning wheel and a stool.

It's one of Alaric's favorite rooms in the house, except now it feels as if he's being brought to his execution. Alia gestures, and Alaric sits in one of the two high wingback chairs. A plate of cookies is on the table—peanut-butter-and-jelly thumbprints—and a pitcher of lemonade and two glasses wait as well.

Alia pours a glass and hands it to him, waits while he drinks.

"I'm glad you came home," Alia says softly, "and while your father will never say it, I know he feels the same."

"He doesn't." Alaric picks up a cookie, pops it in his mouth to distract himself with the explosion of strawberry rhubarb on his tongue. He doesn't need her to reassure him; he's fine with his father's attitude. "I don't want to see him, either."

"You will be polite," Alia cautions, and Alaric nods.

"Yeah," Alaric grumbles. "If I'm coming to dinner, Chris is coming, too." His jaw goes tight as he waits for a reaction.

"I know." Alia reaches across, her fingers light against his wrist. "Chris is your friend, and I am grateful that he was able to give you a ride here today. We would not turn him away."

"He's human."

There's a small twitch in Alia's jaw, a hitch in her heartbeat. "I know. But he is welcome here, as are your other friends. They are a part of your life, yes? I have already lost one son."

Alaric's throat goes tight, a growl building. "I know. Don't tolerate them because you're afraid of losing me."

"I am trying to do more than tolerate them," Alia snaps, a low breath shuddering through as she visibly eases. "I am trying to understand, Alaric. Orson obviously had friends that he made no effort to bring home. You have brought your friends here. You have made an effort; I am trying to ease their way. I want to know about your life, Alaric. We were close, once."

Alaric's gaze shifts to where the wheel sits, remembers sitting with his mother while he first learned to spin. "It's different now," he mutters.

"It is," Alia admits. "But we can only create our new future if we try. So tell me, how is school? Do you enjoy your courses?"

"I like magical studies," Alaric admits. " 's taught by an Emergent Mage. He reeks like magic, and his son's worse. But he's an expert, spent a lot of time talking to Lineage families, trying to understand how Talent works and how different lines work. He's good. Doesn't let anyone be an asshole bigot in class."

"Language."

Alaric grumbles. "He's a Mage, but I think you'd like him. You'd like Rory, if you gave him the chance. I went to his grandparents' place in Vermont."

"Oh?"

"Yeah. They've got sheep." Alaric warms to his topic, describing the ways that they work with hemp for their spinning and some of the work he did there. He tells his mother about the children, and about his plan to exchange ideas and perhaps product. He goes silent then, waits for reprisal.

"Building relationships is a good idea," she says quietly. "Perhaps we have been set apart for too long. It will do us good to exchange ideas with others."

"Even Mages?"

Her lips purse, and her scent is sour as she quietly admits, "Perhaps even Mages. Now, tell me about your football, Alaric. It's clear that it is important to you."

It's not easy to break football down into something that his mother will understand. She's never seen a game and, to the best of his knowledge, has never watched him practice. But she shows interest, and Alaric can't walk away from a chance to talk about it. She asks questions, and it's easy to pretend that she might love it the same way he does, or at least love it on his behalf.

When he sits up, brings his arm back as he's talking through a long bomb sent to Dax, she laughs aloud. He lowers his hand, brow furrowing.

"All that time trying to throw across the river," she says with a soft smile. Her hand rests on his knee, fingers warm and quiet. "All that time where you tried from farther and farther away, testing yourself to see if you could keep the ball from the water, land it safely on the other side. All those balls floating down the river."

"You did watch." He doesn't know what to think. It's been years since he practiced like that, since he first joined the Blended league when he was only fourteen years old. It's been a long time since he tested himself against nature, the only way he knew how to test his skills when at home. Corbin had no interest, and no one else cared.

"Who do you think took the time to fish them out and place them back in storage for you?" Alia asks. "It may not be the Clan way, but you were determined nonetheless. And it was clear that it was your passion. When I could not find them, I sent Orson to buy more."

Alaric can feel the heat in his face. He should have thought to wonder why there was a steady supply despite his failed attempts. He should have wondered who was spying on him, and who cared enough to find the things he'd lost. He lowers his gaze, tilts his head in clear submission. "Thank you."

Her fingers brush against his shoulder and throat. "You are my son," she says, "and I do love you, no matter how far apart from us you believe yourself to be. You are still the child of my heart who knows more about fiber and craft than anyone else I have taught. You are still the boy who helped me lay the gardens while refusing to plough the fields. And you are the boy who found his home in things that I didn't understand. I don't love you any less for that."

"Mom." The word slips free before he knows what comes after, his mouth closing quickly to give himself time to think. There are things he doesn't know how to say or explain, like the dragon that simmers under his skin. And there are things that he doesn't know if they matter, if he should even bother to try to explain, because they may never come to anything.

Alaric's head jerks up as he hears a door close in the distance, the distinct sound of Theobald's steps approaching. "Fuck."

"Language." Her tone is mild.

"I am never going to be who he wants me to be," Alaric says softly. "I'm never going to learn to take any shape—I'm always going to be the kind of Clan I am. I'm never going to perpetuate the line. And I don't want to be isolated. Chris, Rory, Dax—they're all my friends. And our Clan community is going to have to deal with that."

"He knows that, as do I," Alia's tone remains quiet, but holds a note of solidity as well. "Give him a chance, Alaric. Give him time."

"I'm going to give him plenty of time," Alaric agrees. He glances at the door that opens into the back, shrugs one shoulder. "It's best if that time's spent without us having to talk to each other. If we don't talk, we won't fight."

She doesn't try to keep him there, simply opens the door as he drops into the hound and pads out. He doesn't know where he's going yet, but he hears Theobald greet Alia in the distance, and he knows he got away just in time.

60

Alaric is already far from the house when he shifts back into human form and digs out his phone.

Going out for a run. Avoiding my father.

He sends the text to Chris and leans his elbows on his knees while waiting for a response.

Okay. I've actually started writing. Keeping writing is good.

Alaric snorts softly. He's seen Chris start writing three times already, and each time after a half hour, Chris has deleted the file and gone back to his research. Maybe this time will be the right start.

He shifts back into the hound and raises his nose, catching scents on the air. The fading scent of apples has him loping toward the orchard, weaving through the trees with his nose to the ground. It's too late in the season for the apples to be good—there's already been a hard frost, and the remaining apples were turned to cider weeks ago. But it's a comfortable place to explore, catching the scent of extended family and the rest of the community.

The orchard is always a popular place in the fall; the Clan gathers apples for food and preservation. Alaric remembers shimmying up the trees to shake the apples from the highest branches so that Corbin and Drea could collect them.

He pauses, catching their scents, entwined together and bright as if they passed recently. Nostrils flare and he follows the aroma, intent on the path until he stumbles over them.

Entwined, yes.

Lying on the ground together, tangled and hip-to-hip, mouth-to-mouth. Soft sounds that only register after Alaric's stepped on Corbin's foot, in the split second before Corbin jerks upright.

"Fuck!"

Alaric takes several steps back, lowers his body to the ground, tail drooping.

Drea sits up more slowly, combing leaves from her hair and tugging her shirt back to her waist. "Ric? What are you doing out here? If Mom wants us to come in, you could've texted."

Corbin is flushed, his heart hammering, scent a confused mélange of arousal and fear. "Ric, I…we…" He trails off, and Alaric shifts back to human, because he gets the feeling he's supposed to say something.

He kneels there, silent. Cold seeps through his jeans from the damp ground, chilling his knees.

"Ric?" Drea says, and there's worry in her scent now. She rolls into a crouch, one hand out.

"I'm not a wild animal you have to tame," Alaric growls.

"Yeah, well, you might be giving off the wild-animal vibe right now," Corbin says quickly. "Complete with growl. Should I be worried you're going to tear my throat out?"

"Were you hiding this from me?" Alaric knows the answer as soon as he asks, knows he shouldn't have even bothered. Warmth rises under Corbin's skin, and Drea ducks her head, won't look him in the eye. "Why?"

"We didn't want to hurt you," Drea says softly. "You and Corbin—"

Alaric shakes his head. "I love you both. You're my best friends. It's not like…" He trails off because he doesn't have the words for it. "I'm not angry." He means the words to be truth and isn't sure why they taste like a lie on his tongue.

Drea kneels in front of him, reaches out until he leans forward, lets her hug him. She presses her cheek to his, and he turns to take her scent on his skin before he pulls away.

"It's good," he says, and pushes to his feet. "We're good. I'm not going to tear anyone's throat out." When he grins at Corbin, there's a puff of smoke from his nostrils. "I don't need to. If it comes to that, Drea can defend herself. Don't fuck up."

He doesn't know what he'd do if they couldn't stand each other after this. He holds up his hands—Corbin is his right, and Drea is his left—then lowers them slowly, as if maybe they'll understand what this means to him.

Corbin comes to his feet, and Alaric shakes his head before Corbin can approach. "Not now," Alaric says. He lets wings carry him skyward, spots Corbin flying close behind. Alaric wheels tightly in the air, diving back to the ground, daring Corbin to follow.

By the time Alaric levels out, Corbin is gone. Alaric takes another lazy turn, spots Corbin on the ground below with Drea.

He lets the air carry him back to the house. He taps on the window of his room with one claw; it takes three tries before Chris looks up from his laptop and blinks. Alaric taps again, and Chris finally rises and opens the window.

Alaric resolves into human form before his feet touch the ground. He frowns as he looks at Chris, opens his mouth, then closes it again. "Sorry to interrupt your writing," he finally says.

"It's fine. I don't know why I expected you to come back through the door instead of the window." Chris rubs his eyes, glances at his watch. "I could use a break. It's been a few hours. Were you out flying? You're probably starving."

"Started out running. Just following..." Alaric shrugs because it's hard to explain to someone who doesn't live by instinct and nose. "Found Corbin and Drea."

"I'm surprised you're not still out there with—" Chris cuts off abruptly, frowning. "Alaric?"

"They were together." It's not a big deal, and it's not something he needs to worry about. Or worry at, picking at the thought and feeling like it's a scab on his skin. "It doesn't matter. It's okay."

"You don't sound okay."

Alaric tries to taste the words again, and this time they taste more like truth. "No. It's okay. But I don't want to talk about it."

He pushes through the door to his room, not sure where he's going until he stands in the hall. He can smell the *stay away* scent from several doors down, knows that this is the one place his father doesn't want him to go. Alaric strides down the hall, passing Drea's room, and stops at the door to the room that belonged to Orson. He pushes it open, shrinking back from the wave of scent that pours out. He tilts his head before he thinks better of it, baring his neck to his father even without him there.

"Ric?"

"It's okay," he says again, lowering his chin and standing resolutely in the doorway. "My father marked this room to make sure we wouldn't go in."

Chris crowds close behind him, and Alaric inhales that scent instead, familiar and strong, letting it wash away the inherent order in the marking.

"Did your father seriously piss on this room to keep you out?" Chris asks, breath warm against Alaric's ear.

Alaric huffs a laugh. "Not exactly. I think. He wouldn't have harmed anything important."

Chris moves behind him, and Alaric hears the sound of his phone waking up. "So, are we going in?"

Alaric takes a slow step over the threshold, body stiff and wary in the face of the strong scent. Once he clears the doorway, he can breathe more easily, and he takes a moment to steady himself and take stock of what's been brought back.

"Hey," Chris says quietly, and when Alaric turns, he realizes that Chris is aiming the camera at the room, then at Alaric himself.

"Hi, Ric," Thorne calls out. "You've got both of us here. Chris thought that if there's anything in those boxes, we might be able to help out."

"And I figured you'd rather have Rory on the phone than Pawel," Chris says quietly, and Alaric can hear Rory's low laugh on the other side of the call.

"Yeah. Let's start opening boxes."

The boxes are labeled neatly, as if someone had been planning for a move. Bedroom 1. Bedroom 2. Kitchen. Living room. It's as if they somehow have the dregs of the entire apartment here without any of the furniture, whatever might have been deemed important by someone collecting evidence.

Alaric starts by pulling the tape off the living room box. Half-burned candles, and a bag filled with a bowl and herbs that make Alaric sneeze. He holds them up to the camera, and after a moment, both Rory and Thorne chorus, "Sage and thyme."

"There's something else in there," Alaric says. "You might not see it, but

I can smell it, and it doesn't smell like dinner."

"Bring it back with you," Rory tells him. "We'll take a closer look then."

Chris hands the phone to Alaric. "We'll do better if we go through two boxes at a time. I'll start on one of the bedroom boxes."

"Do you know what you're looking for?"

Chris raises both eyebrows. "Nope. Do you?"

He has a point. Alaric points at the boxes, and Chris pulls the tape off and digs in.

It's a lot of little personal things. A bookmark that's a scrap of paper in handwriting that Alaric doesn't recognize. A to-do list in a flourished scrawl, interspersed with Orson's writing, and for a moment Alaric's heart aches. He smells Orson on the books he pulls out, and on one particular throw pillow. He stands there, holding it to his chest for a long moment, inhaling the scent.

"Alaric." Chris is holding up a composition book. "Your brother kept a journal."

Alaric reluctantly sets the pillow on Orson's bed and sits next to Chris as he points the phone at the book. Chris opens the book, and Thorne lets out a sharp bark of laughter. "Is that your brother's handwriting?" Thorne asks.

Alaric runs his fingers lightly over the ridges the pen made in the paper. "Yeah. Most of it is. Some of these notes in the margins aren't, but it's the same handwriting from most of the other notes they found in the living room. Probably his roommate."

"Those are rituals." Rory's voice is cautious. "I mean, that page is a discussion of ritual. A deconstruction, like you'd probably do in Pawel's class. Did Orson major in magical studies?"

Alaric shakes his head, the motion slowing. "Couldn't have. He went to VIT."

"PHU offers classes to VIT students. He could've taken it and not said anything," Thorne suggests gently. Chris nudges Alaric's shoulder, and Alaric leans into him, stares at the book rather than the phone.

He can see what Rory's saying; as he skims through the words he sees things that sound like they could be magical rituals. But more like information about it. Almost as if Orson and his roommate were holding a conversation on the page about how Clan could mix with Mage Talent to do a spell. It twists into a tight knot in Alaric's gut, and he closes the book.

"We should probably take a closer look at that."

Alaric grunts. He can't deny that Thorne's right. But the idea of reading it himself makes him feel vaguely sick. "I'll bring it back."

His nostrils flare, a sudden bright flash of anger in the air. Footsteps land harshly in the hall outside; Alaric stands as the door bursts open, moves in front of Chris.

"Get out," Theobald growls deeply, the sound reverberating in the room. It burrows under Alaric's skin, and he takes a step back, stopping when he bumps into Chris's knee. "This room is closed."

"Because you don't want the truth." Alaric drops the phone into Chris's lap, behind his back where Theobald can't see. He hopes Chris has the sense to end the call before Theobald catches the small sounds of Rory and Thorne breathing. He keeps talking, trying to cover. "Because you don't want to know the real reason why Orson died."

"I already know!" Theobald pushes into the room, gets in Alaric's face, pushes at his shoulder. "I know that it was a Mage that brought this on my son. The same way they're twisting your mind, turning you into something other than Clan. And we will have retribution for Orson's death. For the loss of my son and heir."

Alaric barks out a sharp laugh. "You still have a son, and an heir."

Silence, anger growing in the air around them, thick in Theobald's scent.

"We will have our retribution," Theobald growls, low and dark. "Before they take you as well."

Alaric huffs and smoke swirls around them. He feels the tension in Chris's knees where they press against Alaric's legs, the small jerk of motion backward. "No," he growls, voice rumbling with another puff of smoke. "We aren't going to war."

"We're going to war if I say we are," Theobald counters. "It is past time to make them understand—"

"Make *who* understand?" Alaric shouts. "Mages? *All* Mages? They aren't all the same. They aren't all one person, and neither are we. There are Clan who have communities where they live with Mages. Where they *marry*

Mages. This isn't even *about* magical ritual. I tried to tell you, it's something different. That isn't a symbol—"

Theobald roars, and Alaric's words die in his mouth. He reaches for Chris, getting an arm around him as soon as he rises—a clear statement of his intention to protect his friend. Theobald's gaze narrows, and Alaric stares back at him.

"No," Alaric says, tone flat. "I tried. I came for dinner today, but you want me to be something I'm not, and you're determined to destroy our community. You want to go to war, and there isn't a war that needs to be made. I won't do it. I won't be blind to everything outside of this place. I can't be. I'm angry about Orson's death and I'm going to find out what happened. That's what we need to do, not fight blindly because that's what your father did, and his father before him. This isn't Mages. We don't know what it is, and I'm going to find out. I refuse to go to war on your behalf."

"If you walk out—"

"—don't come back?" Alaric barks out laughter, short and sharp. There are steps in the hall, claws clicking on the floor, and his mother's scent, bright and worried. "I thought I was all you had left, *father*. I'm either your heir, or I'm not. You can't have it both ways. But fine, I won't come back until I know what happened."

He pushes Chris toward the door. Alaric keeps his body between Chris and Theobald, refusing to let Theobald threaten Chris. There's a low growl in Theobald's throat, but Alaric ignores it, just as he ignores his mother standing in the hall and the gathered Clan around them in various shapes and sizes.

Chris heads toward Alaric's room without needing direction, and Alaric follows close behind.

"Alaric."

He almost stops at his mother's soft voice. He pauses, rocks back before stepping forward again. "I'm sorry," he replies quietly. "We won't be at dinner tonight."

"Be safe," Alia murmurs. She makes no move to follow, and by the time Alaric reaches his room, he and Chris are alone.

Chris holds up the book. "I thought you'd want this."

"Fuck." Relief spirals through his chest in a bright, hot spike. Alaric takes the journal, then yanks Chris close for a hard hug, holding on. It's meant to thank him for rescuing the one thing that might help—for daring to smuggle it out in front of Theobald. But it feels more like taking comfort as he inhales Chris's scent, presses his cheek against him, and rubs for a moment as if Chris were Clan.

"I assume we're leaving." Chris's voice is a rumble as they stand pressed close together. Chris's hand moves across Alaric's back, then lightly pats him. "Let me pack up my project, and we can be out of here in five minutes."

Alaric's phone chimes, and he steps back, chest aching as he shivers in the cold. He thumbs it open, stares at his sister's text.

I'm sorry.

Air rushes out. *I'm sorry, too*, he types. *Rumor travels fast?*

I meant about—wait, did something happen?

Alaric stares down at Drea's words, ealizes she isn't in the main house and has no idea of his alteraction with his father. *I'm leaving, sorry. Not you and Corbin. I can't stay here with Theobald.*

What did our father do now?

Chris lays his hand on Alaric's shoulder, warm and heavy. "You about ready to go?"

"Yeah." Alaric types out one last reply. *He won't listen, and he won't investigate to find out the truth. He says he's going to war.*

61

ALARIC CALLS MINNISALE's from the road, and the hostess promises to put something together for them. There's no nearby parking, so Chris stays in the car, keeping it running, while Alaric runs in and pays for the big bag of food. The waitress, Jenny, remembers him, and he vaguely remembers her. She asks after Chris while she tucks what looks like a quarter of an apple pie and a small box of cannoli into the bag as well, after he's paid.

"No charge," she says with a cheerful smile. "No one deserves to eat takeout on Thanksgiving without something nice for dessert."

The place smells like roast turkey, braised beef, and herbed potatoes. The smell of warm apples lingers in the air and tastes like home. Alaric doesn't comment on Thanksgiving, simply thanks her and quickly escapes as an older couple approaches to request their table.

He slides into the car and opens the bag, pulling out a cannoli. The pastry crunches, and the sweet cheese on the inside is perfect. He savors it before he swallows, then holds out the remainder. When Chris opens his mouth, Alaric nudges it in, watches as Chris smiles.

"They have good desserts."

"We didn't stay for dessert last time," Alaric remembers. "We went back to OPT for beer."

"We can have good beer this time, too," Chris points out. He pulls onto campus, then into the small lot near OPT.

Alaric takes the bag as they head inside, the place silent. He doesn't even hear Lewis's heartbeat, so he must have found someplace to go for the holiday.

"Seems like we've got the house to ourselves." After getting used to the noise of the house, it almost seems too quiet. He inhales, tastes the mixed scent that makes up the family that is this house, and relaxes slowly.

Chris takes the bag and walks into the kitchen, spreading everything out on the table. He grabs plates and instead of putting his lasagna on one plate and Alaric's chicken parmesan and ravioli on another, he takes a little of each like it's family style. "Good to be home?" he asks.

Alaric huffs his approval of splitting the meals, then digs into the fridge to unearth two beers. He pours them both, hands one off to Chris, and takes the plate Chris made for him in exchange. " 's more like home here right now, yeah," he admits. " 's good to be back. My father and I—" He sinks down onto the couch in the living room. "I scared you."

"Not exactly." Chris sets his food on the coffee table, pulls it closer, and slides to sit on the floor. He's too tall to fit, his body folded awkwardly. "I thought the two of you were going to try to kill each other, and yeah, that's a little terrifying. I didn't think you'd hurt me."

"Good." It helps to know that. Alaric takes a forkful of the lasagna; it's good, full of meat and cheese and a brightly flavored tomato sauce. He can see why Chris likes it. "Not good that you thought we'd kill each other," he grumbles under his breath. "He won't look past his narrow view."

"Clan's Clan," Chris says, and Alaric looks at him sharply. Chris's head is bent down, focused on his dinner, and Alaric can't tell if he's smiling; there's a faint scent of amusement in the air.

"I wasn't that bad at the beginning of the semester," Alaric mutters.

"You have changed," Chris counters. "It's hard to go from one environment to another, especially when you're coming from a place with a small view of the world. You never brought humans or Mages home when you were in high school, did you? And Orson never brought his friends home."

Alaric rumbles, because Chris has a point, but he doesn't feel like admitting it. "Where'd you pack the journal?"

"It's in the bag." Chris pushes his plate away. "You want me to go get it? I need to work some more on my project. Doesn't seem like anyone's around; we could use the living room."

"Mm." Alaric gets up to grab more food while Chris goes up for the journal and his work. By the time they get themselves arranged, the TV is on in the background with a movie streaming quietly. Chris sits on the floor, papers and his laptop on the table, his back against the couch and leaning against Alaric's leg. Alaric presses his knee against Chris's shoulder as he flips through the journal.

It's not easy reading.

The concepts themselves aren't difficult, but Alaric's brain keeps shying away from the ideas. There's a page which is clearly the development of a ritual, with complicated mathematics and notations for blood. There's another page which seems to be attempting to break down and define the elements of Clan via their magical nature, relating shapeshifting to innate ritual.

The ideas make Alaric's skin crawl, and he changes position, pulling both feet up on the couch, toes pressed against Chris's shoulders.

Chris reaches up to touch Alaric's ankle, and for just a moment, it helps.

Something simmers under Alaric's skin, and he reaches for his phone, opening the stalled text conversation thread with Thorne before he thinks about it. There have been a few conversations since the night Thorne stopped sleeping with him, but not many. Alaric sees him more in person than he speaks to him in text.

Alaric closes the conversation and drops the phone. He picks up the journal, flips a few pages, and starts reading.

There are times when it seems like the shadows are alive in the corners of the room. The living room is pitch black at night—bulbs blow as soon as we put them in the lamps. Dionne refuses to sleep on the couch; she spends her nights with me or Sal. We're working on a ritual to cleanse the house. Sal thinks something is polluted, says he can feel it. Dionne claims there are things in the darkness that we can't see because we move too slowly. I can't smell anything, can't taste anything, can't fight anything. All I know is that all the darkness makes my skin itch.

Alaric's throat closes, and he coughs roughly. He twitches, foot touching Chris's neck, and Chris glances up, brow furrowing.

"Shadows," Alaric says, and Chris nods like that means something. Alaric raises the book. "I'll keep reading."

"Mm." Chris turns his head, his cheek brushing Alaric's ankle for a moment before he turns back to his work.

The phone is in Alaric's hand again, his heart hammering hard. His thumbs hover over the keyboard, and he tosses the phone on the table this time, where it lands face down, skittering to touch the edge of Chris's laptop. Chris moves it over a few inches and keeps working.

Alaric exhales, turns the page.

There's a name and number at the top of a page, notes in two different pens and handwriting like Orson and Sal must have interviewed someone at the same time, writing on either side of the page. Descriptions of Clan and Mage intertwining in one family, and tiny, careful notes about a ritual: *calming the beast*. On the next page is another ritual to raise the beast, and after that, notes on how certain forms might interact differently with magic while attempting to develop a ritual to make something slow.

Alaric drops the book on the couch, nearly kicks Chris in the head as he gets up and walks away.

A whisper of noise and a soft thunk behind him. "Ric."

He turns back, and Chris is still sitting, his hand over Alaric's phone.

Fuck.

"You're upset," Chris says quietly. "You're pacing. And you thought about texting Thorne."

Alaric shrugs, skin heated as Chris watches him. "So?"

"You de-stress with sex, right?" Chris pushes the table out enough that he can come to his feet.

Alaric blinks, the thump in his chest almost too loud to hear over. "Not with you."

Chris stops mid-step, rocks back. "Okay then."

The scent of hurt and disappointment is thick in the air. "Fuck." Alaric scrubs at the back of his head, scrunches his eyes shut as if when he opens them again everything will reset back to before he opened his mouth. "You don't want to have sex with me," Alaric says bluntly. "And I don't want to fuck you up. Like Thorne did."

Chris frowns. "What makes you think it'd screw with me?" He spreads his hands. "With Thorne, I had no idea what I was getting into. He thought I knew, I thought it was something different, and we were both young and stupid enough that we didn't talk about it. I know you, Ric, and I know exactly what you'd be offering. And what wouldn't be involved."

The sound of his heart is louder now, hammering in his ears. Alaric clenches his hands tight, then flexes his fingers, and it does nothing to loose the tension thrumming under his skin. "I feel like I'm going to fly apart," Alaric admits. "Like I..." He trails off, raising his hands, lowering them without knowing how to say it.

"Like you need someone else to help you hold it together?" Chris asks. "Like you need physical comfort—like Clan, only *more* physical?"

Alaric nods, feet stuck like glue to the floor as Chris approaches slowly.

"No strings," Chris says quietly. "No expectations that it's anything else. Just something to help you relax."

Chris is right there in front of him, a heavy warmth that contrasts with the cold wall at Alaric's back. Musk in the air, a deepening scent of arousal that swirls around them, and Alaric needs this. He needs to fall apart, to let go, for the tension to seep from his bones. He nods once, and Chris crowds in closer, catches Alaric's hands in his. He tangles their fingers together, and carefully raises Alaric's hands above his head, presses them back against the wall.

When Chris kisses him, he leans into him, his weight holding Alaric in place even though the touch of his lips is careful. Gentle. Alaric growls softly, and Chris kisses him harder, teases his mouth open with his tongue until Alaric gives way.

Alaric can feel Chris's heartbeat where they lean together; it races as fast as his own.

Chris lowers Alaric's hands, steps back slightly. "You good?"

"Fuck." Alaric blinks, catches himself leaning toward Chris, then sways back to standing upright. "Yeah. 'm good."

Chris smiles, touches Alaric's lower lip with his thumb. "Good. Then let's go upstairs."

Excerpt from *When Magic Entered the World: Interviews With Lineage Talent*, by Pawel Szczek, © 2009

The thing I wonder the most is: *why?*

The world has been the same for so long. There were Lineage Talent, and there was the occasional Emergent Talent. Every person of Lineage I knew could name one or two Emergents. My cousin married a girl who came to our community because she had Emerged when she was only five and her family needed a place where she'd be safe. They found their way from Rhode Island to Minnesota, and then to our small Clan. She preferred to be a vole most often—don't ask me why, out of all the rodents that she could be—and her brothers and sister were perfectly human.

Sometimes that was how it worked.

But now...now it seems that they are coming out of the woodwork. Turn around and there will be seven new arrivals this month, thirty this year. A hundred that you've read about in the news, small stories except for the sensations where something goes horribly wrong.

Some people blame that girl, but that can't be it. What did Kenzie Davis do, other than want to win a gymnastics championship? She could have died if her Talent hadn't intervened.

She didn't start this, but she's a part of it. She's a symptom, not the root of the problem.

Two days before Kenzie Davis Emerged, my grandfather passed away, and a day after she Emerged, his partner was gone. Both leaders of our community dead in the first days of the Emergence, a hollow left in their wake. My father and his brother stepped up, but the community was still unstable. Their position was untenable, and unrest ruled our community. Everyone disagreed about what should happen next—should we be public? Should we retreat? Should we seek out the Mages and go to war over the Emergence? Because clearly they were to blame.

We were being torn apart in those early days, and for the first six months I thought that we might lose everything we had become over the last centuries. Until Sasha Kennedy stepped forward and began to work with them. She wasn't Clan. She wasn't Mage. She wasn't even Talented. But she was the very human mother of the vole I mentioned, who had come to us for sanctuary.

We thought that her family had been drawn to us because they needed us. In the end, I believe it was something more. We needed them to survive the Emergence. We needed to change. To expand. To Emerge as well, to become something more than our Lineage.

And I still wonder why.

Why did we have to change?

AFTERMATH

62

ALARIC WAKES INTO deep warmth and the heavy solidity of a body sprawled half on top of him, tangled skin to skin. He inhales and tastes Chris's scent mixed with his own, and he blinks into the early sunlight that spills into the room.

For a moment, the whole world sharpens into bright, terrifying focus; Alaric's heart thuds once, then feels like it stops. Skips.

Fuck.

What if he's fucked everything up?

Alaric tries to slide out of the bed, and Chris murmurs something. "Need to pee," Alaric mutters, and Chris rolls over, wraps himself in the blankets as he faces the wall.

Alaric stands up as soon as he's free.

He yanks on sweats and a T-shirt, throws on a hoodie, and searches for socks and sneakers. He tiptoes down the stairs; he can hear other heartbeats in the house now. Lewis came back sometime during the night, and a few others that Alaric can't identify other than as familiar. When he steps out and closes the door without anyone waking, he finally breathes easily.

It's a short run to Teas Please, and it does nothing to clear his head. It's early, but there are already cars on the road, and he's surprised how busy the restaurant is on the Friday of a long holiday weekend. Alaric waits at the front for someone to notice him, his hood up and hands shoved deep in the pockets. Nate walks by and stops a few steps past, turns slowly as his brows furrow.

"Where's Chris?" Nate asks. He grabs a menu and motions for Alaric to follow into the back. They end up in an unfamiliar corner populated primarily by tables for two. Everyone seems too awake and too cheerful for

Alaric, and he grumbles and sinks into his chair with his back to the wall.

"Still asleep," Alaric mutters, flushing at the thought of waking up that morning.

"You should let him know where you're sitting, since it isn't the usual corner." Nate taps the table. "You want to bother with the menu, or should I just go get you something?"

Alaric isn't in the mood to make decisions. He grunts softly and shoves the menu back at Nate, glad when he walks away without another question. Alaric pulls his phone out, lays it on the table as he opens up his last conversation with Chris.

Didn't want to wake you. Went to Teas Please.

He hits send and turns his phone over, leaves it facing down on the table. It's warm enough inside that he pushes his hood back first, then after a few minutes unzips the hoodie and drops it on the back of his chair. He catches someone looking at his PHU Football T-shirt, raises an eyebrow and waits to see if they say something; eventually they look away, back to their conversation.

"Here." Nate puts down the pot of ginger tea along with two cups, and a crêpe filled with eggs, ham, smoky cheese, and spring onions. One more small plate offers a blueberry scone, crusted with sugar. "I'll keep an eye out for Chris and bring something out when he gets here."

Alaric narrows his gaze. "He's still sleeping. He's not coming to breakfast."

"But you—" Nate cuts off, mouth snapping shut. "I'll bring more tea if you need it. Just signal, okay?"

It's not quiet when he walks away, but at least no one's talking directly to Alaric. He picks at his crêpe but leaves the tea, the scent of ginger pricking at his senses. It's not that he's not hungry. He just isn't in the mood to eat.

He picks up the phone, flips it over, almost surprised that Chris hasn't responded. Fuck. Just...fuck.

Alaric opens his texts again, finds his constant conversation with Rory. *I think I fucked up.*

Is it something you want to talk about?

Alaric huffs, not really sure about the answer to that. *Probably not.*

Probably should.

Three dots, appearing and disappearing, before the answer finally comes. *Is this going to be the kind of thing I can actually help with, or should we get Thorne involved?*

Alaric winces, because this is going to be awkward. *Thorne would be better at it. Still not sure I actually want to talk about it.*

A fresh group conversation pings from Thorne. *What do you think you did, Alaric?*

Still don't want to actually talk about it.

You started it, Rory points out.

And then Rory got me involved. I'm awake, and it's ridiculously early. Why are we up this early?

Mom's making breakfast before Dad has to actually go to work. Dad's still asleep.

Alaric can almost guess which Dad is which when Rory speaks, but it's still confusing. *So you got up this early for breakfast?*

There's a string of laughter emojis across the screen from Thorne.

The vegetarian food options in the dining halls are not ideal, Rory says. *I am not missing a chance to have a good meal while I'm home. I am bringing back leftovers. If we had a large enough freezer, I could bring back enough to eat until it's December break. If I trusted Thorne's roommates, I'd use his freezer.*

He doesn't trust my roommates.

I got that impression, Alaric responds, smiling slightly.

"You look better," Nate says, sliding into the chair across from him.

Alaric holds up the phone. "Rory and Thorne." It chimes again, and Thorne's message is stark on the screen.

If you need to talk about something, Alaric, you should talk about it.

His smile drops away. *No, I'm fine. Just at Teas Please for breakfast. Nate stopped by to talk. I'll text later.*

Alaric turns the phone to silent and puts it face down on the table, pushing it into the corner.

"You usually eat faster than this," Nate points out, drinking from the cup he has with him. "And you haven't touched the tea. Not in the mood for the ginger?"

"It's Chris's flavor." Alaric doesn't figure he needs to say anything more than that. It's not his choice. It's good. He likes it. But it reminds him of Chris.

"Did something happen between you two since you were here on Wednesday?" Nate asks, leaning his elbows on the table. "Personal question, I know, but honestly, you look like death warmed over and maybe you need to talk. Get it off your chest. Rant to me, then go back and make up with him. Have fantastic make-up sex."

Alaric flushes, skin heated darkly. "We didn't fight, and we already had sex. And I think it fucked everything up."

"Wait. What?" Nate sits back again, arms crossed. "You mean you two weren't already together? I thought this was your standard date location. You're always here together."

"We're friends," Alaric points out, gestures at the general population. "Not everyone who comes here together is dating."

"Not everyone who comes here together sits in each other's pockets," Nate counters. "Or looks at you the way Chris does."

That thought sends a chill down Alaric's spine, that Chris could be harmed by this. Hurt by Alaric taking what he needed and not giving back what Chris needs. Fuck. "We weren't together," Alaric says flatly. "And I don't want to talk about it because I've already fucked shit up enough. I don't need more reminders about it." He picks up the scone, breaks off a piece, and shoves it in his mouth. The blueberry flavor explodes across his tongue, chased by the sweetness of the sugar crystals; when he picks up the tea to wash it down, the flavors meld and it's striking but pleasant.

He closes his eyes for a moment; Nate's still there when he opens them. "Why are you here?"

"Here?" Nate taps the table. "You looked like you could use some company, so I took my fifteen and sat down. Since you're eating now, I think it worked." He motions at the restaurant. "In general? Like I said the other day, I'm local. And I'd rather have the money from working the early shift on Black Friday than have to be home with my dad."

"Don't get along?" That's something Alaric can commiserate on. "Went home for dinner yesterday, argued with mine, and came back before dinner started."

Nate makes a face. "Ouch. Sorry. Mine wouldn't argue with me. He'd have to notice me to do that, and honestly, since I was about thirteen, he hasn't paid much attention. It has its advantages and disadvantages. He didn't care what I did after I got my license. As long as I'm in college, he signs the tuition checks and lets me go. But it's not like he actually cares about anything, either. If I yelled, he'd probably just turn his back and do something else."

Frustration and resignation in his scent; Nate's shoulders slump.

" 'm sorry your dad's a dick," Alaric mutters, and Nate laughs, surprised.

"Same," Nate says quietly. "Is that why you started playing football? To get away from your dad?"

Alaric shakes his head. " 's what pissed him off in the first place. It's not a Clan thing—we don't do organized sports. Don't involve ourselves with humans. Could get them hurt. Could rebound back on us."

"Like what happened in the opener," Nate says, and Alaric nods.

"Yeah. Like that." His stomach rumbles, and he cuts off a bite of the crêpe, taking the time to chew before speaking. "But I fucking love football. Don't give a shit what my father thinks about it. Why? D'you do something to get away from your father?"

"Not exactly." Nate drinks again, sets down the glass as he makes a face. "I started running with my mom when I was little. Everything changed when she left, and I just kept running. Dad was distant, and Mom was gone, and it felt like if I kept running, maybe I'd catch up with her. I never did. But it got me a scholarship to PHU, which is good, and it keeps me busy. The whole world falls away when I'm running." He cocks his head, considering. "The indoor season's starting, if you want something to do over winter. Or in the spring. I run year-round—I'm a long distance runner, so it's everything from cross-country to the 10k"

Alaric shakes his head, digging into the crêpe. He's finally making headway, eating while Nate distracts him. "I don't want to run more than I have to for football. That's not what I love about it. You want someone who runs, talk to Dax."

"I might."

Alaric catches the scent a moment before he spots Chris weaving through the restaurant, heading in their direction. His nostrils flare, and he goes still, setting the fork down carefully.

"Hm?" Nate turns, rises in a fluid motion. "That's my cue to get another pot of the ginger tea and another crêpe, unless you want something different?" He glances at Alaric.

"Do I need to pull up another chair?" Chris asks, his hand on the back of the chair Nate has vacated.

"Just coming off break," Nate says. "Don't worry, I'm not stealing your boyfriend." He pats Chris's shoulder. "I'll be back with your breakfast shortly."

"He's not my boyfriend." Chris pulls out the chair, sinks into the seat. "And I like the booths on the other side better."

"Come at a time when we aren't full of hungry shoppers who've already been hunting Black Friday deals for hours and are pausing for breakfast," Nate mutters. "It'll be quieter later. On the other hand, the tips are good."

Chris's feet bump Alaric's under the table, squeezed in close. Alaric nudges the other half of his scone across the table, and Chris picks it up, takes a bite. "You okay?" Chris asks.

"Guess that depends," Alaric says quietly. "Did I fuck everything up?"

Chris raises his eyebrows. "No? Why would you think you did? It wasn't the 'boyfriend' comment, was it?"

Alaric shakes his head quickly. "Fuck, no, that's fine. We're not, and you're not. I just...you..." He waves a hand at Chris. "We're friends."

"Exactly." Chris nudges him under the table. "We talked about this last night, Ric. We're friends, and that's not changing. I don't regret it, if that's what you're worried about. Do you?"

"No." Alaric exhales loudly. "It was good. I feel better."

"Then we're fine." Chris turns, looks out across the room. "Did Nate say he was bringing me breakfast before I ordered?"

Alaric still has half a crêpe on his plate, so he nudges it toward Chris. "Here. Whatever he brings back, we'll share. You already finished my scone."

He can breathe more easily now, and as Chris digs into the crêpe, Alaric reaches for his phone. He opens the conversation with Rory and Thorne and sends one last text.

Everything's fine.

When Chris brings up the topic of college bowl games to watch, Alaric falls easily into the conversation. It sounds like a good way to spend the day, lounging on the couch back at OPT, watching football with a friend.

63

ALARIC HEARS THE front door of OPT open and close in the distance, then light steps on the stairs coming up. He expects them to pass by, heading down to someone else's room, but they stop outside Chris's room, and there's a tap against the slightly open door. Alaric tilts his head, inhales and listens for the heartbeat, and nudges Chris.

"Nikita's here."

Chris pulls his headphones off, sets them on the bed, and blinks at Alaric. "Why?"

"I don't know. She's still in the hall," Alaric says, as Nikita raps against the door again.

She nudges it open, peeks in. "Hey." Her voice is small, her arms wrapped around her center as she leans against the doorjamb. A scarf that seems like overkill for the current fall weather is looped around her throat, and she's buttoned up in a heavy jacket. "I'm the only one on our floor right now, and I was kind of getting freaked out. Then I remembered that Drea said you were crashing here for the weekend, and I couldn't think of anyone else I know on campus right now, so I figured I'd come over."

"What are you doing here for the holiday?" Chris stands up, pulls the door open the rest of the way, and motions for her to come in. When he holds out a hand, Nikita shrugs out of the jacket but keeps the scarf, wrapping it around herself like a shawl.

"My sister Tammy moved to California, and she's having a baby next week—C-section—so my mom's gone out to stay with her." Nikita shrugs one shoulder. "On the one hand, it means I went home, and Dad and I went out to this awesome diner for Thanksgiving. But on the other hand, Dad figured he'd get some work done on the house while Mom's gone, and

I'm not in the mood for dust and noise, so I took the train back here. And well. It's not going so great over there alone."

There's a crisp scent in the air and a chill that wasn't there before Nikita walked in. Alaric frowns, nostrils flaring. Anxiety. A jittery skip to her heart as her fingers tap against her thigh. She sinks to sit on Dax's bed, pushes off her boots, and draws up her feet to sit cross-legged.

"What's going on?" Alaric asks, trying to keep his voice low and calm. He's not sure exactly why she's here, but she smells upset, and that's bothering the beast under his skin.

Chris sits back on his own bed, shoulder and thigh tight against Alaric's side.

Nikita fidgets, twisting her fingers together. "I keep having nightmares. The kind of nightmares that I don't remember and that are making me get fined for using my Talent indoors. It's been snowing in my room the last two times I woke up. That's why—" She cuts off, indicates the jacket and scarf. "I had mittens and a hat. I was hoping that maybe if I crashed here, the nightmares would stop."

"Or we could at least wake you up," Alaric says. "You fell asleep and made a storm in the middle of Teas Please when there was a crowd of us. I don't think having people around helps."

"Thanks for the comfort," Nikita mutters dryly. She pulls her knees up, wraps her arms around them. "Even if you wake me up, that's better than waking up under a pile of snow going into hypothermia, right? It's not like I want to make storms indoors. I'm supposed to be sleeping. It's that thing you do when your brain turns *off*, and I'm not sure when the last time I did it normally was."

"How'd you sleep while you were at home?" Chris reaches for his phone, comes up with Alaric's instead, and hands it to him. "And if this is something going wrong with your Talent"—he holds up his hands in a clear indication of *don't yell at me*—"maybe you should talk to the one expert on campus to see if he has any ideas. Unless you've already done that."

"I hadn't even thought of it," Nikita admits. "I've just been..." She presses the heels of her hands against her eyes. "I'm so tired. I kind of slept at home. I mean. It didn't rain inside or anything, but I figured it was because Jennifer wasn't there, so like, my stress levels were totally lower. But then I got back here and boom, there we go with the snow. So. Yeah. That's not a bad idea. I mean. Okay. Go ahead. If you've got Professor Szczek in your contacts, do it."

My floormate is a Weather Witch and she's having nightmares and making it snow in her sleep. It's been bad for a while and it's getting worse.

Alaric presses send, doesn't figure that they'll hear back from Pawel any time soon. He has no idea what Pawel would be doing, but he assumes he has family other than Conor. When his phone pings, he blinks down at the quick response.

She's not in control of her Talent?

Alaric looks over at Nikita. "You're fine when you're awake, right?"

Nikita nods slowly. "Yeah. I just can't sleep. Pretty much at all."

It's only when she sleeps. So she's not sleeping. Or when she does, she has nightmares and it rains or snows. She did it when she fell asleep in Teas Please once.

Chris sets his hand on Alaric's thigh, squeezes lightly. "I'm going to see who else is in the house right now."

"Lewis let me in," Nikita offers. She lowers her chin to her knees, stays huddled and watching Alaric while he waits for Pawel to respond.

Where are you? I can come over, see what I can see.

Alaric licks his lips, glances at Nikita briefly before typing, *We're at OPT. I'm staying here over the holiday. Nikita came back early and didn't want to be in the dorm alone because it kept snowing.*

I'll be there shortly. Conor's at a friend's house tonight and overnight, so I have time.

Alaric sends back an *okay*, then sets the phone aside. "Pawel's coming over," he says. "He should be here soon, and maybe he can see if something's wrong."

"Besides me behaving like I'm eight years old and have been startled into spewing a thunderstorm," Nikita mumbles, her head bowed. "I used to be pretty bad about it when I was little. Not when I was really little—I didn't have that much power. I'd make tiny clouds when I was upset sometimes, or if it was going to rain anyway, it'd start if I got upset. But it got pretty bad when I was in grade school. My sister still talks about how when I saw the Emergence on TV, I called down a massive thunderstorm. After that I may have had a kind of crappy tweenhood, but it got better when I got older. I got control. This is just…it's really fucked up, Alaric. This isn't me. I swear."

"You're someplace new," Alaric points out. "This is all different, and you're living with strangers. It isn't easy on me, and I know, I'm Clan, none of this was ever going to be easy. But maybe it's not easy for you, either. Something here might be setting you off."

"Something other than Jennifer?" Nikita smiles wryly.

Alaric snorts softly. "Yeah. I'm thinking something other than Jennifer, since she's not here right now."

Nikita unwinds herself slowly, crosses the space to Chris's bed, and settles down next to Alaric. She pulls her feet up, tilts into him as he puts an arm around her shoulders. She buries her face against his chest, breathes in slowly. "I heard somewhere that Clan gives good hugs," she says softly.

"Been told that. We're kind of touchy." Alaric gets both arms around her, pulls her onto his lap, and holds on tight. She exhales in a rush, and the room gets a shade warmer as they're quiet for a long moment.

"Maybe it's being away from home," she eventually says. "I mean. At home, everyone's a Weather Witch, right? It's comfortable and familiar. And I know other kinds of Mages, but honestly, you're the first Clan I've met face to face. And I still don't know what Pels is. And it feels like being here, everything is so much *more*. Do you feel it?"

Alaric rubs her back, glances up at the sound of the front door. "Rory'd probably say it's all the energy," he says. "To me, it's just strangers, but yeah, sometimes I smell the magic. Pawel smells like a lightning storm about to strike."

"What about me?"

Alaric inhales again, shakes his head. "You taste like ice right now," he says. "Not like magic, not to me. But you're not a typical Mage, either. Not every Mage smells the same."

The door pushes open as Chris returns with Pawel. Nikita unwinds from Alaric's grasp, slides her feet down so she can spill from his lap. She stands there, arms crossed, and tilts her head as she looks at Pawel. "So. Hi."

Pawel looks like they woke him up, his short hair mussed and spiked in several directions at once. He pushes a hand through it as he looks at Nikita, stalks around her. "There are rituals I can try," he says without preamble. "I'm pretty sure Ric isn't going to enjoy that; he doesn't seem to like magic as a rule."

Alaric grunts. "I don't fucking care right now. I'll leave the room."

Pawel stops, hands on his hips. "Actually, we will. It's going to probably stink afterward, at least for a while, and you need to sleep here. Can we use the living room?"

"There are only three people other than us here for the holiday weekend, and two of them are out today," Chris tells him. "Lewis promises to stay in his room because he wants nothing to do with any of this. And he made us promise to order pizza."

"Fine," Alaric agrees.

"Good." Pawel motions at the door. "Frat house isn't exactly where I usually think about diagnosis and cleansing rituals, but I'll take what we can get," he mutters under his breath. There's something about the slump of his shoulders that makes Alaric think he looks younger than usual.

"If you can't figure it out, I'll go home for break in a month," Nikita says, one hand light on the railing as she goes down the stairs ahead of Pawel. "It's better there. It's better not here."

Pawel scrubs a hand through his hair, drags his hand across his face. There's an underlying rancid exhaustion in his scent, low but rank to Alaric's nose. "I'll figure it out," Pawel says. "There are rituals we can do to take a look at your Talent—at your inherent power levels. See if anything's not what I'd expect for a Weather Witch." He glances back at where Alaric stands at the top of the stairs, Chris behind him. "You aren't going to like this, I'm figuring, but I'm also not going to tell you not to watch."

Alaric lowers himself to sit on the top stair, where he can look through the railing and into the living room like a child watching his parents' party. "I'll stay here."

Chris nudges Alaric to move down one step, then sits behind him, knees pressing in where they bracket Alaric. The position lets Alaric drop his hand to circle Chris's ankle, and the point of contact is comforting. Good.

Chris's fingers brush against the back of Alaric's neck, and he shivers.

"What do you want me to do?" Nikita asks.

"Just…sit on the floor," Pawel says, his voice coming from a distance. The sound of the window sliding open, then Pawel comes back into view. "I honestly don't know if magic smells in a way that can be helped by an open window, Ric, but I figured I'd try. It's the best I can do."

Alaric grunts his thanks and leans back against Chris's touch.

Alaric starts out watching as Pawel circles Nikita, the scent of ozone rising rapidly, but he finds it uncomfortable. It's like staring into the sun. So he closes his eyes, turns his face to press his cheek against Chris's palm, and tries to breathe through his mouth. Instead of watching, he catalogs the small sounds of Pawel's breath and the uptick of his heart rate. The little *hmms* and *ahhs* that punctuate other murmurings, and Nikita's strained breath. There's a brief silence, then Nikita's heart slows abruptly, her breath going soft and even.

Alaric's eyes flicker open, and Nikita is lying sprawled on the floor, Pawel kneeling next to her, one hand hovering in the air over her heart.

Alaric growls softly, and Pawel glances up. "She's fine," Pawel says. "Sleeping. Temporarily. I'll wake her up in a moment." His tongue flicks out, jaw sets. "Give me a few more minutes here."

Pawel leans in closer to Nikita, whispers something, and light flares. Alaric sneezes in the sudden brightness of the air, three times before he has control of himself. By the time he's able to breathe again, blinking, Nikita's sitting up with her hand out to hold Pawel farther away from her.

"I'm okay," Nikita says, but it's freezing, and Alaric's not sure whether that's a lie or not.

Pawel sits back on his heels. "No, you're not. But I'm not sure what you are, either," he admits, pushing his hand through his hair. "Your power levels are off the charts. Speaking as an extremely powerful Emergent Mage, I've seen power. My son is ridiculous—he makes accidental sparks on a regular basis and he's still in third grade. But you're something else right now. And it's not only weather."

Nikita cocks her head, gaze narrowed. "Of course it's only weather. I'm a Weather Witch. There isn't anything else in my Lineage."

"There's something." Pawel's voice is flat, careful. "Nikita, I don't know what it is, either because I've never seen anything like it or because it's merged with your Mage Talent. When Lineages combine, they can create wholly new—"

Alaric coughs, interrupting as Pawel's tone slips toward lecturing.

"I've heard," Nikita says dryly, and Alaric wonders if she knows about Dax. "But Professor Szczek, there *are* only Weather Witches in my Lineage. If there's anyone else, they're still a Mage. We can trace back a solid ten generations, into the old country. We kept records. My grandmother has the book that belonged to her grandmother. I've met cousins of cousins. We all know each other. There's no room for some other Talent to slip in."

"Something did," Pawel insists. "Nikita, you are not *just* a Mage. Not anymore, and maybe you never were."

Chris presses his knee into Alaric's back, and when Alaric glances up, Chris motions down the stairs. Alaric rises, reaches back to pull Chris to his feet; he still has Chris's hand in his when they reach the bottom of the stairs.

As soon as Alaric settles on the couch, Nikita is sprawled across both him and Chris, curled into Alaric with her face pressed against his throat. He rubs her back, feels the shivers slow.

"I'm sorry," Pawel says, sitting on the edge of another chair. He rubs at the back of his neck, body tense with frustration. "It seems like everything I do right now produces more questions and no answers."

"We'll get there," Chris says. "If we don't have the questions, we won't know what we're answering."

"That's fucking philosophical," Alaric mutters, but Chris has a point. In his mind, they've found plenty of answers that don't make sense yet. Maybe they haven't matched up the questions.

"Dax found out where Noah is buried," Pawel says quietly. He gestures at Alaric. "That's the kid from VIT. The one who—"

"Like Orson," Alaric says, and Pawel nods.

"Exactly. So Dax is going to visit him over break and try to talk to him, see if he has something more for us than your brother did."

Nikita's breath slows again, evens out. Alaric rubs circles on her back as he nods at Pawel's words. There really isn't much to say about that; they'll find out what they find out. "Hey, Nik?" he murmurs.

"Mm. Sleepy now."

Chris snorts.

"It's later than you think," Pawel says, tapping his watch. "Maybe not late by college kid standards, but Conor had me up at six this morning. So I'm going to head home, just...let me know how it goes tonight, okay?" His hand hovers over Nikita's shoulder once he stands up, expression concerned.

"Yeah." Alaric rises carefully. He and Chris rearrange Nikita so Alaric can carry her upstairs while Chris lets Pawel out. It occurs to him that they never got the pizza, and Lewis never reminded them. And right now, Alaric really doesn't give a shit.

Having that much magic around is exhausting. Once Alaric gets Nikita settled on Dax's bed, he retreats to Chris's bed and lies down. Chris comes in quietly, stands at the door for a long moment.

"I don't think you're going to wake her up," Alaric rumbles. "She's out. I'll move to the floor if you want to sleep."

"You're fine in my bed. It's not like we haven't shared before," Chris points out.

Yeah, but this time isn't starting out with mind-blanking, relaxing sex. This is fully aware and watching while Chris strips off his jeans and T-shirt and pulls on sleep pants before he turns off the light, then crawls over Alaric. This is Alaric sliding out of his own jeans and tossing them on the floor, then stretching out again under the blankets that Chris has lifted.

It's rolling over on his side while Chris spoons in behind him, an arm thrown casually across his middle to keep them close in a too-small bed. It's Chris nuzzling his shoulder, pressing a kiss to his neck. "Stop thinking, Alaric," Chris murmurs against his skin. "You like puppy piles. This is a small pile."

" 's not the problem," Alaric mutters, because this is...it's...it's not appropriate, not with Nikita in the room. This should be easy. Chris is right, it's just people sleeping, except Alaric can't stop thinking about what else they've done in this bed, and what else they could do.

Chris huffs a soft laugh, shakes his head. "Save that thought for another time," he says. "It can be that, too. But not right now."

Alaric grumbles, tries not to think about it. It's awkward, is what it is, and it's probably going to be more awkward in the morning.

It doesn't take long for Chris to fall asleep, arm tight around Alaric, holding him close. Something won't let Alaric let go, not yet. He's aware. Wary. Watchful. His eyes burn in the darkness, growing used to the low light, and he stares at Nikita as she sleeps.

It's cold in the room, but not snowing. Still, he feels like there's something off, and he stares at the shadows for a long, long time before he can finally decide that they aren't moving. That they're all safe, and he really needs to sleep.

64

"WHAT THE FUCK?"

It's too early in the morning for the way Lewis is yelling. A door slams on the hall, then footsteps crash down the stairs. More slamming, maybe from the kitchen, and at least a few more curses, loud and angry and confused.

Alaric rolls over and buries his face in Chris's throat. Chris is warm, and the air outside of their blanket cocoon is not.

Pounding on the door, then it slams open, and Lewis is standing there, already talking. "There's no heat," he says sharply. "No heat, no hot water, no electricity. Nothing. There's a branch down in the road. And there's ice on the trees. Looks like we're in the middle of a hell of an ice storm."

"Hm?" Chris leverages himself up, leans past Alaric to grab a phone. "It wasn't supposed to storm this weekend."

"Wasn't supposed to, but it sure as hell *is*, and right now we don't have a way to make breakfast." Lewis stalks out, stomps back down the stairs.

At least he didn't comment on the way Alaric and Chris are curled together in bed.

Chris huffs out a small puff of air. "It's cold," he says. Alaric grumbles, curling closer.

"Good reason to stay right where we are," he mutters, and Chris laughs.

"We should check on Nik," Chris murmurs, but his hands are warm against Alaric's abdomen, and Alaric can't quite convince himself to get out of bed.

Then the covers are gone, and Alaric's cold.

"Fuck you," he grunts as he gets up. He pads over to Dax's bed, sits on the edge, and nudges Nikita's shoulder gently. "Hey. Nik. Wake up."

She huffs a soft breath and exhales, still deeply asleep.

Sleet hits the window with a soft *tap, tap,* sliding down to join a rising ridge of ice along the sill. Chris leans against the window, looking out. "Shit. It's bad out there. I think there's already a quarter inch of ice on the trees, and it doesn't look like it's stopping."

Alaric looks down at Nikita, then over at Chris. "You don't think…"

"I think it's possible." Chris grabs his phone, motions for Alaric to join him on the bed. "I think we should take a look at how bad things are before we start panicking."

Chris's phone is at 70% power, and Alaric's is already at 50%, even though they were both plugged in overnight. The power obviously went out a while ago, and the repeated buzzing of messages has sapped the battery. Alaric skims through his messages while Chris checks the news.

This is a hell of a storm, Ric. Are you guys okay?

There's more from Drea and from Corbin as well, both worried about how campus will fare without wood stoves and fireplaces to heat in the absence of power. He taps quick notes back, assures them that he and Chris will stay warm.

Dad says we're not coming back tonight, Drea texts. *We don't have a ride anyway. No one's supposed to be on the roads, even though it's not far. It's bad out there.*

"Airports are closed," Chris says quietly. "Trains aren't running. Weather people are freaking out—this came out of nowhere."

"How big is it?" Alaric asks, gaze straying to where Nikita sleeps.

"Most of the Northeast seaboard," Chris admits. "Southern Maine down to Delaware. It's huge, goes inland into Pennsylvania. It's a freak storm."

"I think we need to wake Nik up." Alaric drops his phone on the bed, doesn't care when Chris picks it up as soon as it buzzes. "If that's Drea or Corbin, tell them we really are okay and if all else fails, we'll find a way to build a bonfire somewhere," he says dryly. He kneels next to Nikita, tries nudging her again, adding a soft growl.

"It's Rory," Chris says. "You want me to call him?"

Alaric nudges harder, but Nikita snuffles and burrows deeper under her pillow. "Tell him we're okay, we're not going to freeze to death, and Nik won't wake up."

The way Nikita's sleeping doesn't feel natural. Alaric hesitates, feeling the issue of consent keenly, then slowly slides one arm under her. He lifts her, repositions her on top of the pillow, and she rolls away, hugging the pillow hard.

Not even a murmur of awakeness.

"Won't wake up how?" Rory's voice asks, and Chris holds up the phone, pointing it at Alaric, Nikita, and the bed.

"Pulled her out from under her pillow. Didn't even say a word," Alaric admits. "She's out hard. Plus there's the weather."

"And you think the two are related," Thorne says.

Alaric nods. "Yeah. She came over because she kept making it snow in the dorm, and Pawel says her magic's fucked up, and now this. This shit only happens when she sleeps."

Thorne makes a small, thoughtful noise.

"So you already talked to Pawel?" Rory asks.

"Not today." Chris sits on the edge of his bed, and Alaric joins him. As the camera faces them, he sees Thorne and Rory squeezing close together in one space. Thorne's eyebrows go up, but Rory is looking at something off screen.

"He was over yesterday," Alaric says. "Before all this. This shit happened overnight. Power's out here."

"Yeah." Rory's voice is low. "I was reading the news. It's a completely freak storm—there are people muttering about magic, but this isn't how that works. It'd be localized, not the entire Northeast."

"Maybe things are different," Alaric mutters. "I mean, I'm a fucking dragon sometimes." The two might not be related, but on the other hand, they're both things that are different from normal. Like when Mac Emerged, and then Emergents started coming out of the fucking woodwork.

"Do you think it really matters?" Chris asks, leaning into him, weight solid and comforting.

Alaric's gaze drifts past the phone to where Nikita sleeps soundly. "No. I think we need to wake her up and stop the storm."

"Call Pawel," Rory says. "I'm sending him something because I had a weird thought, and I want to know what he thinks." He focuses on the camera, seemingly staring right at Alaric. "Let us know what happens, okay? We were supposed to come back today, but Dad's bringing us tomorrow since he can take a day off easily enough."

"We could take the van," Thorne says idly.

"Where would we put the van? Parking by your apartment sucks. There's not enough space on the street," Rory points out. "We don't need the van. Besides. Dad's getting the van fixed so we'll be able to go on tour once summer hits. On the road all summer means no van now."

There's a soft *ping* in the background, and Rory looks away again. "Pawel's going to call you," he says, "so we'd better get off the phone."

Alaric nods, and Chris touches the button to end the call. Alaric stands up, flexes his hands as he paces toward the window, and leans on the sill, looking out. When Chris presses in close behind him, Alaric lets his head drop forward, tries to relax with the comforting weight draped across his back.

"Fuck," Alaric whispers.

"We'll figure it out," Chris murmurs, mouth warm on Alaric's neck. There are teeth, then, and for a moment, the rest of the world drops away.

His phone is loud in the silence, a bright tone against the solid sound of heartbeats and the musk that lays an undertone for the room. Alaric twists away, grabs it. "Hi, Pawel."

"I'm already on my way over. I have Conor with me, and we're walking, so it'll be a bit. The sidewalks are bad, but there's no real traffic, which helps." A murmur in the background, and Pawel huffs a low laugh. "Yes, we have to avoid the trucks spraying salt and sand. Anyway, we'll be there in about twenty minutes. I'm bringing cinnamon bread and cream cheese, because we were slicing it when Rory called, and it seems like this is more important than breakfast."

Even through the phone, Conor's indignant "There is *nothing* more important than breakfast" is clearly audible in the background.

"We'll figure out how to make something to go with it so Lewis doesn't eat it all," Alaric rumbles. "He was pissed off about the lack of electricity."

"We'll adapt," Pawel says. "We have magic. Conor, stop that. Not while we're walking. Look, I want to save my battery since we don't know when the power will be back. I'll see you when we get there."

By the time Alaric ends the call, his battery's already dropped below 30%. He sends a quick text to let people know he's turning off his phone, then shuts the power down and drops it on the bed.

"I'm going to go take a cold shower," Chris says.

For a brief moment, Alaric thinks about joining him. It'd be warmer with two people. It'd take the edge off of the itch under his skin.

On the other hand, Lewis is in the house, and Alaric isn't comfortable with that.

"I'm going to show Lewis how to use a grill to make breakfast." Because they've got that, at least, and it won't be the first time Alaric's done it. The hard part will be scrounging through the fridge to find food without letting all the cold out.

By the time Pawel gets there, both Chris and Alaric have managed to clean up and get dressed, and Alaric's made burgers and scrambled eggs. It isn't necessarily traditional breakfast food, but no one seems to mind, especially Conor, who spreads cream cheese on his cinnamon bread, then piles it high with a burger and eggs. He shoves the sandwich in his mouth for a huge bite and declares it perfect before taking his plate into the living room and curling up on the couch.

"He's adaptable," Chris says.

Lewis grumbles something about dishes, and Pawel shakes his head. "Easy. Get a stock pot out."

Alaric pulls out one of the brew pots, and they fill it with water before Pawel focuses on it intently. Alaric smells ozone in the air, swears he feels the prick of it against his skin, and the water slowly starts to steam. They put the pot in the sink, and Lewis rolls up his sleeves to attack the dishes.

When Pawel heads for the stairs, Alaric and Chris follow. Pawel stops on the second stair, holds up one hand. "Alaric, stay downstairs. I can guarantee this is going to go past your comfort level. Chris, if you don't mind coming with me, I don't want to be alone with Nikita." He has a rueful expression. "This is an extenuating circumstance, but I'm still a professor, and she's a student, and I want to make sure everyone feels safe. Particularly because she can't wake up to give consent."

"I want more food," Conor announces from the living room. Chris shrugs and heads up the stairs with Pawel while Alaric follows Conor into the kitchen.

Lewis has his sleeves rolled up and is elbow-deep in the dishwater, scrubbing out most of the dishes from breakfast. "Put them on the counter," he says distractedly.

Conor takes a moment to consider Lewis, looking up at him with pursed lips. "I'm not done eating yet," he announces. "Alaric and me are going to finish everything up. It'll be easier to do the dishes."

Lewis glances over. "While I'm grateful to your dad for heating up the water, let me just say that if you could magic this place clean in general, I wouldn't mind."

"Sorry, nope." Conor splits the last two slices of bread between his and Alaric's plates, then finishes off the last of the cream cheese without an apology. He waits for Alaric to get more eggs before he takes the last of those as well, and solemnly splits the last hamburger between them. Conor wraps the slice around his half burger and eggs, shoves it in his mouth. "If I could use magic to clean, Dad would be happy because my room would be clean," he says while chewing. "It really sucks that we don't have TV, and my tablet is dead. I'm bored."

Alaric is pretty sure that's his cue. On the other hand, when Lewis huffs and twists off the water, toweling his hands dry and tossing the towel on the table, Alaric isn't going to argue if he wants to take over. Lewis motions for both of them to follow him into the living room and opens a cabinet to the left of the fake fireplace.

"Games," Lewis says. "Some more kid-friendly than others." Lewis crouches down, starts pulling things out and sorting them into two piles— one goes on the floor next to his feet, the other handed to Alaric and Conor. "I won't play Monopoly, just so you know, and I refuse to get in trouble for beating a kid at Scrabble. It's not your fault you don't have a vocabulary yet."

"My dad's a professor," Conor says. "My vocabulary's awesome. I can spell antidisestablishmentarianism."

"Do you know what it means?" Lewis pauses, a box in his hands held out toward Conor.

"It means people got pissed off when church and state were separated," Conor says easily. "Are those poker chips? Can we play poker?"

"I'm pretty sure Pawel will lower my grade if we gamble," Alaric mutters. "So no, we're not playing poker."

"But we can play Michigan Rummy." Lewis carries the box to the table. "It uses a poker hand but isn't poker, and no one's using money. We're just trying to collect chips, and most of it's chance."

It's not a game Alaric knows, but he quickly catches on to the rules. It gives him something to focus on other than Pawel upstairs with Nikita as first one hour passes, then another.

It's also a decent game, and he gets the feeling Corbin would love it. He wonders if it's always sold with a plastic game board, or if he could get something nice in wood. Maybe someone would make it for him.

Conor crows as he collects a huge pile of chips for finally managing to get out the 8-9-10 cards in one suit. The door opens upstairs, and Alaric twists, looking over at the stairs as Chris sits down at the top.

"She's awake," Chris says. "You can come up if you want, Alaric."

Chris smells overwhelmed, his scent muted by distance. Alaric pushes to his feet, shoves his chips at Lewis. "If you can play with two people, you'll need these to beat him," he says, indicated Conor with his thumb. "Kid has more luck than anyone should."

Everything smells like ozone when Alaric gets to the top of the stairs, the sharp scent nipping at his skin. He sidles a step closer to Chris, settling when Chris's hand falls at the center of his back. "I don't like it," Alaric mutters.

"It was bad enough that even I could feel it," Chris whispers back. "Like standing in a storm, waiting for lightning to strike."

They push open the door, and the scent is worse. Every hair on Alaric's body stands up, and he shudders, resisting taking a step back.

"Hey." Nikita sits cross-legged on the bed, hunched over, her hair a chaotic mess. "I'm really sorry about this. I mean, I thought coming over here would make things better."

"I don't think being in OPT made things worse, unless one of them is a Dreamwalker," Pawel says. He's lying on the floor, arms and legs spread, eyes closed. "The best guess I have is that somewhere way back in your Lineage is a Dreamwalker, and you're manifesting with a combined Talent."

"What?" Nikita's voice is barely a breath. She looks up, eyes wide, and Chris and Alaric bracket her, giving her something to lean on. She reaches for Alaric's hand, grabs on, and holds hard. "I'm not a Dreamwalker. I've never done that."

"Latent Dreamwalkers sometimes manifest when they're with other Dreamwalkers," Pawel says. "If you are, then someone lost track of you; they tend to keep meticulous records. Or there was an affair no one knew about or something. Or it's Emergent."

Nikita snorts. "I'm Lineage. We don't Emerge."

Pawel leverages himself up on one shoulder. "The one thing I've learned in the last ten years is that all the rules are changing. They've been changing. Things that were true remain true, but other things happen more. Faster. I can't say it's impossible to be both Lineage and Emergent at the same time, I can only say that we've never seen it before. With the number of legends that I've seen come true in the last few months, I can't discount anything, Nikita."

"But I don't even know what I'm dreaming!" she protests. "I thought Dreamwalkers knew. That it was real to them. But I don't remember *anything* when I wake up. I just go to sleep, and then the weather starts, so it's not really like I'm a Dreamwalker. I'm not dreaming."

"It's the best avenue we've got," Pawel says flatly. "Nikita, this can't happen again. If this storm came to you, then we have to head this off before you destroy the Northeast in a storm of the century. And if this is you—if this storm is actually the dream—then there are two of you. There's another active Dreamwalker somewhere on this campus right now, close enough to you that you're intertwining with them. Something's going wrong, and the best way I can come up with to work on that theory is to have you work with another Lineage Dreamwalker. One who doesn't show the Talent and can teach you what you need to know to control the dreams."

"Do we need to find the other Dreamwalker on campus?" Chris asks quietly. "Because it's not fair if Nikita has to leave to fix this and can't come back."

"Wait, who said anything about leaving?" Nikita yells. "I'm not going anywhere."

"There might be a way around that." Pawel inhales slowly. "I've been working on ways of suppressing magic—just so we can keep Conor in check when he's having an explosive day. Nikita, if you're willing to stay at my place tonight, we'll see if we can get your Talent bound for the night at least. This isn't a requirement—I can do it anywhere. But if I'm going to maintain the ritual, I'll need to be there. You can have anyone else stay as well, to make you comfortable."

Chris's phone chimes, and he glances at it. "They've closed campus tomorrow and wish everyone safe travels once the roads are clear," he reads.

Nikita slumps forward, head in her hands. "This isn't real," she mutters. "This isn't happening."

"That's how it usually begins," Pawel says quietly. "You're not insane, Nikita. We can fix this. But we need to get started, and we need to make sure that you're safe, and that everyone else is safe, as well."

"Yeah," she mumbles. "I know. I get it. And yeah, I'll stay at your place. It's okay. I'm just going to walk back to my dorm to get some more clothes first. And a better jacket. Alaric?"

He has a sister, and he has Corbin; that's a statement he knows how to read. "I'll come with you. Do you want Chris and me to stay at Pawel's with you tonight?"

She's silent for a long moment, body bowed, before she shakes her head. "Come over tomorrow. Hopefully we'll get power back. Do you have heat?"

"Fireplace," Pawel says. "Wood stove, plenty of wood. Conor likes to burn things."

A hint of amusement flickers in her scent. "Okay then," she agrees. "That's what we'll do." She sits up, puts her arms around Alaric, and hugs him hard. "Thanks for trying."

"We'll figure it out," Alaric says, and does his best to make it sound like he believes it, because right now it feels like everything's just getting more out of control.

65

POWER IS BACK by the time they wake up on Monday morning. Alaric can hear the shower running down the hall and assumes Lewis has already claimed it. By the time he and Chris manage to get their showers in and everyone's eaten breakfast, more of the OPT brothers are trickling in.

Without classes, it's chaotic in the house, everyone shouting and enjoying the day off. When Dax arrives, Chris and Alaric shove him back out of the house and start rounding people up. Alaric texts Drea and tells her to have Amy drop her off at Pawel's house. Mac's already heading there on her own, and Rory and Thorne's lanky dad Daniel offers a ride to the rest of them.

The roads are fine, the ice melting off the trees. The cool fall day rises above freezing, almost balmy in the aftermath of the storm. Nikita meets them at the door with Conor when they arrive, and they send Daniel off and head inside. Corbin's there, waiting with Drea, and they both pounce on Alaric, rubbing his cheek with theirs as if to claim him.

"Dad was an asshole for the rest of the weekend," Drea says quietly. "Mom's worried about you."

"I'm okay. I'll go home for Christmas." Alaric's not ready to walk away yet, although he can see it coming. He wonders if that's the split Alex was talking about, then wonders if she'd even know the answer if he asked her. "We were going through Orson's stuff, looking for more clues. Dad seems determined to go to war with the Mages. We need to prove to him that that isn't the right answer."

There's a knock at the door, and Conor runs to answer, grabbing his jacket on the way. "I'm going to Alan's!" he yells out, and a moment later the door slams as Pawel comes downstairs.

"I'm assuming that was Emily and not a random kidnapper," Pawel says dryly, looking at the door. "My son's best friend's mother," he clarifies. "She takes Conor often. More frequently than I deserve, really." He drops into one of the chairs, slumps back. With his hair a mess and the dark circles under his eyes, he barely looks older than the rest of them. "I figured we'd be better off without Conor here for this."

They all find space in the living room. Chris, Corbin, Alaric, Drea, and Rory manage to crowd together on the couch with Thorne sitting on the floor, leaning back against their legs. Dax sits in the second chair while Mac perches on the arm, and Nikita sits close to the coffee table, her arms folded atop the wood.

"I guess I should start the information sharing," Nikita says quietly. "So. I slept okay last night. Pawel did something to try to keep me from doing whatever in my sleep, so I didn't start up a storm again. But I'm exhausted, and he's worse because he had to keep it going all night, so this isn't exactly a workable solution."

"I contacted a Dreamwalker family I know, and they're coming here to meet with Nikita tomorrow," Pawel says. He has his hand across his face, his eyes closed as he stretches his legs out. Long fingers hide his expression. "We aren't sure that's what's going on, but it's the first, best angle to explore. This is a woman who hasn't manifested the Talent, but she knows how to work with Dreamwalkers who have, which Nikita might be. We don't want to risk her life or sanity just because we don't think it could be real."

Nikita makes a dissatisfied, pained sound, her head thumping forward against the coffee table.

Rory twitches. Pawel glances over.

"I can help," Rory says, raising his hand. "I can dampen her natural ability while she sleeps tonight, so at least you guys can get decent rest. We can probably work out a way that I can keep touching her while I sleep, too. It sounds like it's a better temporary solution than yours is."

"I should have thought of that," Pawel mutters.

Rory shrugs. "You know I don't like using it; it bothers people. So that's fine, I brought it up now, and we can work with it. I didn't realize it was this bad, or I would've offered before, Nik."

Her laugh is muffled, her head still down on the table. Her voice sounds like a muted echo. "Are you saying that if I'd crawled into your bed ages ago, this would've stopped?"

Rory leans forward, elbows on his knees. "You aren't exactly my type, so getting you in my bed wasn't something that really crossed my mind."

She looks up, smirks. "You aren't my type either, Rory, so don't worry. I get it. This is platonic. What is it?"

"My natural magical ability is to nullify Talent," Rory says quietly. "I can calm it. It should keep you from Dreamwalking, if that's what you're doing, and at the least you shouldn't be able to play with weather in your sleep."

Nikita nods her agreement. "Thanks."

"What does any of this have to do with Orson?" Corbin spreads his hands when they look at him. "What? We're all thinking it, aren't we? Orson died. The guy from VIT died. Shadows attacked Mac and Ric. And this." He gestures at Nikita. "Maybe these things aren't linked, fine, but the timing of all the weirdness seems to indicate we should think about it. Right?"

"I went to talk to Noah," Dax says. He clarifies, "The guy from VIT. He wasn't there."

Pawel frowns, leans forward. "Wasn't there? Or wasn't talking to you?"

"I didn't even get an itch," Dax tells him. "I know when there's a restless spirit around, and Noah's not restless. I went to his grave, and I went to the place he died—he wasn't in either place. So what happened either destroyed him completely, or he crossed over without any complaint. Either way, he wasn't around for me to talk to."

Pawel leans back, tapping a finger against his chin. "Darrik Malone's been found, and he's been cleared of the murder," he says slowly. "I went to talk to him, and he wasn't particularly interested in the conversation. Can't blame him—they incarcerated him for three nights, and the parents at his school called for him to be fired. He's back on even ground now, but he figures his chances of getting tenure are slim. The problem is, he has no idea what happened."

"Was he there?" Drea asks, and Pawel nods.

"He was there. It was a questioning ritual." When everyone looks at him curiously, Pawel elaborates. "There are many ways to invoke predictive Talent, and it's easiest when you have someone with that particular Talent around."

"Like Carolyn."

Pawel blinks at Drea, nods once. "Yes, like Carolyn. But apparently they wanted to ask questions without someone like her, so they did a questioning ritual. Darrik can't remember what he planned to ask. They had gotten as far as each putting their blood in, and the next thing he knew, he was waking up in a hotel in Albany with blood on his clothes. His own blood and unidentified blood—they tested it and it's not Lorraine's or Noah's. Darrik did mention darkness rising up, so it's definitely possible they were also attacked by Shadowwalkers."

"Also known as Deathstalkers, which could explain why Noah's nowhere around," Corbin says solemnly.

"But also Shadow*walkers*," Pawel emphasizes. "It's possible that Darrik was transported against his will to Albany and left there."

"It's also possible the unknown blood belonged to the Shadowwalker," Alaric says slowly. "Are the clothes still in evidence?" It's a lot of information to take in, but blood is something he knows what to do with. Scent is something he can use.

"Pretty sure he got everything back and has washed or destroyed it by now." Pawel looks over at him. "His boyfriend died. I don't think he'd want something around to remind him."

Chris's fingers trail across the back of Alaric's neck, and Corbin leans into him from the side. Alaric stops growling as soon as he realizes that he's the one making the noise, but the idea of what's happened still disturbs him. That something is stalking them, stealing those who are important.

"We were talking about how maybe it's Emergent Talent calling the Shadowwalkers," Alaric says gruffly. "Maybe it's the ritual, but that wouldn't explain why one came after me and Mac."

"That might have been because they know we're investigating," Drea points out.

"Or it could be a combination. Ritual is a strong magic, and it seems like in both cases, the rituals were ones that were a little different," Mac says. "I'm not a Mage, but if you're customizing something, you're putting something of yourself into it. Do we know how powerful the Mages involved were?"

Pawel shakes his head. "No, but we know that Nikita's power levels are very high right now. And Alaric…" He glances over, considers him. "Alaric Emerged, in his own way, that night, manifesting a form that he never had before."

" 'm not powerful," Alaric mutters. It's been a common theme throughout his life, that he's broken as a shapeshifter. Adding one more form doesn't change how broken he is.

"Clan follow one line," Chris says quietly. "Corbin's a bird. Drea's a mammal. You're a hound, a bear, a lizard, an eagle, and a dragon. You might not have as many forms, but that you're powerful could be argued because you cross between different types of animals, and one of your forms is legendary."

Alaric shivers, uncertain whether it's because of Chris's words or the way he leans in close, breath warm against Alaric's cheek. He never thought of it that way. "I—"

"I have an idea." Pawel blinks at them, stands up abruptly without apologizing for the interruption. "Thorne, Rory, let's talk about this. Dax, I can use you too, possibly. I need more information. We need some time to figure this out. There are going to be several pieces; we need to be safe. But we can do this."

He's already halfway out the door before Alaric manages to ask, "Do what?"

Pawel turns back, meets his gaze. "Trap the Shadowwalker."

66

CORBIN SHOULDERS HIS backpack, then slings a duffle over one shoulder. "Time for me to catch the bus."

Alaric is halfway to his feet when he pauses in an awkward crouch, hanging over the couch. Drea is by Corbin's side, her fingers wound with his, hands clasped palm to palm. He coughs uncertainly, sits back down.

Corbin frowns. "Aren't you going to walk with us to the stop? I barely saw you when you were home."

Alaric pushes to his feet, wavers until Drea rolls her eyes, a wave of fond irritation in her scent. Rory's already gone, following after Pawel, Thorne, and Dax. Mac's chatting with Chris and Nikita, and it's not like Alaric needs to stick around. Alaric puts his hand on Chris's shoulder, leans in. "Tell Rory I'll see him back at the room."

"Do you need anything from my place?" Chris asks. "Dax is probably going to be a while. I can get whatever you need and drop it back at your room."

There's a faint shiver at the casual familiarity. Alaric lets go, takes a step back as he shakes his head. "Nothing I need right away," he says. "I'll pick up whatever's still there after classes tomorrow. Tell Dax I'm sorry I didn't wash his sheets after borrowing his bed."

Nikita laughs softly. "It's not like you're the only one who crashed there," she points out. Her smile is sad, her scent thick with disappointment. "I'm not sure when I'll see my own bed again. I mean, it's not like I have the best roommates, but still, couch surfing was not in my plans."

"If you have to go with the Dreamwalker family tomorrow, make sure to let us know," Drea says. "We're going to worry."

"Yeah, well, I'm worried, too." Nikita shrugs. "There isn't much I can do right now. Maybe I'll be able to sleep tonight with Rory's help."

Oh. Right. "Are you crashing in our room, then?"

"I don't know." Nikita worries at her lower lip. "Would it bother you if I did? I mean, last night—"

"It's fine." Alaric doesn't like the way she smells, scent thickening with something unpleasant and upset. "Wherever. If I see you later, that's fine. You and Rory just let me know, okay?"

"Come on." Corbin claps his shoulder, shoves him toward the door. "If I don't catch the bus, I'm sticking around another hour, and I really do need to get back to VIT. No matter how much time I spend here, I don't plan on transferring to PHU."

"You're the one who decided to go to a different school. Could've made it easier on yourself." It's easy to fall into the familiarity of it as they head out the door. The warmth outside seems at odds with the chill of the day before. Everything glistens, wet with melting ice.

As they start walking, Corbin bumps Alaric's shoulder with his duffle, Drea walking on his other side. "You okay?"

Alaric's pretty sure what Corbin's trying to ask, but it isn't even the first thing on his mind right now. "Yeah," he rumbles with a one-shouldered shrug. "It's been kind of a busy few days. Nik's power going out of control was just one thing."

"You left abruptly," Drea says, tone careful and soft.

"It wasn't you," Alaric responds. "Dad and I argued again. I have this journal that Chris and I managed to get out of Orson's stuff. When Chris said we should go, I didn't want to stick around."

Drea's expression is soft. "I like Chris. He's a good friend. And he's not scared of our father."

"He's scared." Alaric knows he is. Chris has said as much, and besides, Alaric can smell it on him. "But he refuses to back down. He's determined to be there when I need a friend."

Corbin looks over at him, gaze narrowed and sharp. "Alaric."

Alaric feels the pointedness of his gaze, poking and prodding at him. He stops walking, and Corbin stops too, leaning in close to examine him. "What?" Alaric snaps.

Corbin raises an eyebrow, and Alaric's resolve crumbles.

"Fine," Alaric mutters. "We had sex."

"I'm not surprised." Corbin heads down the sidewalk a bit faster than before. "The two of you have been tilting at each other since I met him. I figured you were dating and hadn't told us yet."

"I don't want a boyfriend," Alaric says flatly. "I'm not dating Chris."

"What does dating mean to you?" Drea asks. She slides closer to Corbin, her arm across his back. "I mean it, Ric. Explain dating."

"It's romance," Alaric says, spreading his hands as if that's going to make sense of it for him. "It's 'I love you' and roses and being all—" He cuts off, waving his hand at Drea and Corbin. "Being linked. Affectionate. I don't know. It's just—more than I want. Or need."

"So this is a one-time thing?" Corbin asks, snorting when Alaric glances away without answering. "That's what I thought. Have you talked to Chris about this?"

Alaric gathers himself, fixes his expression into a glare for Corbin. "Yes. It's a one-time thing. That's all it has to be. It doesn't need to be anything else, and Chris is fine with it." That's what Chris said, but Alaric isn't sure he believes him. He knows Chris's brain works differently than his own. On the other hand, he knows Chris understands where he's coming from. He grumbles his frustration under his breath.

"You could try talking about it again, if you're not sure," Corbin says gently.

"As long as your friendship is fine, you're fine." Drea grabs the duffle off of Corbin's shoulder. "Your bus is arriving soon, and you're being slow."

"Sounds like you want to get rid of me," Corbin teases, and Drea slides in close, cradles his head as she kisses him.

"I'd keep you, but you keep pointing out that you go to a different school," she reminds him, "and I don't think Alaric actually wants his sex life deconstructed, no matter how well-meaning you think you are. He's going to be fine, and Chris is going to be fine, and even if they're not, you poking at the cracks is only going to make things worse."

Corbin licks his lips, looks away as she steps back.

Drea huffs. "Fine. You're both overprotective assholes. Get it out of your system. I'll make sure the bus doesn't leave without Corbin." She turns on her heel, walks toward the bus station where a few others are waiting with bags.

"She's not actually angry at us," Corbin says, glancing at Alaric.

Alaric knows his twin, and he knows that it's all for show, her way of saying "just talk already" without saying that she expects either of them to open up emotionally. He inhales, shoves his hands into his pockets, shoulders hunching forward.

"How about us?" Corbin asks softly, swaying closer until he can nudge Alaric's shoulder. "Are we okay?"

It's impossible to avoid the topic this time. "Do you want me to tell you that if you hurt her, I'll bury your bones in a place where not even Clan will find you?" Alaric mutters. "Pretty sure you already know that."

"Pretty sure she's already as important to me as she is to you," Corbin responds. "Ric, we all grew up together. She's like—she's not a sister. That would be weird. But she's already more than anyone else would be. What-ever's between us, we're still Clan. We're still family."

"You're my right hand," Alaric says solemnly. "She's my sister. I can't be anything without you. Both of you. And I definitely can't lead without you. So don't fuck this up, Corbin."

"Don't plan on it, dude." Corbin pats his chest, then yanks Alaric in for a hug. "Honestly, feels like this is where I've always been heading," he says quietly. "Don't let her know that. She'll never let me live it down."

" 's exactly why I should tell her." Alaric laughs, rubs his cheek against Corbin's, then hugs him harder again, holding on several beats too long. "If I'm honest, if you're going to be with someone, Drea's pretty much perfect. Same for her with you." He steps back, shrugs. "Simplifies things, 'cause I'm already keeping you both. Don't have to worry about more people."

"Ric, you keep saying you hate people, but I'm beginning to think that's a lie," Corbin says, patting his chest again. "You have an entire community here, one you've found all on your own. Luckily, it turns out I like them."

It's already impossible to imagine a life without Rory and Thorne, with-out Chris being solidly there. Without Dax. Even without people like Nik and Nate and Sera and Pat, along with everyone else who seems to cycle through Alaric's daily life. He huffs softly. "Yeah. Well, so do I. Guess I'm keeping them."

"Corbin! Bus is here!" Drea calls out.

The stench of diesel fuel gives Alaric a headache as the bus idles nearby. He wrinkles his nose, and Corbin laughs at his expression. "We'll figure it out," Corbin says. "Let me know what happens. I want to be a part of this, however it shakes out. Count me in, okay?"

"Okay," Alaric agrees, even though he has no idea how they're going to do this. If it isn't safe for Corbin and Drea, he has no problem leaving them out of it. But that's something to figure out once they actually have a plan.

67

RORY RETURNS TO the room late, long after dinner. When Alaric asks if he's hungry, he waves off the question with a comment of "Pizza" before sitting down at the one desk, hunched over a pile of paper, scribbling notes with an expression Alaric recognizes from when Rory's composing.

Except this time, instead of a guitar or keyboard, Rory's using detailed notes and symbols that make Alaric vaguely uncomfortable.

"So," Alaric asks slowly, "does that mean there's a plan?"

"There's a plan for a plan," Rory says, still focused on what he's writing. "We're working on a plan. There's a skeleton." He glances up, looks at Alaric. "You'll be involved."

"Kind of figured I would be." Despite the discomfort, Alaric knows this is something that he needs to do. "Can you tell me about it?"

Rory holds up a finger, keeps scribbling with his left hand. Alaric tries to get comfortable, but he can't sit still, not now. He starts pacing, stopping only when Rory glares at him.

"Stop worrying and let me finish this thought," Rory grumbles, and returns to what he's doing.

Alaric leans against the bed, inhales deeply to try to force calm through his body. He leans forward slightly as Rory's writing slows, then back again when he spots the sigils on the paper.

Finally Rory sets the pen down, rubs at the bridge of his nose. "Sorry. I just…I didn't want to lose that thought."

"Can you tell me anything about it?" Alaric asks again, and Rory makes a face.

"Not that would make sense, no. I mean, not much." Rory turns the chair to face Alaric, crosses his arms, and leans back with his long legs stretched out. "We're pretty sure the Shadowwalker is being summoned by high-level, unique magic. Like Orson's ritual. And Nik's dreams. And your dragon." Rory huffs. "Speaking of Nik, the Dreamwalker managed to get here today. Evelyn's actually the daughter of an active Dreamwalker, and her own son manifested the Talent as well, so she's got experience in dealing with experienced and inexperienced Dreamwalkers. She and Nik talked for a long while, and Nik decided to sleep on her own with Evelyn watching over her instead of me trying to keep her from using her Talent. It'll probably help her learn more about whatever's going on, and besides, neither of us know each other well enough to feel really comfortable climbing into bed together."

"Think she's safe?" They aren't close, not like Alaric's close to Rory or Chris, but Nikita's one of his floormates, and he gets along with her. She's a member of the larger friend group he's become a part of, and he worries for her safety.

"It seems like Evelyn knows what she's doing." Rory reaches back, grabs the paper, and stares down at it, touching the symbols on the page. "More than we do, anyway. At least she has experience with the concept, and if that's what Nik's doing, Evelyn'll be able to identify it. And if Nik isn't Dreamwalking, we'll know by tomorrow, hopefully."

"So." Alaric nods at the paper because he knows Rory is avoiding it. "The plan?"

"Like I said, we don't have much," Rory admits. "We have the lynchpins. The hard part is designing both the ritual and the trap around it."

Alaric arches one eyebrow, waits.

"You," Rory admits. "Mac, Pawel, me. Pawel and I can do the ritual, and you're the bait. We're hoping that I can nullify its ability to walk through shadows. And Mac's our failsafe. Because I really think we need one."

"She might also be bait. We don't have any proof that I'm the one it was after when it attacked us," Alaric points out.

Rory leans forward, elbows on his knees. "I think if it was going to attack her, it would've done it back when she Emerged. Her Talent is stable. She's not changing, not evolving. Nik is. You are. Which is…really interesting," he admits reluctantly. "We had a whole long discussion about it, how Talent can continue to evolve over time, and how Emergents don't always Emerge on their own, and how Talent interacts. Dax says his family believes that sometimes Emergent Talents stay dormant until the right conditions are met, which might be what's happening."

"I wasn't going to be a dragon until I was here," Alaric says, and it makes sense when he says that. "I needed to be around people who weren't Clan. People who would push me."

"Your skin needed to feel Talent that was different to call the legend out from where it was hiding, yes," Rory says. "The thing is, we think the Shadowwalker is drawn to that. Which means we have to focus on getting you to manifest the dragon."

"That would be easier if I could do it on demand."

Rory makes a face. "Yes. So unless you figure out how to do that soon, we're going to work on a ritual to force it out." Alaric shudders. "I didn't think you'd like it." Rory sets the papers down, shoves them under a text-book at the back of the desk. "If we come up with something else, we'll do that, but right now it's the best idea we have."

"I get it." And Alaric does. He understands the need, and he won't say no even though he hates the idea. "I just don't want Corbin or Drea anywhere involved with this. Or Chris. They need to be safe."

"We're trying to keep it very focused," Rory says softly. "Dax is helping with the design, and so's Thorne, but when everything happens, we don't want them there either. It'll be too easy for something to go wrong."

Alaric can't help but feel it'll be his fault if something goes wrong. This all started because Orson died. The Shadowwalker is drawn to campus because of him. "Yeah." He pushes away from the bed, reaches to grab his toiletry kit. "You're going to keep working on that, right?"

Rory's gaze strays to the papers, then to the beds. "Is it going to keep you from sleeping? Because I really should."

"I'm not going to enjoy it, but yeah, you work on it," Alaric says gruffly. "I'm going to get ready for bed."

He changes into sweats and a T-shirt, and by the time he walks down to the bathroom, Rory is already engrossed in his notes again, muttering under his breath.

Alaric takes as much time in the bathroom as he can. He showers before bed just to feel the water running over his head, to let his body go loose and calm under the heat. He stands there and lets it beat down on him, eyes closed, inhaling as deeply as he can.

The red heat of his skin fades quickly as he dries off, brushes his teeth with a towel wrapped around him. He nods to Jackson when he comes in, turns when Pat yells out about the stuff Alaric left by the shower. It only takes a moment to dress and gather his things up while Pat mutters something about casual nudity.

Alaric processes the words and emotion after Pat's already under the water: *some people are so comfortable with casual nudity that they forget not everyone is.*

Alaric presses his lips together, leans close enough to the shower that he'll be heard, but not so close he's intruding on Pat's privacy. "Sorry," he calls out. "Guess I'm still getting used to the fact that not everybody's like Clan."

The water twists off, and Pat calls back, "What was that?" After Alaric repeats himself, there's silence for a long moment. "It's okay," Pat finally says. "I'm still getting used to sharing space with a bunch of other guys. You're not a bad guy, Alaric, even if I'd rather not see you drop your towel in plain sight."

The water turns back on, and Alaric takes that as a sign he's not supposed to answer. When he turns to leave, Jackson is leaning against the sink, watching him.

"You okay?" Jackson asks. "You seem quieter than usual tonight."

Alaric snorts, relieved when there's no puff of smoke in the air around him. " 'm fine," he lies, because he will be. Eventually.

Rory's in his own bed when Alaric makes it back to the room, lying on his stomach, still scribbling furiously. He has headphones in, music loud enough that Alaric can hear the sound around the earbuds. Alaric hangs up his towel, shoves his things out of the way, and climbs into his own bed. It's one of those nights where he wants to close everything out, so he puts his own headphones on to cancel out the ambient sound, plugs in his phone, and starts up the music.

He sets the phone down and lies back, eyes closed and arms crossed. He can't find peace or sleep, fidgeting on the bed and rolling over, trying to find a comfortable space where there is none. His phone vibrates, the music skipping in his ears with the notification.

If you're still up, stop thinking so loudly and get some sleep.

Alaric smiles at the text from Chris. *Can't get comfortable. Rory's working on a ritual and it makes my skin itch.*

As long as you're not lying there worrying about other things.

Alaric bites his lip, touches the screen. *I wasn't,* he types. *Should I be worrying about things? Did we fuck everything up?*

Dots appear and disappear before the response comes again. *Nothing's fucked up. We're friends, right?*

You're the kind of guy who likes things to be more than friends.

That's the part that Alaric can't let go of. He knows how much Thorne hurt Chris, and he doesn't want to be that person. He gives a shit about Chris. They're friends, and he doesn't want to lose that.

I'm okay. The text comes through on its own, just those two words. A moment later, dots appear. *And we're okay. And if it makes you uncomfortable, we won't do it again. Don't think about it if you don't want to think about it. It can only be that once.*

This is so fucking complicated. Alaric has no idea how to deal with this, how to put anything into words. *It was good. I liked it,* he admits. *But you know that.*

A picture comes through of Chris lying in bed, laughing. *Yeah. You made that pretty obvious at the time. And if you do decide you want to blow off steam again, I'm open to it.* The words stop, replaced by dots that appear and disappear several times without Chris sending another text.

What. Alaric licks his lips, waits.

If we do it again—if we keep doing it—there's one thing I'd want.

Alaric feels the bottom drop out of his stomach. *What.*

I'm not asking for high romance. I know that's not you. But if we're having sex, I'd rather that you not do it with someone else, too.

Alaric thinks back to how it felt to watch Thorne flirt with other people. That part wasn't what bothered him, it was knowing that if Thorne was with them, then he wasn't with Alaric right then. Alaric frowns, tries to figure out the right way to explain it, and shrugs to himself. *I'd want that too*, he finally says, even though that doesn't make it clear.

Don't let it get under your skin, Chris sends. *If you need something, let me know. We can talk more after everything's done. We've still got the Shadow-walker to deal with.*

And finals. He can almost hear Chris's laugh.

And finals, Chris echoes. *We'll talk after the chaos is done.*

Alaric sends back one final *Yeah*, then sets the phone aside. He rolls over and shoves his hands under the pillow, letting the pressure of his head weigh them down. When he closes his eyes, he thinks of the comfort of having someone else in his bed, of that anchoring weight. And he's finally able to shake off the prickling of Rory's work and fall asleep.

Excerpt from *When Magic Entered the World: Interviews With Lineage Talent*, by Pawel Szczek, © 2009, new forward © 2014

I grew up believing in magic.

It was almost a game between my mother and me, when I was very small. She told me about the faeries that lived in our backyard, and I'd go out hunting for them. We pretended to light fires with our fingertips and to read minds. When she died, I thought the magic was gone from the world, and I was desperate to hold onto it. I read everything I could on ritual, on paganism, on every possible belief in magic I could find.

I arrived at Pine Hills University steeped in the belief that the truth was hidden somewhere in the myth I'd read, that it was written between the lines of the stories people told. I declared a major in classics, focusing on mythology, and a minor in sociology.

I graduated, eventually, with the first PhD in magical studies.

I Emerged my freshman year, around the same time as Kenzie Davis. I discovered that magic *was* real, and that I was an Emergent Mage. I learned that there were people who already knew everything there was to know—about themselves, but not about other Talent. And I decided that someone needed to learn it all, to bring that information together. To create a new field of study, and to understand the truths of the world around us.

This collection of interviews was the result of my first attempt to learn everything that I could. I met with Mages, Clan, and other Lineage Talent. I searched out rumors to determine whether they were real. I cataloged everything I could find and made notes about the differences between communities.

Over the five years since this thesis was published as my first textbook, I have learned one important thing about magical studies: no matter how much we learn, it will never be everything. Ritual changes. Magic changes. Talent changes. Every year, every month, every day...we need to keep our eyes open, and our hearts wide, and our minds unobstructed by preconceived notions.

When Kenzie Davis Emerged, the entire world discovered what I had always suspected, perhaps had known in my heart: magic is real.

It exists, and we must learn how to live with it. Whether Lineage or Emergent, whether Talented or not. We coexist. We inhabit this same world. And we must never stop learning about each other.

DENOUEMENT

68

WAITING FOR THE ritual is the worst part.

Nikita returns to the dorm three days after the ice storm. Alaric manages to find out from Pels that she's fine but doesn't get to talk to her. They're all too busy trying to get through the final few weeks of the semester, with papers and projects looming and finals coming right after that.

Alaric feels as if he should be stressed, should be ready to jump out of his skin, but there's no time. Instead, he goes through the motions, focusing on working hard at taekwondo practice and getting his essays done for magical studies. Eating with groups, then everyone dispersing to their own classes. When Alaric goes to OPT, he falls asleep on the couch in the middle of a party, the noise crashing around him. But it's easier to be there than in his dorm room.

The ritual scrapes at his skin even when Rory's just writing it down, making notes and marking runes on paper. Alaric sleeps fitfully; Rory simply doesn't sleep enough. There are nights when Rory doesn't come home, staying at Pawel's with Thorne and Dax while they dig through notes and try to come up with a way to do what needs to be done. Alaric doesn't sleep then, either, his mind spinning with worry over Rory's wellbeing.

When Rory finally comes home on Friday morning and says, "It's done," Alaric doesn't know whether to be relieved or anxious. Rory climbs into his bed and falls asleep.

Alaric doesn't ask questions, doesn't bring it up. Doesn't talk about it around anyone else, wanting to keep everyone as far away from it as he can. When Corbin and Drea ask for details, Alaric puts them off. He can't outright lie to them, but he can defer.

And when the time is set, when he knows when everything will happen, he avoids them altogether.

He has dinner at OPT that Saturday night, sits through a meeting with his fraternity brothers, then corners Chris at the end.

"Can you give me a ride to Pawel's place?"

Chris's jaw goes tight, his scent sour. He motions at the door, and Alaric heads outside first. There's noise from inside, music starting. Classes are over, and everyone is studying for exams that will begin on Wednesday; Saturday's a good day to let off steam for the evening.

Chris closes the door, follows Alaric down the steps. "You could walk to Pawel's place," he says, voice low.

"I know." Alaric shrugs one shoulder. "Figured you'd rather drive me. But you can't stay. I don't even know where we're doing this—Pawel's in charge. All I know is that we don't want to be on campus."

"How dangerous is it?" Chris bumps Alaric, nudging him toward where the car is parked. "How worried should I be?"

"Coaches would be pissed off if I fucked up now," Alaric grumbles, trying to make light of it. "Nothing's going to happen."

"If you believed that, you wouldn't be keeping everyone so far away from this." Chris pushes Alaric back against the car, traps him there with his hands on either side of Alaric's shoulders. "If you don't think the plan is ready, don't do it. No one else has died. We have time."

"We don't have time—what if we wait and someone else dies?" Alaric's been thinking about it for the last two weeks, worried that another person he cares about is going to be stolen by the Shadows. This is their only option, and they have to do something.

"Fuck." Chris has a palm against Alaric's face, thumb light against his lip. "Don't fuck this up, Ric."

"Not planning on it." Alaric goes with it when Chris presses close, rests his entire body against Alaric's like a heavy blanket. Chris kisses like he's going to drown in Alaric, or perhaps like he expects Alaric to drown in him. Alaric sinks into it, forgets what he's about to do, until the catcall of someone walking by reminds him where they are. He nudges Chris back, licks his lips. "I need to get over there."

"Get in."

The ride is silent, and Chris drops him off without fanfare. From the set of his jaw, the tension in his shoulders, Alaric expects to smell anger. Instead he smells resolve and concern. Fear.

"I'll be fine." Alaric leans on the open window, holding onto the car so Chris can't drive off immediately. "Might not be back tonight, but I'll text you when it's all done."

"Call me," Chris says quietly, and Alaric nods before he lets the car go.

Rory leans against the doorway of Pawel's house, arms crossed, lanky legs crossed at the ankles. He raises one eyebrow, and Alaric grunts rather than offer an explanation. "Where are we doing this?" Alaric asks.

Rory's breath hisses out; he jerks a shoulder toward the house. "Here. Pawel said he can control the environment better if he's in his own warded space. Also, he's got a privacy fence around the backyard, and there's enough room for you to go all dragon. We think." He unfolds himself, knocks into Alaric as Alaric passes by. "Mac and Pawel are waiting out back. We've got barely enough light to get started, then it'll become dark enough for the plan to work."

"Did you tell anyone it's tonight?" Alaric asks, voice low.

Rory ducks his head, one quick nod. "Thorne knows. He promised not to tell Mom and Dad and Dad until it's too late for them to get here to try to stop me. Mom's going to be pissed as hell. She's already worried after what's been happening, but she hasn't tried to stop us so far. This, though? She'd think this is suicide."

Alaric laughs dryly. "Great. That's a fantastic recommendation for the plan, Rory."

"How about you?" Rory leads the way through the house, straight into the kitchen, and pushes open the back door. It seems empty, smells dark and dank, like an old basement. Alaric tunes his senses for any sign of Conor, but other than the constant prickling of ozone that seems to linger in the Szczek household, there's nothing.

"Haven't talked to Drea and Corbin since you came back yesterday morning," Alaric admits. "Chris knows, though."

A low snort of laughter, punctuated by the bang of the door behind them as they step out. "Figured," Rory says. "Scale of one to ten, how pissed off is he at you for being an idiot?"

"He isn't," Alaric says quietly. "He's scared. So am I."

"So am I," Pawel says, and that's not reassuring. "We're chasing a legend, something that half the magical world doesn't believe exists. We're chasing something that, if it does exist, is known for stealing people away."

"Something that literally has death in its name, we get it," Mac says, leaning back in a camp chair, her feet kicked up on the edge of a cold fire pit. "This is war, Pawel, and war sucks. I know that, and I've known it for a long time. If I'm going to be your weapon, let's get this over with before I reconsider."

There's a darkness to her tone that Alaric hasn't heard before, a rank edge to her scent, sweet like burning flesh. Her skin is cast gray in the twilight, her eyes dark. She's dressed in black, her hair pulled back from her face with a thick headband but left natural otherwise. When she pushes to her feet, she hesitates, grabs the arm of the chair to catch her balance. It takes her a few steps before she moves with her usual grace.

When she reaches Alaric and Rory, she drags them both in, her arms around them, head dropped against Alaric's chest. "Don't die. Okay? Just, don't die."

"That's the point of all this preparation," Rory says quietly, his hand curled around the back of her head. "So none of us die."

"And so no one else dies," Alaric adds.

Pawel clears his throat, and Mac steps back, lips pursed as she looks at him. "We need to get started before it gets so dark we can't see," Pawel says quietly. "We need some tactical advantage."

"Do I get to know what the plan is?" Alaric asks, because he has a feeling he's the only one who's been left in ignorance.

"You're bait," Mac says dryly, "and the weaponized tank. I'm the rescue crew. Rory's the water we dump on the fire. Pawel pulls the trigger."

"Not quite how I would've put it, Mac, but it's close." Pawel motions for Alaric to step away from the house, moving into the more open area of the yard past the fire pit and patio. "We don't know enough about the Shadow-walkers or Deathstalkers," he admits, "but we do know that magic—high power, unique ritual or Talent—seems to summon the ones that attacked you. And we know they move in the darkness. We have worked to develop a ritual that should, if things go as planned, slip the dragon from your skin."

"So both a new ritual and my dragon," Alaric mutters. "And all your power."

"And all my power," Pawel echoes. "You aren't the only bait, Alaric. We've done what we can to overload this plan as much as possible, so we can hope for success. We need to lure the Shadowwalker here so we can trap it."

"What do we do with it then?"

Pawel's gaze narrows. "What do you want to do with it?"

Rip its throat out. Devour it while it screams and regrets that it ever had anything to do with... Alaric deflates before he finishes the thought. He shakes his head. "Revenge," he says slowly. "But that's not killing it. Do you think you can make it safe for us to transport it, if we catch it?"

"Catching it is the hardest part," Pawel says. "If we can trap it, I'm reasonably certain that we can continue to use the same methods for keeping it trapped."

Alaric nods sharply. "Then I know what we're going to do." There's no point in going over it. If they capture it, good. He'll deliver it appropriately. If not, they'll need a new plan, and hopefully a war won't start while they're coming up with one.

"Come here." Mac sinks to sit on the ground, pats the space next to her. "I trust you not to hurt me when you become a dragon. You didn't last time."

"I'm still me," Alaric protests, even though it's half a lie. He doesn't remember a thing from the last time the form came out. On the other hand, he doesn't remember what the bear did to Marks, either; everything he knows is put together from watching the tape after. His mouth thins, shoulders hunch. "Pretty sure I'm still me."

She leans her shoulder into his. "Take a good sniff and file it in the part of your brain that remembers *friend* has this scent."

He dutifully inhales even though he already knows Mac, already has her scent tucked away with the sound of her heart.

Pawel and Rory stand back, fire lighting in the pit with a *whoosh*. Flames make the shadows flicker, coming alive in playful dances around the edge of the yard. Alaric blinks at them, tries to makes sense of them and search for meaning, while the rise of magic pricks against his skin.

Mac shivers, pulls away. She twists around to watch Pawel and Rory, but Alaric can't do it. He sits with his back resolutely toward them, spine hunched, arms around his legs as he keeps his knees drawn to his chest. The magic plays over his skin, skips across the exposed spaces, sparks against him. He blinks, exhales a rough cloud of smoke.

Mac shudders again, pushes to her feet. Thick, sour anxiety rises in the air, and she makes a sound under her breath. She twists behind him, her fingers brushing against his hair before she pulls back quickly. "Fuck," she whispers.

"You okay, Mac?" Pawel's voice is tight, concerned. Alaric feels the pause in the magic, growls softly.

"I'm fine," she snaps. "Keep going. If I'm not fine, I won't be here. You know that."

Alaric inhales, choking on the thickness of magic in the air. He exhales in a rough cough, and there's a spurt of flames that has him scrambling up, hands and feet spread as he crouches.

"Again," Pawel murmurs, and the magic shifts, wrapping around Alaric and slipping under his skin.

The dragon roars, exploding outward with a thunderous cry, wings flapping.

The shadows roil, and Mac disappears. She reappears at the far end of the yard, diving into the shadows that push toward Alaric. She reaches for something, but it's gone, moving in a thick line, then disappearing before it reaches the light. Mac disappears again.

Alaric roars once more, not sure what to do. Magic itches in his nose: ozone from Pawel and Rory, but also a different scent, one he recognizes from the traces lingering around Orson's belongings.

This. This creature.

It was there when Orson died.

He flaps his wings, and Rory shouts, but Alaric can't hear the words.

He dives into the darkness, sweeping with claws, searching for solidity. Mac taps his shoulder, and Alaric spins, feels something brush against his spine. He swats at it, and they dance as Alaric chases the Shadow and Mac bounces around them.

Alaric stops when there's something in the darkness hanging in front of him. A face, two eyes burning as they peer at him. A smile sharp and pleased, scent bright.

Mac wraps her arms around the Shadow from behind and wrenches. They both disappear.

"Fuck, not on top of me!" Rory yells out. "It's gone. Mac!"

Alaric dives at them both, feels something grab his neck. He growls angrily, a gout of flame bursting forth.

"Watch it!" Pawel snaps, and Alaric rolls in the air, wings flapping, the air putting the fire pit out with a heavy *whoosh*.

Snapping around, Alaric tries to loosen the grip of the thing. It tightens across his throat; he knows that if he were human right now, he'd be losing consciousness. He spots Mac, flies toward her as she blinks out of existence. Her weight settles on his back, pressing the thing down against him. "Get us back to Rory!" she shouts.

Why doesn't she teleport? There's no time to argue as he twists in mid-air and flies back to Rory, landing on the ground and rolling as Mac flies free. Rory lands on Alaric, and Alaric feels the dragon slip away. By the time Rory reaches past his shoulder, Alaric is nothing but human, darkness wrapped around his throat and squeezing tightly. He grunts, tries to change, but with Rory flattened against him, magic at full power, there's nothing he can do.

There are bright spots of light at the corners of his eyes; he squeezes them shut, tries to gasp in a breath. "Fuck." The word is a low rasp, barely audible.

"I've got you." Mac's fingers wrap around his wrist. He feels her intake of breath, smells the resolve as she steels herself, and a moment later they're ten feet away, watching Rory fall on top of the darkness, straddle it, and hold it down.

Alaric can breathe, but the stench of ozone in the air strangles him. He coughs, turns his head, and closes his eyes. Pawel chants, the magic intensifying, wrapping around that corner of the yard while Alaric shrinks away.

"Do you need me to get you out of here?" Mac asks, and Alaric shakes his head.

"I'm not leaving them alone with it," he rasps, coughs again to clear his throat.

"I think we've got it." Rory's voice is strained. "As long as I don't let go, I think we've got it."

There's a low laugh, sound reverberating in the darkness. It almost looks human where Rory's wrapped around it, vaguely feminine features set into writhing shadow.

Rory's expression twists wry. "It's not easy to hold onto."

"I've bound it. I'm not sure how long my spell will last, and I think that whatever plan you have, Alaric, we'd better do it now." Pawel's scent wavers, thickens again like sparks around a fire.

"Give Mac your keys," Alaric says, "and let's get in the car. We're taking it to Haverhill."

It's disturbing the way the Shadow laughs at his words, as if Alaric hasn't managed to surprise it at all.

69

THEOBALD MEETS THEM at the turn off from the main road onto Clan land. His wolf is huge, back arched and feet spread as it growls, blocking the road. Sharp teeth are bared in a snarl, and Alaric tumbles out of the back of Pawel's SUV while it's still moving.

Alaric's bear emerges before he fully gains his footing, lumbering forward. There's a screech as the emergency brake pulls the SUV to a stop, and then Mac is right next to him, one hand on his front limb.

"Ric," she says, and he hesitates, then roars.

Theobald answers with a howl of anger.

"We have something in the car and two very exhausted Mages," Mac says quietly. "Nothing's going to get better if you rip each other's throats out."

Theobald's attention shifts to her, nostrils flaring as he inhales deeply. The growl drops low in his throat; Mac stands her ground despite the thickness of fear in her scent.

Alaric forces the bear back, comes back to humanity with hands in fists tight at his sides and Mac's fingers gripping his forearm. "You wanted an answer," he says, voice low and rough.

Theobald's change is quick, becoming human in a blink. He stands with his arms crossed, eyes glinting yellow in the moonlight. "I can smell the answer. Get the Mages out of here."

Alaric shakes his head, steps forward into Theobald's space. "The Mages aren't the problem. They're the ones keeping that thing in the car from attacking you. Or any of us. That thing killed Orson, or something like it did. You wanted an answer, so I brought one. You need the Mages if you want a chance to talk to it."

Theobald pushes Alaric out of the way, stalks to the car, and yanks the door open. He looks into the backseat, where Rory and Pawel have their hands on the writhing Shadow. The Shadow grins at Theobald, teeth shining sharp within the darkness, and laughs softly.

"What is this?"

"Shadowwalker," Alaric says, at the same time as Pawel bites out "Deathstalker," from between gritted teeth.

"Impossible."

"Not impossible," Pawel says. "Just highly improbable. Legends have to come from somewhere."

"If you're going to question this, I'd really appreciate it if we could do it soon," Rory says softly. "I'm tired."

"Just let go," the Shadow hisses. "I'll only take your soul."

"Also called Soulstealers," Pawel comments as Theobald takes a step back.

"The Berman homestead," Theobald snaps, falling back into wolf form. He barks once, then lopes away, pausing and snarling when the SUV doesn't immediately start to move.

"Put it in all-wheel drive," Alaric says quietly when Mac's back in the driver's seat. She switches it as they start up, following Theobald down the road.

"So many people," the Shadow whispers. "I can taste them, ripe for the harvest."

"No," Alaric grinds out. "You won't touch my Clan."

"They're dull, flavorless. Not like you."

Alaric swears the Shadow licks its lips before it laughs again, the sound full of chimes and gravel.

Theobald veers from the main path, the road getting narrower and rougher as they go. Alaric can't remember the last time he went out to the Berman place; it's been empty for almost ten years. They came to the community when he was a toddler and left not long after the Emergence. He barely remembers them, other than the vague memory that they had a daughter only a year older than himself, Drea, and Corbin.

"I'm going to need you to hold it here on your own," Pawel says quietly.

"Do you have enough energy left for that, Rory?"

"When this is done, I'm going to sleep for a week, then eat like I'm Clan," Rory mutters. "I'll do my best."

Theobald yanks open the back door of the SUV. "You can bring it in here. Do whatever you want to this place; it's far enough from the rest of my Clan not to taint them. No one will live here again."

"It's just magic." Pawel disengages slowly, hands out, making sure that the Shadow remains trapped with Rory. "You're magic. We're all magic. Emergent, Lineage, Clan, Mage…it doesn't matter. We all have our roots in the same power."

Theobald's lip curls; it's obvious that he's not impressed.

"Let him do what he needs to do," Alaric growls, and Theobald snarls in return.

"I'll go with them." Mac's shoulders are stiff, her scent flat and angry. "I can take care of myself and Pawel, and I can certainly take care of your father, if it comes to that."

Compared to Theobald, Mac's tiny and fast, but nothing impressive. At the same time, Alaric doesn't doubt her capability, and he wonders if Theobald will underestimate her. "I'll stay with Rory."

Mac nods, turns to follow Pawel and Theobald inside.

"Why here?" Rory asks, and the Shadow laughs.

"Can't you feel the way this place is steeped in magic?" the Shadow whispers. "Threaded through the land, woven into the wood of the house. The foundation is built on magic; the darkness already swallowed it once. Give it time. It will spread, despite what he tries to keep it at bay."

"Stop talking," Alaric mutters, and the Shadow goes silent. Rory's breath eases slowly, and Alaric twists in his seat, manages to get a hand back to rest on Rory's shoulder in silent strength.

Alaric closes his eyes for a moment, centers himself as he inhales deeply. The Shadow is a dank scent invading his senses, but he can catch hints of something similar in the space around them: sifting in through the window are the moldy remains of something left behind. He wrinkles his nose, almost sneezes.

He refuses to admit that the Shadow might be right.

He jerks upright when the back door opens again, Pawel leaning in. "Come on, Rory, let's get this inside."

" 'It'…'this'… Am I not a person?" The Shadow's features shift, taking on a feminine cast. It untangles itself, unfolds into something spiky and not quite human, as if it mimics life rather than is a part of it. They rush it indoors, pushing past where Theobald waits. Rory and Pawel manage to wrestle the Shadow into one corner of the room and release it, stepping back quickly as it bursts into a flow of darkness all around them then recedes.

It stands on two legs when it's done, hands pressed against an unseen wall. "I am as human as you are," it whispers. "There are none of us that remain untouched."

"I don't like this," Theobald snarls. "This place is fouled."

"I don't like you," the Shadow hisses. "You foul this place as much as I do. There are cracks in your Clan, cracks in the earth that let things bubble through. The split will break apart, and you'll fall in, Theobald Herne. Let the split swallow you. Let it take you home."

The wolf returns, darting forward, only stopping at a sharp call of Theobald's name from the doorway. He cries out, sits back on his haunches at Alia's voice. She stays where she is, arms crossed, lips pressed thin.

The Shadow cocks its head. "Alia Herne. There are few things that are the same between the worlds, and you are one. Bedrock."

"What is it talking about?" Rory slumps next to Alaric, leans on him when Alaric gets an arm around him.

Alaric shakes his head. "No idea."

"Some historians used to think that Dreamwalkers and Shadow-walkers were the same thing," Pawel says idly. "Both were able to move between realities, and both were unknown legends. But we've tracked and found Dreamwalkers, and until now, there's been no proven sighting of a Shadowwwalker."

Alia comes forward slowly, twists a hand in Theobald's ruff. He comes back to human in a crouch, head bowed forward under her touch, gaze fixed on the Shadow.

"Did you kill Orson?" Theobald asks quietly.

A soft, dark chuckle. "He was delicious."

Theobald's lip curls; his growl matches Alaric's.

Rory rests a hand on Alaric's forearm, but Alaric shakes his head. "I'm okay," he says. He can maintain control. He can stay human.

He's not certain his father can do the same.

Even under Alia's touch, Theobald seems to flicker between human and wolf.

The Shadow laughs again, steps back and crosses shadowy arms. "Most of you would taste good enough," the Shadow muses. "I'd save her for the main course"—it nods at Mac—"and sip him for afters, like a sweet dessert wine." It stares at Rory. "You couldn't even defend yourself now, little Mage, could you? I can feel the exhaustion dripping from you, seeping magic into the air. You've never taken so much for so long."

Rory blinks. "I don't take anything. I just stop it."

"So you say."

"Leave me." Theobald pushes to his feet, stalks to the edge of the Shadow's confinement. He stands almost toe to toe with the thing, and it stares back at him, elongates until it looks down on him. Theobald growls low in his throat, air thick with fury. "Leave me with it."

"I don't think that's the best—"

Theobald cuts Pawel off. "Is it contained?"

"For now." Pawel gestures at the ceiling, then the floor. "This isn't a perfect situation, and the containment will need to be updated—"

"I won't take that long."

"You can't go in with it," Alaric says sharply. "It'll steal your soul."

"Not his," the Shadow replies, voice flat. "He's bitter. Cold. Flat and tasteless. There is nothing of him that I want. Let him stay. Let him try his worst. I don't care."

Alaric inhales, tastes no lie on the air. He has no idea if Shadows have tells in their scent, no clue if he should worry. When Pawel looks to him, Alaric shrugs and looks to Alia. "Mom?"

"I think your father is making a poor decision, but it is his right to make that decision." Alia's fingers drift along Theobald's cheek briefly before she steps back. "We'll go."

Alaric ushers the others out first. Mac slips an arm around Rory's waist, and Rory leans on her as they exit, Pawel trailing slowly in their wake. Alia's touch slows Alaric's steps, and he lingers outside the door.

In the fresh air, the dank scent of the Shadow lingers but isn't as oppressive. There's a clarity in Alaric's mind now, and he catches a whiff of ozone that isn't Pawel or Rory, but something else. Something deeper that might be a part of this place. He tilts his head, nostrils flaring.

"Your father is calling a conclave for the New Year," Alia says. Alaric shifts his attention to her. She stands with her hands clasped before her, as if there's nothing odd about the old Berman homestead. She raises her eyebrows, questioning silently.

"No." Alaric knows what it will be, as all the Clan of the Northeast and perhaps from farther west come to Haverhill, gathering to discuss what has happened. "He won't allow me to lead this Clan, and I refuse to take part in something that is solely a means to an end he wants to put in place. I will not start a war against the Mages."

"Then speak against it," Alia says plainly.

Alaric snorts. "He won't allow me to. You know that as well as I do. If I'm there, I'm there only as his heir. I have no voice, no vote of my own. I'm there to show that, despite Orson's death, and despite every infirmity I have, his line will go on. I won't blindly follow him. His case will be hurt more if I'm not by his side."

"You could have a say if you simply say it," Alia says, and Alaric shakes his head.

It isn't that simple. He's been fighting with Theobald for so long that it feels ingrained under his skin, a part of who they are. "He would muzzle me," Alaric says quietly. "Until he's ready to let me lead by his side, I can't lead this Clan. I'm sorry, Mom."

She reaches for him, pulls his head down so she can rub her cheek against his. He wraps his arms around her and leans on her as if he's still a child, taking comfort in her scent. There is strength here.

"He's going to destroy us," Alaric whispers.

"I won't let him," Alia murmurs, pressing a kiss to his cheek. "And neither will you." She steps back, pats his chest. "Now go, Alaric. You still have finals, and your friends are exhausted. We will see you when we come to get you and your sister for break."

Alaric hesitates, glances past her at the door that stands closed. He can't hear anything from inside, can't smell blood or anger. He has no idea what's happening, and it worries him. "You'll let me know if anything happens," he says, and Alia nods.

"Nothing is going to happen." She walks, and he goes with her, lingering for one more hug when they reach the SUV. "Go home, Alaric. You've brought him the evidence he needs. Give him time with it, time to understand. Make your case when you come home for the holidays. He'll listen then."

Alaric isn't so sure. As they pull away, all he can think is that he left his father alone with the Shadow, and he doesn't know what's going to happen next.

70

"There's nothing I can do, Dax." Alaric spreads his hands, tries to keep the gruff growl from his voice. "Pushing the Shadowwalker to talk wasn't helping us. Leaving it with Theobald will hopefully stop a war. I can't be there until finals are over, and Theobald won't let the Mages stay to do anything."

"I get that." Dax pushes fingers through hair that's grown out, curly and scruffy. He huffs, rubs a hand across his face. He's scruffy all over, like he doesn't care, although Alaric can tell that the beard has been trimmed down to the one small spot on his chin. "I get it, but it's not enough, not yet. I can still feel—" He cuts off, motions at his temple. "Orson's not satisfied."

"Orson was like that." Alaric shifts slightly, arms crossed. When Chris nudges closer, Alaric takes his weight against his shoulder, relaxes slowly at the touch.

"Is it possible that Orson doesn't think this stopped the war?" Chris asks.

"He's dead, Chris," Dax snaps. He makes a face. "Fuck, sorry. I don't think he knows any more than we do. He's dead. This is what's keeping him here so yeah, he doesn't think we stopped the war, for whatever reason. He's not satisfied. The thing is, maybe you did. Maybe bringing the Shadowwalker out to Haverhill fixed things. Or maybe it didn't. Or maybe there'll be a war three years down the road. We don't know. And until there's something that's enough to satisfy Orson, I'm stuck with him in the back of my head. It's making it hard to go home and not try to stick around Alaric and protect him."

"Go home when your finals are done," Chris says quietly.

Dax scowls, presses fingers to the bridge of his nose. "You have no idea what this feels like."

"I don't," Chris admits.

"Visit me over break." Alaric shrugs at the look they both give him. "I'm going home. It'll make my mom happy, and my father is going to have to deal with the friends I have visit. Rory might come visit me; I might go to Vermont at some point. Chris—" He stops abruptly.

"If you want me to visit, Theobald doesn't scare me."

"Lie," Alaric says, and Chris doesn't deny it. "But if you want to visit, I'd like it. So Dax, come out there over break. Talk to Orson again. See me and Drea and Corbin, talk to my mom, see that we're all safe. Maybe it'll help get him out of your head."

"Maybe." Dax's expression is dubious as he rubs at his forehead. "Right now it's distracting, and I have my first exam tomorrow morning. I'm going to Maxwell to meet up with my orgo study group. I have a blanket in my backpack. I'm napping there if they don't kick us out."

"If you want to go back to the room, I'm sleeping tonight. I have a project due tomorrow by midnight," Chris says. "My major project isn't due until Friday. I'm going to work here for now."

Alaric pulls open the door to Douglass, motions Chris inside as Dax heads for Maxwell. "I'm not going to be much company," Alaric mutters. "Rory's got Coven, though, so it's quiet."

"I have a paper due tomorrow, and so do you," Chris says easily. "I'm not looking for conversation, just a quiet space where I can work. I find it easier to concentrate when there's someone else in the room."

Alaric knocks into him on the way up the stairs. "You like being around people."

"Don't need a puppy pile, but yeah," Chris admits. "It feels better. And you're decent people to be around."

It's a thought that warms Alaric, like Chris is Clan. Someone inside his inner circle. Someone that makes him comfortable as well. He nods once, pushes open the door.

It takes time to find a method that works for them. They both end up on Alaric's bed, high above the floor, leaning against the wall shoulder to shoulder. Chris's foot hooks over Alaric's ankle, a comfortable, hot weight.

Alaric's focus is on the laptop balanced on his knees; Chris sifts through notes, searching for information more often than typing.

Alaric manages to lose himself in the paper, working his way through the final topic for magical studies. When the door to the room opens, he jerks out of the fugue, elbowing Chris in the side.

Rory blinks at them. "Oh. Hey. Sorry. Am I interrupting?"

Alaric lifts the laptop. "Working on my paper for Pawel. Chris is doing some art history thing."

"This is psych," Chris mumbles. "Art history isn't due until Friday." He reaches for a paper that's fallen on the other side of Alaric, pulling it back and making notes in a file on his laptop. "Almost at the point where I can start writing it." He glances up when they're silent, blinks. "Okay, so sometimes I procrastinate." He rolls his eyes, gets back to work.

There's a sour scent in the air. Rory shrugs out of his jacket, tosses it over Alaric's on the chair. He rubs at his wrist, looks around until his gaze falls on the guitar on its stand. Rory takes the instrument and climbs onto his own bed, sitting cross-legged as he picks at chords that jangle against Alaric's senses.

"What's wrong?" Alaric asks quietly.

"The ritual tonight didn't do what we thought it would." Rory shrugs. "We put a lot of energy into it. Volunteers from Coven, and we were the only ones there. Tonight would've been optional, anyway. Last week was our last real meeting." He glances up from under the long fall of hair across his face. "Nik was there. She's looking better. Said she's got her first psych exam at noon tomorrow."

The idea of a ritual gone wrong makes Alaric's skin itch, but the stink of Rory's skin makes it worse. "What went wrong?"

"Don't know." Rory strums a minor chord. "It was this ritual that Pawel worked out with Ángel and Hayley, and it seemed like it was going to be really simple. The hardest part was the energy needed, and that I had to give energy instead of nullifying it. But when we were done, it didn't work."

Alaric has no idea who Ángel and Hayley are, but he figures that's not important to the story. "It bothers you," he says, and the next chord twangs painfully.

"Yeah," Rory says quietly. "It bothers me. They were really disappointed. They were looking forward to this. Kind of like…imagine being engaged for two years and then the wedding doesn't happen."

Alaric shakes his head. "Not a great analogy."

Chris snorts.

"The point is, it was something they'd been looking forward to for a long time, that was incredibly important, and it didn't work." The sounds from the guitar remain discordant, pinging against Alaric's eardrums. Rory's fingers slow, stop. He inhales slowly, closes his eyes. "If I play something that doesn't sound like shit, will it bother you?"

Chris waves, and Alaric shakes his head. " 's good," Alaric mutters.

Alaric has gotten a page written, and whatever Rory's working on is starting to sound more like a song, by the time Chris finally sets his laptop aside. "Did you say Nikita was there?" he asks.

Rory glances up. "Yeah. She's doing okay now. The Dreamwalker worked with her; said she raised a son who showed the Talent. She doesn't think Nik's a Dreamwalker, but it's close enough that whatever they did means Nik hasn't had nightmares since."

Alaric's phone buzzes. He lifts it, expecting it to be Drea, but a message from his mother pops up instead: *The Shadow is gone.*

Rory laughs a little, strums. "I think Nik's more excited that Jennifer moved out Sunday night, before the study days really got started. As soon as she turned in her last paper, she was gone. Nik's done by Friday; Pels still has another final next week."

Alaric's still staring at the phone, fingers hovering over the screen. His mother's message feels like an accusation, and his stomach clenches. He types back slowly: *Dad?*

"Ric?" Chris leans into him.

"Shadow's gone." Alaric forces himself to breathe evenly, one breath at a time, until the response comes back and he can inhale fully again. "My father's okay." He reads each message as it comes in, translates for Chris and Rory. "Mom says it's like it was never there. My father still says the Berman place is fouled, warned everyone away from it. Mom thinks it's been gone for a day, maybe, and he didn't say anything until she went out there, found him sitting in the room alone."

"At least nothing happened to your father." Rory's scent thickens again, sour and dark. "We knew this could happen. Pawel left a lot of residual energy there, but it couldn't hold the Shadow forever."

"I honestly thought he'd kill it," Alaric mutters. Chris rests a hand across the nape of his neck, and Alaric leans into the pressure. "I thought he'd kill it instead of keeping it and trying to talk to it. Or it'd try to kill him. Or he'd let the community tear it apart. Didn't figure it'd last long enough to escape."

"I'll let Pawel know." Rory slides off the bed, puts the guitar back on its stand. He pulls open the door, stops when he sees Nikita standing on the other side, her hand raised to knock.

"You could text him," Chris says, and Rory ducks his head, pulling back into the room and giving Nikita room to come in.

"Alaric," Nikita calls out, pausing when she sees Chris. She cocks her head. "Perfect. Can I ask you a personal question?"

"You're going to ask anyway." Alaric knows this by now, even after only one semester living on the same floor with her.

"You don't have to answer," Nikita points out. "I was just wondering— how did you come out to your families? I'm thinking of coming out to mine and I'm not sure how they'll take it. So advice might be nice."

"Haven't." Alaric isn't even sure what he needs to tell them more—that he's gay or that he can become a dragon. "Don't think I'm going to bother. They'll figure it out or they won't, and I don't really give a fuck what my father thinks."

Nikita edges closer. "He won't cut you off, will he?"

"Do you think your parents will cut you off?" Chris sets his laptop aside, slides to the edge of the bed so his legs hang over and he can look down. "You don't have to come out to anyone, Nik, not even your parents."

"They won't cut me off." Nikita shrugs. "It's just that since Tammy had the baby, Mom's all about asking me when I'm going to meet a nice guy so I can get married, have babies after college, settle down like Tammy did. And I keep getting the urge to tell her that it's not guys I go for."

"They aren't very open-minded?" Rory asks, his thumbs moving across the keyboard of his phone. "Mine never really assumed anything, but then, I have one mom and two dads, so our house was pretty much ready for anything. Which is good, considering they ended up with me and Thorne."

"I told mine when I was a senior in high school," Chris says. "I was scared to tell my dad before then. I knew he loved me—I knew that wouldn't change—but there's this whole image in football, and well, I'm Black. There are a lot of stereotypical expectations and even though I trusted my parents not to push me out for not fitting that, it was still terrifying."

"What made you decide to come out?" Nikita asks.

Chris laughs dryly. "Locker room talk. This guy joined the team, and he was out, and everyone knew it. And there were a few guys giving him shit, and I wasn't going to let that happen. They tried saying some bullshit about how being gay makes a guy weak. Pete wasn't weak; he was a damned good kicker, and he could outsprint most of the guys on the team. They were just looking for some reason to put him down.

"I didn't want to start a fight, so I got together with my co-captain and we came up with a plan. Then I had to present it to my coach, and before that, I wanted to tell my parents. Because if the team was going to know, I wanted them to know first."

"How'd it go?"

"Fine," Chris admits. "Maybe I'm lucky, but my family was cool with it. One of my brothers said that he figured one of us had to be—and the youngest one talked to me privately about a week later because he thinks maybe he's bi. He's still figuring it out. But I did it over dinner one night—'please pass the potatoes, oh by the way, I'm gay and I'm coming out to the team tomorrow so we can stop the bullying.' "

"Seriously?" Nikita laughs, the sound louder when Chris nods.

"Hey." The door nudges open, TJ poking his head in. "Quiet time in ten minutes, right after primal scream. Time for guests to get out."

"You could come study at OPT if you want?" Chris offers as he pulls his stuff together.

Alaric glances at Rory, not sure he wants to leave his roommate on his own. Rory's still distracted by his phone, tapping away at his messages, and while his scent has eased, it's not quite right. "I think I'm staying here tonight," Alaric says. "Rory?"

Rory blinks at him. "I'd appreciate that," he says quietly. "If you don't mind."

"Don't mind," Alaric tells him. " 'm gonna walk Chris out and go scream, okay?"

Rory winces. "Yeah, don't do that in here. You were leaning out the window last night and it was still loud enough to hurt my ears."

"Not a fan of primal scream," Alaric murmurs as he follows Chris out. Nikita's slipping into her own room, and Alaric can hear TJ in the distance talking to Pat and Jackson over the sound of their music. "I like it. Get to lose control."

Chris smirks. "You like that."

There's heat under his skin, warm and rosy. Alaric ducks his head, then glances up to see Chris at the bottom of the stairs waiting for him. "Yeah," Alaric says softly.

Chris crowds him as soon as he gets to the bottom, pushes him back against the wall and kisses him. Alaric groans softly, opens his mouth under Chris's. When he gets a hand on Chris's shoulder, fingers wrap around his wrist, holding tightly as Chris grips the nape of Alaric's neck.

It's better than the primal scream.

Chris pulls back, rotates them so someone can pass by and head upstairs. Alaric licks his lips, stares at Chris with his body aching.

"Take care of Rory," Chris says quietly. He leans into him again, heavy and warm against Alaric's body. A slow kiss this time, lingering before Chris speaks again. "Dax is going home Friday. He's coming back Saturday for the concert, but he's not in the room Friday."

"I'm done Friday. Not going home until Monday when Drea's done." Alaric licks his lips, thinks about what Chris has said. What he's offering.

"Finish your finals," Chris tells him. "Focus on that. Get through the paper, the exams, and on Friday, we'll get Chinese food and watch movies. Okay?"

It sounds like a date.

It also sounds like what they've been doing all fucking semester.

"Minnisale's," Alaric counters. " 'm paying."

"Fine, you pay. I pick the movies." Chris kisses him again, hard and fast and brutal enough to leave Alaric breathless and hungry. "Come on. Let's go scream, and I'm going to get out of here."

As Alaric steps out of the building, he can hear windows being thrown open, doors being pushed wide. It's as if the campus collectively draws a breath and lets it out, all at once, in a blood-curdling shriek. Alaric joins in, howling while Chris screams, and it feels good to stand side by side and let go.

71

THIS TIME, THEY get to the concert hall in Clifton Park long before the crowds. Chris and Alaric consider squeezing into the Phoenix Rising van, which Daniel drove out with their equipment, but in the end, they decide to follow the band over in Chris's car. Stormy and Andy are up for the day, and Alaric meets them in a whirlwind of noise before everything is packed into the back of the van and Daniel escapes into a car with Lucy and Rowan.

Alaric ends up helping carry things in, pulling Corbin and Drea to help when they arrive. There are more people backstage than the venue expects, but Thorne smooths everything over with the staff, and they're distracted shortly after that when someone spots Daniel staying off to one side.

By the time the stage is set and Phoenix Rising is doing their sound-check, Alaric has no idea what he's participated in, only that it's hard work. Much harder than he expected.

"I'd say that usually they have roadies for this, but while the kids are popular enough to pull a crowd, they're still small enough to travel on their own in a van. I'm Rowan." He sticks his hand out, and Alaric clasps it, then Chris does the same.

"I remember." Alaric inhales. "You smell like Thorne."

Rowan laughs, and it's a familiar sound. "Not surprising, since he's my biological son. I'd say the red hair had to come from somewhere, but then we've got Lucy." He gestures, and Alaric spots her across the room, leaning against Daniel. Her hair is streaked with pinkish red and black. "It's naturally that way. But neither of the boys came out with stripes."

"Dad." Rory slips into view, hands shoved in his pockets. "Don't tell everyone everything about us."

"Pretty sure Thorne's already done that," Rowan points out. "I know how your brother makes friends."

Alaric feels the heat in his cheeks, steps back to brush against Chris. Rory makes a face, protests, *"Dad."*

They get pushed apart by stagehands coming through, working with a local high-school band setting up to open for Phoenix Rising for this special concert tonight. At Rory's urging, Alaric and Chris head out onto the floor, find spots near the front barrier with their friends. Corbin stands behind Drea, his arms around her as he presses his cheek to hers. Chris glances at Alaric, and when he reaches out, Alaric moves closer; Chris's arm falls behind his shoulder with a comforting weight.

The doors open, and crowds press in, pushing them up against the barrier. By the time the opening band starts to play, Alaric's ears are ringing with the sound of excited heartbeats, his nose filled with the scents of strangers. Chris moves behind him, wraps his arms around him until Alaric is surrounded and centered and held in place, and finally he can breathe again.

The opening set flies by, leaves his ears ringing. Drea and Nikita talk to each other during the changeover, yelling to be heard over the background noise and music.

"You okay?" Chris gets his mouth right by Alaric's ears, teeth almost catching on the earlobe.

Alaric's breath catches. He nods. " 's okay. 's good, like this." He crosses his arms over Chris's, pinning him in place. "Don't stop."

"Not going to." Chris laughs softly, leans his head down on Alaric's shoulder. "I've got you, Ric."

A drum riff pulls their attention to the stage, and when Alaric looks up, Thorne is standing at the edge, his hands lifted.

"Hello, Clifton Park!" Thorne calls out. "I don't know about you, but I only have one more final left, and I need a study break. Are you ready to make some noise?"

The crowd screams, and Alaric winces, but then the music slams to a start. He gets lost in the emotion, the swell of excitement in the scent around him. Chris keeps him anchored as they move to the music.

It's strange seeing Rory on stage, as if he's a completely different person. Thorne's bouncing around, his outgoing yells—that all makes sense. But the way Rory moves with confidence, pulled up to his full height, strutting when he needs to—it jars Alaric's senses. Rory leans against his brother, playing while Thorne sings, a small smile as he plays.

He's comfortable on the stage, and as different as it is, Alaric recognizes that this is Rory, too.

Somewhere in the middle of the show, the current song winds down, and Stormy and Andy retreat from the stage. Two stools are brought forward, and Thorne and Rory sit, each holding an acoustic guitar. The way they sit, both facing the audience, makes it even more obvious that Thorne is right-handed and Rory is left-handed, the necks of the guitars stretching in opposite directions. They take a moment to tune their instruments while a mic stand is brought out, placed between them.

Thorne looks out at the audience, gaze sweeping across before it falls on Alaric and Chris, and he raises his eyebrows. "So, this is a new song. Rory and I have been working on a lot of songs because we're hoping to go into the studio sometime this spring." The crowd erupts, and Thorne raises a hand. "You have to be patient while we figure out how to pull off recording while we're all spread out between three different schools!" he calls out.

Rory knocks into him with his knee, and Thorne nudges back, smiling.

"The point is," Thorne says, "this particular song is something that we wrote because, well, sometimes things just need to be said. And it's not perfect, but we figured we'd give it a shot here tonight. So you'll need to tell us what you think after the show. Hashtag takeachance if you want to talk about it online, okay? We'll be looking."

"Thorne spends his life online," Rory says dryly. "You know he won't miss a thing. It'll be interesting getting him to get some sleep tonight."

"I won't stay up all night reading responses," Thorne protests. "You want to know too."

Rory plays two chords in response, then Thorne plays as well and starts to sing.

It's slow and soft at first, almost wistful before Rory comes in with a counterpoint on his guitar, and the beat starts to drive the song forward. By the time Thorne sings the chorus a second time, people are singing along, and Alaric's pretty sure it's going to be a hit with their fans.

Does it matter where we're going?
Does it matter where we've been?
Does it matter what they think
About all the things they've seen?
All that matters here is you.
All that matters here is me.
And all I'm asking is that maybe
We take a chance and let it be.

There's a low huff in his ear, and Alaric presses back against Chris, squeezes the hands that are still wrapped around his center.

The guitar drops away, sound echoing faintly in the hall. Thorne's voice is low and sweet again as he finishes the song.

I know what everyone says,
But we're not everyone here, dear.
Who needs love when we've got
Each other? I'll be here.
Take a chance and let it be.

Alaric licks his lips as Thorne's voice fades away. Thorne and Rory stand and hand off the acoustic guitars while the stools are taken away. It takes a moment to reset the stage before the music is thundering again, leaving Alaric's heart pounding in time with the bass and his ears still ringing with Thorne's words.

By the time the final encore ends, Alaric is ready to escape from the crowd. Chris takes his hand, and Alaric grabs Drea while she grabs Corbin. They form a human chain as the crew from his floor and their friends make their way through security and backstage. Alaric and Chris find a place out of the way where it's quiet enough that Alaric can filter out the random smells and heartbeats.

Rory finds them there. He has sweat dotting his forehead and an almost-empty bottle of water in his hand. He leans his back against the wall, lets his head fall back.

"I am completely out of energy," Rory says, and Alaric can smell the exhaustion under his skin. "Love the show. Hate the aftermath."

"It was good," Alaric tells him. "Didn't expect it."

"It's different up there," Rory admits. He slides down the wall until he sits on the floor, knees bent, arms across his knees. His hand falls to his wrist, twisting around it as he rubs it. "Up there, it's about the band. All of our energy together. And it's about Thorne. I can do it because I'm with them, and because the music has to come out."

Alaric and Chris join Rory on the floor. "Kind of like having a beast inside of you," Alaric comments. Chris touches his knee, and Alaric covers Chris's hand with his own, holding it there.

Rory winces, pushes at his wrist again. "Yeah. Maybe. Something like that."

There's a sourness to his scent, something that wasn't there a moment ago. "What did I say?"

Rory looks up sharply. "It's nothing."

Alaric snorts. "I can smell that you're upset. It's not nothing."

Rory licks his lips, gaze flicking between Alaric and Chris. "Look." His voice drops low. "You can't say anything, okay? And honestly, I wouldn't be telling you, except—you'll see." He rotates his wrist, showing the inside with an out-of-focus swirl of ink that seems to shift as they look at it.

"We did that ritual Tuesday," Rory says, voice low. "I told you how it didn't go the way we expected, right? The thing is, it was supposed to prove that Ángel and Hayley are soulmates. And at the end of it, they were supposed to touch, and they'd have these matching marks on the insides of their wrists. Or maybe something that represented each other. Either way, it was supposed to be something that linked them together. But when we finished, the marks they had were indistinct, like they haven't actually touched the right person yet. And it shouldn't have happened to me when it happened to them."

Alaric's brows draw together in a deep frown as he tries to follow.

"So that's supposed to tell you about your soulmate?" Chris asks.

Rory nods. "If it's like theirs, yes. When I touch my soulmate, it'll be something that matches them somehow."

"Is it Alaric?"

Alaric's snort is too loud, and he waves off the attention it gets from Stormy, who looks over from across the way. "Not my type," he says, at the same time as Rory says the same words. Chris motions between the two of them as if to point out that they've proved his point, and Alaric grumbles.

Soulmate is an even more difficult word than *love*, and Alaric doesn't want to contemplate it. But when Rory holds out his hand, Alaric clasps it.

Nothing changes.

"I'd still say you're platonic soulmates," Chris says, his hand curling on Alaric's knee, squeezing.

"Best friends," Rory says. "This means there's someone else out there. Someone that it thinks is different for me." He tucks his wrist close to his body, expression wry. "I'd better go make sure everything gets packed out to the van. If you don't want to get stuck helping, you can wait outside. Watch the stuff for us." His gaze rests on Alaric. "Should be quieter out there."

Chris winds his fingers through Alaric's, tangling them together. "We can do that." He stands and tugs Alaric to his feet.

Alaric takes a moment to grab Rory, yank him into a hard hug and hold on until he feels the tension bleed away. Thorne calls out, and Rory raises a tired hand before going to him while Chris and Alaric head outside.

They end up leaning against the van with Alaric's jacket over Chris's shoulders in the chill of the December air. "Why did you do that?" Alaric asks quietly, and Chris glances over at him.

"If you were soulmates, wouldn't you want to know?" Chris asks. "I'm not talking about something sexual. Rory would hate that. But you two are close; anyone can see it. It could be possible."

"But wouldn't you be jealous?" Alaric's still trying to understand this thing they're doing that makes no sense to him.

"Not really," Chris leans against him. "I know both of you, and I know that your friendship with Rory has nothing to do with us."

Alaric's breath hitches. "Because there's an 'us.' " He swallows. "I'm still trying to figure that the fuck out."

"Is it bad so far?" Chris asks, and Alaric shakes his head.

It's not bad. He likes the sex with Chris. A lot. He likes knowing that he's the only one Chris is sleeping with, that if he wants sex, Chris is there, and he wants it too. He likes the solidity and weight of him. "I'm not sure I'm in love with you, and I don't know if I can be," he admits. "You're going to want more than I've got."

"It's okay." Chris tangles their hands together again, warm and comfortable. "I like where we are right now, Ric. I like what we've got, where we've been so far. 'Friends with benefits' seems to be working out."

"I like where we are, too," Alaric says quietly, looking down at their joined hands. "You're a good friend. Hard to think about what it'd be like here without you. Even if we weren't having sex."

"Good." Chris turns, twists his hands in Alaric's shirt, and drags him into position. Alaric ends up leaning against Chris, keeping him warm against the car while Chris holds him in place. Chris locks gazes with Alaric for a moment, then kisses him slowly, one hand coming up to cup his jaw, fingers spread and tightening down against his skin with a strong grip. Alaric whines softly in the back of his throat, and Chris chuckles.

"Good," Chris says again, a murmur against Alaric's lips. "You like where we are. I like where we are. Let's just see where we go from here."

It's uncertain, but then, Alaric's entire future is filled with uncertainty. He can do this, and take a chance, and commit to going forward and seeing what happens next.

Acknowledgements

The series *Welcome to PHU*, of which this book is a part, was a long time coming. So long, in fact, that I struggle to thank everyone involved in its creation.

Many of these characters have lived in my head for years, and in some cases, decades. I'm not sure who came first—Mac, possibly, who is a derivation of a character originally created for a role-playing game back in the early '90s, and who still owes pieces of her personality to that event. I have dabbled with these characters over the years, some of them first appearing in games, some in early stories, some even as OCs in fics I wrote. I am thankful to everyone I have ever played RPGs with, or who has read and commented on any of my work over the years; you have encouraged me and helped me round out and create the personalities inside my head.

I have to thank my family. My parents, who encouraged me when I was still young, always made time to read and support my words. My husband: Kevin, you had no idea what you were in for marrying a writer, did you? And to my kids, who grew up with "please, just give me an hour, Mommy's writing," you have become amazingly patient, and I love you and treasure you. To all of you who have been with me when I needed you, supported my time to write, and pulled me out of my own shell to be part of this wonderful family, I love you. I wouldn't be here without you.

To those who have read *Commit to the Kick* and other parts of the PHU series online, thank you for reading, for commenting, for hitting the little heart button, for supporting me on Patreon, for helping signal boost the Kickstarter. Thank you for being here, for reminding me that I'm not writing in a vacuum, and for hopefully falling at least a little in love with this world and characters.

And finally, thank you to the voices in my head. You are loud, obnoxious, and relentless. This is your story, and I am so thankful that you made me tell it.

About the Author

Tris Lawrence has been writing since she was a child, filling notebooks with the worlds, dreams, and voices from inside her head. She declared in sixth grade that she wanted to be a writer, promptly started drafting her first novel in seventh grade, and never looked back.

Tris has always been fascinated by the way people work: how their relationships fit together, how they work socially, how they learn and discover. She has read avidly her entire life, devouring mysteries, romance, science fiction, and fantasy novels, and as an adult still loves all of these genres, as well as reading YA constantly. Her favorite stories center around people who are learning or discovering new things, and coming-of-age stories top that list, which is how the school of *Pine Hills University* came to be. She wants to share stories of people who are learning how to relate to each other, how to adult, how to college, and how to just be. She hopes to share stories about diverse characters with representation of everything she wishes she could have read growing up, and she hopes that these stories will touch the lives and hearts of those who read them.

When not writing, Tris is a wife, a mother (to two children, two cats, and a dog), a knitter, a system administrator, a third-degree black belt in taekwondo, an avid reader and obsessive writer, and a music aficionado. Sleep, she claims, is optional.

You can find Tris online in several places, including Twitter (https://twitter.com/tryslora), Facebook (https://www.facebook.com/trislawrencewrites/), Pillowfort (https://www.pillowfort.io/tryslora), and Mastodon (https://wandering.shop/@tryslora).

Available Books by Tris Lawrence

Welcome to PHU

Twinned Trilogy

> Book 1: Commit to the Kick
>
> Book 2: Missed Fortunes
>
> Book 3: Into the Split

Marked Trilogy

> Book 1: Not Your Destiny
>
> Book 2: Not Your Love Song
>
> Book 3: Not Your Guardian Angel

The Summer Break Series

> The Meaning of Home

Welcome to PHU Side Stories:

> Best Friends AND…
>
> Live Like There's No Tomorrow
>
> so he won't fly away

Books and short stories in the Welcome to PHU 'verse are available at

- https://duckprintspress.com/about-duck-prints-press/creators-we-work-with/authortrislawrence/
- https://welcometophu.tumblr.com/
- https://www.pillowfort.social/community/WelcomeToPHU/

Other Publications with Duck Prints Press

> Add Magic to Taste (author contributor)
>
> He Bears the Cape of Stars (author contributor)
>
> Warm Anything You Want

About Duck Prints Press LLC

Duck Prints Press LLC is an independent publisher based in New York State. Our founding vision is to help fanwork creators navigate the complex process of bringing their original works from first draft to print, culminating in publishing their work under our imprint. We are particularly dedicated to working with queer creators and publishing stories and artwork featuring characters from across the LGBTQIA+ spectrum.

Find us online at our website https://duckprintspress.com/ or on social media:

cohost!: https://cohost.org/duckprintspress
Dreamwidth: https://duckprintspress.dreamwidth.org/
Facebook: https://www.facebook.com/duckprintspress
Instagram: https://www.instagram.com/duckprintspress/
ko-fi: https://ko-fi.com/duckprintspress
LinkedIn: https://www.linkedin.com/company/71237377/
Mastodon: https://pettingzoo.co/@duckprintspress
Patreon: https://www.patreon.com/duckprintspress
Pillowfort: https://www.pillowfort.social/duckprintspress
TikTok: https://www.tiktok.com/@duckprintspress
Tumblr: https://duckprintspress.tumblr.com/
Twitter: https://twitter.com/duckprintspress

Goodreads: https://www.goodreads.com/user/show/129902473-duck-prints-press-llc
Storygraph: https://app.thestorygraph.com/profile/unforth

If you enjoyed this story, don't forget to leave us a review!

Commit to the Kick on Goodreads:
https://www.goodreads.com/book/show/57826902-commit-to-the-kick
Commit to the Kick on Storygraph:
https://app.thestorygraph.com/books/4a8d0f15-9ed0-437a-9467-dec-ce0941870

www.ingramcontent.com/pod-product-compliance
Lightning Source LLC
Chambersburg PA
CBHW060755030726
47503CB00002B/249